LINDA CASTILLO

NEW YORK TIMES **BESTSELLING AUTHOR OF**
SWORN TO SILENCE

D0034598

A
WHISPER
IN THE
DARK

B

**BERKLEY
SENSATION**

$7.99 U.S.
$9.99 CAN

ISBN 978-0-425-21138-0

EAN

A WHISPER
IN THE
DARK

LINDA CASTILLO

BERKLEY SENSATION, NEW YORK

THE BERKLEY PUBLISHING GROUP
Published by the Penguin Group
Penguin Group (USA) Inc.
375 Hudson Street, New York, New York 10014, USA
Penguin Group (Canada), 90 Eglinton Avenue East, Suite 700, Toronto, Ontario M4P 2Y3, Canada
(a division of Pearson Penguin Canada Inc.)
Penguin Books Ltd., 80 Strand, London WC2R 0RL, England
Penguin Group Ireland, 25 St. Stephen's Green, Dublin 2, Ireland (a division of Penguin Books Ltd.)
Penguin Group (Australia), 250 Camberwell Road, Camberwell, Victoria 3124, Australia
(a division of Pearson Australia Group Pty. Ltd.)
Penguin Books India Pvt. Ltd., 11 Community Centre, Panchsheel Park, New Delhi—110 017, India
Penguin Group (NZ), 67 Apollo Drive, Rosedale, North Shore 0632, New Zealand
(a division of Pearson New Zealand Ltd.)
Penguin Books (South Africa) (Pty.) Ltd., 24 Sturdee Avenue, Rosebank, Johannesburg 2196,
South Africa

Penguin Books Ltd., Registered Offices: 80 Strand, London WC2R 0RL, England

This is a work of fiction. Names, characters, places, and incidents either are the product of the author's imagination or are used fictitiously, and any resemblance to actual persons, living or dead, business establishments, events, or locales is entirely coincidental. The publisher does not have any control over and does not assume any responsibility for author or third-party websites or their content.

A WHISPER IN THE DARK

A Berkley Sensation Book / published by arrangement with the author

PRINTING HISTORY
Berkley Sensation mass-market edition / August 2006

ISBN: 978-0-425-21138-0

BERKLEY® SENSATION
Berkley Sensation Books are published by The Berkley Publishing Group,
a division of Penguin Group (USA) Inc.,
375 Hudson Street, New York, New York 10014.
BERKLEY® SENSATION is a registered trademark of Penguin Group (USA) Inc.
The "B" design is a trademark belonging to Penguin Group (USA) Inc.

PRINTED IN THE UNITED STATES OF AMERICA

10 9 8 7 6 5 4 3 2

A WHISPER IN THE DARK

PROLOGUE

John Merrick had always liked the takedown. He liked the adrenaline rush of walking into a dark warehouse, knowing he had only his partner, his Heckler and Koch .45 semiautomatic and his own nerve to back him up. As far as he was concerned, the more risk, the better the rush.

He moved through the dark warehouse with the stealth of a big cat on the prowl. Gripping the pistol, he slid soundlessly along the wall, his every sense homed in on the pallets and crates stacked ceiling high and dead ahead. He could feel the scream of blood through his veins, the burn of adrenaline in his gut, the heady zing of nerves crawling just beneath his skin.

Chicago PD had received the tip just that morning. A ton of Bolivian cocaine had been trucked in from Guadalajara, Mexico, and unloaded in this South Side warehouse. Tomorrow, the drug would be broken down into smaller shipments, loaded into trucks with hidden panels and shipped all over the nation. Within days, one ton of pure poison would hit the streets across America.

It was John's responsibility to make sure that didn't happen.

Big Joe Hartigan had been eluding the narcotics task force and DEA for the better part of four years. Tonight, Chicago PD had him squarely in their crosshairs, and there was no way in hell they were going to let him slip away. It would be the largest bust of John's twelve-year career—and the biggest takedown in the history of the department.

John fully intended to be the one doing the taking down.

His heart thrummed steadily as he sidled into an aisle, the H&K leading the way, a hollow-point bullet ready in the chamber. The warehouse was immense and as dark and silent as a tomb. But John knew there were at least six other cops making entry simultaneously. Two at the loading bays at the rear of the building. One at the second-level fire escape. Three more at the front door. John had been assigned the side exit. And like a finely choreographed ballet, the seven men moved in from all directions as a single, deadly unit.

John rounded a corner, found the first aisle clear, and moved silently to the next. In the back of his mind he wondered when the rats would start jumping out . . .

The air hung thick with tension and the dark anticipation of violence. He could feel both of those things edging through him, like a blade nicking just deep enough to draw blood. He wasn't superstitious, but the hairs at his nape prickled with a sensation he could only describe as foreboding.

He cleared another aisle then approached the next. Peering around a crate, he found the row deserted. Puzzled, he lowered his firearm and listened, hearing only the pound of blood through his veins.

Where the hell were Hartigan's thugs?

Movement at the end of the aisle drew his gaze. John dropped into a shooter's stance, spread his legs, raised the pistol. Adrenaline stung his gut when he spotted the man in blue jeans and a ponytail holding a sawed-off shotgun the size of a cannon.

"Police officer!" John shouted. "Drop your weapon! Do it *now*!"

As if in slow motion, the shotgun came up. A quiver of fear ran the length of John. He heard the sound of shoes against concrete behind him. Shit, he thought. Backing toward cover, he spun in a half circle. A second man behind him raised a pistol.

Instinct kicked in. John's finger jerked against the trigger. The .45 bucked in his hand. The explosion deafened him, made his ears ring. Cordite stung his nostrils. The man crumpled to the floor.

John swung the pistol around to the other man to find him gone. "Shit," he muttered. "*Shit!*"

He hit his mike. "Shots fired! North exit! Gimme backup *now*!" Without waiting for a response, he started toward the downed man.

The perp lay motionless on the concrete floor, in a widening pool of blood. John kicked away the gun. It was too dark to see exactly where the man had been shot, but John could tell from the amount of blood that the injury was bad. Maybe even fatal.

Trying not to think about that, he knelt. "I'm a police detective. Chicago PD. You've been shot. Just . . . take it easy. An ambulance is on the way."

The man stirred, tried to say something, but his voice was low, the words unintelligible.

"Don't try to talk," John said.

The man opened his eyes. Within their depths John saw pain, incredulity and a damning measure of humanity. The power of those things had icy sweat breaking out on his back.

The man lifted his hand, reached out. "I'm a . . . cop."

John felt the words like a blade, plunging and going deep. Disbelief rose in a violent tide. He stared hard at the man, looking for a lie, praying for a lie, reminding himself that a suspect would say or do anything to save his ass.

"DEA . . . undercover . . ."

John didn't want to believe it; he desperately didn't want

it to be true. But he saw the truth in the man's eyes. And he felt the horror of it twist like barbed wire in his heart.

Aware that his hands were shaking violently, he tore the tiny halogen flashlight from his belt. He ripped open the man's shirt, barely noticing when buttons popped and scattered. The earth seemed to shift beneath him when he saw that the Kevlar vest had been breached. Everything inside him froze into a solid block of ice when a Drug Enforcement Agency I.D. shined up at him.

Oh, dear God in heaven, he'd shot a cop . . .

He read the name on the I.D. *Franklin Watts*. A DEA agent working undercover. A man fighting the same war he was. Shot down like a criminal . . .

"Oh, man. Oh, Jesus." John grappled with his radio. Vaguely he was aware of his fingers fumbling. His heart pounding wildly in his chest. The bitter taste of bile rising at the back of his throat. "I've got an officer down!" he screamed. "Officer down! Officer *down*! Where the *fuck* is the ambulance?"

Holstering the H&K, John yanked off his jacket, covered the agent with it, then looked into his eyes. "I didn't know you were a cop," he said.

"Undercover." Franklin Watts closed his eyes. "Guy behind you . . . was going to plug you with that shotgun."

Only then did John realize that this man had saved his life. Another layer of queasiness settled over the horror churning in his gut.

"How . . . bad?" the man asked.

Taking his hand, John squeezed it hard. "You're going to be all right."

"Yeah, and spring's going to . . . come early this year."

John had never shot anyone before, never even had to draw his weapon. That he'd shot a cop made him feel physically ill. None of the intel Vice received had given any indication that DEA would be at the scene. The enormity of the mistake dropped onto his shoulders with the weight of a thousand boulders, and he felt every ounce as if it were a ton.

How in the name of God had this happened?

Careful not to cause his fallen comrade pain, he opened the Kevlar vest and used his flashlight to locate the wound. He found it to the left and center of his breast-bone. A sucking wound. Too much damage. He'd never seen so much blood, wondered how a man could bleed so much. All the while the burden of responsibility pressed down on him, crushing him so that he could barely take a breath.

"I need to stop the bleeding," he heard himself say. "I'm going to apply direct pressure, okay? It's going to hurt."

"Already . . . hurts like . . . son of a bitch."

John's hands quivered when he set his palm against the wound. "You doing okay?"

"Can't . . . breathe . . ."

"Hang in there. You're doing fine." But John could plainly see that he wasn't. He could hear air bubbling as it escaped the hole in the other man's lung.

Where the hell was that ambulance?

Franklin Watts's breathing turned labored, and John knew that his lung was filling with blood. That he would either drown or bleed to death in a matter of minutes if help didn't arrive soon.

Feeling helpless and more frightened than he'd ever been in his life, John leaned close to him. "I'm here, Frank. Hang tight, buddy. Paramedics will be here in a few minutes."

Closing his eyes, the DEA agent took quick, shallow breaths.

"That's it. Nice and easy." John tried to stay calm, but he could hear the hard edge of fear in his voice now, the underlying pitch of panic. He reached for his mike. "*Where's that fucking ambulance?* Goddamn it, I need it *now*!"

The radio crackled a response, but the voice barely registered. He heard sirens in the distance, shouting, and the pound of footsteps a few yards away, but he'd never felt more alone in his life. He looked down where his hand was pressed against the man's chest, saw the blood leaking between his fingers, and he knew this man didn't have much time.

He squeezed his hand. "Stay with me, buddy."

But when he looked into the other man's eyes, DEA Agent Franklin Watts had already slipped away.

ONE

New Orleans
Two months later

*Julia Wainwright stood on the sidewalk in the chill morn-*ing air, a box of warm beignets in her hand, a stack of books tucked beneath her arm. She stared through the storefront window, taking in the display of leather-bound tomes artfully arranged on a red and gold tapestry, not quite able to convince herself it was her creation.

"Not bad for a kid who flunked second-grade art class," she murmured, unable to keep the grin off her face.

The sun rising over the French Quarter's St. Louis Cathedral warmed her back as she tugged the key from her coat and stuck it in the lock. Hugging the books to her body, expertly balancing the beignets, she shoved open the door with her foot.

The aromas of old building—paper dust and vanilla candles—greeted her like an old friend as she stepped into the Book Merchant, the antique bookstore she owned and operated.

Julia had had a love affair with books even before she'd learned to read, which had occurred at the ripe age of four. Immersing herself in wonderful stories, with characters who were every bit as real as her friends from preschool, had transformed a rather lonely childhood into a world filled with enchantment and adventure. She had understood and appreciated the power of the written word long before most of her classmates had even read their first book.

As she'd grown older, her love of books burgeoned to include rare and old books. She could sit for hours with a battered volume, thinking about all the people who'd held it in their hands over the years, wondering if they'd wept or laughed at the passages within.

Two years ago the Book Merchant had been nothing more than a pipe dream. Then she'd discovered the derelict storefront in a historic building in the French Quarter—and known it was perfect. The space had been damaged by water and suffered with years of neglect. But Julia had a gift for seeing potential—whether in people or old buildings—and she'd refused to listen to the naysayers telling her the place couldn't be saved. Risking her life savings, she'd procured a loan, purchased the narrow space and begun the monumental task of transforming a dilapidated room into her dream. After months of backbreaking work and countless sleepless nights, the Book Merchant had been born.

Setting the books on the scarred surface of the old-fashioned counter, she worked off her coat. By the time she reached the coffeemaker, she'd already fished a beignet from the box and taken an enormous bite that would have sent her mother scrambling for her *Miss Manners' Emergency Handbook*.

It was the one book Julia didn't carry.

She chose a dark roast with chicory, and while the coffeemaker ground beans, she set her mind to the task of opening the shop. She lit the dozen or so scented candles she burned throughout the day. Yesterday had been vanilla. Today was hazelnut. Tomorrow maybe she'd try the café au lait she'd picked up at the candle shop on Magazine Street.

She'd just begun the task of counting petty cash when she spotted the envelope on the floor just inside the front door. Someone had slipped it through the old-fashioned mail slot, and she'd somehow missed it when she walked in. A chill that had nothing to do with the damp February weather ran the length of her.

Refusing to acknowledge that her heart was pounding, Julia crossed to the envelope and picked it up. The absence of a postmark indicated it hadn't come through the mail system. This one had been hand delivered. The others had been mailed. The realization that he knew where she worked raised gooseflesh on Julia's arms.

She slit the envelope. Like the others before it, the letter was off a laser and printed on ivory linen stationery in an Olde English font. Hating it that her hands weren't quite steady, Julia unfolded the letter and read the short passage.

Her tainted pen spills sin onto the page
like the fevered blood from a sickle slash.
Soon thine blood will be hers
and vengeance will be mine.

"What is that supposed to mean?" she whispered.

But deep inside, Julia knew. And the realization chilled her almost as much as the letter itself.

She jumped when the bell on the front door jingled. Relief swept through her when she looked up to see her sister, Claudia, enter the shop.

"Hi," she said, tucking the letter into her pocket.

"Don't 'hi' me." Glaring at her, Claudia Wainwright crossed to the counter and hefted a cardboard box onto the scarred surface. "I can't believe you sent me to pick up these books without warning me," she said, brushing paper dust from her slacks.

"Would you like coffee to go with your bad mood? It's fresh." Unfazed by her younger sibling's wrath, her mind still on the newest letter she'd received, Julia crossed to the coffeemaker and poured French roast into a tall mug.

"Black," Claudia grumbled.

"What has you in such an uproar this morning?"

"Mr. Thornbrow is the rudest old codger I've ever had the misfortune of dealing with," Claudia said.

Julia withheld a smile. The accused Mr. Thornbrow was a fellow antiquarian who ran a bookstore near Tulane, where Claudia attended law school. "He does have a knack for being difficult," Julia said diplomatically.

"He tried to charge me twice for these books."

Julie winced. She'd already paid fair market value for the books in question. "He's a little forgetful."

Claudia snorted. "He's a crude little man and uses his age to try and cheat people. I honestly don't know why you continue to do business with him."

"I deal with him because he has one of the most extensive collections in the city." More interested in the package her sister had brought her than her wily competitor, Julia tugged open the flaps and peered inside the box. "There are beignets next to the coffeemaker if you'd like one."

"I am not going to let you appease me with beignets," Claudia said, but her eyes were already drifting to the pastries. "Next time you can pick up your own books."

Anxious to see the gems her sister had brought from Mr. Thornbrow's shop, Julia pulled out one of the old tomes and her chest clenched with pride. "Oh, my. Victor Hugo," she whispered in reverence. "A first edition. I can't believe he parted with this."

Claudia grumbled something about grouchy old goats, but Julia wasn't listening. A flutter of excitement went through her when she slid the first book back into the box and pulled out the second. The redolence of aged leather and dust met her as the ancient volume in her hand came into view. "*Alice's Adventures in Wonderland*," she murmured. "First English edition. London. 1865. Oh, Claudia, it's lovely."

Rolling her eyes, Claudia took a bite of beignet. "I don't think I've ever seen a book I would consider lovely. Especially one as dusty and old as that one. They make me sneeze."

Julia felt the burn of tears behind her lids at the thought of all the reading pleasure the book in her hand had brought to so many people in the century and a half since it had been published. Feeling foolish, she blinked rapidly and slid the book back into the box. "In any case, thank you for braving Mr. Thornbrow and picking them up for me. I would have had to open the shop late if you hadn't volunteered."

Claudia poured coffee and took it behind the counter. "Lunch at Arnaud's would probably make up for it . . ."

Thinking she might treat her sister to her favorite French Quarter restaurant, Julia hefted the box and started for her desk. "I'd better get these books logged," she said over her shoulder.

"Julia?"

"Hmmm?"

"You didn't tell me you received another letter."

The words stopped her cold. Putting on her best smile, Julia turned to see her sister brandishing the envelope she'd inadvertently left on the counter. Damn.

"It was delivered before I arrived this morning," she said.

"I'm sure it hadn't crossed your mind to hide it from me, had it?"

"Why would I try to hide it?"

"Because you know I'm going to make you to do something about it." When Julia didn't respond, Claudia raised the envelope and rattled it. "How many does this make? Seven? Eight?"

"Six." Julia set the box on her desk. "If you're counting."

"I'm counting. And you should be, too." Claudia put her hands on her hips. "Where's the letter? I want to read it."

Knowing she was busted, Julia slid the letter from her pocket and handed it to her sister. "It's the same as the others."

Claudia read the letter aloud. "Her tainted pen spills sin onto the page like the fevered blood from a sickle slash. Soon thine blood will be hers and vengeance will be mine." Her gaze met Julia's. "That is freaking creepy."

Hearing the passage spoken aloud made the hairs at Julia's nape prickle. "Creepy is a good word."

"Do you recognize the author?" Claudia asked.

"Not this one, but the one I received on Monday came to me last night." While she'd been lying awake, worrying about who might be sending her threatening quotes from books.

"Which one?" Claudia bent and slid from beneath the counter the manila folder containing five other letters.

"The sins ye do by two and two ye must pay for one by one." Julia quoted the passage from memory as she walked down one of the narrow aisles and pulled out a book. "Kipling, maybe." She carried the book to the counter, set it down and both women began paging through it. "Let's see. Oh, here it is. Rudyard Kipling's 'Tomlinson.' "

Silence reigned for a moment while both women read the poem. Then Claudia blew out a breath. "This guy is obviously some kind of nutcase, Julia."

"I'm getting that impression, too."

Claudia looked down at the letter in her hand. "What does it mean? Why would someone send letters like this?"

"I don't know." But after this latest letter, Julia had an idea as to the why, and it disturbed her almost as much as the letters themselves. She was going to have to do something about it. The question was what. "This one was hand delivered, Claudia."

Her sister's eyes widened. "He was *here*? He knows you run this shop? My God, I always thought he was, you know, in another state or something."

Julia nodded, resisting the urge to rub the gooseflesh that had come up on her arms. "No postmark."

Both women were silent for an instant, and then Claudia said, "I think it's time you reported this to the police."

"I'm not sure what the police can do. I mean, it's not against the law to send letters."

"These are more than just letters. They're . . . disturbing. Threatening. Julia, this creep could be dangerous."

More than anything, those were the words she hadn't wanted to hear. "He's quoting books, Claudia."

Her sister made a sound of annoyance. "He could be some kind of wacko stalker. He could be watching you. He could walk right into the bookstore and you wouldn't even know it." She looked at the letter and quoted. "Soon thine blood will be hers and vengeance will be mine? It sounds like he wants revenge for something you've done."

Julia hoped her sister didn't notice the shiver that went through her. In the two weeks since she'd received the first letter, she'd found herself jumping at shadows, watching her customers more closely than normal. For the first time since opening the Book Merchant, she was uneasy working alone and staying late at night, both of which she did often.

She knew her sister was right. To ignore the situation any longer would be not only foolhardy, but also potentially dangerous. The problem was, she wasn't sure how to address it without opening a can of worms she had absolutely no desire to deal with.

Julia chose her words carefully. "Do you have any idea the embarrassment this could cause Dad if the wrong person caught wind of this and decided to sensationalize it?"

"A few cryptic letters aren't exactly a scandal."

"For God's sake, Claudia, I'm not talking about the letters."

"Oh. *Oh.*" Understanding dawned in Claudia's eyes. "You think this is related to your book?"

Julia slid the letter from the folder. "Read the latest letter again." She tapped her nail against the ivory paper. "Her tainted pen spills sin onto the page like the fevered blood from a sickle slash." She sighed unhappily. "I think it's obvious."

Claudia bit her lip. "There's got to be a way to keep you safe without spilling the beans."

The beans her sister was referring to were the publication of Julia's first book, which had been released six months earlier under the pseudonym of Elisabeth de Haviland. Few people knew about Julia's writing. Certainly not her father, pillar of the community and New Orleans's religious icon Benjamin Wainwright. Julia wanted to keep it that way. "Dad has worked long and hard to get where he is. I would hate for my writing to affect him in any way."

"Or embarrass him."

"Thank you for stating the obvious," Julia said dryly.

"Maybe it's time you told him. I mean, come on, you're his daughter. He loves you."

Julia couldn't help it; she laughed even though the humor of the moment eluded her. "I don't think he's prepared for Elisabeth de Haviland."

"You don't have to tell him *what* you write."

"You know how Dad is. Once he finds out his daughter is an author, he'll tell all of his friends and rush out to buy the book." *And they'll all get the shock of their lives*, she thought with a shudder.

"Look, the fact of the matter is there's some weirdo out there sending you threatening letters. You can't ignore something like that these days."

Julia knew her sister was right. She should have done something when she'd received the first letter. "I hate it when you make more sense than I do," she muttered.

"At least file a report with the police. I'll check, but I think Louisiana has a stalking law."

"That will help. Thank you." Julia sighed. "If the police ask, I'll simply tell them the stalker must be referring to a book I carry here at the shop."

"I think it's a good compromise."

Taking the letter from her sister, Julia looked down at the cryptic words and felt a stir of anger. She'd finally found her place in the world, and now it seemed some warped individual had his sights set on disrupting her life. She wasn't going to let him do it.

"And in case you're wondering, there's nothing wrong with what you write." Sipping her coffee, Claudia looked at her over the rim.

Julia smiled. "Thanks. But I still don't want anyone to know about the book."

"You know your secret is safe with me."

"Is there a but coming?"

"I just hate for you to feel you have to keep such a big part of your life hidden."

"Come on, Claudia. Dad is about to become director of the Eternity Springs Ministries, the third largest church in Louisiana. There are people out there who think what I write is pornography and would use that to hurt him. He's worked hard to get where he is. He's got so many wonderful ideas on how to help people and families in need. It would kill him to lose that." She shook her head. "Besides, I just don't think Dad is prepared to find out his daughter is writing something so . . ."

"Hot?" Claudia smiled.

"Misunderstood," Julia finished.

"Or maybe you're the one who's not prepared."

An unexpected quiver of emotion went through Julia at the wisdom of her younger sister's words, and she surprised herself by smiling. "Since when did you get so smart?"

"I have a really smart older sister." Claudia crossed to her and gave her a smacking kiss on the cheek. "My lips are sealed, Julia. But whenever you're ready to tell him, I want to be there because I have never seen Benjamin Wainwright speechless."

He stood naked inside the door of her bedchamber, his body trembling with anticipation and a dark wanting he was helpless to control. Arousal was like a slow burning fire inside him, taunting him until he thought he might scream. The wanting was an agony that ripped through him with every violent thrust of his heart.

She lay on her side, anticipation dark in her eyes. A fallen angel with lips the color of blood. The flickering light of the wall torch danced like warm fingers over the silk of her flesh. His eyes drank in the sight of her. The round, golden flesh of her breasts. The thatch of dark curls at the apex of her thighs. The full force of her beauty snatched the last of his breath from his lungs and his head spun. He couldn't bear to look at her and not have her.

"You've no right to be here," she said.

"You've no right to look at me that way and not expect me to go mad with wanting you."

He crossed to her then, his jutting sex moving from side to side. He almost smiled when her gaze flicked over the bulbous purple shaft. He saw the thin layer of fear she tried to hide in her eyes, and it struck him that she was an innocent. But he'd long since stopped caring about right and wrong. He was delirious with the fever of wanting her. He would finally have her, tonight and every night for the rest of eternity.

Lust was as dangerous and reckless as a wild beast turned loose inside him. Her innocence called to him, a siren song that sang through his blood like a fever. She would be a woman when she left his bed. He would free her of the burden of her innocence. He would taste the blood of her maidenhead. He would mark her. Make her his. He would plant his seed in her womb.

He could have her in every way that a man could have a woman . . .

Fury blurred the words on the page. He slammed the book closed, the sound coming like a gunshot in the silence of his study. Filth. Filth. *Filth!* He was aware of his heart pounding, the blood rushing hotly to his groin, where his penis swelled uncomfortably against his fly.

He couldn't believe she could do this to him. *Him!* He wasn't weak like other men. He had the highest moral convictions. He had beliefs. Faith. And yet this whore could make him lust. A powerful lust that tore down his resistance and left him sweating and hot and weak.

She was a whore. A woman without virtue, contributing to the moral decay of a society already in the throes of ruination. New Orleans was filled with them. Sinners. Men and women of weak moral character.

But Julia Wainwright was worse than the others. Not only did she look like an angel, but she was the daughter of a religious man. She knew better and yet she continued to spread sin using the pages of her books. He thought about Benjamin Wainwright and wondered how a man with such strong religious convictions had raised such a harlot. Hadn't he taught her that lust was the devil's tool?

The Bible foretold how the devil would return in the form of an angel. Julia Wainwright looked like an angel in every sense of the word. Only she was an angel of Satan. He was duty bound to stop her. The only question that remained was if he was strong enough to withstand her deadly charms.

He looked at the photograph. She was standing behind the counter in that dusty little bookstore. She wore a turtleneck, just snug enough to reveal the curves of her breasts. The kinds of curves that made a man weak. Her brown hair had fallen into her eyes and she'd raised her hand to shove it back, giving him that woman's smile when he'd snapped the shot. She wanted everyone to believe she was good. Innocent. But he knew better. He knew her secret. And when she'd looked at him with those gypsy eyes, he'd smiled back, but deep inside he'd hated her.

He'd hoped the letters would stop her, but they hadn't. He was going to have to step up his efforts. He hadn't wanted to hurt her. But he knew all too well how powerful and utterly deceitful Satan was. It was going to take more than gentle persuasion to stop her. He was going to have to hurt her in order to save her from herself and deliver her from evil . . .

The image of his hands around her slender throat sent another hot rush of blood to his groin. He looked helplessly at the bulge at his crotch, and shame cut him like a blade. She made him weak, and he hated her for it. Hated himself.

Embarrassment choked a sound from his throat, but the lust was stronger. It had taken hold of him like a fever. She did this to him. It was her fault. Her *fault*!

The need pulsed inside him. An agony he could no longer stand. He was weak. A mortal in the hands of Satan.

"Forgive me," he whispered as he unzipped his fly.

His hands trembled as he wrapped his fingers around his swollen penis and began to pump his hand. He stared at the photo, pleasure wrapping around his brain like a powerful narcotic. A drug he would never get enough of.

He could hear his breaths rushing between his clenched teeth. His hips moved in time with his hand. Oh, God. Oh, God! So good.

"Whore," he spat. "Bitch."

Shame sent tears to his eyes. He could hear his father's voice inside his head. *You're an evil boy. A demon. You've got the devil inside you!*

"No," he whimpered. "It's her fault."

But when he closed his eyes, the memories descended.

TWO

John Merrick stood beneath the green and white striped canopy outside the Book Merchant and watched the traffic along Royal Street bump and grind into the night. Around him, a cold February rain fell in sheets, bringing a rise of fog. He'd been in New Orleans for almost two weeks, but it wasn't long enough for him to forget why he'd come back—or why he'd run in the first place.

His lieutenant had tried to persuade him to stay in Chicago, but John had turned him down flat. As far as he was concerned all of the things that had once made him a good cop had died the night his bullet had killed DEA Agent Franklin Watts.

After the grand jury cleared him of charges and Internal Affairs ruled Watts's death a friendly fire incident—a euphemism John had come to hate—he'd resigned from the force and walked away from a career he'd invested twelve years of his life building. He'd broken the lease on his apartment, loaded all of his worldly possessions into his restored 1971 Mustang fastback and headed to his hometown in the hope of putting the incident behind him and moving on with his life.

Yeah. Right. The way things were going he figured he'd be lucky to find a way to live with himself.

He'd found a one-bedroom apartment in a shady neighborhood on the east side of the Quarter, and set his sights on getting a job. But for the life of him he couldn't figure out what the hell to do. All he'd ever known was law enforcement. Who wanted a broken-down ex-cop with a ruined career and a shitload of baggage? An ex-cop who hadn't been able to pick up his gun since that terrible night . . .

He'd been surprised as hell when he'd gotten the call from an old friend of his father's, Benjamin Wainwright. Something about his daughter needing some additional security at her French Quarter shop. John hadn't wanted to do the rent-a-cop thing. He'd tried to wriggle out of the meeting, but Wainwright wasn't a subtle man when it came to getting what he wanted, especially when it came to his two daughters.

John knew he should go inside and make nice with her, but he wasn't in the mood for nice. He sure as hell wasn't in the mood for small talk. He barely remembered Julia Wainwright; hadn't so much as given her a single thought in all the years he'd been away. Last time he'd seen her she'd been a chubby fifteen-year-old with bottle-cap glasses and a mouth full of braces. He didn't even want to think about what she might look like now. She'd had a crush on him if he recalled, though John had never so much as spared her a second glance. He'd never gone in for the bookish type, especially the quiet, brainy ones.

He was considering walking away from the whole damn situation when Benjamin Wainwright's Cadillac slid up to the curb. The reverend threw open the door and stepped out.

"John! Good to see you!" he said in a booming voice as he crossed to the sidewalk.

John put on an expression he hoped looked friendly and extended his hand. "It's good to see you, Mr. Wainwright."

"Don't 'Mister' me, son. It's Benjamin to you. How've you been?"

Wainwright was as tall and thick as a century-old cypress, and as wily as a bayou fox. His white hair contrasted sharply with black brows that arched over intelligent eyes the color of antique pewter. He had a loud voice, a quick laugh and eyes that didn't miss a beat, no matter how subtle.

John recognized the shrewdness behind those Southern gentleman eyes, and he knew that while Benjamin Wainwright might look like someone's favorite uncle, he hadn't gone from minister to the head of one of New Orleans's largest religious organizations on his charm alone. Behind all that Old South charm lay a cunning man who knew how to get what he wanted and didn't mind stepping on toes to get it.

He wondered what the hell Wainwright wanted with him.

"I was sorry to hear about the trouble you had up in Chicago." Wainwright pumped his hand. "If there's anything I can do . . ."

John felt the words like a slap, but he didn't flinch. Two months had passed since he'd pulled that trigger and killed a fellow cop, but not a moment went by that the incident didn't eat at him. "I'm fine," he said.

Glancing through the display window of the Book Merchant, Wainwright lowered his voice. "I need you your help with a problem. You remember Julia, don't you?"

John remembered enough about her to know he didn't want to be here. "Sure."

"Well, some troubled individual has been sending her letters."

"What kind of letters?"

"Vague threats. Strange stuff. Enough so that I became concerned."

"Are these letters coming through the U.S. mail, or what?"

Wainwright grimaced. "Claudia told me the latest was hand delivered."

"Did she go to the police?"

"She filed a report, but you know how that goes. The NOPD has one of the highest murder rates in the nation. They're spread pretty thin. They don't have the manpower to do much but drive by the shop a couple of times a week. That's not enough to suit me."

"It sounds like she's doing everything she can."

Wainwright's face went taut. "I'm afraid those letters might have more to do with me than her."

John got a bad feeling in the pit of his stomach. "Why do you think that?"

"You've heard the old adage, don't talk about politics or religion?"

John nodded, wondering where the conversation was heading.

"I break both rules. My position with Eternity Springs Ministries is more political than ever these days. The national convention is being held here in New Orleans next month. There've been whisperings of a faction of the church breaking away."

"Because of where you stand?"

"I'm a conservative, and some people don't like my stance on certain issues."

"You think someone from the church is behind the letters?"

Wainwright shrugged. "Could be someone trying to distract me or trying to get me to pull out."

"Seems like a roundabout way to do that."

The old man's expression remained troubled. "The truth of the matter is I'd never forgive myself if Julia was hurt because of me."

"What exactly do you want me to do?"

He leaned close, his eyes taking on a diamond-hard glint. "I want you to find out who's sending those letters and put a stop to it."

"Mr. Wainwright, with all due respect, I'm not sure I'm the right man for the job."

"I'd feel better about this if someone of your caliber were keeping an eye on her."

John didn't have anything to say about his caliber. "To be honest with you, I was thinking about heading out to the cabin to do some fish—"

"I'll let Julia fill you in on the details." Wainwright plowed past him and started toward the door. "I suspect she's going to be stubborn about this."

"I can't imagine where she got that," John muttered under his breath.

Wainwright grinned at him over his shoulder. "Her mama, of course."

As John followed Wainwright through the front door of the shop, he assured himself he could handle this. A quick look at the letters. A canned speech on personal safety. And he was out of there. If all went as planned, he'd be on his way to the cabin at first light.

The Book Merchant was exactly the kind of place John would never venture. It was a narrow, crowded shop that smelled of old wood, musty paper and some flavored coffee he'd never developed a taste for. Floor-to-ceiling shelves jam-packed with books of every shape and size formed four rows that stretched from front to rear like ancient canyon walls. To his right, an antique cash register sat atop a scarred wooden counter. To his left, a small sitting area, replete with a settee, tiffany lamp and silver coffee service, invited customers to sit and read or whatever the hell it was people did in shops like this one.

Despite the old world ambience, there were telltale signs that someone's tastes leaned toward the contemporary. Yellow light rained down from snazzy little pendant lights suspended from the ceiling. A sleek laptop lay open and humming on the desk—right next to an antique typewriter. Expensive chocolates wrapped in gold foil were neatly displayed on the counter—free of charge to the

book-buying public. Colorful bookmarks, depicting everything from Labrador retrievers to stars, dangled from a
small rack next to the cash register.

John did a double take when he spotted the woman behind the counter. Her back was turned, but he didn't need
to see her face to know she was attractive. She was standing on a short stepladder in high heels and a snug suit that
revealed some very intriguing curves. She was reaching for
a book on a shelf above her head, and her skirt had ridden
up to reveal legs so long and shapely he thought they ought
to be illegal. A cell phone was jammed into the crook of
her neck, and she was in the midst of a lively conversation.

"Mr. Thornbrow, if you would just give me a moment,
I'm sure I can find the book and have it back to you first
thing tomorrow morning." She tugged out a tattered volume, turned slightly toward the light in order to read the
spine and shoved it back. "I know it's here somewhere."

Her voice was throaty and Southern and as intoxicating
as aged bourbon—the kind that went down like warm silk,
then knocked a man flat without his ever knowing what hit
him. But John was barely aware of the conversation. His attention was focused exclusively on those mile-long legs
and one of the nicest derrieres he'd ever laid eyes on.

She wore a rust-colored jacket that hugged slender
shoulders and a narrow waist. Beneath the jacket, a cream
colored sweater flowed like wet silk over the swell of generous breasts. The fabric was so finely woven he could see
the lace of her bra and the faintest impression of her nipples . . .

Holy Moses.

Aware that his pulse was up and his blood was heating
fast, John tore his gaze away to stare out the display window, and tried hard to concentrate on the traffic moving
along Royal.

"Darlin', are you sure you ought to be on that stepladder
in those high heels?"

The woman turned at the sound of Benjamin Wainwright's voice. John felt something go soft in his chest

when she smiled. It had been a long time since he'd noticed a woman's smile. Even longer since he'd experienced a moment so fundamentally male. That he did now made him feel just a little bit more human.

"Oh, hi, Dad. I'll be down in just a moment. Help yourself to coffee. It's vanilla, I think. And there are some beignets left from this afternoon."

Dad?

The word ricocheted inside John's head like a stray bullet. Then it registered that the stunning creature with the thousand-watt smile and killer curves was none other than little Julia Wainwright all grown up. He didn't surprise easily, but this one smacked him right between the eyes like a sucker punch. He simply couldn't get his mind around the idea of the klutzy ugly duckling he'd once known blooming into such a magnificent swan.

She'd returned her attention to her phone conversation. "Look, Mr. Thornbrow, I've got a couple of visitors I need to take care of. No, I'm not trying to put you off. Fine. I'll call you tomorrow. I promise."

His eyes did another slow, dangerous sweep of her as she climbed down the ladder, and all he could think was that she was innocence and sin rolled into one very intriguing package. But when she turned to face them, it was her eyes that sucked the breath right out of his lungs. She had the most incredible eyes he'd ever seen. Gypsy eyes, he thought, as bottomless and mysterious as the bayous surrounding New Orleans. They were large, fringed with sooty lashes and as blue as the Gulf of Mexico on a sunny day. Her hair was as glossy as mink and cut into a chic style that curved under at her jaw, a stark contrast to her magnolia-blossom complexion. Her mouth was sulky and full and painted the color of a wet hibiscus petal. It was the kind of mouth that could bring even the most impervious man to his knees.

John had never cared for upper-crust sophistication when it came to women. Women like that were too much trouble, when most of the time all he wanted was a few laughs and an expeditious roll in the hay. Still, he thought Julia Wainwright might be worth a bit of trouble, and for a moment he wondered what it would be like to peel away those fancy outer layers and take a peek at the woman beneath all that class . . .

Snapping the cell phone closed, she gave them her full attention. Her gaze swept from Wainwright to John. He saw a flicker of recognition. Her mouth opened slightly in an instant of surprise. Her eyes cooled a few degrees, and he suddenly knew that his wish of being off the assignment before he'd even really begun was about to become reality.

"John Merrick?" Her gaze flicked to her father, then back to him. "Well, um . . . what a surprise."

John snapped out of his lust-induced trance and stuck out his hand. "It's good to see you again."

A moment of hesitation, then she reached over the counter and accepted his handshake. He felt the contact like the heady shock of a first kiss. Her hand was small and soft, but her grip was surprisingly firm. Pleasure ran the length of his body, like a lit fuse burning short and a few degrees too hot.

"What's this all about?" She released his hand, and her gaze swept to her father.

"Claudia told me about the letters you've been receiving," Wainwright said.

She blinked, and John knew immediately there had been some kind of confidentiality breach between the two sisters.

"I was handling it," Julia said.

"I don't think you can handle something like that on your own."

"I filed a report with the police."

"Which was the smartest thing to do," John said.

"But it's not enough," Wainwright added.

Her eyes went from John to her father. A woman who sensed a conspiracy and had just realized she was outnumbered. "Dad, I'm handling this."

"And how are you doing that?"

"For starters a beat cop from the eighth precinct stops in almost every afternoon for coffee," she said.

"What else?" John asked.

Her expression cooled. "And this has what to do with you?"

John smiled, but it felt stupid on his face. "We're working up to that," he said.

"Working up to what?" she demanded, cool being replaced by outright suspicion.

The elder Wainwright sighed. "Look, honey, I heard that John was back in town and between jobs, so I gave him a call and asked him to meet us here."

"Why would you do that?"

Wainwright looked at a loss for an instant. "Well, I thought he could help out."

"I have a part-time clerk. I don't need any help."

"I mean with security, darlin'."

She gave him a you've-got-to-be-kidding look. "Security?"

"I thought he might start with a security check." Wainwright turned to John. "Right?"

Feeling like an idiot, John nodded. "A security inspection would be a good starting point."

"Oh, good grief." She all but rolled her eyes. "What does this security inspection entail?"

"I have a checklist." John looked around. "Exterior and interior lighting. Locks. Alarm system." He smiled. "Might even get you a break on your insurance."

She didn't smile back.

"It's painless," he said. "Twenty minutes max."

Julia frowned at her father. "I suppose if it will help you sleep better at night."

Wainwright looked mildly annoyed. "Honey, look, I thought maybe John could keep an eye on the shop for a few days," he said, obviously trying for diplomacy.

"Dad, I appreciate your concern, but I don't think that's necessary," she said.

"Julia, you're too smart not to do something about those

letters. I'm a public figure in New Orleans and not every-one agrees with my views. Unfortunately, I think there are a few people in this city who wouldn't hesitate to take their displeasure out on my family."

"Dad, I don't think the letters have anything to do with you."

"Then what?"

She blinked. "Well, maybe a book I carry here at the shop has displeased someone."

"Maybe." But Wainwright didn't look convinced. "I'd never be able to live with myself if something happened to you because of me."

She softened. "People have been passionate about the written word for centuries. Books have been burned and banned by governments. Authors had been threatened with death." As if realizing she'd strayed into territory best left alone, she added, "I carry books that undoubtedly offend some individuals. Political. Religious—"

"The letters mention sin," he interjected.

"*Fanny Hill.*"

Looking pained, Wainwright made a sound beneath his breath. "Even so, darlin', I feel it's my responsibility to see to it that you're safe."

"I have no qualm about John conducting a security in-spection here at the shop." She came around the counter, a little house cat protecting its den from the neighborhood pit bull. Her gaze flicked to John, and he could see she was reining in impatience.

"And your apartment," Wainwright added.

"I'm sure John has better things to do than babysit me." She gave him a pointed look. "Don't you?"

It was the opening John had been waiting for. His chance to get the hell out of there and still save face. If he was lucky, he could make it to the cabin by first light and spend the next couple of days communing with nature and trying to put things into perspective.

He stared at her, indecision tugging him in different di-rections. Part of his brain screamed for him to jump at the opportunity to run—something he had become quite adept at. But there was another part of him that wasn't quite so logical, a part of him that knew Benjamin Wainwright didn't jump at shadows. If Julia was receiving threats, she probably needed him a hell of a lot more than he needed to spend the next few days getting lost in a bottle of rotgut.

"With all due respect," he heard himself say, "if you're receiving threats, you should be taking them seriously, particularly with your father vying for the director position at Eternity Springs."

She turned those gypsy eyes on him, and in their depths John saw a flicker of stubborn. "I am taking this seriously," she said. "I've filed a report with the police, and I've just agreed to a security inspection by you."

Wainwright sighed then scowled at John. "Talk some sense into that hard head of hers. I've been trying for twenty-nine years and still haven't succeeded."

"Dad, it's not like we're talking about a mad axe murderer here. I've received a few letters."

"Threatening letters," Wainwright injected.

"I have an alarm system."

"You have a mass of wires that are at best a fire hazard."

John watched the exchange with interest, curious about the source of Julia's resistance. She was too smart not to realize the situation could become serious. A threat—no matter how subtle—wasn't the kind of thing you ignored, especially if you were the daughter of a controversial, high-profile religious icon in a city full of sinners. He wanted to think this was working out exactly the way he'd hoped it would. A quick security inspection and he was out of there. But in some small corner of his mind, he wondered if Julia's resistance had to do with the incident in Chicago. If she somehow knew about it. If maybe she thought he was incompetent because he'd shot and killed a fellow cop. The shame that followed cut with unexpected force.

"This is exactly the kind of thing that could escalate and turn into something ugly if you're not on top of the situation," he said.

Sighing, she looked to the heavens in exasperation. "I'm outnumbered."

"What you are," John said, "is smart enough to know when you need help."

Benjamin Wainwright stepped forward and set his hands on her shoulders. "Julia, darlin', you've known John since you were a kid. Be reasonable and let him take a look at those letters." He looked around the shop with mild distaste. "Let him hang out for a couple of days and keep an eye on things for you."

"Dad—"

Wainwright's cell phone chirped. Giving his daughter a final frown, he yanked the phone from his belt, glared at the display for a moment, then growled, "Honey, I've got to take this. It's the folks from Our Lady of Saint Agnes. 'Scuse me." The bell jingled when he pushed open the door and stepped onto the sidewalk.

"Saved by the phone," she muttered.

John stood his ground near the counter, wondering who'd won the tug-of-war. He told himself that even if the old man claimed victory and John ended up spending the next few days here, the assignment would be a piece of cake. The problem was that John was in no frame of mind to be playing rent-a-cop. He had enough problems just getting through the day without some high-maintenance, difficult-minded female complicating things.

Without speaking to him, Julia went back to her place behind the counter. Pulling cash from the drawer, she began counting, slapping each bill down with a little too much force. "I apologize for my father putting you on the spot."

"I'm sure he has your best interest at heart."

"I want you to know . . . none of what was said has anything to do with you personally."

John winced. "I didn't take it personally."

"Please don't feel an obligation to—"

"Babysit you?"

She didn't stop counting bills, but her mouth quirked. "Something like that."

"He's only trying to protect you."

She stopped counting and looked at him, her expression softening. "I know."

"You'd make him a happy man if you let me hang out here for a couple of days."

She banded the bills. "He's never approved of my having this shop."

"Why not?"

She lifted a shoulder, let it fall. "He wanted me to get my master's degree. Get involved with the ministry, either teaching or missionary work."

"He got a bookstore instead."

"Not nearly as respectable."

"Respectable is overrated."

John watched her place the bills in the register, trying not to notice that her hands were as pretty and slender as the rest of her.

"Are you speaking from experience?"

He looked up, found her eyes already on him. "I'm an expert on disrepute."

She was about to say something when the bell on the door jangled, announcing Wainwright's reentry. "Honey, I've got to go. Parker and I have to go meet with members of the Historical Society. Charlie Bouchet is pressuring me to buy and restore Our Lady of St. Agnes, and I'm just not sure it's a wise use of funds."

"I think John and I can handle the rest of this without your input," Julia said sweetly.

Frowning at her, Wainwright turned to John. "Don't let her railroad you out of here. She's tricky and tough."

"I think I can hold my own," John said.

Wainwright didn't look too sure. "While you're here, you may as well take a look at the locks on her apartment, too. She lives upstairs."

"Why don't you just move him into the storage room across the hall?" Julia said dryly.

"Not a bad idea," Wainwright said.

She rolled her eyes. "I'm kidding, Dad."

John might have smiled if he didn't have a stake in this. But he did. On too many levels, if he wanted to be honest about it. First and foremost there was the very real possibility that Julia could be in some kind of danger from whatever wacko was sending her threatening letters. Second, he owed Benjamin Wainwright. Twenty years ago, the man had been chaplain with the NOPD. He'd gone above and beyond after John's father was killed in the line of duty. That wasn't the kind of thing a man forgot.

John's capitulation, he assured himself, didn't have a damn thing to do with the way that skirt swept over those curvy hips of hers.

Wainwright kissed the top of her head, then looked at John and winked conspiratorially. "Let me know what you think about those letters, will you?"

John watched him exit, feeling as if he'd just been neatly manipulated, though he wasn't sure by whom. As he turned back to the counter, he suddenly had the sinking feeling he wasn't going to make it to the cabin tomorrow.

THREE

Julia couldn't believe her father had hired John Merrick.
Of all the cops he could have turned to from the days he'd
been a chaplain with the NOPD, why did it have to be
John? Why couldn't he have hired some retired cop with
gray hair, a spare tire around his middle, and a wife and five
kids instead of this dangerous-looking ex-cop who'd once
been the object of her most forbidden teenaged fantasies?

She tried not to think about that as she watched him
prowl her shop, his cop's eyes taking in every detail. The
eighteen-year-old bad boy she'd known a lifetime ago had
been replaced by a brooding man with troubled eyes and
danger written all over his six-foot-plus frame. The man
who stood before her now looked as if he'd earned every
one of his thirty-five years—the hard way.

He wore a black leather jacket and gray slacks. His dark
brown hair looked as if it had gone quite some time without
a cut, and he swept it straight back from a face that was as
lean and uncompromising as his body. His eyes were the
gray color of a Louisiana storm. The kind that was chock
full of thunder and lightning and maybe even a tornado or

two. Julia had gotten caught up in the maelstrom of those eyes a lifetime ago. And like the silly teenager she'd been, she'd felt her heart breaking when he left for Chicago without so much as a good-bye. It had been a hard lesson for a fifteen-year-old caught up in the throes of her first love.

Picking up a book, she slid it onto the shelf behind her and tried not to be angry with her father for complicating things. Julia was no fool; she knew he was right. What didn't sit well was the idea of him hiring John Merrick without consulting her first.

"Last I heard, you'd run off to Chicago and became some hotshot detective," she said.

"Yeah, well, you got the Chicago part right."

An instant too late she remembered the shooting incident. Her father had told her it ended John's career, and she felt a quick kick of guilt. "That was a stupid thing to say. I'm sorry—"

"You don't have to dance around the subject. It happened." He sighed, but it was a haggard sound. "It's over."

She might have believed him if she hadn't caught the quick flash of some dark emotion in his eyes. And she wondered if it truly was over for him. If a person ever got over that kind of tragedy. Even a tough guy like John Merrick.

She watched him cross to the nearest shelf and slide out a book. "How long have you owned this place?" he asked.

"Two years now."

"You like it?"

"Do cops like donuts?"

Smiling, he slid the book back into place without looking at it. When he turned back to her, his face was composed and as hard as a piece of granite. "I didn't know what to say when your father approached me. I didn't realize he hadn't discussed this with you."

"He makes it difficult to say no sometimes."

"I was planning to turn him down until he mentioned the letters." He shrugged. "Then I figured you might appreciate the help."

Julia couldn't dispute that without sounding like an idiot. "I do. Thank you."

"How about this. I take a look at the letters. If I think they warrant your getting some personal protection in place, we'll handle it. I'll recommend a few security measures here at the shop and your apartment upstairs to appease your father, and we're both off the proverbial hook. Fair enough?"

She nodded, relieved that he was being so reasonable. She crossed to her desk and pulled out the manila folder where she kept the letters. "There have been six so far."

John crossed to her and took the folder. "Have you touched them? Handled them much?"

"Just to open and read them."

"Has anyone else touched them?"

"Claudia."

His eyes met hers, and Julia thought she saw the hint of a smile. "Last time I saw her she was all pigtails and freckles."

"She still has the freckles." She smiled. "She's going to Tulane now and works here part-time."

John set the folder on the desk and opened it. Taking the first letter by the corner with his thumb and forefinger, he read. *The sins ye do by two and two ye must pay for one by one.*

He looked up, saw Julia watching him, biting her lip, and he wondered if she was more frightened by the letters than she was letting on.

"It's a quote from a book," she said.

"What book?"

"It took me a while to figure it out." He tried not to check out her calves when she walked halfway down the second aisle and paused to pull out a thick book with a tattered cover. "It's Rudyard Kipling's 'Tomlinson.'" She carried it to the counter and began paging through it. "Right here."

He crossed to the counter. Silence reigned while they read the poem, then she turned her eyes on him.

"What do you think?" she asked.

"If you read it literally, it's a threat." He glanced at the other letters, picked the next one up by its corner and read.

Her tainted pen spills sin onto the page/like fevered blood from a sickle slash./Soon thine blood will be hers/and vengeance will be mine.

"I couldn't find the author of that one."

"Not quite as subtle."

"I agree."

"Any idea what the reference to writing means?"

When he glanced at Julia, her gaze skittered away. "I thought perhaps he was referring to one of the books I carry here at the shop."

"Maybe." But not for the first time, John was getting an odd vibe from her, as if she weren't quite being honest with him. Of course, that didn't make any sense. Julia Wainwright wasn't the kind of woman who kept secrets. And she had no reason to lie to him.

Or did she?

He turned his attention to the third letter. *Death is here and death is there,/Death is busy everywhere,/All around, within, beneath,/Above is death—and we are death.*

"That one is from Shelley's 'Death,' " Julia said. "It's old, 1820 or so."

"So this guy probably knows books. You tick off any of your competitors recently?"

"Not that I know of."

He flipped the page to find that the next letter was even more chilling: *The wages of sin is death.*

"It's from the New Testament," Julia put in.

"Another reference to sin. To death. Threatening, considering its context. Same paper as the others. Same font. Looks like it's off the same laser." He looked up, his expression devoid of emotion. "Do you have any idea who might be sending these?"

"I've racked my brain trying to come up with some logical culprit, but I have no earthly idea." She watched him compare the letters. "What do you think?"

"I'll tell you what I don't think. These letters don't have anything to do with your father. These letters are about you."

"Why do you say that?"

"These messages are too personal, with too much focus on books and writing. That leads me to believe it has to do with you or your shop." His gaze met hers. "Someone put some thought into these letters. Someone who knows old books and wants to convey a message to you."

Julia suppressed a shiver. Not because his words were a surprise, but because she'd already drawn the very same conclusion. "Who would do something like this? I mean, who would go to this kind of trouble?"

"Someone who's fixated. Obsessed. To him, it's not trouble. It's a compulsion. Judging from the dates on these letters, that compulsion is pretty powerful. See the dates?"

He was right. The last two letters had been delivered just two days apart. "Why is he doing it?"

"Evidently he's unhappy with you because of something he perceives that you've done." Intensity shone in his eyes and for a moment he looked very much like a cop. "Any idea what that might be?"

"I don't know."

"You sure?"

"Of course, I'm sure." She pressed her hand to her stomach. "Do you think it's someone I know?"

"Most stalking victims know their stalkers," he said. "I would venture to say this person has at least met you. We're probably talking about a male." He shrugged. "Could be a customer. A vendor. Someone you've come in contact with through the shop. Anyone come to mind?"

She shook her head. "I can't imagine anyone I know doing something like this."

"Has anyone shown an unusual amount of interest in you? In the shop? Spending an unusual amount of time here?"

"No."

"What about boyfriends? Neighbors? Any suspicious people hanging around the shop?"

"No and no." She laughed, but heard the tension in her

voice. "And half the people in the Quarter are suspicious-looking."

He smiled, but the humor was thin. "No recent falling out with anyone? Disgruntled employees? Have you fired anyone recently?"

"Claudia and Jacob are my only employees."

"Who's Jacob?"

"He's my part-time clerk."

"Is he religious?"

"He goes to church."

John pulled out a small pad. "What's his last name?"

A rise of annoyance had her shaking her head. "There's no way he's involved in this," she said.

"Won't hurt to run a background check on him then, will it?" he asked and waited.

"Brooks," she said after a moment.

"That wasn't so hard, was it?"

"I'm not trying to be difficult. I just know he isn't in-volved."

"Yeah, well, that remains to be seen." Frowning, John looked down at the letters, his brows knitting. "There's a common theme to these letters."

"I've noticed," she said. "They appear to revolve around sin and redemption. Punishment. Revenge. Absolution."

"And death." The muscles in his jaws worked as he seemed to consider that. "Do you carry any risqué or con-troversial books?" he asked. "Anything that might offend someone? Anger someone?"

"Well, I have a first edition of Sir Richard Burton's translation of the *Kama Sutra*. Some Victorian erotica. Oh, and I have a copy of *Fanny Hill* that was published on the black market in 1898. First edition." A priceless book and one that had caused plenty of controversy over the years, but Julia knew in her heart it wasn't the book that had an-gered the letter writer.

"Do you have a Web site with an inventory of books?" he asked.

"I'm working on it, but the site isn't up yet."

"If a book or author you carry is, indeed, the reason behind the letters, that means the letter writer has been in the shop or somehow knows your inventory."

Gooseflesh raced up her arms at the thought.

"Have you received any strange phone calls? Any hangups? Unfamiliar cars parked outside?"

"I'm usually pretty observant, but the shop has been busy and it's possible I just haven't noticed." She raised her gaze to his. "John, do you think this guy is dangerous?"

"I'm not going to sugarcoat this for you, Julia."

No, she thought, he'd never been good at that, but then that had always been part of his appeal. "So what am I up against?"

"He's stalking you. There are some strong emotions involved. That makes him dangerous."

"How dangerous?"

"If his compulsion gets out of control, he could try to get to you."

"How do I protect myself?"

"Don't underestimate him. Be vigilant. Be alert. Take some measures to keep yourself safe."

"Like what?"

"Commonsense stuff. Alarm system. Locks. Secure windows and doors. Keep someone with you at all times."

"Oh, jeez . . . like that's going to be practical."

His gaze moved around the shop. "Do you mind if I take a look around?"

"Oh, um . . . sure. I can show you around, if you'd like."

"Let's start with the back door."

Her heart was beating a little too fast as she led him down the aisle toward the rear of the shop. She was keenly aware of him behind her, the steady tread of his boots against the floor, the rustle of his leather jacket. The faint hint of his aftershave reminded her of pine forests and summer storms.

At the rear of the shop, she opened the door to the storage room, flipped on the light and stepped inside. "This is where I do most of the inventory work and boxing for shipping." She motioned toward the exit door. It was a dented metal antique with a push bar and knob that rattled like old bones. "That door leads to an alley behind the building. It winds through a couple of courtyards and eventually cuts over to Bourbon Street."

John walked to the door, squatted to inspect the lock and shook his head. "This lock wouldn't keep out a determined four-year-old."

"In the two years I've owned the shop, I've never had any problems."

"Yeah, well, you don't want that first time to happen." He straightened, turned to her. "I can arrange to have a new lock installed tomorrow."

"That would be great. Just . . . let me know how much I owe you."

"Did I hear you mention that you have an alarm system?"

For the first time, Julia felt foolish, because she knew upgrading the old security alarm was something she should have done ages ago. "I do, but it's not exactly state-of-the-art."

John frowned at her. "Tell me your security system is not a four-and-a-half-pound Chihuahua."

"It's not." She smiled. "It's just . . . old."

"How old?"

"Well, I've been meaning to upgrade."

"I'll find a reputable company and get them out here in the next day or so." He pulled out the pad and made another note. "Any other windows in this place?"

"Just the display window at the front."

He scribbled, then slid the pad into his jacket pocket. "Your father mentioned your apartment is upstairs."

An uneasy quiver of nerves ran the length of her. "Oh, well . . ."

As if discerning her reluctance, he said, "I figure the sooner we get this done, the sooner your father will get off your back."

"There's an incentive." But as she left the storage room and started toward the steps that led to the second level, she tried hard to remember if she'd cleared her desk . . .

The only sound came from their shoes against the wooden steps and the occasional creak as she took him up the narrow staircase to the landing outside her apartment door. At the top, she inserted her key into the lock and swung it open.

A quick sweep of the room told her she had, indeed, tidied things up that morning. "It's small in square footage, but it makes up for it in character."

"Nice place."

Despite her apprehension, she felt a quick swell of pride. Her apartment wasn't designer or roomy or elegant, but it was hers and she loved every square inch of it right down to the creaky cypress plank floor. The walls were heavily textured and painted an eye-pleasing terra cotta. The woodwork was painted fresh white. Bookshelves crowded with volumes of all shapes and sizes encompassed the wall to her left. The sofa was overstuffed, piled high with fussy pillows and designed for spending quality time with a book.

"One bedroom?" John crossed to her bedroom, paused in the doorway.

"Two actually, but I use the second one for an office." She watched him stride to the window and check the lock. His gaze went briefly to the queen-size iron bed where she slept, and she was suddenly ridiculously grateful she'd taken the time to make it.

"The screws have nearly rusted off the lock." He glanced back at her. "It wouldn't take much for someone to climb up the fire escape, sidle along the ledge and pry it open."

She walked over to see for herself. "This building is really old. Circa 1835. Most of it is original."

"Original is good except for when it comes to locks."

"Right."

He made a note on the pad, then turned from the window and nearly ran into her. For an instant she found herself staring into the turbulent gray depths of his eyes. She saw a measure of surprise. A warning she didn't quite understand. And a heady dose of male awareness that made her feel breathless and a little dizzy. She felt that same awareness flash through her body like a lightning strike on a hot night.

She was about to heed the warning and step back when he reached out to steady her. The unexpected contact jolted her. She could feel the heat of his fingertips through her jacket. The beat of his pulse against her bicep. The zing of nerves that had nothing to do with cryptic letters and everything to do with the way he was looking at her.

Unable to hold his gaze, she let her eyes skim down his face, past the straight slash of his nose, the chiseled lips, to the crescent scar on his chin he'd gotten when he was fifteen. She remembered that day perfectly. He'd jumped into the swimming pool, but didn't clear the diving board. He'd bled like a sieve and had to get six stitches. But he'd been incredibly brave. And she thought maybe that was the day she'd lost her nine-year-old heart to him . . .

Gently, he pushed her to arm's length. "I need to check the fire escape door," he said, then stepped around her and headed toward the kitchen.

Julia stood her ground in the bedroom and assured herself the wild skitter of her pulse had nothing to do with attraction. She'd gotten over him years ago. She was just uneasy about the letters. Besides, she didn't like people poking around her apartment. Any other reason was too ludicrous to consider. Schoolgirl crushes didn't last twenty years.

John Merrick might be a sight to behold with those stormy gray eyes and that chiseled mouth, but Julia was a hell of a lot smarter than the naïve teenager she'd been a lifetime ago. Experience had taught her caution when it came to men, and she'd learned how to steer clear of the ones who spelled trouble. John hit the danger zone in that category, and Julia had never been attracted to danger. She liked her life safe and predictable, just the way it was.

"This is your office?"

His voice snapped her out of her reverie to see him push open the door to the bedroom she'd transformed into her work area. She didn't want him in there, but couldn't think of a viable excuse without making him suspicious, so she held her ground in the doorway while he crossed to the single window and checked the lock.

"This one's rusted, too." He pulled the pad from his pocket and made a note. "You probably ought to have the windows wired to the alarm, too. It'll cost more, but it's worth it in terms of security."

His eyes skimmed the crowded bookcases while he spoke. Julia knew it was silly, but she felt like a secretive teenager whose parent was inspecting her room for contraband.

"Nice collection of books," he said.

"Thank you. It's taken me a while to accumulate." Pride swelled as she skimmed over the leather spines and embossed titles. "These are the ones I could never bring myself to sell."

His gaze swept from the books to her. "I'm glad you've found your place in the world," he said quietly. "Some people never do."

She sensed an inference to his own failed career and didn't know what to say. "There were times when I thought the shop was a pipe dream. Times when other people in my life thought the same thing."

"You pursued it anyway."

"You can't please everyone. But then you already know that, don't you?"

He stared at her for so long she wanted to squirm. Julia had always been good at reading facial expressions and body language. But John's face was so utterly inscrutable, she hadn't a clue what he was thinking or feeling.

Shaking himself as if from a dream, he stepped back. "I'll check the kitchen and get out of your hair."

Before she could say anything, he'd turned away and disappeared into the hall.

*His heart was still pounding when he reached the galley-*style kitchen. He stood there for a moment, trying hard to convince himself it wasn't attraction that had arced between them just a moment earlier. He might have screwed up his career, but he wasn't stupid enough to get involved in a situation simply because his hormones thought it was a good idea. Hormones rarely steered a man in the right direction.

Julia Wainwright might have a body made for sin, but there was no way in hell he was going to concede to some primal instinct to mate and get tangled up with her, physically or otherwise. With the shooting weighing heavily on his mind and his life in upheaval, he was in no condition to act on some animal impulse.

Determined to finish the security inspection and get the hell out of there before he did something stupid, he strode to the fire escape door and tugged it open. The lock appeared to be as old as the building. The striker plate was bolted to wood that was rotted in places and warped with age. One hard kick and the door would give.

"Terrific," he muttered.

The fire escape stairs led to a narrow courtyard littered with empty clay pots, a single upended garbage can and a crumbling old fountain that had long since seen its glory days. Deserted and poorly lit, it was the perfect place for an ambush . . .

"So, do I pass home security 101?"

He closed the door and turned to her. She was standing a few feet away, watching him with those gypsy eyes. She'd taken her shoes off, and he could see that her toenails were painted an intriguing shade of burgundy, that her feet were every bit as sexy as the rest of her. And he found himself wishing the kitchen wasn't quite so small . . .

"You get points for locking the doors," he said. "Not that any of these locks would hold."

"That's a comfort."

He thought about the courtyard. "You don't use the back door, do you?"

"Only when I'm in a hurry and need to cut over to Bourbon Street."

"Points off for that." He frowned at her. "I don't want you using the alley at all. At least until the letters stop."

She bit her lip. "What if they don't stop?"

Because he didn't want to make promises he couldn't keep, he didn't answer. "I made a list of repairs and other work you need to have done. I'll contact a locksmith tomorrow and have them replace your locks. I should be able to get an alarm company out here in the next day or so." He thought of the fishing trip he'd had planned, realized he could make the calls in the morning and be at the cabin by afternoon . . .

"So, just how hard do I need to be looking over my shoulder, John?" she asked.

He met her gaze levelly. "Just be aware, Julia. Your surroundings. The people around you. You need to take this guy seriously."

She pursed her lips. "Okay. I can do that."

He knew it was stupid, but he was feeling territorial and a little protective of her. He wanted to believe it was because he'd known her since she was a chubby kid with braces. Because her father had asked him to look after her. Because she was an innocent in a world full of wolves. But if John wanted to be perfectly and bluntly honest about it, he knew that hard edge of territoriality had more to do with the way that suit swept over curves even a saint would have a hard time resisting.

He sure as hell never claimed to be a saint.

But he was smart enough to know that things would work out better for both of them if he put her in somebody else's hands. He was in no frame of mind to keep anyone safe from anything. He needed some time alone to get his head together and decide what he was going to do with the rest of his life.

He was pulling his notepad from his jacket pocket to make a note about the alarm when the lights flickered and went out. "What the hell happened to the lights?" he growled.

"It's a fuse. Happens sometimes."

"Don't tell me. It's original to the building."

"I don't think they had elec—"

John made a sound of exasperation. "Jesus, Julia, I don't have to mention that this could be a small security problem, do I?"

"Don't start yelling at me. I have no control over what my landlord does or does not do."

"Yeah, well, if your landlord won't repair the electrical for you, maybe he'll do it for the city inspector." He moved toward the sink, where dim light slanted in through the window, only to knock his shin hard against something heavy and sharp. "Son of a—"

"Oh, sorry. I forgot about that bookcase. I'm refinishing—"

Cursing, he rubbed the bump that had come up on his shin. "How the hell do you get your electricity back on?"

"The fuse box is in the storage room. I just need to grab my flashlight and a new fuse and go downstairs to screw it in."

Annoyed, John shoved the bookcase out of the way with a tad too much force. He could hear Julia moving around a few feet away. The sound of a drawer opening. The shuffle of paper. A resonant click sounded, and then a beam of yellow light cut through the darkness.

When she shone the beam between them to illuminate their faces, a teasing smile curved her lips. "You're not afraid of the dark, are you?"

Not amused, he held out his hand for the flashlight. "I

have no desire to break my friggin' leg on some damn bookcase. I can't believe you put up with this crap."

"This building is historical," she said a little defensively. "Mrs. Langston, my landlord, is trying to preserve as much of it as possible."

"Preserve her wallet maybe."

She shoved the flashlight at him. "Be careful on the steps. I wouldn't want you to fall and break your neck."

"Funny." John took the flashlight, crossed the living room and opened the door into the hall. The wooden steps creaked as they descended the stairs. He could hear Julia behind him. Beyond, the shop was as silent as a tomb. Outside, the rain was coming down in sheets, and he could hear the hard ping of raindrops against the roof. At the bottom of the stairs he opened the door to the storage room.

"Where's the fuse box?" he asked.

"To your right."

John shone the light to his right in time to see Julia step up to a rusty metal electrical box mounted on the wall. "Don't tell me," he said dryly. "It's an antique."

"Some people have no appreciation for the ancient."

"Especially when it's a pain in the ass."

"This will just take a second."

John held the flashlight while she worked off her jacket, draped it over a metal chair, then opened the metal box mounted on the wall and unscrewed the spent fuse. He tried to hold the beam steady on the box, but his attention kept drifting back to her. To the way that sweater flowed over curves he had no right to be noticing at a time like this.

"Do you mind?"

Realizing he'd let the beam stray, John jerked the light back to the box. "Sometime today," he growled.

An instant later the lights flicked on. Julia turned to him, her expression triumphant. "Good as new."

"If you don't mind a fire hazard."

He spotted her jacket draped over a nearby chair back, and for the first time he had an unencumbered view of her without it. He saw silk flowing over lush curves, the outline of lace and the hint of large nipples puckered with cold . . .

Disgusted with himself, he stepped back, figured now would be as good a time as any to make his exit. He turned off the flashlight and handed it to her. "I'll give you a call tomorrow and let you know when the locksmith and alarm people will be out."

"Great. I'll be here all day."

He left the storage room and entered the main portion of the shop. Aware that he'd broken a sweat, that he was walking too fast, he headed toward the door. He could hear Julia behind him, but he didn't slow down. He didn't want her to ask him to stay for coffee. He didn't feel like making small talk or reminiscing about old times. He didn't like the way he was reacting to her, didn't want to get caught up in the way she looked or the way his body jumped to attention every time he looked at her.

But he knew if she asked him to stay, he would . . .

He reached the door. Vaguely, he was aware that Julia had gone behind the counter. That she was humming a tune, and he could still smell the sweetness of her perfume. He twisted the knob, tugged open the door. The cold, wet air registered at about the same time as the realization that the door hadn't been locked.

He was trying to decide if he should give her a quick education on all the things that could happen to people who didn't lock their doors when her scream stopped him dead in his tracks.

FOUR

*Julia didn't scare easily. She wasn't particularly squeam-
ish or skittish.* She'd never even been afraid of bugs or ro-
dents or any of the other creepy things that launched most
people into panic mode. But the sight of the knife stabbed
into the book and surrounded by the stark red of blood sent
a scream pouring from her throat.

She scrambled away from the counter just as John burst
back into the shop. "What is it?" he snapped, but his eyes
were already on the counter.

Julia pointed, surprised to see her hand shaking.
"Someone . . . must have come in while we were upstairs."

He crossed to the counter. "What the hell?"

Taking a calming breath, she moved closer and stared
down at the macabre sight in utter disbelief. Someone had
driven a nasty-looking knife through the center of a book
and dribbled what looked like blood all over the cover and
surrounding countertop. The serrated blade had gone
through both the front and back covers and penetrated the
wooden counter beneath.

"My God," she murmured, but her voice was high and tight. "What do you—"

John's gaze met hers, his eyes flat and dangerous. "Did you lock the front door after your father left?"

"I'm sure of it."

"It wasn't locked." He glanced toward the rear of the shop. "Stay put. Don't touch anything. I'm going to check the back room."

Sudden understanding dawned: the intruder could still be in the shop. Julia's heart began to pound. She watched John move soundlessly down the aisle and disappear into the storage room. Still not sure if she was frightened or angry—or maybe a little of both—she glanced down at the book. A shudder moved through her as she took in the length of the knife, its stainless blade stained with bright red droplets. The cover of the book had been slashed multiple times, as if the culprit had been in a frenzy. It almost looked as if the book was bleeding . . .

Leaning close, she was able to make out the title on the spine, and a second, deeper chill barreled through her. *A Gentleman's Touch* by Elisabeth de Haviland.

"Oh, my God." Dread and a pristine new fear unfurled inside her. For a moment Julia couldn't catch her breath. Pressing one hand to her stomach, she leaned heavily against the counter. She couldn't believe this was happening. She'd been so careful. How could anyone know?

"The storage room is clear. The back door was locked." She turned to face John.

"They must have come in through the front door," he said.

"That's impossible because I locked it."

"Are you absolutely certain?"

"Of course, I am," she snapped. "I live in the French Quarter. I always lock my doors."

He didn't look convinced, but she gave him credit for not pressing her. "Any idea who might have done this?"

She glanced at the chilling scene on the counter, then looked away, shook her head. "I can't imagine."

"Who has a key to this place?"

"Claudia and Jacob. My landlord. My dad."

"Jacob again, huh? His name keeps coming up."

"You can be suspicious all you want, but there's no way he had anything to do with this."

He removed the pad from his jacket. "I need his contact information."

"Why? What are you going to do?"

"I'm not going to send him a goddamn Christmas card."

"John, I don't think—"

"Julia, for God's sake, I'm not going to rough him up. I'm just going to talk to him. Now, give me his phone number and address."

Realizing the smart thing to do at this point was cooperate, even if she disagreed with him, Julia walked to her desk, pulled out a memo pad and jotted down Jacob's address and phone number. She crossed to John and held the piece of paper out. "Be nice to him. He's a good kid."

"Yeah, well, that's what everyone said about Ted Bundy."

"That's not funny."

"Who's joking?" He took the paper and slid it into his pocket without looking at it. "I need your landlord's number, too."

Making a sound of exasperation to cover the fact that she was still feeling shaky, Julia recited the number from memory while he jotted it on his pad. "Don't be rude to her. She's old and sweet."

"As long as she cooperates, we'll get along just fine."

Shaking her head, Julia looked toward the counter, the ghastly sight sending a shiver through her. She simply couldn't reconcile herself to believing someone she knew was doing such a thing.

She jumped when he set his hand on her shoulder. "You okay?"

"I'm . . . ticked off more than anything."

One side of his mouth curved. "Ticked off is better than hysterical."

"Yeah, well, you can relax. I don't do hysterical." She

couldn't stop looking at the book. "For God's sake, is that *blood*?"

He grimaced. "Smells like it."

"Where would someone get blood? I mean, he could have . . . It could be hum—"

"For all we know he could have gotten it at the neighborhood butcher. We can have the police test it." His eyes narrowed. "It took some strength to get that knife through that book and into the countertop."

"It's almost as if he was in a frenzy."

"Or a rage."

Unnerved by the thought, Julia rubbed her hands over her arms. "Who would do something like this?"

"Evidently someone who's unhappy with something you've done. Some perceived wrong." He tilted his head slightly, as if to get a better look at her. "Any idea what that might be?"

She forced her gaze to his. "None."

He stared at her, his eyes probing with an intensity that unnerved, but she held his gaze. For a moment, the only sound came from the rain pinging against the window and the quickened beat of her heart.

After a moment, John looked away and focused his attention on the book. "There's something wedged between the pages."

On impulse, Julia reached for it, but he stopped her by grasping her wrist. "Don't touch it," he said. "If it's blood, it's a biohazard. Plus, we don't want to contaminate any possible evidence."

She looked down where his fingers were wrapped around her wrist. His grip was warm and surprisingly reassuring. His skin was dark against hers, and for a moment Julia couldn't look away.

"You're shaking," he said.

"Yeah, well, I'm not used to finding bloody books on my counter."

He released her and unsnapped a cell phone from his

belt. "The police will be able tell us if this is human or animal."

Julia hadn't wanted the police involved any more than they already were, but she was smart enough to know she no longer had a choice. The situation had just taken a hard turn left into dangerous territory.

"What will the police do?" she asked.

"They'll file a report. A minor crime like this— trespassing and vandalism—doesn't warrant much attention from PD. We'll be lucky to get a crime scene team out here to dust for prints. On the other hand, if the blood turns out to be human, they're going to want to know where it came from."

The thought made her shudder. "Let's hope it's not human."

"I'll give Mitch a call, see if he can help get a CSI out here."

"Mitch as in Mitchy?"

John grinned. "He'd probably prefer if you didn't call him that."

She smiled back. "He's a cop?"

"A damn good one. If we can get someone to dust that book for prints, Mitch can help us cut through some of the red tape. Get the prints entered into AFIS. If our perp's in the system, we'll I.D. him."

Hope swept through her at the thought of the police catching the stalker.

John punched keys on his phone and slipped into cop mode as he reported the crime. Watching him, Julia suddenly realized that he had probably been a very good cop. That he missed police work. That he was a hell of a lot more disturbed about what had happened in Chicago than he was letting on.

He snapped the phone closed. "A unit will be here in a few minutes." He glanced at the book and frowned. "In the meantime, I thought we'd see what this sick son of a bitch had to say." Removing a small pocketknife from his slacks, he opened it and used the tip to slide the paper from its nest.

Julia watched, not sure she wanted to know.

The paper appeared to be the same expensive linen as the others. Using the knife, John unfolded it on the counter.

Something went cold inside her when the words came into view. *The harlot's ink is her lifeblood. Bleeding sin onto the page. Words that maim the hearts of the innocent and taint the souls of the weak. Soon the blood will be hers. The world will be purged of her sins. And vengeance will at last be mine.*

"Holy shit," he muttered, "I think the crazy bastard really *did* write this in blood."

She stared at the perfectly executed red calligraphy, aware that her heart was pounding. She could feel her breaths coming too short, too fast. And for the first time since the letters began, she acknowledged the fear that had taken up residence deep inside.

"Do you recognize the book?" John asked after a moment.

Julia closed her eyes briefly, pressed her hand to her stomach against the slow curl of dread. She didn't want to tell him about her book. She wanted that part of her life to remain private. But there was no way she could continue to downplay the situation.

"Maybe," she whispered.

"What do you mean 'maybe'?" He looked at her sharply, his thick brows knit with impatience. "If you know something, Julia, now would be a good time to enlighten me."

When she said nothing, he used the tip of his knife to open the cover flap of the book and turn to the first page, where the title and author's name were visible. "Elisabeth de Haviland." He turned his attention back to Julia. "Are you familiar with this author?"

"Yes."

"Is she a friend of yours? What?"

"Not exactly."

"What do you mean 'not exactly'?" He looked at the book. "Can you think of any reason why this book might upset someone? Why they would take that anger out on you?"

She nodded. "I can think of several."

"Is it controversial? What?"

Heat rose in her cheeks. She could feel the guilt on her face, the rise of panic in her chest, her brain scrambling for a lie. But she knew there was no way she could keep her secret and still hope to find the person responsible. As much as she didn't want to acknowledge it, the two were as intertwined as the blood and paper of the pages inside the book.

John closed the book and turned stormy gray eyes on her. Within their depths, Julia saw questions, cool suspicion, and an impatience that was tempered with the resolve to satisfy both.

"You're not telling something," he said. "Come on, Julia. Talk to me. Who is Elisabeth de Haviland?"

She met his gaze levelly, refusing to drop her eyes or look away first. She didn't have anything to be ashamed of, she told herself. Damn it, she didn't. But she could feel the burn of a blush rising into her cheeks . . .

"Me," she said and tried not to think about what the confession would set into motion.

FIVE

John hung back and watched the single CSI work the scene. Big city police departments were invariably stretched tight with regard to manpower. Dispatch had sent only one investigator. At his brother's prodding, no doubt. John didn't miss the politics or the bullshit, but he sure missed being a cop.

It had been over two months since he'd worked a crime scene. In the past he'd always felt at home among the chaos, the pain and death and bad jokes. Tonight he felt like an outsider. A civilian. But then standing on the sidelines had never been his cup of tea. John figured he'd better get used to it. In his current state of mind there wasn't a police department in the country that would hire him.

Julia sat at her desk, looking pale and frazzled even through the smile she'd worked up for his younger brother, Mitch. But John knew from experience the facade wouldn't last much longer. She might put up a brave front, but he'd seen the fear in her eyes. She was scared—and rightfully so.

Why had she been so reluctant to tell him about the book she'd written?

He liked to read as much as the next guy—thrillers and police procedural mostly—but for the last few years his life had been too busy for such indulgences; it had been months since he'd read a novel. He wondered what kind of book she'd penned. More to the point, he wondered why some sick son of a bitch had seen fit to slink into her shop after hours, put a knife through the cover and drizzle it with blood.

"You got a sec?"

John turned to find his younger brother standing behind him. An unexpected frisson of pride swept through him at the sight of the uniform. Mitch Merrick might be a rookie, but you couldn't tell by looking at him. John had watched him work the scene, and his younger brother was as competent as any veteran detective.

Both he and Mitch came from a long line of law enforcement. It was in their blood. Both boys had wanted to be cops as long as John could remember. Their father, Carter, had tried to break the tradition by urging them to pursue other careers. But John and Mitch had no interest in anything but police work. After their father was killed in the line of duty when John was eighteen and Mitch was sixteen, there was never any question as to which profession they would choose.

"Sure," John said.

Taking a final look at Julia, he followed his brother to the front door.

"So what do you have?" John asked.

"I thought we were dealing with a simple B and E and vandalism until the CSI told me the blood is human."

"Damn." He hadn't wanted to hear that. "You think someone's been hurt?"

"Tech said there's not enough blood to indicate serious injury or death."

"Guy definitely made a statement."

"No shit. Tech'll type it. We'll run DNA, see if we get a hit in the database, but it's a long shot."

"Did the tech get latents off the book or knife?" Running prints through the Federal Bureau of Investigation's Integrated Automated Fingerprint Identification System (IAFIS) was routine.

"Whoever handled that book and knife wore gloves."

"Pretty careful for a vandal, don't you think?" But John figured both men knew they were not dealing with an ordinary vandal.

Mitch looked over his shoulder toward where Julia sat at her desk, pretending to do paperwork. "So what's up with Julia? How did you end up here?"

John thought about Benjamin Wainwright and shook his head. "Long story. I'll fill you in later."

"Looks like the little bookworm is all grown up." Mitch grinned. "Last I recall, she had one hell of a crush on you."

John didn't smile back. "Yeah, well, she's older and wiser now."

"Someone hassling her?"

"She's been receiving threatening letters. Weird shit."

"Stalker?"

"Yup."

"So you going to keep an eye on her, or what?"

John frowned, not liking the insinuation in his brother's voice. Not liking it even more that he'd somehow ended up in the middle of a situation he wanted no part of. "Something like that."

"Or maybe you're worried she'll put a crimp in your style. God forbid you might have to come back to the land of the living."

John shot his brother a warning look. "What I do is my business, bro."

"For chrissake, John, it's been two months—"

"I know how long it's been."

"If you think drowning yourself in a bottle every night is going to help, you're sorely—"

"I killed a man, goddamn it," John ground out.

"It was an accident. You were cleared."

The radio strapped to Mitch's hip crackled, saving John from having to respond. It wasn't the first time they'd had the conversation. He hoped it was the last. The way John saw things, a good man was still dead and John still had the man's blood on his hands.

Mitch spoke into the radio clipped to his lapel. When he looked at John, his expression was all business. "I gotta run. I got a domestic over on Rampart."

"Thanks for getting the CSI out here. I know that took some doing."

"I'll let you know if we get a hit on that DNA." Mitch started for the door. "Good luck finding your stalker."

John watched his brother walk out the door, wishing like hell he'd never returned Benjamin Wainwright's call.

It was nearly midnight by the time the CSI left. He'd bagged the book and knife, along with a sample of the blood and several fingerprint strips, to take back to the lab. John stared at the blood that remained on the counter, wishing the CSI had cleaned it up. But, of course, that wasn't his job, so John had asked him to leave a pair of rubber gloves. Julia provided the bleach. He spent ten minutes scrubbing the counter.

"I could have done that," Julia said.

Peeling off the gloves, John tossed them into the trash bag and tied it off. "Where do you put your trash?"

"There's a Dumpster in the alley." She reached for the bag, but he frowned at her and carried it to the back of the shop. He opened the rear door to a narrow alley lined with scarred metal doors, garbage bags and an array of trash cans. A beat-up Dumpster with a broken lid stood just to the left of the door. John tossed the bag and walked back inside.

He found Julia standing at her desk, looking exhausted and frazzled—and like she'd rather be anywhere but here with him.

"Look, I know it's late," John said, "but I think now is probably a good time for you to tell me about this book you've written."

Her eyes skittered away and he got the feeling the book was the last thing she wanted to talk about. But why?

"It's a novel," she said. "A love story."

"Love story?" He sighed, sensing there was more. "You want to elaborate on why you think a love story would set someone off?"

"It's not the first time a book has sent someone into a tizzy."

Wondering why she was stalling, he motioned toward the counter. "A butcher knife stabbed into one of your books and drizzled with human blood is a hell of a lot more than a tizzy."

When she didn't respond, he sighed with impatience. "Julia, if you want me to help you, you're going to have to level with me."

She fidgeted. "It's called literary erotica."

"Literary erotica, huh?" He was no scholar when it came to books, but he had a pretty good idea what she was talking about. "You mean you write about sex?"

"I write about a man and a woman having a consensual and loving sexual relationship."

Not knowing what to say to that, John scratched his head and tried to imagine what this rather benign woman could have written that would anger someone to the point of stabbing a bloody knife through one of her books.

"Do you think your book is the reason this guy is sending you letters?" he asked.

Her eyes met his. Within their depths he saw knowledge and the kind of fear a woman like her should never have to feel. "If you read the letters in that context, it makes sense."

"Any ideas who you might have offended? A religious zealot? What?"

"I think it's someone who feels that, perhaps, sensuality

shouldn't be part of literature. That maybe I'm perpetuating something sinful."

Sensuality, he thought, was the politically correct word for sex. Jesus. "So, this could be based on religious beliefs." He let the idea roll around in his head for a moment. "But then I guess the Puritans were always cramping the sinners' style."

"Certain kinds of literature have been controversial since man began scratching symbols onto the walls of caves."

"Do you think this might have something to do with your father or Eternity Springs Ministries?"

"I don't know." Turning away from him, she sank down into the chair behind her desk. "Probably not."

"What's Benjamin's take on this?"

She looked away, sighed. "I haven't exactly told him."

"You told him *something*, because he called me."

"Claudia told him someone was leaving notes. Thankfully, she didn't tell him about my book." She pursed her lips. "I'd like to keep it that way."

"Any particular reason why?"

"You can't possibly be that dense."

"I am," he said, deadpan.

She laughed. It was a throaty sound that rippled over him like warm waves, hitting every pleasure center in his brain.

"Julia, I don't see what the big deal is."

"The big deal is that my father has worked hard to get where he is. He's about to be elected director of the Eternity Springs Ministries." She put her face in her hands for a moment, then raised her gaze to his. "As unreasonable as it sounds, I think if word got out that his daughter is writing . . . explicit novels, it could hurt his chances of getting the directorship position. It's an elected position, and he needs the votes of all twelve of the board of directors."

John considered that for a moment. "Benjamin Wainwright is no dummy, Julia. He probably already knows—"

"He doesn't," she cut in. "I write under a pseudonym. There's no way he could know."

"So then who *does* know about the book?"

"Claudia and Jacob. My editor in New York. My agent, also in New York."

Jacob again, he thought. "Do you have a Web site?"

"Yes, but there's no photograph."

"What about an address or e-mail address for fan mail?"

"I have both. A P.O. box here in the Quarter and an e-mail address."

"The letter you received this morning was hand delivered?"

She nodded. "I don't know how he could have found out about the bookstore."

"Unless he works here."

"It wasn't Jacob."

John didn't say anything. His cop's mind was already jumping ahead to other ways some overzealous fan or religious fanatic could have found out where she lived. "Someone could have been waiting at the post office box when you picked up your mail. He could have followed you here."

She looked a little sick. "I thought of that."

"Have you noticed anyone suspicious? Anyone watching you? Showing a little too much interest in you or the shop?"

"No, but . . . most days I'm so busy here I wouldn't notice."

"You need to start being aware of your surroundings."

"Okay."

"Even though it's probably already too late, next time you go to the post office, I go with you."

She didn't look happy about it, but she nodded. "All right."

"I'll drop by tomorrow and install new locks on all your doors. I'll see what I can do to expedite that new alarm system."

"Thank you." She rose.

Not for the first time John had a difficult time keeping his eyes on her face. They wanted to roam. In the background rain pinged against the roof. He could hear the hiss of traffic on the street. The low rumble of thunder in the distance. Even though she was standing several feet away, he could smell the sweet, erotic scent of her perfume. The aroma of the candles she'd been burning. The leather and dust smell of the store. Looking into her eyes, he felt as if his senses were suddenly hypersensitive, and he wondered what it would be like to run his hands over her . . .

Suddenly anxious to leave, he pulled the Mustang keys from his pocket. "Keep your doors locked, including the bolts," he said and started toward the door.

"I will."

He had crossed to the door and set his hand on the knob when it struck him that it might be helpful for him to take a look at the book she'd written so he could decide for himself what could possibly have offended someone into threatening her.

He turned. She was still standing at the desk, watching him. "I want a copy of your book," he said.

For an instant, she looked taken aback. She blinked at him, and even in the dim light he thought her cheeks reddened. "Oh . . . well, I think I have one on the shelf."

He watched her walk to the third row, trying hard not to notice the way her skirt brushed against her calves. Trying even harder not to wonder what the rest of her looked like beneath all those practical clothes.

Her jacket opened as she reached for the book. He saw the curve of her breasts, the outline of her bra through her blouse, and he broke a sweat beneath his leather jacket.

She put the book in his hand. "It was released about a month ago."

He took the book and looked at the cover. It was a trade-size paperback. The cover was colorful and sophisticated, depicting the slightly faded silhouette of a woman straddling her lover. "I'll take a look, just so I know what we're dealing with."

She finally looked into his eyes. "Thank you for doing this. For—"

"Keeping your secret?" He smiled.

"For getting involved when I know you have a lot of other things on your mind."

She was referring to the shooting, of course. No one ever came out and said "the shooting." Invariably, they called it "The Incident" or otherwise found some euphemism, a way to dance around the cold hard fact that he'd shot and killed a fellow cop.

Not wanting to get into a topic he spent far too much time thinking about anyway, he turned and walked through the door without responding.

Six

He stood in the shadows of the warehouse, hidden from view, his heart pounding. He could feel the sweat running between his shoulder blades beneath his coat. The hard press of fear crushing the breath from his lungs.

Twenty yards away, he could hear the perp moving toward him. Leather soles against concrete. The brush of denim against denim. The rustle of a nylon jacket.

He pressed his back hard against the crate and closed his eyes, trying to focus, trying to calm down. But his palms were sweaty as he gripped the H&K .45. And like a movie he'd seen a thousand times before, he knew what would happen next.

He stepped away from the crate. Movement at the end of the aisle drew his gaze. John dropped into a shooter's stance, spread his legs, raised the pistol. Adrenaline stung his gut when he spotted the figure holding a sawed-off shotgun the size of a cannon.

"Police officer!" John shouted. "Drop your weapon! Do it now!"

As if in slow motion the shotgun came up. A quiver

of fear ran the length of him. He heard the sound of shoes against concrete behind him. Shit, he thought, and spun in a half circle. A second man behind him raised a pistol.

Instinct kicked in. John's finger jerked against the trigger. The .45 bucked in his hand. The explosion deafened him, made his ears ring. Cordite stung his nostrils. The man crumpled to the floor.

John swung the pistol around to the other man to find him gone. "Shit," he muttered. "Shit!"

He hit his mike. "Shots fired! North exit! Gimme backup now!" Without waiting for a response, he started toward the downed man.

The figure lay motionless on the concrete floor in a widening pool of blood. John looked for the weapon, but there was no gun in sight. Kneeling, he set his hand against the perp's shoulder and rolled him over.

Only it wasn't Franklin Watts staring up at him.

Horror ripped through him at the sight of Julia Wainwright's face. She looked up at him, her eyes filled with pain and accusation. "You did this to me," she said.

John reached for his mike, but it was gone. There was no one to call. No one to help him. He felt for his cell phone, but that, too, was gone.

"You're going to be all right," he heard himself say.

"Everything you touch dies, John. You're death."

"No . . ."

"My blood is on your hands, just like Franklin Watts's."

When John looked at his hands, they were covered with blood . . .

John came awake abruptly and sat bolt upright, his heart pounding. He looked down at his hands, expecting to see blood. Relief swept through him when he saw they were clean and dry.

Just a nightmare, he told himself. But the horror of it clung to him, as dark and putrid as decaying flesh. He couldn't get the sight out of his head of Julia's blood on his hands.

Untangling himself from the blankets, he sat on the edge of the bed and put his face in his hands. His skin was slick with sweat. He could still feel himself shaking, both inside and out.

"Jesus Christ," he muttered. Scrubbing his hands over his face, he rose and walked barefoot to the kitchen. He found the bottle of gin next to the toaster, uncapped it and drank straight from the bottle. The alcohol burned a path down his esophagus. It would probably eat a hole in his gut one of these days, but even an ulcer would be better than the nightmare.

He snagged a glass from the cupboard and poured. It was too much alcohol and he was drinking it for all the wrong reasons. But he downed the glass in two gulps. After *The Incident* in Chicago, the department shrink had prescribed a mild antidepressant, but after three weeks of taking it, John hadn't liked the way it made him feel. Not that the alcohol was any better, but at least he knew what he was getting.

He hadn't eaten dinner and could already feel the gin going to his head. Salvation, he thought, and it frightened him that he didn't know what he'd do without the booze. Another glass and he would be well on his way to a drunken stupor. A third and he would fall back into bed and sleep like the dead until noon.

If he was lucky, anyway.

He poured a second glass and carried it to the bedroom, pausing at the dirty window to look out on the deserted street beyond. The neighborhood was derelict and fraught with crime, and not for the first time he wondered why he'd chosen this place. It was a one-bedroom dump furnished with broken-down furniture and a few mismatched dishes. But John had known what he wanted. A place where he wouldn't be noticed. A place where he could slide into oblivion. A place where life would not intrude upon the dark place he'd landed. A place where he could decide if he wanted to go on or end it right here and now and finish his slow descent into hell.

Lowering himself onto the bed, he opened the night-stand drawer and pulled out the lockbox. His hand trembled slightly when he opened the box and peeled away the chamois cloth. A shiver moved through him when the gun came into view.

The shrink had called it hoplophobia. Fear of firearms. John called it fucking shameful. He hadn't been able to so much as touch his own weapon since the night he'd shot and killed Franklin Watts. He was a cop, for God's sake. A cop who couldn't bring himself to pick up a gun was one useless son of a bitch. He wondered if he'd be able to pick it up if he took a mind to expedite his trip to hell . . .

The laugh that squeezed from his throat was a harsh sound in the utter silence of his apartment. And for the first time in his life, John acknowledged the fact that he was lonely and scared and hanging onto some frayed thread with the desperation of a man facing a fatal fall. He didn't know what to do. Didn't know how to reach out. Wasn't sure he wanted to.

What a fucked up mess.

Draining the glass, he closed the box and put it back into the night table. He staggered slightly as he made his way back to the kitchen. At the counter he refilled the glass. All the way to the top this time. He drank deeply, hating it that he needed the anesthetization of alcohol just to make it through the night.

"Fuck it," he said and took another long pull.

He closed his eyes against the slow burn of the gin. He thought about Julia Wainwright and her stalker, and it struck him that he was not capable of protecting her. You can't even pick up your gun, Johnny-boy, came a taunting little voice. How the hell are you going to keep her safe?

He couldn't. The admittance shamed him. When he closed his eyes, he remembered the dream. He saw the way she'd looked at him when her pretty body was covered with blood. *Everything you touch dies . . .*

He wondered if Mitch could help him find some retired cop or PI who could look after her until the stalker was caught. John simply wasn't up to the job.

He looked down at his hands, remembering the way they'd looked when they'd been covered with blood. He couldn't bear another death on his conscience. It would kill him as effectively as any gun. Maybe that was best . . .

He picked up the glass and the bottle of gin and carried both back to his bedroom.

As usual, Julia was in a blinding rush. She should have been back at the shop an hour ago. If it hadn't been for her one-hundred-and-fifty-dollar Via Spigas with the three-inch heels, she'd be running instead of walking.

The day had been a whirlwind from the moment she'd left her apartment and stepped into the shop at eight o'-clock that morning. A rare and used book convention at the historic Orpheum Theatre sent a steady stream of buying customers into the shop all day. At three o'clock she'd held a poetry reading and high tea for a local author. At just after six, she'd made an appearance at the convention to speak on valuating rare and old books. Afterward, she'd spent some time chatting with some of the conference go-ers and lost track of time. Somehow it had gotten to be nine P.M.

Claudia had been at the shop since noon. She and her boyfriend, Rory, had dinner plans. Julia didn't know what time the reservation was for, but she was pretty sure they'd missed it.

At Canal Street, she spotted a cab and darted into the street with her hand up—something she'd learned from her editor in New York—but the cabbie sped off, leaving her in a cloud of exhaust.

Resigned to a long walk back to the shop, she crossed Canal and entered the French Quarter at Royal. It was the tail end of the dinner hour, and as always the area was abuzz with activity. Julia loved the colorful madness of

French Quarter living. The contrast between the quiet sophistication of Royal, with its antique shops and high-end shopping, against the anything-goes attitude of Bourbon Street, with its topless bars, gay bars and drink-until-you-can't-stand mentality, was keen.

She passed storefronts chock full of Mardi Gras masks, crude T-shirts, Cajun cooking spices and postcards. As she ventured deeper into the Quarter, the zydeco music gave way to the bass-drum rumble of some local rock band. Mardi Gras revelers in colorful shirts and hurricane-to-go glasses crowded the sidewalks. A lone saxophone player and a fortune-teller vied for space at the opening of a narrow courtyard. Julia took it all in, loving that she was right in the center of it.

The day had been so hectic, she'd had little time to dwell on the incident last night. But several times she'd found herself looking over her shoulder. And thinking about John Merrick.

He was no longer the grinning teenager she'd been half in love with a lifetime ago. The years had added some hard edges to him that hadn't been there before. Edges so sharp they'd undoubtedly cut if anyone got too close. When she'd looked into his eyes last night, she'd felt locked out. It was as if he'd posted a huge NO TRESPASSING sign and then dared anyone to encroach.

But Julia was a true lover of people; it was in her nature to reach out, to know them, to care. She had seen the dark and unsettling layers that lay within John. She discerned the shadows, and she instinctively knew he was dealing with demons she couldn't begin to understand. She didn't like seeing him suffer. It only made her want to peel away those dark layers and heal him.

She suspected much of his unhappiness was because of what had happened in Chicago. The friendly fire incident that had ended a man's life—and John's law enforcement career. She knew he'd ultimately been cleared of any wrongdoing. Evidently he hadn't been able to forgive himself.

Around her the night was so cold she could see her

breath. In the distance, thunder joined the low rumble of the bass drums of a nearby club. A light rain had begun to fall—just enough to turn her hair into an unruly mop, and she was glad the shop was closed and she had nothing else planned for the evening.

At Toulouse, her cell phone rang. Seeing the shop number come up on the display, Julia winced and hoped her sister wasn't angry. "Hi, Claudia."

"Don't 'Hi Claudia' me. You're late and now I'm late."

"I'm sorry. I got tied up at the convention."

"Julia, you turned off your phone."

"Well . . . I turned it off right before I walked up to the podium, and forgot to turn it back on."

Claudia made a sound of frustration.

"I'm glad you're not mad."

"I *am* mad."

"What time are you supposed to meet Rory?"

"Ten minutes ago."

"I'm sorry, sis. What about *Phantom*?"

"Curtain time is in an hour."

Picking up her pace, Julia glanced at her watch, relieved that her sister would not miss her favorite musical. "I'll be there in five minutes."

"I'll call Rory and let him know I can't make dinner."

Part Goth, part rock star, Rory was a guide for one of the local cemetery tours. Somehow he'd managed to snag two coveted tickets to the opening night of *Phantom of the Opera* at the historic Saenger Theatre. He and Claudia had been going out for about two months now, and she seemed to be crazy about him. He seemed nice enough, but Julia had always thought he took his job a little too seriously.

"Where are you, anyway?" Claudia asked.

"Just past Toulouse."

"Please tell me you took a cab."

"I tried to grab one at Canal, but the convention had just let out."

"Julia! That's not a very good excuse when there's some wacko sending you bizarre letters."

Julia knew her sister was right. It wasn't exactly wise for her to be walking the French Quarter after dark. But having lived and worked in Vieux Carre for the last two years, she'd learned to be cautious.

Sensing that she was about to get a lecture, Julia ended the conversation. "See you in two minutes."

"Be careful. And hurry up, will you?"

Julia disconnected and turned the corner onto St. Peter. She smiled at the sight of the old-fashioned street lamp outside the Book Merchant at the end of the block. She was wondering if there would be any beignets left from this morning when a man wearing a Mardi Gras mask stepped out of a narrow courtyard and blocked her path.

Julia started to smile, but something about him gave her the creeps. Never breaking stride, she veered right in an attempt to maintain a safe distance between them. But before she could get out of arm's reach, his hand snaked out. His fingers clamped around her arm like a vise. A scream tore from her throat when he yanked her into the narrow courtyard.

For an instant the swift violence of the act stunned her. Terror and adrenaline tangled and spread inside her. She had the presence of mind to reach for the can of mace in her bag. But before she could grasp it, he shoved her hard against the brick wall.

Julia's back struck the wall hard. Her head snapped against the brick. The impact knocked the breath from her lungs. She raised her hands to shove him away, but he grasped her upper arms, yanked her toward him and then slammed her a second time against the wall.

"*Bitch.*"

The force of the attack dazed her. A moment of dizziness swirled in her head. The Mardi Gras mask looked macabre in the semidarkness. She caught a glimpse of a dark jacket. Blue jeans. He was taller than she was, but not by much.

Before she could get her wits about her, he yanked her arm and pulled her more deeply into the courtyard. All she could think was that if she didn't get away he was going to hurt her. Maybe even kill her.

"Help me!"

She dug in her heels and tried to yank her arm from his grasp, but lost her footing and went down to her knees. He dragged her several feet, but she barely felt the rough cobblestone cutting her.

"Let go of me!" she screamed.

A jagged spear of terror swept through her when he turned to her. She could hear his breaths rushing through the tiny hole in the mask. She imagined his face contorted in rage beneath it. She could feel the fury coming off him in terrible, black waves. Oh, dear God, she thought, he's going to hurt me.

She lashed out with both fists, but he blocked her efforts. She tried to tear off the mask, but before she could his hand shot out, his fingers clamping around her throat, cutting off her oxygen. Keeping his arm straight, he backed her toward the wall, slammed her into it.

"You've got the devil in you, don't you?" he hissed.

The words barely registered. Julia couldn't breathe. She clawed at his hands, scratching herself in the process, and for the first time she noticed the leather gloves he wore. She lashed out with her boots, tried to kick him, but he danced aside.

"Don't fight me." His grip on her throat tightened.

Panic tore through her when she realized she couldn't get away. That he could choke the life from her here and now and no one would notice until it was too late.

He squeezed brutally. She opened her mouth to draw a breath, but her windpipe was crushed. Her tongue felt huge, and it bulged from her mouth. Her vision blurred. Her head began to spin. Darkness edged into her sight. She could feel her hands beginning to tingle. She stared at the hideous mask, wondering why he was doing this to her.

An instant before she passed out, he loosened his grip. Julia sucked in a ragged breath. He leaned close, so that the mask was only a few inches from her face. "You knew I was watching you tonight, didn't you? That's why you wore that dress. You whore."

For an instant it was as if he'd spoken in a foreign language she didn't understand. Then the meaning of the words registered. She opened her mouth to scream, but he tightened his grip on her throat and she managed only a hoarse sound.

"Succubus."

Julia gripped his forearm with both of her hands in an effort to force him to release her throat. Her vision swam. She could feel the blood pounding in her head. If she passed out, she would be at his mercy . . .

"Cheap harlot," he whispered.

Something wet splashed onto her face. In her peripheral vision she saw something in his hand. He shook it at her, spewing more liquid on her face and throat. She didn't know what it was, but all sorts of unpleasant scenarios converged on her mind. Acid. Blood. Dear God . . .

She couldn't believe this was happening. A minute ago all she'd been worried about was getting to the shop so her sister could go to the opera with her boyfriend. Now she was in an alley a scant fifty yards from the shop and fighting for her life . . .

Vaguely, she was aware of one of his hands fumbling with her jacket. At first she thought he was trying to get to her purse, which was slung over her shoulder. Dread enveloped her when she realized he was trying to get his hands beneath her jacket.

Julia had one hand jammed against his chest. The other was wrapped around his wrist, trying to break his grip on her throat, but he was too strong. She could reach her cell phone, but she knew there was no way she could dial 911 without his stopping her. Her best hope was the canister of pepper spray in her purse.

"Let go," she croaked.

He snarled something indecipherable through the mask. His fingers tightened, cutting off her oxygen once again. "Tell me you want me to save you."

Confusion swirled. The words made no sense. She tried to speak, hoping he would release his grip on her throat. When he did, she sucked in a breath. The sound was animalistic, but she didn't care. "Why are you doing this?" she croaked.

"I'm going to save your soul," he whispered. "But you have to want it. *Say it!*"

She let her right hand drop from his chest, dipped her fingers into her purse. She felt her wallet. Her hairbrush. Where was the pepper spray? Hope burst through her when her fingers closed around the canister. She wondered if the mask would protect him. If she could aim well enough to get the spray into the eye cutouts . . .

His fingers dug into her throat. Out of time, Julia thought. She gripped the canister. Brought it up with a numb hand. Somehow her finger found the trigger. Aiming for the eye cutouts, she sprayed.

A sound that was part roar, part scream tore from his throat. He released her immediately, his hands flying to his face. Julia fell against the brick wall, gulping air. He reeled backward. Vaguely, she was aware of the spray arcing toward him and realized she was still holding down the trigger.

He made a terrible sound as he stumbled back. His foot caught on the edge of a broken pallet and he went down on his butt. "Fucking whore!" he screamed as he scrambled to his feet. "Succubus bitch!"

She didn't wait to hear more. Throwing the canister at him as hard as she could, she spun and flung herself into a dead run for the street.

SEVEN

The pre–Mardi Gras revelers were in full swing when John crossed Esplanade and entered the Quarter. He could have driven, but driving during Mardi Gras week was for tourists who didn't know any better. He was in no mood for a fender bender with some drunken idiot from Iowa. Besides, he needed the walk to clear his head. Not only did he have the mother of all hangovers, but he wasn't looking forward to telling Julia and her father that he was ditching the assignment.

He fingered the business card in his pocket. He and Earl Milkowski had worked the mean streets of South Chicago a lifetime ago. After some research, he'd found out Earl had retired and moved to New Orleans. Bored with retirement, he'd gotten his private detective license and opened an office near the warehouse district. John knew Earl would take good care of Julia. John sure as hell couldn't.

A phone call would have been easier, but a damnable sense of responsibility—of pride—forced him to relay the news in person. Besides, John had never been one to take the easy way out.

Normally he loved the Quarter, but tonight he barely noticed the tourists lined up at Café du Monde or the *clop!* of the carriage horses' steel shoes against concrete. A cold front had pushed down from the north, giving the evening air a bite. The streets glistened beneath the antique street lamps. The exotic rhythm of zydeco from one of the tourist shops blended with the bass drumbeat drifting from the open door of a bar down the street.

Head down against the cold wind coming off of Lake Pontchartrain, John headed north on St. Peter. He stopped outside the Book Merchant and took a moment to get his lines straight. He had business to take care of back in Chicago. He'd already contacted Earl Milkowski. Earl had been a good cop. John could vouch for him.

Right.

Scrubbing his hand over his face, John pushed open the door. The bell jingled as he stepped inside. Warmth and the sweet scent of candles greeted him. Some pseudo-classical music flowed in a slow current from tiny speakers mounted high on the wall. Unexpectedly, he was struck by the warm hominess of the place. And he suddenly found himself looking forward to seeing the woman who owned it.

"Hi, John."

For an instant he thought the voice was Julia's, and his heart skipped a beat. But when he spun, he found himself looking at her sister, Claudia. She was standing behind the counter, looking at him as if he were a moose and had wandered out of the Alaskan woods and into the shop.

"Is Julia here?" he asked.

"No, but I expect her any moment." Claudia came around the counter. "Is there something I can help you with?"

"No. I'll just wait if that's all right."

"Of course it is." She looked at him quizzically. "Did you find out something about the stalker?"

"Not yet." He shifted his weight, glanced toward the door, wishing Julia had been in so he could get this done and get the hell out of there.

Her eyes narrowed. "Is everything okay?"

"I had something come up," he heard himself say. "In Chicago. I've got to fly up there."

Liar. Coward!

Claudia was several years younger than her sister, but her youth didn't make her any less astute. She cut him a sharp look. "You mean you're bailing?"

"I'm not bailing," he said, hating the defensive ring in his voice. "I've already called a private detective friend of mine."

He reached for the business card in his pocket and handed it to her. "He's ex–Chicago PD. He's good. Reliable."

She accepted the card and gave him a kind look. "I hope your leaving doesn't have anything to do with . . . what happened. I mean with the . . . incident in Chicago."

The incident.

"It doesn't," he said quickly. But he hated the fact that no one could seem to say it. He'd killed an innocent man. A fellow cop with a wife and two kids. Four lives destroyed, not to mention his own . . .

"I briefed my friend on Julia's stalker," he said. "He's expecting a call from her. He'll take good care of—"

The door to the shop swung open. John looked up to see Julia burst in. He knew instantly someone had hurt her. She was disheveled. Her face was ghastly pale, her eyes wild with terror. She was wearing a skirt, and he could see that at least one of her knees was bloody.

"Julia!" came Claudia's frightened voice. "Oh, my God. What happened?"

Every cop's instinct John had ever possessed jumped to attention. "Call 911," he snapped.

Julia stood just inside the front door. Even from ten feet away he could see that she was trembling violently. A dark emotion he didn't want to identify rose inside him at the sight of the red marks on her neck.

He crossed to her, aware of the wild look in her eyes. "Are you all right? Did someone hurt you?"

Her hand went to the marks on her throat, and she

rubbed at them with trembling fingers. "A man. He . . . jumped me. In the alley."

"Are you hurt?"

She shook her head. "I'm . . . okay. Just . . . shaken up."

Fury swept through him at the thought of some son of a bitch roughing her up. Gently, he put his arm around her. "Come over to your desk and sit down for a moment so I can have a look at you, okay?"

Vaguely he was aware of Claudia on the phone with the 911 dispatcher. He guided Julia to the desk. Even through her coat he could feel her shaking. So small, he thought, and another hard punch of rage made his heart pound.

"Let me take your coat," he said before she sat. Not because he was polite, but because he wanted to see for himself just how badly she'd been roughed up.

She didn't look at him as she worked the coat off her shoulders. He took the coat from her and, gingerly, she lowered herself to the chair.

She was wearing an off-white sweater made of some fuzzy material. The neckline dipped low, and for the first time John got a good look at the deep red marks at her throat. Someone had put his hands around her neck, and he hadn't been tentative about it. John could see each individual finger mark. Jesus Christ. The son of a bitch had tried to strangle her . . .

"I need for you to tell me what happened," he said.

Claudia came up behind him. "The police are on the way." She looked at her sister. "Honey, are you all right?"

Julia lowered her face into her hands. "No."

"What happened?" John repeated, wanting the details while they were still fresh in her mind.

She raised her eyes to his. Her eyes were dark against the pale cast of her complexion. At some point she'd been crying. He could see the tear streaks in her makeup.

"I was walking home from the convention, heading toward the shop on St. Peter. There's a courtyard near Mr. Goubeaux's antique shop." She drew a deep breath, shook her head. "He must have come out of the courtyard. I didn't even see him coming."

Walking alone, he thought, and made a mental note to rake her over the coals later. Right now, she looked too damn fragile.

"Who?" John asked.

Julia shook her head. "I don't know."

"Oh, Julia." Claudia went to her and brushed her fingertips against the angry red marks on her throat. "Honey, you're bruised. Are you sure you're okay?"

"Did you get a look at him?" John cut in.

Julia shook her head. "He was wearing a Mardi Gras mask."

"What kind?"

"A jester. An expensive one, I think."

Like a thousand other people walking the Quarter tonight. "What about his clothes?"

"All I remember seeing is a dark jacket. It happened so fast." Julia bit her lip. "That's not much help, is it?"

"You're doing fine," John said, but he wanted more. He suddenly wanted badly to get his hands on the sick fuck who'd put his hands on her and hurt her. He told himself it was more of a big brother kind of anger than anything more complicated. But he was keenly aware of the male need to protect that rose up inside him. "Did he say anything?"

"Just . . . weird things." A shudder moved through her. "He called me a . . ." Her voice broke. She closed her eyes briefly, then continued. "He called me a whore. A succubus."

A chill moved down John's spine. "Succubus. That's an odd term."

"Medieval Latin origin, I think," Claudia said.

John felt her gaze on him, but he didn't take his eyes off of Julia. "What does it mean?"

"Something like an evil female demon that descends on hapless sleeping men to have intercourse."

Julia shot her sister a withering look. "And you know that how?"

Claudia shrugged. "I learned it in my humanities class last semester."

It was suddenly clear to John that this was no random attempted rape or mugging or assault.

Absently, Julia used the back of her hand to rub the tears from her cheek. "It's him, isn't it? The guy sending the notes?"

"I don't know," he said. But he fit the profile. John bent slightly to make eye contact with her. "Can you tell me exactly where this happened?"

Julia nodded. "It happened just past Goubeaux's Antiques. There's a narrow courtyard. I was on the sidewalk. He . . . came out of nowhere. Grabbed me, dragged me into the courtyard."

John rose abruptly. "You two hang tight. The police should be here any moment. Lock the door behind me."

"Where are you going?" Claudia asked.

"I'm going to see if that son of a bitch is still hanging around." But as John started for the door, he knew the stalker was already gone.

Julia couldn't stop shaking no matter how hard she tried. In the minutes after the attack, Claudia had brewed herbal tea and tried to make conversation while they waited for the police to arrive. John had questioned her; Julia did her best to answer, but everything had happened so fast she didn't think she was much help. All she could do now, it seemed, was sit at her desk and try not to relive the terror of the attack.

She knew it could have been worse, but she'd never been subjected to violence, and she couldn't get the terrible shock of it out of her mind. The stark feeling of helplessness. The sensation of being unable to breathe. The keen sense of vulnerability. The incident had probably lasted no more than three or four minutes, but she knew that tiny moment in time would haunt her for the rest of her life.

She sat at her desk, gripping the mug of tea, wishing the warm brew would melt the ice jammed inside her. She'd lost track of the number of police officers she'd talked to. Toward the end, a detective had arrived and asked her the same questions all over again. Claudia had been hovering like a mother hen, brewing tea and talking too much in an effort to put her at ease. But Julia wasn't sure she'd ever be at ease again.

She'd lost sight of John. After making sure she was all right, he'd left and gone to the scene. By the time he'd come back, the police had arrived and she spent what seemed like an eternity answering questions. Mitch had even stopped by to check on her after hearing the address come across his radio.

It was nearly eleven P.M. by the time the last police officer left.

"Are you sure you don't want me to take you to the emergency room to have those bruises checked out?"

Julia looked up to see John approach, his expression grim. "The last place I want to go is the hospital," she said.

Kneeling in front of her, he reached out and touched her throat. "You're abraded. You've got some swelling here. Bruises." He glanced down at her bloody knees, and some dark emotion she didn't quite understand flashed in his eyes. "At the very least you need to get those knees cleaned up."

"For God's sake, will you two stop hovering?" Julia fought unexpected tears. "I'm fine."

Claudia picked up a cup of the tea and shoved it into Julia's hands. "Sip this and we'll give you some space, okay?"

Feeling like a fool, Julia rolled her eyes, but sipped the tea. Nobody said anything when her hands shook so badly she nearly spilled it.

Claudia looked at John. "Do you think the police will catch him?"

He lifted a shoulder, let it fall. "If they can lift some latent prints and get a hit in the system, there's a good chance they'll get him."

"The police won't get prints," Julia said. "He was wearing gloves."

Claudia's cell phone chirped. Frowning, she glanced at the display and quickly put the call to voice mail. But Julia knew it was Rory calling for the dozenth time. And it suddenly dawned on her that her sister had missed the first half of *Phantom*.

"You should have gone ahead with your plans," Julia said.

Claudia rolled her eyes. "Like I'm going to leave you here alone after what you went through tonight."

"I'm fine. In fact, your hovering and tea brewing are driving me nuts." When Claudia only continued to stare at her, she added, "Besides, John is here."

In the beat of silence that followed, John felt a mild rise of panic. Suddenly he found himself in a position he did not want to be in. A position he was probably not qualified to handle.

Claudia's gaze snapped to John's. "He's got to go to Chicag—"

"I'm not going anywhere," he heard himself say.

After seeing Julia bruised and bleeding, he knew there was no way he could walk away from this. He sure as hell had no intention of leaving her alone.

"But I thought—"

He cut her off. "I changed my mind."

Julia looked from John to her sister. "Changed your mind about what?"

John held Claudia's gaze. "I don't want you walking to the theater alone. Call a cab or have your boyfriend pick you up."

Claudia sighed. "Okay," she said and looked at Julia. "Sis, are you sure you'll be okay?"

Julia nodded. "Of course, I'm sure. Go. I'll see you in the morning."

John watched the two women embrace, pleased that Julia had a good support system. With the stalker becoming increasingly violent, she was going to need all the support she could get.

Claudia went to the counter and picked up the phone to call a taxi. Julia turned to John. "Don't look at me that way."

"What way?"

"Like I'm going to fall apart. I'm not."

She was playing it tough. Good for her. But he didn't put too much stock in the facade. He'd seen the terror in her eyes when she'd burst through the front door. He felt some of that terror himself every time he thought about how things might have turned out if she hadn't gotten away.

She spent a moment straightening some papers on her desk that didn't really need straightening. "You mentioned earlier that the police might be able to get fingerprints. He was wearing gloves, John. How could they get prints?"

"Our perp left behind a couple of items."

"What items?"

"A crucifix and some kind of glass vial."

Her eyes widened. "My God, I forgot to mention that at some point I thought he splashed something in my face. I was so scared I wasn't sure. But now I remember him holding some kind of small glass container."

"Any idea what the liquid was? Did it have a smell or sting your skin?"

She shook her head. "I didn't notice either of those things."

The situation just kept getting stranger and stranger. "Did you see a crucifix at any time during the attack?"

Her brows knitted. "I saw something in his hand. It flashed in my mind that maybe it was a gun or knife, but I didn't get a good look at it." Her gaze met his. "That's strange about the crucifix. Are you sure he dropped it? Maybe it was already lying in the courtyard."

"The cops are pretty certain it was his."

"How can they know that?"

"Because the crucifix was covered with blood."

EIGHT

"*Blood?*" *The word reverberated inside her head like the* echo of a gunshot. Julia found herself looking down at her clothes, looking for signs of blood, and she shivered with revulsion.

"Mitch told me," John said quietly, his gaze sweeping to Claudia as she spoke on the phone.

"Human blood? Animal?" Julia looked down at the drying blood on her knees. "Could it be mine?"

"CSI took a sample of your blood. They'll test to see if it matches."

"But you don't think it will."

"I think we're dealing with one sick son of a bitch."

Queasiness seesawed in her stomach at the thought of how blood might have gotten on a crucifix of all things. Good Lord.

"Did you tell the police about the notes you've been receiving?" John asked.

"Of course I did."

His smile was wry. "But you didn't tell them about the book."

Julia blew out a breath, ruffling her bangs. "I'm not in the mood for a lecture, John."

"It would have been smarter to tell them everything and let them do their job, Julia. This is serious. Dangerous—"

"I know," she snapped.

"Things could have turned out a hell of a lot worse," he snapped back.

"John, the detectives can still investigate this without knowing about the book. They have all the evidence."

"True, but they're not operating with all the facts. For example, motive."

The memory of her attacker's whispered words shivered through her. *You've got the devil in you* . . .

"This is exactly the kind of thing I was trying to avoid," she said. "Dad's already been in the news because of his views. If the media gets wind of the fact that I've written a novel, they'll be all over it. I can see the headlines: *Religious Leader's Daughter Writing Smut*."

An emotion she couldn't quite identify flashed in his eyes, and she realized he knew all too well about the media's penchant for sensationalism. They'd been all over him after the shooting. More than one so-called journalist had suggested John was guilty of murder.

"You're suggesting we let the cops operate on the assumption that this guy is obsessed with you?" he asked.

"That's not too far from the truth." But she felt foolish for feeling the need to hide something so trivial when just over an hour ago she'd been fighting for her life.

"Cab's here."

Julia turned to see Claudia approach, her bag slung over her shoulder.

"Don't go anywhere alone," John said to her. "Keep your doors locked. Alarm system engaged, if you have one. Keep your cell phone under your pillow tonight."

"He really knows how to make a girl feel safe." Claudia smiled.

But Julia saw through the bravado. Claudia was rattled, too. She hugged her younger sister tightly. "Thanks for hanging out with me tonight. I'm so sorry you missed the show."

"Don't worry about it. If you need anything, just call."

A horn sounded from the street. Claudia pulled back, her gaze going to John. "Take good care of her."

"I'll be fine." Julia motioned toward the door. "Tell Rory I said hello."

With a wave, Claudia dashed to the door. "See you to-morrow." The bell jingled as she opened it and rushed outside.

John followed her as far as the sidewalk and watched to make sure she got into the cab safely. Once the cab had pulled away, he engaged the lock, tested it, and closed the miniblinds, effectively locking them in for the night.

A quiver of nerves swept through Julia when he turned to face her. She wanted to blame her jumpiness on what had happened; pan assault in a dark alley was enough to rattle anyone. But she knew the sudden case of nerves had more to do with the man and the way his eyes swept over her.

"I'm staying here with you tonight," he said.

Alarms started going off in her head. The instinct to ar-gue was strong, but Julia didn't. The truth of the matter was that for the first time in her adult life, she was afraid.

"There's a cot in the back room." Needing something to do, she crossed to her desk and looked desperately for something to straighten. "Or you're welcome to use the sofa upstairs."

"The cot will be fine."

"Are you expecting him to come here tonight?"

"No."

When she ran out of things to do at the desk, she crossed to the counter. "So then why do you feel the need to stay?"

His gaze sought hers, held it. "I don't trust fate."

She knew it was crazy, but for an instant she didn't know if he was talking about the stalker or his spending the night with her.

Discomfited by the notion, she bent and straightened the

novelty bags beneath the counter. "So what's our next move?"

"We let the cops do their jobs."

"And tonight?"

"There's nothing we can do tonight." He shrugged. "Check the doors and windows."

She smiled. "Check for monsters under my bed?"

He didn't smile back. "Yeah."

"That was a joke."

A shiver moved through her when his gaze swept down the front of her. He grimaced when his eyes landed on her knees. "Since you're too damn stubborn to go to the emergency room, why don't you let me see to those abrasions?"

She'd almost forgotten about her scratched knees. But now that the adrenaline had ebbed, the scrapes were beginning to burn, the bruises beneath coming to life. The wounds needed tending. But having John do it somehow seemed far too intimate.

"If you're up to it, I'd like to go over what happened one more time," he said.

Dread rose inside her at the thought of reliving it. The logical side of her brain knew any small detail could possibly help find her attacker. But the more emotional side of her brain did not want to venture back.

"I'm up to it," she replied. "I'll just check the doors."

Before she could move, he started toward the rear door. "Front door is locked down tight," he called out over his shoulder.

Because she needed something to do, Julia rechecked the front door lock anyway, then walked to the rear of the shop. John had already opened the door and stepped into the alley, leaving the door open. From where she stood, Julia saw spindly fingers of fog rising from wet pavement. The slightly unpleasant odor of garbage hung in the air. John was standing stone still a few feet from the doorway, looking around.

She came up beside him. "What is it?"

He looked back at her, then motioned to the darkened light fixture across the alley. "Is that light always out?"

She hadn't noticed before, but now that he'd pointed it out, the alley seemed darker than usual. "I think it's usually lit."

He crossed to the light and reached inside the globe. An instant later, dim light flooded the alley.

"Loose bulb?" she asked.

"Or maybe someone unscrewed it."

A chill went through her at the thought. "John, I don't understand why someone would do this."

"The mentality of a stalker is so outside the normal realm of a normal person's mind, it's hard for anyone to grasp."

Julia wasn't sure she wanted to understand, but she knew this was one of those times where ignorance was not bliss. "You think he's obsessed with me?"

"I think he's fixated on you and/or some perceived wrong that you've done."

"My book?"

He crossed to the door and ushered her inside, locking it behind them. "A lot of stalkers are disenchanted with reality, or unable to cope with reality, so they create their own. They tend to blame their problems on others. For example, if this guy has created a world where your novels cause him or others problems, he may feel compelled to somehow rectify the situation. At that point you become the focus of his obsession. His obsession becomes the center of his imagined universe."

Julia shivered as they started up the stairs to her apartment. "Scary thought."

"I'm no profiler," John said. "But this guy probably thinks you've wronged him. He may even have convinced himself that you are the one who needs help."

"Or saving."

"Exactly."

She unlocked the door to her apartment and stepped inside. A sense of comfort flooded her at the sight and smells of her ordinary things. The overstuffed sofa and chair in front of the television. The clutter of books on the coffee table. The cup she'd left on the kitchen counter this morning. The pleasant scent of the citrus and peppercorn potpourri she'd picked up at the candle shop on Poydras the day before. Until this moment she hadn't realized just how badly she'd needed to be safe in her own home.

Normally when she closed the shop for the evening, she would make dinner or perhaps grab something to eat at the Cajun restaurant two doors down from the shop, then settle down with her laptop until bedtime. It was her relaxation, her escape. Tonight, however, writing was the last thing on her mind.

"Do you have a first aid kit?"

She turned to see John close the door behind him and engage the lock. He looked large and out of place in her small apartment, and it struck her just how seldom she had male visitors.

"In the bathroom. I'll get it." She started toward the hall.

"I'll get it." He motioned toward the chair. "Have a seat. I'll be right back."

Sighing, Julia crossed to the chair and sat. She turned on the reading lamp beside the chair and for the first time got an up-close-and-personal look at her knees. Her panty hose were torn and sticky with drying blood, exposing deep abrasions. She could already see the swelling where the bruises were beginning to bloom. Realizing her hose would be in the way, she rose and walked into the kitchen, peeled them off and dropped them into the wastebasket.

"You're going to be feeling those bruises tomorrow."

Julia looked up to see him standing in the living room, the small red and white first aid kit in one hand, the bathroom water glass in the other.

"I'm already feeling them." She crossed to the chair and settled into it.

"How's your throat?"

"Sore."

He offered three ibuprofen tablets and the glass of water. "These might help."

Julia downed the pills and drank the entire glass of water, all too aware that her throat hurt with each swallow. "If I hadn't maced him, he would have . . ." She set the glass on the table next to the chair. "He would have—"

"He didn't," John cut in.

That she could have been killed tonight made her feel sick and intensely vulnerable. Julia had never thought of herself as weak or defenseless; she'd never been afraid of anything in her life. But suddenly she found herself very glad that John was there.

"It keeps playing in my mind like a bad movie," she said.

"A dozen different scenarios could have happened, but they didn't. You're okay. You're safe." His expression softened. "If it's all right with you, I'd like to keep it that way."

"You're not going to get an argument from me."

"There's a first." Lowering himself to the ottoman, he opened the first aid kit. "Now let me have a look at those knees."

Julia leaned back in the chair and propped her feet on the ottoman. She tried to relax, but the fact that someone had purposefully done this—injured her not only physically, but emotionally as well—was beginning to eat at her. "The more I think about what he did to me, the angrier I get."

"It's okay for you to be angry." He looked away from her knee and made eye contact. "It's normal."

Her thoughts faltered when he gently set his hand on the backside of her knee and raised it so that her leg was slightly bent. The sight of his hand on her leg sent a shock through her system. His fingertips were warm and slightly rough against her flesh. The sensation was heady and startlingly pleasant. She could feel heat rising into her cheeks. Her heart beating like a drum in her chest.

"You have some gravel imbedded in your skin that needs to be scrubbed out."

He wetted a sterile gauze pad with peroxide and began to gently scrub at the tiny gravel particles. Julia was so caught up by the sensation of his hand wrapped around her bare leg that she barely noticed the sting.

"John," she said after a moment, "I don't want this to disrupt my life."

"It already has."

"I don't want to give him that kind of power. It's almost as if that's what he wants."

"What he wants is to get his hands on you."

A shudder ran the length of her before she could stop it.

John looked up from her knee and grimaced. "Look, if you want to play this smart—and safe—you're going to have to make a few lifestyle adjustments."

"I'm not going to lock myself in my apartment or cower every time someone walks into the shop," she said with some heat.

"I'm not telling you to do either of those things. What I'm saying is to exercise caution."

"My life isn't exactly a walk on the wild side."

"You walk alone in the Quarter after dark. Julia, that's incredibly irresponsible."

"I've been doing it my entire adult life."

"That doesn't make it smart."

Julia knew he was right. But she didn't want to concede. She hated it that the stalker was going to force her to make changes she didn't want to make. She was in a good place in her life. She was happy and independent. She didn't want to allow some madman to turn everything upside down.

"Look, all I'm asking is that you incorporate a few commonsense things into your routine."

"Like what?" she asked, not liking the defensive ring in her voice.

"Don't walk alone after dark. When you're here at the shop, make sure there's someone with you. I'll take care of the locks and the new security system." He smiled. "Try to keep in mind that this is only temporary."

"I like my life the way it is, John. I hate it that this happened. That I feel the need to look over my shoulder every time I leave the shop. He had no right to do that to me."

"No, he didn't." Having scrubbed the gravel from her right knee, he set the used gauze aside and applied a thin layer of antibiotic cream. "The situation isn't going to rectify itself, Julia."

"What do you mean?"

"Stalkers usually don't stop stalking on their own."

"So how do we stop him?"

His eyes glinted. "Next time he comes after you, we make sure he gets me instead."

The plan was good in theory. Big, bad ex-cop from Chicago coming to the rescue of a young woman being stalked by some wacko dipshit. But John knew reality couldn't be further from the truth. He knew there was nothing big or bad about the man he had become since *The Incident.*

Hell, two hours ago he'd all but decided to quit the assignment. He'd been prepared to turn the whole mess over to some second-rate PI because he could barely deal with his own problems, let alone someone else's. If Julia hadn't burst through that door when she had, he would have walked away and never looked back.

But she had come through that door. And the sight of the bruises on her throat, her bloodied knees and the horror in her eyes had changed everything. Seeing her like that had brought to life the age-old need for male to protect female. His head might be royally fucked up at the moment, but he wasn't so far gone that he could walk away from a woman whose life was in danger.

So how are you going to protect her when you can't even pick up your gun, hotshot?

The question taunted him. It burned. Humiliated. Worse, John didn't have an answer. The brutal reality of that scared him almost as much as the thought of this woman being hurt. Yeah, one hell of a bodyguard he was going to make.

"You can hardly be with me twenty-four hours a day."

Realizing he'd zoned out, he looked away from her knee and met her gaze. The bottomless eyes that stared back at him were no longer the eyes of a love-struck teenaged girl in the throes of her first crush. They were a woman's eyes. Gypsy eyes, he thought. Dark and exotic and filled with a woman's secrets. Eyes that could put a man under a spell if he wasn't careful.

John was good at being careful.

Not that a woman like Julia Wainwright would have anything to do with some has-been ex-cop . . .

"No, but I can start spending time here at the shop."

She seemed to consider that, nodded. "I can live with that. For now."

"Good thing, because you don't have a choice." Before she could protest, he set his hand on the underside of her untreated knee. He lifted it for a better angle, bending the knee slightly. The movement caused her skirt to slide up. Only an inch or two, but enough so that every male cell in his body jumped to attention. For several dangerous seconds he couldn't take his eyes off the silky flesh of her thigh.

Fifteen years ago, the kids had called her "canary legs" because her legs had been so skinny. She'd been like a gangly little bird, tiny and awkward and homely. But there was nothing awkward or homely about the woman sitting so close he could smell the exotic scent of her perfume.

His fingers were large and dark against her skin. At some point she'd removed her stockings, and he was keenly aware of the velvet softness of her skin. The supple strength of the muscle beneath. The warmth emanating from her into him. The electric current of something else he didn't want to name.

In his mind's eye he saw his hand slide up her thigh, beneath the hem of her skirt. He imagined his palm sliding over silky flesh, his fingers touching soft, secret places. Sinking into wet heat. He envisioned the way she would look at him, her eyes heavy with desire as she leaned back into the pillows and opened her legs to him, let him inside . . .

The hot rush of blood to his groin stunned him. He went hard. His hand stilled. Her flesh burned his palm, but he withstood the sizzle. A tremor ran the length of his body. Caution and the sharp edge of sexual attraction tugged him in different directions. The power of it shocked him, and for a moment he could do nothing but stare stupidly at his hand wrapped around her leg.

He didn't want this. Hadn't asked for it. Goddamn Benjamin Wainwright for dragging him into this. John was in no condition to take on this kind of assignment. He was in no frame of mind to even consider the possibility of a sexual relationship or any other kind of relationship for that matter. He was clinically depressed and plagued with nightmares. Aside from the bottle of gin in his kitchen, guilt was his one and only friend these days.

So what the hell are you doing with your fingers wrapped around her leg?

Shifting to accommodate his erection, John dragged his gaze away from Julia's thigh. He rushed through the process of bandaging her knee. He didn't do a very good job of it, but he had to get out of there. She was too close. He was feeling too many things at once. If he wasn't careful, he might just do something stupid. Like lean close to get a taste of that full mouth. In the back of his mind he wondered what she would taste like. If she would be sweet or spicy. If she would pull away or kiss him back. If she would groan low in her throat and lean close . . .

Finished with the bandage, John slid back and stood abruptly. "Where's the cot?" he heard himself ask.

She set her feet on the floor and looked at him oddly. "Are you sure you won't take the sofa?"

"I need to be downstairs." He nearly snapped the words.

"Oh. Of course." She rose and started for the door.

He knew better than to watch, but his eyes took on a life of their own and he drank in the sight of her curvy backside beneath that skirt.

"The cot is downstairs in the storage room. I'll just go down and get—"

"I'll do it," he cut in.

"Oh, well . . . sure."

He barely spared her a glance as he brushed past her and started for the door. But he could feel the blood pooling low. The attraction tugging at him like a choke chain on a dog.

In his frame of mind, the thought of getting involved with a decent woman like Julia scared the hell out of him. He didn't trust himself. Didn't know what he was capable of. Some days he felt like a ticking time bomb. It was as if the guilt of taking another man's life had unleashed something inside him. Something that was ugly and mean and unpredictable.

He heard her say something as he reached for the door and yanked it open. But he didn't respond. He didn't turn to her. He didn't even look her way.

"John," she said.

He slammed the door in her face. He knew it was rude. But he didn't care. He didn't want to be attracted to her. He didn't want to feel *anything*. For her or anyone else.

He took the steps down to the shop. He could smell the remnants of vanilla candles. But it was the memory of her perfume that titillated him. For a moment he stood in the dark silence of the shop, listening to the traffic on the street. The patter of rain against the window. The hard beat of his own heart.

"What the fuck are you doing?" he muttered.

Reaching into his pocket, he withdrew the keys to his Mustang. At the alley door, he disengaged the locks and stepped into the night. Mist swirled down from a black sky. John raised his face to the sky, hoping the cold rain would clear his head.

Around him the sounds of the French Quarter reverberated through the alley. The bass beat of a drum from the club down the street. Lively conversation drifting on the breeze. He should have been pleased taking on this assignment. It was work. He liked and respected Benjamin Wainwright. He'd known Julia since she was a skinny, knobby-kneed kid. Only she wasn't a kid anymore and his feelings for her were a hell of a lot more complicated than he wanted them to be.

Muttering beneath his breath, he crossed to the Mustang he'd parked a few yards down and unlocked the door. Bending, he reached into the glove compartment and withdrew the flask. He uncapped the lid, tipped the bottle and took a long pull that burned all the way to his gut.

He'd never developed a taste for alcohol, but then this wasn't about pleasure. It was about escape. About pain. About punishing himself for fucking up and costing a man his life. It was about two children losing their father. A wife becoming a widow at the age of thirty-two.

Lowering the flask, he slammed the car door. He took another drink as he crossed to the shop. A third as he walked inside, closed the door and locked it behind him. By the time he found the cot in the storage room, the alcohol was beginning to do its job.

Thank God he'd thought to fill the flask before leaving his apartment.

He dragged the cot to the center of the storage room and unfolded it. He glanced at the blanket and pillow Julia had brought down, but he wasn't going to use them. They smelled like her, and he didn't want to be reminded of her while he slept, while his guard was down.

John took another drink. He hadn't had anything to eat since lunch and his head was beginning to spin. But he welcomed oblivion. Anything was better than the hell his mind had become. But there wasn't enough alcohol in the flask to do the job. There wasn't enough alcohol in the whole goddamn world to get the knife out of his heart.

He sat down hard on the cot, unlaced his boots and set them aside. Leaning forward, he put his elbows on his knees and closed his eyes and tried to shut down his mind.

But his thoughts refused to give him peace, and for an instant they transported him back to that warehouse. He remembered the ice-pick stab of terror when he'd pulled the trigger. The black cloak of dread that had dropped over him when he'd realized he'd shot a cop. The greasy nausea that rose into his throat when he'd looked down at his hands and seen the other man's blood on them.

John took another drink. Then another. And another. The flask was almost empty now, but he no longer cared. He lay back on the cot and stared at the ceiling and tried not to think.

He didn't want to be here. Wasn't even sure why he'd left Chicago. But deep inside John knew. He was a man about to come apart at the seams. He knew enough about himself to know that when it happened it would be violent.

He thought about the last woman he'd had a relationship with, and the keen blade of shame cut him a little deeper. In retrospect, he knew she was one of the reasons he'd fled.

He and Alison had been together for nearly a year. He'd liked her as a person, cared for her. He'd even entertained the notion of being in love with her. Then one night a few days after the shooting she'd pressed the wrong button and he'd gone off on her. If he hadn't pulled back, he might have done something he would have spent the rest of his life regretting.

But she wasn't the only reason he'd left Chicago. John knew that if he'd stayed, the darkness would have swallowed him whole. He knew if he'd had the guts to pick up his gun, he would have taken the easy way out. He knew he would have put the barrel in his mouth and pulled the trigger.

Nine

She came to him in the night, an angel riding a summer breeze. Her presence whispered across his consciousness like a lover's caress across skin. She was stunningly lovely in the slant of light coming in through the window. So beautiful she took his breath away. Innocence and sin rolled into a single devastating package.

She was his greatest desire and his biggest fear. He wanted her with everything that made him a man. One look into her siren's eyes and he was hard and aching with a need that could drive a man insane. Like a man dying of thirst, all he could think of was quenching it. Like a shipwrecked sailor willing to drink saltwater, knowing it would bring a slow and agonizing death.

Like a hundred men before him, he found himself willing to risk death to have her.

She wore a sheer gauzy gown that fluttered in the wind. The old hunger rose inside him at the sight of her woman's curves. The silhouette of her breasts and the dusky peaks of her nipples. The dark nest of curls at the juncture of her thighs. The need was like a bullwhip snapping inside him.

Wordlessly, she went to him. Her gown flowed behind her. He jolted when she put her hands on his shoulders. A whimper escaped him when she opened her legs and came down on top of him.

"Elisabeth," he whispered. "Ah, God."

She sat on his stomach and looked down at him. A smile played at her full lips. He could feel the wetness between her legs against his abdomen. Her woman's scent titillating him. He knew she was laughing at him, but he didn't care.

Bracing her arms on either side of his head, she leaned down and kissed his mouth. His hips jerked convulsively with the intimate contact. Need exploded, an agony he would do anything to end. He had to have her. Now and forever. Already, he was about to come.

"Let me touch you," he whispered. "Please."

She threw her head back and laughed. The gown opened and he could see her breasts. Need consumed him like a madness. All he could think about was touching her. Having her. Ending this agony of desire.

Tentatively, he lifted his hands to her breasts. An instant before he touched her, she slid forward, trapping his face between her legs. Pleasure and fear tangled inside him when her curls brushed his face. He tried to turn his head to draw a breath, but couldn't. It was as if she'd paralyzed him. He couldn't move. Couldn't breathe. Oh, dear God, she was going to kill him this time.

"You're pathetic and weak," she hissed, reaching behind her to grasp his swollen penis. "Look at you. You have the body of a little boy."

He came the instant she touched him. His entire body shuddered uncontrollably. He cried out with each hot spurt, but the tight grip of her thighs muffled the sound. Shame warred with the ecstasy of his release, the humiliating loss of control. But dear God, he wanted more. If only he could breathe . . .

Panic ripped through him. He clawed at the thighs that

gripped him like a vice. His body bucked beneath hers. His chest heaved with the need for oxygen.

Vaguely he was aware of her laughing. A maniacal sound that drove home the madness of what was happening. The very real fear that she could kill him here and now if she so chose. And that he would allow it.

Please.

The single word echoed inside his head like a scream.

He opened his eyes. Terror crashed over him at the sight of the monstrous thing on top of him. His lovely Elisabeth had transformed into a vicious beast with tangled white hair and green, glowing eyes. Its lips pulled back into a snarl. Saliva dripped from large canines. A huge phallus jutted from a thatch of white hair between its legs.

"Succubus," he whimpered.

Its vile tongue snaked out, licked his cheek. "Yes."

He'd known what she was, but lust had made him weak. Her beauty had blinded him to the truth, seduced him. Her treacherous heart had tricked him. He'd embraced evil for the pleasures of the flesh. Now he was going to pay a terrible price.

"Don't," he whispered.

"Now I'm going to give you what you really want," it said in a deep, gravelly voice.

"No!" He twisted, tried to rise.

Swiftly, its hands snaked out, gripped him. With inhuman strength it flipped him onto his stomach. A hard punch landed against his spine, and for an instant all he could do was gulp oxygen into his air-starved lungs. Then he felt icy hands against his back, the slide of a reptilian penis against his buttocks.

Oh, dear God no . . .

A scream tore from his throat as he was penetrated. Agony tore through his body as the violation began, as swift and violent as the lash of a bullwhip. Pain and humiliation rose inside him like vomit. He tried to scream, but his face was crushed into the mattress.

"No! God, please, *no!*"

The horror of the nightmare sent him bolt upright. La-bored breaths mingled with whimpers of pain and tore harshly from his throat.

I'm going to give you what you really want . . .

The evil words reverberated inside his head. He could still feel the agony of the violation. The evil lingering in the room. He desperately wanted to believe the entire episode had been nothing more than a nightmare.

But he knew better.

She was coming for him.

In the darkness, he reached down and touched his pa-jama bottoms, felt the cold wetness of semen. Succubi were known for causing men to have nocturnal emissions. Even good, religious men of high moral character. Like him.

Shame cut him at the thought of what he'd done. Of what had been done to him. A whimper escaped his lips. He put his hand over his mouth, but he could not keep the tears at bay.

The succubus had violated his body. His mind. But he knew she wouldn't stop. Not until she was finished with him. Then she would kill him.

He wondered if he was the only man she had visited. How many more men would she rape and torture and maim? How many souls would she steal? How many men would not survive?

Throwing his legs over the side of the bed, he stood. On trembling legs he walked to the tiny bathroom and flipped on the light. The sight of his tear-streaked face shocked him. At some point he'd bitten his lip hard enough to make it bleed. Or had she struck him? He'd been in so much agony, he didn't remember.

The only thing he knew for certain at the moment was that he had to stop her. She was the embodiment of evil. A demon preying upon men of faith. Some wouldn't believe anything so utterly unbelievable. But he did. He believed with the fervor of a man who'd lived the terror.

Feeling soiled and dirty, he spent several minutes washing up, trying hard not to think of the vile things that had been done to him. All the while a pristine new fury built inside him like a storm. He had been violated. He could not allow the succubus to get away with it. He couldn't let her steal his soul.

He dressed in blue jeans, black sweatshirt and dark sneakers. Leaving the bathroom, he went to his desk and switched on the lamp. His hand shook as he opened the drawer. The crucifix stared up at him. Next to it, the titanium blade of the ancient dagger glinted silver in the light of the desk lamp.

Tonight, the hunted would become the hunter.

TEN

"What's a pretty girl like you doing in a place like this?"

Felicia nearly spewed her hurricane all over the bar at the tired line. Turning on the bar stool, she glanced at the man standing next to her and laughed. "That's a real original pickup line you got there, Elvis. Maybe you ought to trademark it."

His mouth curved. "Who says I'm trying to pick you up?"

"You're in this dump at one A.M. Why else would you be standing there looking like some scraggly little mutt begging for scraps?"

"Maybe I just want to have a good time."

Felicia sucked on her straw. He wasn't the man she'd hoped to take home tonight. She'd had her sights set on the older guy in the Armani suit and Rolex watch at the end of the bar. But he'd been hanging all over that redhead with the big boobs for the last half hour. Why couldn't it ever be the *rich* guy whose eye she caught?

But it was late and she was feeling lonely. Elvis wasn't exactly a heartbreaker, but he was attractive in a boy-next-door sort of way.

He caught the bartender's eye and ordered a hurricane for her.

"You're not drinking?" she asked.

"Designated driver."

Responsible, she thought, and her opinion of him went up a notch. She smiled when he removed the money clip and wad of bills from his pocket. Maybe Elvis wasn't a loser. Maybe the night wasn't a total wash after all.

"Make that a double," she told the bartender.

"In a to-go glass." He laid a twenty on the bar.

Big tipper, she thought. The night was definitely looking up.

"Want to take a walk?" he asked.

She drank deeply and contemplated him. "Where to?"

"Your choice." He shrugged. "There are plenty of pretty places in the Quarter."

Reaching out, he ran his finger along the side of her face, to her chin, then brushed his fingertips over her arm. "How about if I give you a tour of the cemetery?"

Felicia had never fucked anyone in a cemetery before. She was all too aware that the old cemeteries surrounding the Quarter were frequented by muggers. But with the alcohol humming through her veins and the feel of his fingertips against her face, she thought it might be exciting.

"What's in it for me?"

"You mean besides me?" He smiled.

Felicia threw her head back and laughed. "Sorry, Elvis, but it's going to take more than you're pretty face to get me into some cemetery."

Never taking his eyes from hers, he pulled the money clip from his pocket. "Name it."

She stared at the wad of cash, her heart pounding just a little too fast. Felicia didn't consider herself a prostitute. Prostitutes were drug addicts who gave ten-dollar blow jobs in back alleys and had some ruthless pimp taking all their hard-earned cash. Felicia, on the other hand, was a businesswoman. Yes, she accepted money in exchange for sex. But she chose who she slept with. She believed the men she slept with paid her because they liked her. Because they enjoyed her company. Because she was so damn good at what she did.

"Two hundred and I'm yours for the night."

He didn't look like he could afford it. But he didn't so much as flinch when he tugged two hundred-dollar bills from the wad and passed them to her.

Felicia slid the bills between the buttons of her blouse and tucked them into her bra. "St. Louis or Lafayette?"

"Both," he said and took her hand.

She gripped the headstone and thought about her grocery list while he pumped in and out of her from behind. He'd grown silent after leaving the bar. He'd gotten downright sullen as they'd entered St. Louis Cemetery. Felicia regretted her decision, but she'd had worse dates in the two years she'd been having sex for money. He'd balked at the condom she'd insisted upon. Then he'd wanted to take her from behind like some kind of a damn dog. "Whatever rings your chimes," she'd told him and hiked her skirt. Now, with the drizzle coming down and the night having grown cold, she just wanted him to finish so she could go home and take a shower.

"Oh God. Oh God. Oh God." He gripped her hips hard as he thrust into her, his fingers digging uncomfortably into her flesh. "Forgive me," he grunted. "Please forgive me."

Some men liked to talk during sex. Elvis was a mumbler. Felicia caught about half of what he was saying, and it was getting downright weird. From what she could gather, he was some kind of religious nut who felt he needed God's forgiveness for having sex. Get over it, she wanted to tell him. But she was afraid if she ticked him off now it would take even longer for him to finish.

"Oh baby, yeah," she cooed, hoping to help him along. "Give it to me. Yeah, right there. Oh, you're going to make me come."

"Bitch," he panted. "Whore."

An electric current of anger zipped through her at the words. "Zip it, Elvis," she snapped. "Or I'm going to call it quits and you can spend the rest of the night jerking off."

"*Succubus.*"

Felicia didn't know what the word meant, but she didn't like it. Using her elbow, she tried to push him away, force him to withdraw, so she could straighten. But his hands went from her hips to her throat. Adrenaline sparked in her gut when he squeezed. She let go of the headstone and tried to pry his fingers from around her throat. But he was too strong. His fingers were digging in, crushing her throat. His body continued ramming violently into hers. All the while he hissed. "Whore. Cunt. Succubus bitch."

Felicia had survived twenty-six years of hard living. She'd survived some things she probably shouldn't have. Cheated fate once or twice along the way. But until this very moment she'd always believed she would die of old age. Never at the hands of man she was having sex with.

Oh, dear God, he's killing me . . .

Panic exploded inside her. She thought of her parents back in Shreveport. Her sister in Baton Rouge. The little niece she would never meet. What would they think of her? How could she let them know what she had become? How could she break their hearts this way?

The primal will to live thrashed inside her. Her scream came out as a choking roar. She clawed at the hands crushing her throat. She lashed out with her feet, trying to injure him with her heels. She opened her mouth to gulp desperately needed oxygen. But he only squeezed harder. Her strength beginning to wane. The ghostly crypts around her dipped and spun. She could barely feel his body slamming into hers. Vaguely, she was aware of him speaking, but she could no longer make out the words.

Help me! her mind silently screamed.

But no one heard her.

No one came to her aid.

And as a steady rain pounded down, conscious thought

ebbed and slipped away. Her body went slack. Her knees hit the ground. She saw darkness. She heard the roar of an angry sea. And then she was spiraling down into a vortex of nothing.

ELEVEN

Consciousness came to John by degree. The first thing he became aware of was the ruthless little bastard in his head gleefully stabbing his brain with an ice pick. The second thing he became cognizant of was that he was pretty sure he was going to throw up. To top things off he had to piss. A fact he wasn't going to be able to ignore much longer.

A groan escaped him as he rolled onto his side and realized he wasn't in a bed. The ice pick stabbed harder and faster. John's mouth filled with bile, but he swallowed it back. The floor felt as cold and hard as concrete beneath him, as if his bones were bare and scraping against stone. Vaguely, he wondered how he'd ended up on the floor.

He'd had worse nights, but not by much. The nightmare had started the instant he'd fallen asleep. It was always the same. John walking into the warehouse. The silhouette of a man raising his weapon. The blast of a gunshot. The smell of death and Franklin Watts's blood on his hands . . .

"Fuck," he muttered, pressing the heels of his hands into his eyes.

For an instant the darkness gave him reprieve. No thoughts. No feelings. Just . . . nothing.

Then the chatter started. At first John thought he had finally gone around the bend. Voices echoing inside his head like a bunch of goddamn chipmunks. If he hadn't been so hung over, he might have laughed.

"I walk into the storage room for cash register tape and see a half-naked man collapsed on the floor next to the cot."

"On the floor?"

"Half-naked?" The two voices came simultaneously.

"What's he doing in the storage room anyway?"

"What's *who* doing in the storage room?" came a male voice.

"Maybe he's sick."

"Has anyone asked?"

"Has anyone checked to make sure he's still alive?"

The pain in John's head hit a high note. A moan squeezed from his throat as he forced himself to a sitting position. He cracked open one eye to see the room spin sickeningly. He was lying on the floor, beside the cot. Judging from the pain in his neck and spine, he'd spent the night there.

"Son of a bitch."

Muttering the words beneath his breath, he set his hands on the cot and carefully got to his feet. The room dipped and he closed his eyes. He tasted the sour remnants of gin at the back of his throat, and a wave of nausea washed over him. He looked around for a trash can in case he needed to hurl, remembered belatedly that he was in the storage room of Julia Wainwright's bookstore—and it all came flooding back.

Jesus Christ. What was he thinking taking on this assignment when he could barely drag his sorry ass out of bed—or in this case off the floor—in the morning?

"John?"

He jerked his head toward the voice, winced when pain shot through his neck. Dread joined the nausea and churned in his gut at the sight of the three people crowded into the doorway, staring at him as if he were an alligator that had wandered in out of the swamp.

He squinted, trying to discern if there were three people looking at him . . . or if he was seeing in triplicate. Blinking the faces into focus, he realized two of them belonged to Julia and Claudia. He wasn't sure about the wimpy-looking guy standing behind them.

"What the hell do you want?" he croaked.

Jesus. Had he just said that?

"I thought you might want some coffee."

He looked at Julia, saw the cup in her hand, and for the first time realized he was making one hell of a bad impression. "Set it down on the file cabinet," he said. "I'll get it in a minute."

"While you're at it you might want to put on your pants."

That came from the guy. Frowning, John looked down, realized he was wearing only his boxer shorts. He wasn't easily embarrassed. He normally wouldn't have given a rat's ass if someone saw him in his skivvies. But he had a piss hard-on, and hangover or not, he much preferred to keep that part of his anatomy private.

Cursing beneath his breath, he turned away, snagged his jeans off the cot and stepped into them. "Do you fucking mind?" he snapped.

"Oh . . . sure."

He looked over his shoulder as he zipped his fly. Julia looked embarrassed. Claudia looked like a fifth-grader who'd just been told laughing would get her a detention. The wimpy dipshit looked like he was enjoying the entire stupid scene.

"Close the door behind you," John added.

In unison the three people backed away from the doorway. Julia reached in to pull the door closed. For an instant, their eyes met. An apology hovered on the tip of his tongue, but John didn't voice it. He was in no mood to grovel. He wasn't even sure he cared.

"This is the guy who's supposed to be *protecting* you?" came the wimp's voice as Julia closed the door.

The door closed with a resonant click.

John stood there a moment longer, telling himself he wasn't ashamed. Goddamn it, he didn't care enough to be ashamed. But deep inside he was a hell of a lot more than ashamed.

The problem was he didn't know what to do about it.

*Julia sat at her desk, her right hand flying over the calcu*lator keypad, her left flipping through the month's invoices as she tallied them. Claudia perched a hip on the corner of her desk, sipping a tall café au lait from the coffee shop across the street. A few feet away Jacob rolled a cart down the nearest aisle, shelving the books Julia had bought at auction last week in Shreveport.

"My God, you could have been killed," Jacob said, shoving a Steinbeck first edition onto the top shelf.

"I was mostly just . . . shaken up," Julia said.

Turning to her, the clerk put his hands on his hips. "Honey, that turtleneck only goes so far to hide those bruises that bastard put on your neck."

She'd done her best to hide the bruises, but the smudges had deepened overnight and makeup only covered so much. In the end she'd opted for a turtleneck, but it didn't cover the bruises high on her throat. It sure didn't do much for the pain. The night before the adrenaline had anesthetized her to a degree. This morning, she felt every bruise with an intensity that told her just how violent the attack had been.

"At the very least you should have called me," Jacob said, looking perturbed.

"It was late," Julia said. "Claudia was here. So was John."

"You mean the guy passed out in the storage room?" His voice was incredulous. "A lot of good he would have done. From the look of him, you'd be lucky to wake him up. What was your dad thinking, hiring a guy like that to protect you?"

"Maybe he was thinking John was once a good cop," Claudia put in.

"If super cop is so damn good," Jacob motioned toward Julia, "where was he last night when that maniac was trying to strangle her?"

"I was in the back room getting shit-faced and planning my next fuckup," came a gravelly voice from the storage room doorway.

Jacob spun at the sound of John's voice, nearly dropping the book he was shelving. Claudia slid from the desk, looking like a teenager who'd just been caught smoking.

Julia leaned back in her desk chair and watched John approach. He looked rumpled in the same jeans and flannel shirt he'd been wearing the night before. His hair was sticking up on one side. The pale cast to his face combined with bloodshot eyes told her his night had probably been every bit as bad as hers. Maybe even worse. She could tell by his dark expression that he'd heard every word of their conversation.

He walked to the coffeemaker and poured. His hand shook as he raised the cup to his lips. When he turned around, his eyes were hostile and landed on Jacob. "While we're on the subject of last night, where were you?"

Jacob choked out a sound of incredulity. "You can't be serious."

John's gaze didn't falter. "As a heart attack."

Jacob shot a look at Julia. "Do I have to answer that?"

John didn't give her time to respond. "Unless maybe you have something to hide."

Jacob snorted. "I was home all evening. Reading."

"Alone?"

"I live alone."

"That's convenient."

"That's the truth." Jacob turned to Julia. "This is ridiculous."

Knowing the situation was a nanosecond away from getting out of hand, Julia opened her desk drawer for the bottle of aspirin she kept on hand. Tapping three into her palm, she carried them to John. "Be nice," she said, shoving the pills at him.

John scowled, but took the aspirin. "Thanks."

Julia smiled sweetly. "I don't think you two have been formally introduced."

Jacob snorted.

Claudia ducked her head and pretended to be interested in the invoices on Julia's desk.

Julia made the introductions, but the two men only sneered at each other. Terrific, she thought, and tapped out two aspirin for herself.

The bell on the door jingled.

"Saved by the bell." Claudia rose.

Julia looked up to see John's brother Mitch walk in flanked by a second, bald-headed man in an ill-fitting suit. She knew it was an overreaction, but her heart began to pound.

"Hi, Mitch," she heard herself say. "Is everything all right?"

The grim-faced bald man hung back near the door. Julia thought he resembled a Mafioso. Mitch was all business this morning. His scowl lingered on John, then landed on Julia. "Is there a place where we can talk?" He shot a pointed look at Claudia and Jacob. "In private?"

"Yes, of course." She motioned toward the storage room at the back of the shop. "Has something happened?"

"What's this about, bro?" John asked.

Both Mitch and Julia turned to him. Mitch paused, sighed. "You need to hear this, too."

Julia led John and Mitch into the storage room. John had folded the cot and stacked the pillow and single blanket neatly on top, but the small room was still crowded with three people inside.

"Close the door," Mitch said.

Julia pulled the door closed behind them. The instant the door was closed, Mitch glared first at Julia, then John. "Why didn't you tell me about the goddamn book?"

Arms folded on his chest, John leaned against a shelf,

unimpressed by his brother's wrath. "She wanted it kept confidential."

"That's a bullshit answer. I'm your brother. A cop. I'm trying to help and you have me out breaking my ass without bothering to show me the respect of giving me all the information I need."

"It's my fault," Julia said. "I didn't want anyone to know."

He frowned at John. "You knew I'd find out."

"We didn't think it was relevant," John said.

Mitch glared at him. "You're a cop and you didn't think it was relevant?"

"Ex-cop," John said easily. "I don't see what the big deal is."

"The big deal, bro, is that some sick bastard murdered a woman last night."

Julia felt the words like a punch, so hard that for an instant she couldn't catch her breath. A hundred questions descended at once. And suddenly she had a very bad feeling about Mitch's being here. That somehow the murder was connected to her.

She could see that Mitch now had John's full attention. "What does that have to do with Julia?"

Mitch pulled a notepad from his jacket. "A city worker found a woman's body this morning at the St. Louis Cemetery No. 1. She'd been strangled and stabbed. We'll know more when the ME does the autopsy." His grim gaze swept to Julia. "There was a book found at the scene with some weird shit written inside."

Her heart stumbled, began to race. "Oh, no."

Mitch looked down at his note. "*A Gentleman's Touch* by Elisabeth de Haviland. Sound familiar?"

"Yes," Julia mumbled.

"No thanks to either of you." Mitch jabbed a thumb toward the door. "Detective McBride called the publishing house in New York and got the surprise of his life when he learned Elisabeth de Havilland is no other than Julia Wainwright." He glared at John. "I don't like being kept in the dark, bro, especially when I have a dead body on my hands. You want to explain to me what the hell is going on?"

John scraped a hand over his face.

Julia figured it was her responsibility to explain. "I asked him to keep this information confidential," she said.

"Why?"

"Because my father is about to be voted in as director of the Eternal Springs Ministry. He's worked hard to get where he is, Mitch, and I think if the members or the board found out I was writing . . . erotica it could hurt his chances."

Mitch looked uncomfortable for a moment. "What exactly is erotica, Julia?"

Heat suffused her face. "It's sensual writing. About emotional love and a physical relationship between a man and a woman."

Out of the corner of her eye she could see that John was hanging onto her every word.

"There's a lot of sex in the book?" Mitch asked bluntly.

Julia nodded. "Yes."

"We think that's what set this guy off, got him interested in Julia," John put in.

Mitch's gaze sharpened on her brother. "What makes you think that?"

"The notes. Some of the things he said to her when he assaulted her last night." He shrugged. "It's an assumption, but it fits."

Mitch appeared to digest that for a moment. "Do you think he finds her work offensive or is he turned on by it?"

"Offensive," Julia said.

"Both," John said simultaneously.

"Shit." Mitch scrubbed a hand over his face, his gaze meeting John's.

"He's turned on, but he doesn't like it," John finished.

Julia didn't miss the silent communication that passed between the two men, and a chill crept up her spine. "What do we do now?" she asked.

"You let the cops do their job." Mitch met her gaze. "I'll need a copy of your book, Julia."

She hesitated. "Will you be able to keep my identity in confidence?"

"I'll do my best, but I can tell you the investigation will take precedence over your privacy."

Now that someone had been killed, her privacy—her father's fast-track career—didn't seem as important.

Turning away, she left the two men to get a copy of the book—and for the first time since she'd begun *A Gentleman's Touch*, she wished to God she'd never written it.

TWELVE

"You look like you got caught in a meat grinder," Mitch said after Julia had left the room.

John figured a meat grinder would have been a hell of a lot kinder than the abuse he'd put his body through last night. "Thanks," he muttered.

Mitch looked him up and down, then sniffed. "You smell like a goddamn bar."

Because he didn't know how to respond to that, John walked over to the door, closed it and asked the question that had been burning in the back of his mind since his brother had walked into the shop. "So what aren't you telling us about this murder?"

"It's bad shit, John."

"Yeah, well, murder is always bad shit."

Mitch shot a pointed look to the flask on the floor next to the folded cot. "Can I trust you to keep your mouth shut?"

That his brother would even ask irked. But John figured better men than him had succumbed to the mouth loosening effects of alcohol. "You know you can."

Mitch grimaced. "I talked to the ME while I was at the scene this morning. NOPD isn't going to make it public, but the son of a bitch that killed the woman inscribed something on her abdomen. Carved some weird bullshit into her flesh."

"Jesus." John thought about the possibility of the man who'd accosted Julia in the alley and the murderer being one and the same, and shuddered inwardly. "Was the inscription legible? What did it say?"

"CSI took a bunch of photos." Glancing once toward the door, he pulled a few laser prints from his jacket pocket. "It's some sick shit, that's for sure."

John had seen plenty of crime scenes in the years he'd been a cop. He'd seen the vicious things one man could do to another, and he'd long since stopped letting any of it bother him. But he'd never seen anything like the sight that accosted him when he looked at the photo.

The wages of sin is death.

John stared at the crude words. Blood red against pasty white flesh. The dried blood that had streamed from the cuts told him the words had been carved into her flesh while she'd been alive . . .

"That's the same as one of the letters Julia received."

"I'll need a copy."

"You got it." John sighed. "What else?"

"We won't know exactly what happened to her until the ME finishes. Looks like he tied her up, cut her, then strangled her. There was a bloody crucifix inside her body. Prelim exam says she was raped and sodomized with it. She was torn up pretty bad, like he was in a frenzy." Mitch's gaze met John's. "I don't have to remind you that there was a crucifix found in the alley where Julia was accosted."

"I made the connection." The hairs on the back of John's neck prickled. "They the same?"

"Similar enough for me to drop by and tell you this."

"Shit," John said.

"Any idea who the wacko is?"

John shook his head. "No idea, but I'm working it. I'm

running backgrounds on her employees. Skinny guy out front, Jacob Brooks, doesn't have an alibi."

Mitch scribbled something in his notepad. "I'll plug him into the database and see if anything pops."

"Thanks."

Mitch motioned toward the flask lying on the floor a few feet away. "This might be a good time for you to clean up your act, bro."

Because he wasn't sure if he was up to that task, either, John frowned. "I'd rather you assign her an officer."

"NOPD doesn't have the manpower for that. You know how it works."

"Maybe you could pull some strings."

"I'm sick of pulling strings for you. For chrissake pull yourself together." Mitch shook his head as if in disgust. "The NOPD is recruiting. I added your name to the list."

"Mitch, I'm in no shape to be taking on a job . . ."

"Instead of wallowing in all that self-pity, maybe you ought to be thankful you walked out of that warehouse that night. You're alive, man. For God's sake, it could have been you who'd taken a bullet. Do you ever stop to think about that?"

John stared hard at his brother, his heart pounding. "A day doesn't go by that I don't think about it, goddamn it."

What he didn't say was that for the last two months he'd wished it *had* been him who hadn't walked away.

"You're going to what?" *Julia wasn't one to raise her* voice—not much anyway—but she couldn't keep the incredulity out of it.

John didn't look the least bit fazed. "I said I'm going to move into the storage room."

"Move in?" she repeated stupidly.

"In light of the attack on you and the murder last night, Mitch and I both think it's a good idea."

Julia didn't agree. Not that she didn't feel safer with John around. She did. But after seeing the shape he was in this morning—and taking into consideration the way she was reacting to him—she didn't think his moving in was a good idea at all.

"You won't be comfortable there," she blurted.

"My apartment's not much bigger. The cot is fine. I can use the little half bath off the hall."

"There's no shower."

"I'll have to use yours."

The image of him naked and soaping his sculpted male body rendered her speechless. An author of erotica, Julia was no prude. But it didn't keep the heat from creeping into her cheeks. A naked John Merrick using her shower was not a thought she wanted to have at the moment.

"Don't you think Mitch is overreacting?" she asked.

"Mitch doesn't overreact." He tilted his head and frowned at her. "Neither do I."

The intellectual side of her brain knew his moving in temporarily was a good idea. But another side of her that wasn't quite so logical was beginning to feel hemmed in. It was a feeling she'd been dealing with since childhood. A feeling brought on by an overbearing father whose love could be oppressive. As an adult, Julia had learned to deal with her father; she loved and respected Benjamin Wainwright. But having seen the crumble of her parents' not-so-perfect marriage, she guarded her independence with a fierceness not many people understood.

Not that she would ever consider a relationship with John. He hadn't talked about it, but she knew he was in a very dark place right now. She could see the pain etched into his every feature. While she was willing to be a friend, that was where she drew the line.

"How long?" she asked after a moment.

"At the very least until NOPD can rule out the possibility that the murder last night is related to the attack on you." He lifted a shoulder, let it drop. "Preferably until your stalker is found and stopped."

"Do you think the police will find him?"

"Sooner or later he'll screw up. Or the police will get

lucky." His eyes met hers. "In the interim, I think this is the best way to keep you safe."

She sighed, hating the thought of how this would affect her life. Julia came and went as she pleased. She saw whom she pleased, when she pleased. She loved socializing, but she also valued her privacy. Unfortunately, she didn't see a way out of this.

"I'll do my best to make the storage room comfortable for you. In fact, I've got an old recliner upstairs that I'm not using. And there's an antique floor lamp I can bring down."

"Don't go to any trouble."

"I'll see if I can get Jacob to help me with them." She started toward the cash register counter, where Jacob had just rung up a sale.

"Hey you," she said, walking up behind him.

"You're not going to believe this." The thin young man turned to her and smiled. "I just sold the autographed copy of *In Cold Blood*. Capote signed it in 1963."

Julia glanced at the amount on the cash register and grinned. "Holy cow. Nice job."

"He's a collector from Baton Rouge."

"Did you get his card?"

He passed her a business card. "Of course."

She dropped the card into her pocket, making a mental note to enter the information into the customer database she had on her laptop upstairs. "I was wondering if you would help John move a couple of pieces of furniture to the storage room from my apartment."

Jacob looked past her at John, his smile dwindling. "Why are you moving furniture from your apartment into the storage room?"

"Because until this stalker is caught, John is going to be staying there."

"Does that mean we get to watch him stagger around half-naked every morning?"

Julia had always liked Jacob, but he had a difficult streak that ran a mile deep. She could see it in his eyes now.

And even though they were friends, she was glad she'd never let him forget that this was a business and she was his boss.

"That means," John cut in, "that you need to get your skinny ass moving and give me a hand."

Folding his arms at his chest, Jacob rolled his eyes. "Oh brother."

"None of us are happy about this stalker situation," Julia said as she brushed past them and started toward the stairs at the back of the shop, "but I would appreciate it very much if you two didn't act like a couple of surly teenagers."

Julia heard the two men behind her as she ascended the stairs to her apartment. She unlocked the door and flipped on the light. She caught a hint of vanilla and the aroma of this morning's hazelnut coffee and smiled. Crossing to her bedroom, she opened the door and motioned inside. "You can start with the recliner there in the corner."

John stepped into her bedroom. Not for the first time Julia was aware of his size. He was at least six three and seemed to tower over her five-feet-four-inch frame.

"You sure you can get by without it?" he asked. "I don't need it."

"I rarely use the recliner or the lamp. And I think they'll make your stay in the storage room a lot more comfortable."

He crossed to the recliner, set his hands on the back and frowned at Jacob. "Sometime today, Ace."

Giving Julia a withering look, Jacob crossed to the chair and the two men lifted it and wrestled it through the door.

Julia chose a small table from her bedroom and a lamp from her office. She pulled a second blanket from the linen closet in the hall. She knew the storage room was poorly insulated and could get cold at night. She could hear the men arguing in the stairway and sighed. It was definitely going to be an interesting week.

She'd just finished emptying the single drawer in the table when she heard someone behind her and spun. John stood in the doorway, watching her with interest.

"You startled me," she said.

"Probably good for you to be jumpy."

She motioned toward the table and lamp. "You can take these, too."

He didn't even look at the table. "How long have you known Jacob?"

"Since college." Realizing where he was going with that, she shook her head. "He's not the stalker, John."

"I'm sure you know friends and family are always the first suspects, don't you?"

"Even so, Jacob is no stalker. For God's sake, I see him here every day. He's funny and kind—"

"He works here part-time?"

"Yes."

"Is this his only job?"

"He is also working on a book."

"What kind of book?"

"A thriller, I think."

"Do you know what it's about?"

"He doesn't talk about it."

John seemed to mull that over for a moment. "Does he have a girlfriend?"

"Uh . . . not exactly."

His eyes sharpened on hers. "What does that mean?

"That means his significant other is . . . not female."

He looked surprised for an instant, but quickly covered it with a frown. "Okay."

"Jacob is a great guy, John. Be nice to him, okay?"

Bending slightly, he picked up the small table and lamp. "Nice isn't part of my persona."

"It would be if you let it."

Giving her a dry smile, he carried the lamp and table out the door and went down the stairs.

THIRTEEN

A *steady stream of customers kept Julia busy the rest of* the day. Once he had moved the table and lamp to the storage room, John had asked to use her shower. Julia had given him the key and tried not to think about it. She worked the cash register and chatted with Claudia and Jacob and several customers that had come to New Orleans all the way from London. But the whole while she was keenly aware of the pipes clanging, and she couldn't keep her mind from conjuring images of John with water sluicing over taut male skin . . .

At noon, Claudia left for class at Tulane. Jacob manned the cash register while Julia stocked a box of old books she'd ordered online. She'd just slid an Agatha Christie first edition on the shelf when Jacob's voice right behind her made her start.

"So what's the story on Macho Man?" he asked.

Casting him a frown, she slid another book onto the shelf. "You mean John?"

"Yeah. John. The whole time we were moving furniture,

he treated me like some kind of criminal, asking me all sorts of questions. For God's sake, Julia, he thinks I'm the stalker."

"He's just covering his bases."

"Or maybe he's a homophobe."

Julia bit her lip. "He didn't know you were gay until a while ago when I told him."

Jacob rolled his eyes. "Great. Now he's probably going to want to beat me up."

"Come on. He's not like that. He's tough on everyone, Jacob. Even himself."

"Well, knowing he's an equal opportunity jerk makes it all better." Shaking his head, he usurped her latte and sipped. "What, is he going through a divorce or what?"

Julia had assumed Jacob knew about the shooting by now. She stopped shelving books. "A few months ago he was a detective with the Chicago PD. I don't know the details, but during a bust there was some confusion and he accidentally shot and killed a fellow officer."

Jacob looked appropriately solemn for a moment. "That's heavy stuff."

"So cut him some slack, will you?"

"I'll think about it."

"Thank you." Smiling, she reached for her latte and sipped. "And leave my coffee alone, too."

John spent the first part of the afternoon at the hardware store picking up new bolt locks for Julia's shop, and the second half of the afternoon installing them. He spent twenty minutes on the phone with a local security company, negotiating prices and trying to get the new security system installed sooner than next week. In the end he settled for five business days.

More than once during the day he found himself watching Julia. She was charming and funny with her customers, many of whom were eccentric. But she could be serious and knowledgeable when the situation called for it. He kept an eye on Jacob. The guy seemed normal. But John knew all too well that behind even the most benign of faces a monster could lurk. He knew most stalking victims knew their stalkers. Did Julia know hers? Was her stalker the same man who'd murdered the young woman in the cemetery?

At five o'clock, business began to wind down. Jacob sat on the stool at the cash register, reading a book. Julia sat at her desk, calculating the day's receipts. John knew better than to stare, but he'd been telling himself that all day, and yet here he was, unable to take his eyes off her.

The black turtleneck she wore swept over her slender frame like velvet skin, revealing subtle curves that made his hands itch to touch. Her slacks were just snug enough to let him know she had one of the nicest asses he'd ever laid eyes on.

He wanted to blame his lack of willpower on the hangover—or maybe the need to protect that rose inside him every time he saw the bruises—but deep inside he knew his watching her had more to do with good old-fashioned sexual attraction.

Of course, he wasn't going to do anything about it. He hadn't so much as thought about women since that terrible night in Chicago. His head was too fucked up to consider anything more complicated than getting out of bed in the morning and putting on his shoes. That wasn't to say sex wouldn't be a nice distraction. It definitely would, especially with Julia. But he knew she was not the kind of woman to partake in a one-night stand. Anything more and John was simply not interested.

He'd just finished with the lock on the alley window when the bell on the door jingled. He looked up to see a tall, well-dressed man with sandy blond hair enter the shop. He wore a long London Fog raincoat. Expensive wingtips. A lawyer or banker type, John thought.

The man looked around, spotted Julia at her desk, and a

grin the size of Lake Pontchartrain split his face. "You're never going to believe what I have in my hand," he said, crossing to her desk.

Curious, John stopped what he was doing and straightened. He didn't know who the man was. Didn't know what he wanted or why he was staring at Julia as if she were some coveted prize. But he was damn well going to be ready if Mr. Investment Banker got out of line.

Looking surprised by the man's presence, Julia rose. "Hi."

The man leaned close and kissed her cheek, his hands settling comfortably on her shoulders. "How are you?" he asked.

"Fine." She leaned into him and pecked air. "I wasn't expecting to see you until the weekend."

John knew it was stupid, but he was inordinately pleased that she had pecked air instead of skin. He wanted to describe the feeling jabbing his gut as suspicion, but he was honest enough with himself to realize he didn't like the familiar way the other man was touching her.

"This wouldn't wait," he said excitedly.

The man didn't acknowledge John or Jacob. It was as if he didn't even realize there were two other people in the room. One hundred and twenty percent of his attention was focused on Julia.

"What?" she asked.

He pulled a small envelope from the pocket of his Armani jacket and waved it like a flag. "I've got two tickets for *Phantom of the Opera*. Box seats at the Saenger Theatre."

She blinked, and then her surprise turned to pleasure. "How did you manage that? The show has been sold out for weeks."

"One of my clients gave them to me. He and his wife are going out of town." He slapped her playfully on the shoulder with the tickets. "Will you go?"

"Are you kidding? When?"

"Tonight."

John glanced at Jacob, who, he noted, was watching the

man with a little too much interest. Jealousy? he wondered. Or something else?

"Please?" the man said.

"Oh, Julia, you should!" Jacob brought his hands to-•gether. "I've heard it's a fabulous show!"

"I'd love to go," Julia said.

"Fabulous! We can grab dinner, too."

Julia's gaze swept to John, and in that instant, she realized the two men had not yet been introduced. That there would be questions she wasn't sure how to answer. As if on cue, the man noticed John. His questioning gaze ran from John to Julia and back to John. "You have a new clerk or is he the bouncer?" he said in a lowered voice.

John almost smiled at the territorial way the other man put his hand on her shoulder. A caveman telling him in no uncertain words that she was off limits.

Wiping her hands on her slacks, Julia approached John, Mr. Investment Banker trailing her like a puppy. "John, this is Skip Stockton."

John crossed to the man and tried to look civil.

The man stuck out his hand a little too quickly. "Nice to meet you."

John waited a beat before taking the other man's hand and growling his name.

"Are you two friends?" Skip was curious.

"John is an old friend of the family," Julia said. "We've known each other forever."

John didn't like the way she'd used the word "old." As if he were her older favorite uncle or something. Which he definitely was not. In fact, he didn't have an uncle-like feeling in his entire body when it came to Julia.

"Ah. I see." But Skip didn't understand. John could see the questions burgeoning in the other man's eyes. Questions like: So what is he doing here?

"Are you a collector?" Stockton asked.

"I'm here to keep an eye on Julia."

Stockton laughed, but when no one joined him he sobered. "Keep an eye on her?"

"I've been receiving threatening letters," she said.

"She was assaulted in the alley down the street last night," John put in.

"*Assaulted?*" He looked from John to Julia, his expression shocked and, John noted, concerned. "My God, were you hurt?"

Something male and uncomfortable rose inside John when Stockton put his hands on Julia's shoulders and turned her to him. "Let me look at you."

"Really, I'm fine."

She tried to move away, but he set his palm beneath her jaw and lifted her chin. "How did this happen?" He looked at John as if *he* were the guilty party, which only served to piss him off.

"Where were you last night between ten and ten thirty?" John asked.

Stockton looked as if he'd swallowed his tongue. "I beg your pardon?"

John repeated the question.

Stockton's gaze flicked from John to Julia and then back to John. "What is this? Some kind of interrogation?"

"Maybe you should just answer the question."

"I don't like the insinuation."

"I didn't make an insinuation. I simply asked you where you were last night between ten and ten thirty."

"Guys. Please." Julia stepped between the two men, but her anger was focused on John. "That's not necessary."

"It's okay, Julia." Stockton glared at John. "I was with clients all evening. You can check."

"I will."

Shaking his head, Stockton turned to Julia. "Look, I've got to run to a quick meeting." He glanced at his watch. "I'll be back in an hour to pick you up for dinner."

"I'll be ready," she said.

Stockton bent to give her a chaste kiss on the cheek. Giving John a final triumphant look, he walked out.

*   *   *

John spent the next hour cleaning up the mess he'd made while installing the new locks. But he was keenly aware of the water running through the pipes, and he knew Julia was taking a shower. It was bad enough imagining her beneath the spray, but knowing she was getting ready for a date with some investment banker type put a cruel twist on the situation.

He knew he'd acted like a jerk earlier. He wanted to believe he'd called his brother and asked him to run a background check on Stockton because everyone was a suspect until he or she was cleared. But John knew that wasn't the case. He didn't believe Stockton was the stalker. The truth of the matter was that John was jealous. A petty, stupid emotion that was a total waste of time and energy because he had absolutely no intention of making any advances toward Julia. Not that she would ever re-ciprocate. No, he thought darkly, Julia Wainwright had too much sense than to get tangled up with a man like him.

"John?"

He looked up at the sound of her voice. She was stand-ing in the storage room doorway. In an instant, he took in her silhouette and could have sworn his blood heated ten degrees. She was wearing a silky black dress. Even though the neckline and hemline were conservative, there was ab-solutely nothing conservative about the way the material swept over her body.

Looking quickly away, he finished sweeping the chips of paint and wood shavings into the dustpan. "Yeah?"

"Do you have a minute?"

He dumped the debris into the trash can and turned to her. "I've got all night."

She stepped into the storage room and stopped a few feet away from him, her sultry eyes steady on his. He was keenly aware of her proximity. The exotic scent of her per-fume. The fact that he was responding to her in a way he did not want to respond.

"I just wanted to tell you that you don't have to worry

about Skip. He's a good guy. I've known him for almost two years now. My father introduced us."

"Do you only go out with men your father approves of?"

She blinked. "I go out with whomever I choose."

"You sure about that?"

"Frankly, I don't think the men I go out with are any of your business."

"Ninety percent of stalking victims know their stalkers."

"Skip is no stalker."

John knew now was probably a good time for him to tell her he'd run a background check on the man in question and let her know it had come back clean, but he wasn't feeling particularly hospitable at the moment.

"I didn't want you to worry."

"I appreciate that."

Her gaze flicked to the brown paper bag he'd set on the desk. The top of a bottle of gin peeked out. "That's not going to help."

"You let me worry about that."

"John . . ."

"Let it go, Julia."

She hesitated. "You make it difficult to know you. You don't let people in."

"You don't want to know me."

"Why don't you let me be the judge of that?"

John said nothing. As far as he was concerned there was nothing left to say. "Be careful tonight."

Julia rolled her eyes and started to say something flippant, but John cut her off. "I mean it. Make sure that pencil-neck date of yours escorts you to and from the ladies' room. To the concession stand. Everywhere."

She sobered. "Okay."

She was still looking at him when he stepped back and closed the door in her face.

John had never been good at doing nothing. But as had been the case for the last two months, there wasn't anyone he wanted to see. There was nothing he wanted to do. He hated to admit it, but his brother was right. The only thing he seemed to do well these days was feel sorry for himself. And, of course, get drunk.

He'd felt like an idiot, but he'd stood at the front door of the shop when Stockton had come to pick up Julia. He'd drilled him on a few safety measures, told him not to let her out of his sight. Stockton had agreed. But John could tell the other man thought he was overreacting.

They left at just before seven P.M. John went into the storage room, sat down on the cot and broke the seal. The first sip went down like a ball of fire. The second made him want a third. By the time he got around to the fourth, his head was already beginning to spin . . .

He knew this was the last thing he should be doing. Julia was in very real danger. He should be keeping a more vigilant eye. But already he could feel the walls closing in, the nightmares knocking at his door. When he looked down at his hands, he could almost see Franklin Watts's blood. The guilt churned like vomit in his gut. He would never forget the pain in the eyes of Watts's wife and two children the day of the funeral. He could still hear the blasts of the twenty-one-gun salute. Angela Watts had made eye contact with him as she'd folded the flag over the casket, but there had been no forgiveness in their depths. John hadn't expected it. Hadn't even wanted it.

He thought about Julia and reluctantly acknowledged that the reason he felt so crummy tonight was because he was jealous. But John knew she was better off with Stockton than she would ever be with him. He was in no condition to even entertain the idea of a relationship. He liked and respected her too much to do that to her.

Turning on the floor lamp, he set the bottle on the table and put his face in his hands. He wasn't proud of what he had become. Like a thousand other troubled cops before him, he had turned to the bottle for solace because nothing else worked. It was pathetic that he'd arrived at a place where he preferred the oblivion of alcohol to life. He'd learned to settle for less. A whole fucking lot less.

Sudden fury had him reaching for the bottle. Grabbing it by the neck, he flung it as hard as he could. Glass shattered as it struck the steel shelving. Gin spewed onto the floor. And John found himself facing a night without the anesthesia of alcohol.

Trying not to think about that, he rose and mechanically cleaned up the shards and spilled gin. He tossed the paper towels in the trash and looked around, ashamed and feeling trapped. If things got bad, he could always make a run to one of the bars on Bourbon Street and buy a bottle.

He spotted Julia's book lying facedown on the recliner. It had been months since he'd read a book. And while the thought of reading one now did not appeal, he knew that in this case the contents might give him some insights as to why she was being stalked.

He crossed to the recliner and picked up the book. Settling into the chair, he opened it and began to read. In the back of his mind, he prayed it would be enough to keep the demons at bay, at least for the night.

Fourteen

Phantom of the Opera *was Julia's favorite musical.* She loved the powerful score, the colorful costumes and the gothic tone of an ageless story. Combined with the beauty of the historic Saenger Theatre, the night had been truly magical. Skip had been funny and witty and attentive, walking her the ladies' room twice, once during dinner at Arnaud's and then once during the intermission at the Saenger.

Julia had always enjoyed his company. Skip was a handsome man with a sharp mind and a kind heart. He was well educated and fun to be with. He was a successful investment banker with a bright future. One day he would make some lucky girl a wonderful husband. He would be a loving father.

But Julia was not in the market for either of those things. She liked her life the way it was. She liked her independence, the freedom to do whatever she wanted whenever she wanted to do it, and without having to answer to anyone.

She'd been blessed with good parents. Benjamin and

Jillian Wainwright had loved each other, but it hadn't been enough to make the marriage work. An astute child, Julia had seen more than they'd intended. She'd watched her domineering father break her mother's spirit. She'd seen the kinds of things a man and a woman could do to each other when they were unhappy. Finally, unable to cope, Jillian left and filed for divorce, leaving her two small daughters behind. Though Julia had been only ten years old, she had been mature enough to understand her mother's motives and to this day Julia had never blamed her.

She'd come to terms with her parents' failure at marriage. She had a loving relationship with her father despite his overbearing nature. She flew to San Diego a couple of times a year to spend time with her mother. But at a formative age, Julia had learned that marriage didn't always work and she'd come to believe that it was not for her.

"I'll walk you to the door."

Skip's voice jerked her from her reverie. Julia looked up and realized he'd parked the Jaguar on the street outside her shop. "It's okay," she said quickly, but he was already out of the car and crossing to her door.

Always the gentleman, he opened it for her and offered his hand. "I had a great time, Julia."

"So did I. I love *Phantom*, and the tickets were a wonderful surprise."

They walked in silence to the door of her shop. It was after midnight and around them the Quarter was nearly quiet. Julia was keenly aware of her hand in Skip's. That his palms were warm and damp against hers.

At the door she extricated her hand from his and dug in her purse for her keys. Skip stood silently at her side while she opened the door. "Thanks for a lovely evening."

"The pleasure was all mine." He shoved his hands into his pockets. "I mean that, Julia."

She knew he wanted her to invite him inside. The last few times she'd gone out with him, he'd made it clear that he wanted more than a good-night kiss. He wanted to be more to her than a friend.

Julia was fond of Skip and enjoyed his friendship. But her interest in him stopped there. At times she found herself wishing she felt something more. But the truth of the matter was she didn't. There were no sparks. No spike in her pulse. Just a vague need to get in the door quickly so he didn't have the opportunity to act on the heat she saw in his eyes.

"You have time for a nightcap?" he asked.

"Oh, well . . . I've actually got an early morning."

"At the very least I should check the place out before I leave."

"It's okay, Skip. John is staying in the storage room until my new security system is installed next week."

"You trust him to keep you safe?" His eyes glittered with meaning. "His screw up in Chicago was all over the news . . ."

"He's going through a tough spot, but from what I've heard he was a good cop."

"Still, I'd feel better if I checked out your apartment for myself." Not giving her the chance to decline his offer, he pushed open the door.

The shop was quiet and semidark, as Julia had expected. The only light came from the antique banker's lamp on her desk. She could still smell the faint scent of coffee and the sweet aroma of hazelnut from the candles she'd burned earlier. She walked inside, her boots rapping dully against the wood plank floor. "See?" she said. "No monsters."

"That's good."

She went immediately to the coffee station and reached for the teapot. "I'll make us some tea."

"Julia . . ."

"Can you hit the lights?"

"I'd rather keep the lights off if that's all right with you."

She tensed when his hand landed on her shoulder. Dread curled inside her when he turned her to face him and looked into her eyes. "How long are you going to try to avoid what's happening between us?" he said earnestly.

"Skip . . ."

"I care for you, Julia. For God's sake, I couldn't take my eyes off of you all night."

"You tell all the girls that."

He laughed, but there was a tightness to it she'd never noticed before. "You know that's not true." Setting his hands on her shoulders, he backed her slowly to the desk. "Look at you. You're beautiful." His gaze skittered down the front of her. "I like the way you look in that dress."

Julia had known this moment was inevitable. The moment when he wanted something she wasn't prepared to give. She'd been dreading it. She only hoped her turning him away now didn't affect their friendship.

"Skip, I know we've been—"

The next thing she knew his mouth was on hers. Stunned, Julia went back a few steps. She tried to turn her head, but he set his hands on either side of her face, holding her in place. All the while his mouth roamed hers, his tongue seeking entrance. Julia put her hands on his shoulders and pushed.

Only when he dropped one of his hands to cup her left breast did she succeed in turning her head. "Skip . . . cut it out."

"You want this," he panted.

"No."

"I see it in your eyes."

"This isn't what I—"

He stuck his tongue in her mouth. She hadn't realized she was being pushed slowly backward until her backside came in contact with her desk. A jolt of alarm went through her when he squeezed her right breast. Then his hand slid downward, over her pelvis to her mound, where he tried to cup her through her dress.

Shoving him hard with her right hand, Julia twisted away. "Stop it!"

Skip stumbled back, his expression a mosaic of confusion and hurt. "Julia . . ."

"I think she wants you to get the fuck off her, Slick." John's voice was little more than a low rumble.

Sweeping the hair from her eyes, Julia glanced toward the storage room. In the semidarkness, she saw John in silhouette. He was leaning against the bookshelf, a bottle in his right hand, watching them with the uneasy patience of a predator.

"I can handle this," Julia heard herself say, surprised by the high breathlessness of her voice.

"Yeah, I can tell by the way he was grabbing at your crotch."

"This is a private moment," Skip said.

"That's where you're wrong, Slick."

"You have no right to eavesdrop."

"Good thing for her I'm an insomniac, isn't it?" John raised the bottle and took a long pull. "Were you planning to paw her all night or were you going to take it a step farther?"

"That's enough," Julia snapped. "Both of you." She turned to Skip. "Maybe you should go."

"Maybe I should." Staring at her as if she'd just told him she was converting to atheism, he wiped his mouth. "I'm sorry."

"Sorry I showed up," John asked from across the room, "or sorry you didn't get that dress off her fast enough?"

Skip pointed a shaking finger at John. "Stay away from me," he said and started toward the door.

Saying nothing, John took another long pull from the bottle.

The other man jerked open the door, then turned to give Julia a long look. "I'll call you tomorrow," he said.

"I'll speak to you then," she said.

Shaking his head, he slammed the door hard enough to rattle the pictures on the walls.

*Julia wasn't sure who she was angriest with, Skip for act*ing like a jerk, John for intervening when she could have handled the situation herself, or herself for being so damn stupid as to get herself into the situation to begin with. Since John was the only one handy, she took it out on him.

"What the hell do you think you're doing?" she demanded.

"In the old days they called it protecting your honor."

"Skip is harmless."

Something dark and unnerving glittered in his eyes. "Skip is a now my number one suspect. You would be wise to remember that next time you decide to let him put his hands all over you."

"He didn't. I mean, I didn't—"

"That's not what I saw."

Realizing what she was doing, Julia blew out a breath and looked to the heavens. "I don't have to explain any of this to you."

"Good. Because I don't want to hear the details."

"There are no details."

"Really?"

He had one of the most shuttered faces she'd ever encountered, making him almost impossible to read. He could go from cutting to mocking in a nanosecond, and Julia was having a difficult time keeping up.

She glanced down at the bottle in his hand, the anger she'd felt earlier transforming into something closer to sympathy. "John, what are you doing?"

"Drinking gin." He offered the bottle. "Want some?"

"No, thank you."

"Because of your religious convictions?"

"Because I don't like it."

"You don't know what you're missing."

She looked into his eyes, trying to understand why he was torturing himself this way. But she came up short. "You must really hate yourself," she said after a moment.

"You don't know the half of it."

Her surprise must have shown in her expression, because he smiled.

"Why do you hate yourself?" she asked.

"You mean besides the fact that I shot and killed a cop?"

"John, you were cleared . . ."

"Yeah, well, tell his wife and kids that."

The harsh reality of what he was going through broke her heart. "Please don't do this to yourself. Don't blame yourself for what happened in Chicago."

"I pulled the trigger. Why wouldn't I blame myself?"

"Because it wasn't your fault."

"How the fuck would you know? You weren't there."

"You made a mistake."

"A mistake is when someone backs into the garage door and dents the car. What I did was a hell of a lot worse than a mistake. I killed a man. A good man, Julia. I shot him in the chest and watched him bleed out on the floor." He scrubbed a hand over his face. "Do you have any idea how many lives that devastated?"

"Don't let it devastate yours."

"Too late."

"It's not too late."

"I left two kids without a father. A young woman without a husband. Two grieving parents."

"You can't let this ruin your life, John. You're a good man, too."

"Am I?"

"Yes."

He took another drink from the bottle and wiped his mouth with his sleeve. "If you had any idea the thoughts running through my head right now about you and that dress you're wearing, you'd know exactly what kind of man I am, and it ain't even close to good."

Heart pounding wildly, she resisted the temptation to look down at the dress in question.

He gave her a lethal smile. "You're refreshing as hell."

The way he was looking at her unnerved her. Made her feel stripped bare, both inside and out. Without even touching her he'd made her heart beat faster, something Skip hadn't been able to do even when his mouth had been pressed against hers. Julia knew it was crazy comparing the two men; they were nothing alike. Skip was predictable and safe. John was volatile and troubled and there was no way in hell she would ever get involved with him. But on some fundamental level, she knew he was the kind of man who could turn a spark into an explosion.

"Go to bed, Julia," he said in a low voice that sounded more like a growl.

She stood there for a moment longer, knowing if she passed by him he would act on some of those thoughts running through his head. She held her ground.

After a moment he raised the bottle in a salute, walked into the storage room and closed the door behind him.

Fifteen

The roses arrived at ten A.M. Two dozen red Chrysler
Imperials surrounded by baby's breath and salmon-colored
tea roses in a lovely lead crystal vase. It was a beautiful
arrangement, but Julia took little pleasure in it. Last night,
she'd seen a side of Skip she didn't like. A side she did not
want to see again.

Her feelings for John Merrick, however, were a different
story altogether. She'd gone to bed thinking of him. She'd
wakened thinking of him. She'd dreamed about the scene
that had transpired between them the night before. Only in
her dreams he hadn't turned away. He'd acted on the heat
she'd seen in his eyes, and the outcome had left her heart
pounding. She didn't know what to do about it. Ignore her
feelings and hope they went away? But she didn't think
they would.

She'd opened the shop at eight o'clock, the way she had
every morning for the last two years. She went about her
morning routine of making coffee and lighting candles.
She spent fifteen minutes logging new books and entering

the ISBN numbers into the database she had set up. But Julia's thoughts were not on her work. No matter how hard she tried not to think about John, she invariably found her mind drifting back to him. The way he'd looked at her. The dark glint in his eyes. Words that had made her pulse race . . .

If you had any idea the thoughts running through my head right now about you and that dress you're wearing, you'd know exactly what kind of man I am, and it ain't even close to good.

Closing her eyes, she put her face in her hands and sighed. "Do not go there," she muttered and forced her concentration back to her work.

At ten thirty the bell jangled and Claudia arrived with a box of beignets from Café du Monde. A distraction Julia welcomed.

"How was the show?" Claudia carried the pastries to the coffee station and worked off her coat.

"Breathtaking." Julia laid a linen napkin in an antique wire-mesh basket and began arranging the beignets inside.

"And your date with Skip?"

"Not so breathtaking."

Claudia poured dark roast into a cobalt blue mug. "Details."

Sighing, Julia relayed what had happened the night before, leaving out the part about John. "It was a bad scene."

"I didn't know Skip had it in him."

"Believe me, he does."

"I told you not to wear that dress."

"Evidently, I should have listened."

"So what are you going to do about Skip?"

Julia snagged a pastry from the basket. "I don't know."

"Do you like him?"

"I like him." She bit into the pastry. "But that's all."

The door to the storage room swung open. Both women looked up to see John stagger out. He was wearing blue jeans, the top button undone and no shirt. Without so much as sparing them a glance, he stumbled to the back door, flung it open and stepped into the alley. Julia winced at the sound of him getting sick.

"Well, at least someone had a fun night," Claudia said.

"I think he had a rough night," Julia corrected.

Claudia's questioning gaze met hers. But before Julia could explain, John staggered back into the shop. He disappeared into the storage room, then reappeared with a bundle of clothes.

"I need to use your shower," he said.

It was the first time she'd seen him without a shirt and the sight of his chest rendered her momentarily speechless. He was broad shouldered and narrow in the hip. He was more sinew than bulk, but his muscle definition was like nothing she'd ever seen . . . up close and personal, anyway. His pectoral muscles were covered with a thin layer of black hair than ran down his flat abdomen to disappear in the waistband of low-rise jeans she really, really wished he'd buttoned.

"Of course." Her own voice came to her as if from a great distance.

"Good morning," Claudia said.

Giving her a withering look, he turned and started up the stairs.

For several seconds neither woman spoke. Then Claudia broke the silence with "Oh, my God."

Julia looked at her sister. "What does that mean?"

"That means John Merrick is one breathtaking hunk of man flesh. No wonder you don't like Skip."

"Oh, good grief."

"What can I say, Julia? I'm a chest woman." Claudia shot her a mischievous grin. "Looks like I'm not the only one who noticed. Your face is red."

"I'm embarrassed for him."

"Liar. You're hot for him. I see it in your eyes."

"What you see is your concern." She heard the pipes clang as he turned on the water, and she sighed. "He was in bad shape last night."

"If the last two mornings are any indication, he's been

in bad shape for quite some time." Claudia made a sound of dismay. "I never imagined a tough guy like John Merrick with a drinking problem."

Julia didn't want to imagine that, either, but she'd always been honest enough to call a spade a spade. "He blames himself for what happened in Chicago." She relayed the conversation she and John had had the night before.

"He was officially cleared, though, wasn't he?" Claudia asked.

"That doesn't seem to matter to him. He seems bent on self-destruction."

"How sad." Claudia bit her lip and turned to her sister. "Julia, look, I sympathize with what he went through. But do you really think he's capable of looking out for you? I mean, the guy's obviously a mess."

Absently, Julia fingered the fading bruises on her throat. As much as she didn't want to admit it, she'd been uneasy since the incident in the alley. More than once last night at the theater, even with Skip watching over her, she'd found herself looking over her shoulder, jumping when someone got too close or when a man she didn't know made eye contact with her, even just to smile.

"The thought occurred to me," she said after a moment. "Maybe you could talk to him."

"I can try. I don't know what I'd say." She shrugged. "I don't know if he'd listen even if I found the words."

"After what happened the other night, I don't think this is the kind of thing you want to take any chances with."

"He's here in the evenings. That's a comfort."

"Judging from the way he looked this morning, last night he probably wouldn't even have known it if some screaming madman crashed through the front window."

Julia didn't mention that even though John had been drinking and obviously intoxicated, he'd looked plenty capable last night. "I'll talk to him tonight. I'm sure he'll be reasonable about it."

"If he doesn't straighten up his act, maybe we should fire him and hire a rent-a-cop or something."

"We'll cross that bridge when we come to it."

"Have you received any more letters?"

Julia shook her head. "Maybe he got bored with me and decided to move on."

But she could tell by the expression on her younger sister's face that neither of them believed it.

Fifteen minutes later John came downstairs, went directly to the coffee station and poured. His wet hair was spiked as if he'd run a towel over his head and left it. He wore faded jeans, a navy pullover and leather boots.

"There's aspirin in the drawer on the left," Julia said.

Without speaking, he opened a drawer, tapped out what looked like a handful of pills and downed them all with a gulp of hot coffee. Breakfast of champions, she thought, and shook her head.

When he turned to her, she didn't miss the pallor of his complexion or the bloodshot eyes. "Have you checked with your publisher to see if they've received any letters?"

"No," Julia said. "I can check with my editor today."

"We might get lucky if he sent a letter to New York and left a return address, hoping you might correspond."

Bolstered by the prospect of a lead, Julia sat down at her desk and dialed her editor's number from memory. They chatted for a few minutes and then Julia asked about fan mail. She was surprised to find that the New York office had, indeed, received several dozen letters and cards. Julia asked her editor to overnight the letters and hung up.

"She's going to overnight them."

"Let me know when they arrive."

"All right."

John refilled his coffee. "Sorry about throwing up in your alley," he said when his back was to her.

Julia looked over at him and knew he must be carrying a heavy load for it to bow those broad shoulders. "You were in bad shape last night."

"Never could hold my liquor." He turned to face her, his expression grim and shuttered.

"If there's anything I can do to—"

"There's not." As if realizing he'd been rude, he sighed and his voice softened. "You heard from Chip?"

"Skip," she corrected and motioned toward the roses on the counter.

John arched a brow, some of the old humor coming back into his eyes. "You going to forgive him?"

"I'm going to tell him I'd like to remain friends."

"He's going to be crushed."

Because she didn't know how to respond to that—because this was not a appropriate conversation to have with John—she crossed to the coffee station and poured herself a cup of hazelnut. "I'm sure he'll get over it."

"Judging from the way you looked in that dress last night, I doubt it."

A quick slice of heat low in her belly sent a blush to her cheeks. She hated feeling so transparent. What was it about John Merrick that had her feeling like a silly schoolgirl?

"I have to get to work," she said.

"I need to make some calls." He hesitated. "If you need any help around here, let me know. I'll try to make myself useful."

Her gaze met his. "Thank you."

"Don't mention it," he said and started for the storage room.

The mail arrived at noon. The mailman, a stout little man by the name of Crosby, always helped himself to a truffle or beignet as he dropped the stack in the antique wicker box on the counter. Julia always thanked him and smiled. It was one of those small rituals she loved. While Claudia rang up a sale at the counter, Julia carried the mail to her desk, where she slit each piece, separated the bills from the correspondence and junk mail, and filed what needed to be filed.

She held the phone in the crook of her neck. Mr. Thorn-brow was accusing her of borrowing and never returning a

Keats first edition. Absently, Julia slit the letter with an antique opener.

"If you continue to borrow books and refuse to return them, I'll be forced to stop our book sharing program," he said.

"Mr. Thornbrow, Claudia returned the book to you last week."

The contents of the letter spilled onto her desk. Julia's eyes were drawn to a flash of color. At first she thought it was one of the many junk advertisements she received every day. Then she looked down at the dozen or so photos spread out before her and her blood ran cold. Vaguely, she was aware of Mr. Thornbrow speaking. Of Claudia shuffling paper at the register. Then her heartbeat became a roar. Horror spread through her body like ice.

She saw pasty white flesh and the shocking red of blood. She saw bound hands and a face contorted in horror. Her eyes saw, but her mind could not comprehend. Shock and revulsion punched her like fists.

"Mother of God." Julia dropped the phone and stood abruptly, her heart hammering. The phone clattered to the floor.

"Julia?"

Vaguely, she was aware of Claudia's voice. But it couldn't penetrate the veil of horror stealing through her. She stared down at the photos. Graphic images of murder and death stared back at her. Images she would carry with her the rest of her life.

A gasp escaped her when she felt a hand on her shoulder. She spun to see her sister hang up the phone, her face concerned. "What is it? My God, you're pale as death." Her eyes flicked to the photos. "Oh, my God!"

Both women jumped when the phone rang. The normalcy of the sound brought Julia back. "Don't look at them," she said. "Get John." When Claudia only continued to stare at the horrific pictures, Julia gave her a gentle shove. "Go."

Relief went through her when her younger sister turned and ran toward the storage room.

The phone rang again. Mechanically, Julia picked it up. "The Book Merchant."

"How do you like the photos?" a whispered voice asked.

The words shocked her brain. Several seconds passed before she found her voice. "Who is this?"

"Look at them carefully, Julia. The terror on her face. The pain in her eyes. What do you think?"

"I think you're a sick bastard."

His laugh chilled her, sent a shiver barreling through her. "Ah, such language."

"What do you want?" she asked.

"I want to hurt you. I want to hear you scream in agony. I want you to pay for your sins."

A small part of her brain told her to keep him talking. John would be there in a few seconds and maybe he could get something out of the guy that would be helpful. But his words, the chilling tone of his voice, overwhelmed her with fear. She couldn't bear to listen.

"You're next, Julia. Get ready because I'm coming for you. When I get my hands on you you're going to wish you were never born."

Sixteen

Julia gripped the phone and listened to the terrible voice.
She could feel her skin crawling. Her heart slamming
against her ribs. Her hand gripping the phone so hard her
knuckles hurt.

The next thing she knew John was prying the phone
from her hand. He put it to his ear, his expression taut as he
listened.

An instant later his eyes met hers and he shook his head.
"He hung up."

Julia pressed her hand to her stomach. "It was him."

"The stalker?"

Nodding, she motioned at the photos on the desk. "He
sent those."

John's eyes darkened as he took in the photos spread out
on her desk like macabre playing cards. Using the letter
opener, he looked carefully at each one.

Because she couldn't bear to look at them, Julia turned
away and crossed to Claudia. "Are you okay?" she asked.

Claudia looked shell-shocked. "I've never seen anything like that in my life."

"I'm sorry you had to see them."

"Same goes. You've nothing to be sorry for. It's not your fault."

Julia took her younger sister into her arms. "Thank you."

After a moment she pulled away and turned to John. "Please tell me those photos are not real."

"I'm no expert," he said. "But they look genuine." His jaws clenched tight. "The big question now is, who is the woman in the photo?"

John had seen a lot of disturbing things in the years he'd been a detective, but he'd never seen anything like this.

There were seven photos, each graphic and stark. Five of the photos depicted a young woman bound and terrified. In two of the photos she appeared to be dead. He knew they could be fake. That some backroom photographer could have set up the scene or doctored the photos. But John had seen enough death in the course of his career to recognize it when he saw it. His gut was telling him these were real.

Across from him Julia stood rigid and still. Her eyes were dark with outrage, but her face had gone pale. Even from three feet away he could see that she was visibly shaking. He wished he could spare her the questions, but he knew now was no time to coddle. A witness was much more apt to remember details if questioned immediately.

"What did he say to you?" he asked.

She closed her eyes briefly, then her gaze met his. "He asked me if I liked the photos."

So he knew they had been delivered. "What else?"

"H-he wanted me to look at the photos. He said he wanted to hurt me. That I was next."

"Did you recognize the voice?"

"No. But I think he was trying to disguise it, because he spoke in a guttural whisper." She set her fingertips against her temple and rubbed. "I am so creeped out."

"You're doing fine. I want you to walk over to your

desk, get a piece of paper and write down everything you remember about the call while it's still fresh in your mind."

She nodded.

Touching her briefly to reassure her, John unclipped his cell phone from his belt and punched in his brother's number. Mitch picked up on the first ring with a brusque utterance of his name.

"Our stalker's been a busy boy," John began.

"What have you got?"

John told him about the photos and the call.

Mitch cursed with the proficiency only a cop could manage. "I'll be right there."

*Using the letter opener, John slid the envelope and pho-*tos into a Baggie Claudia had supplied, on the outside chance that when Mitch dusted them for prints something would pop. But John knew that would probably not be the case. The man who'd sent those photos might be twisted, but he was not stupid.

He handed the Baggie to his brother. "I'll pick up the software for tracing incoming calls today," he said.

"Chances are he's using a disposable cell."

"Probably, but it's still worth a shot." John motioned toward the photos in the bag.

"The woman murdered in the cemetery?"

Mitch nodded. "Yep."

"Any idea who she is?"

Mitch shook his head. "I'll check with Homicide and Missing Persons, but a face-only I.D. is a long shot, especially without prints."

"It's possible he's killed before but the body of the vic was never found."

"Yeah." His eyes went to Julia. "How's she holding up?"

John glanced over to see her at the cash register with a customer. She was smiling, but he could see the stress in her eyes. Claudia had left for class at Julia's urging, leaving them alone. Again.

"Shook her up," he said.

"Can't blame her." Mitch scrubbed his chin with his fingertips. "You're looking kind of rough, bro."

Because he didn't want a lecture, John said nothing. But Mitch didn't do well with subtle, and he didn't take the hint. "How hard are you hitting the bottle?"

"Just enough to take off the edge."

"Yeah, and I was born yesterday." Mitch shook his head. "For God's sake, John, don't frickin' lie to me. I saw the bottle in the trash. You've got hangover written all over you."

"I had a few drinks last night."

"A few?" Mitch laughed. "You look like shit, bro."

"Look, it's no big deal."

Mitch motioned toward Julia. "It's going to be a big deal if this joker shows up and you're passed out." He lowered his voice. "I don't want to see that pretty face in a goddamn body bag next time. Think about that before you pick up the bottle tonight."

John ground his teeth, wishing he could dispute his brother's words. It irked the hell out of him that he couldn't. But the thought of facing the night without the anesthetization of alcohol was not a pleasant one.

"Do yourself a favor and cut it out while you've still got a handle on it." Mitch shook his head in disgust. "I've got to go."

Shoving his hands in his pockets, John held his ground at Julia's desk and watched Mitch walk toward the door. He knew he should thank his brother for coming so quickly and offering to help, but he was still pissed about the drinking comment.

Julia called out to him, and Mitch waved as he went through the door.

"What was that all about?" Julia had put on her reading glasses and tucked a pencil behind her ear. She was wearing a red turtleneck today. Not tight, but snug enough for him to be needlessly reminded that she was nicely put together. The bruises peeked out at him from the high neck, reminding him why he was here.

"Nothing," he muttered.

It's going to be a big deal if this joker shows up and you're passed out.

Mitch's words rang uncomfortably in his ears.

"You didn't tick him off, did you?" she asked.

"Probably."

"You're good at that, no?" She softened the words with a smile.

"An expert, evidently." Shoving his own shortcomings aside, he sighed. "You okay?"

She sobered. "Those photos scared me, John."

They'd scared him, too, but he didn't say the words. "Mitch is going to check with Homicide and Missing Persons to see if they can figure out who the woman is."

Rubbing her hands up and down her arms, she crossed to the desk then turned to him. "I don't understand why he's targeted me. Yes, I write erotica, but I'm not the only sinner in this city."

"It's hard for a normal person to understand what drives the demented mind. Evidently, he feels as if you've committed some wrong, either to him personally or, perhaps, to society. He's blinded to everything else."

She shook her head. "So where do we go from here?"

"I need to use your computer to take a look at some software online."

"What kind of software?"

"The kind that will trace incoming calls. A long shot since this guy is probably using a disposable cell, but it's worth a try."

"Knock your socks off." She crossed to her computer and closed the program she'd been using. "I can log these books later this evening, after I close."

John thought about that a moment and decided this was probably a good time to lay down some rules. "Starting today, I don't want you alone in the shop, Julia. In fact, I don't want you to open the shop at all unless I'm here."

"Whoa." She raised her hands as if to stop a speeding semi rig. "Look, I know I need to be cautious. I can handle that. But I will not close my shop. This is my livelihood. My business. A major source of income—"

"You can get by for a few da—"

"No, I can't. I will not close the shop. I will not let this bastard force me to do it."

Frustration ground through him. "Julia, if you want me to keep you safe, you're going to have to cooperate and make some concessions."

"Maybe she's not the only one who needs to make concessions," came a male voice from behind him.

John spun to see Jacob standing between two rows of books. He must have entered through the rear door and neither John nor Julia had heard him.

"This is between me and Julia, so do yourself a favor and butt out," John said harshly.

"This is my gig, too," Jacob maintained. "For God's sake, man, I don't see how you can keep her safe when you're passed out in the freaking storage room, slobbering all over yourself and puking in the alley."

"Jacob." Julia warned.

The other man looked at her and shook his head. "I'm sorry, Julia, but you're my friend. Someone's going to have to say it. God knows we've all been thinking it." He jammed a finger in John's direction. "Before you start making demands on her and pointing your finger at her friends, maybe you ought to take a good, hard look at the way you're going about this."

John stared at the other man, his heart pounding. The urge to put him on the floor was strong, but he resisted. As badly as he wanted to wipe that smug expression off Jacob's face, what little self-respect John had left wouldn't let him do it.

"Stay out of this," he heard himself say.

"I've stayed out of it long enough." Jacob tossed a pointed look at Julia. "She's my friend, and I'm not going to let you get her hurt because you can't keep your head out of a bottle."

The words struck a nerve, but John didn't let himself react. But he could feel the rage building. The knowledge that he was teetering on the edge of a very steep precipice. It wasn't often that he lost control, but he knew it he didn't get out of there pronto he was going to do something all of them would be sorry for later.

"I'll check out the software at the store," he said and started for the door.

"John, wait—"

"Don't." He jerked open the door, then turned. His eyes sought Jacob's. He jabbed a thumb at Julia, hating it that his hand was shaking. "If anything happens to her while I'm gone, I'm coming after you."

The other man made a sound of disgust.

John slammed the door hard enough to shake the antique plates on the wall.

Julia hated it that Jacob and John were at each other's throat. She considered both men friends and didn't want to take sides. But in the end she was compelled to agree with Jacob. Not because she was concerned for her own personal safety, but because she was concerned about John.

She could see the heavy toll the shooting in Chicago had taken on him. He blamed himself. A heavy load she wished she could somehow lessen. Julia had never been good at watching people she cared about self-destruct. But John was in a place she didn't know how to reach. She didn't know how to help him.

But her father would. Benjamin Wainwright might be overbearing as a father, but as a man of faith he was a good listener. He was good at helping people put their problems in perspective. She resolved to give him a call and ask him to speak to John. As his friend, she felt it was the least she could do.

They hadn't spoken since the exchange between him and Jacob earlier in the day. John had left to pick up the tracing software and spent the entire afternoon installing it on her computer. Julia had caught herself watching him several times throughout the day. And she found herself liking what she saw just a little too much.

When he was working on a task, his concentration was complete. His brows knit. Hands steady on the computer keys. Eyes level on the screen. She wondered what it would be like for that concentration to be focused on her . . .

Realizing what she was doing, she quickly shoved the errant thought aside. John Merrick was not the kind of man she should be having those kinds of thoughts about. He was deeply troubled and in no condition to partake in a relationship. Not that she was interested. She wasn't. But a girl could look . . .

At five o'clock Claudia left for her evening class. Jacob left shortly thereafter. Julia spent the next hour filling out the daily sales report, cleaning the coffee station and replenishing spent candles.

"You got a minute?"

She started at the sound of John's voice and spun to find him standing at the counter, his hands in his pockets.

"Sure." She set down the rattan tray of flavored teas and came around the counter. "Look, if you want to talk about what happened this afternoon, there's no need—"

"Actually I want to show you how the software works."

Julia couldn't help it. She smiled. "All right."

He walked to her desk. She noticed he'd moved the phone and put it next to the computer. A wire ran from the computer into the phone. He pointed to a tiny box the size of a cell phone next to the tower. "This box relays the caller information to your computer. Your computer in turn will relay the information to the tracing company. They need three minutes to complete the trace. So, if our boy calls, try to keep him talking."

She nodded, impressed by the sophistication of what he'd done. "Of course."

"Don't turn off the computer—keep this software running at all times."

"Will it tell us where he's calling from?

He hit a key, brought the monitor to life. "A dialogue

box will pop up the instant the trace is complete. If he's calling from a physical address, we'll get it. If he's calling from a cell phone, they'll have to run what's called a triangulation grid, which will tell us the location of the nearest tower." He hit another key and a box popped up. "Chances are he's using a disposable cell phone, but I thought this was worth a shot."

"Do you think he'll call?"

"Yeah, I do. I think he's escalating. Even if he's cautious, he won't be able to resist the compulsion that drives him. He's not finished. Hopefully, he'll make a mistake."

Julia suppressed a shiver. It was unnerving to know there was some stranger out there who at the very least wanted to hurt her. Or at the worst, wanted her dead.

"I'm going to finish your book tonight," he said. "See if I can figure out what has this guy so pissed off."

Discomfort rippled through her at the thought of him reading the book. "All right." She cleared her throat. "Just be prepared . . . I mean, it was written with a female audience in mind."

"I noticed!" One side of his mouth curved, and for an instant the old John was back. "But I think I can handle it."

Julia hoped so, because she wasn't so sure she could.

SEVENTEEN

*John closed the storage room door behind him and stud-*ied his new living quarters. Julia had done her utmost to make the room comfortable. She'd added floral sheets to the cot. A water glass, carafe and a vase of fresh cut flowers adorned the tiny wooden table next to the cot. She'd moved some boxes and set a radio on the shelf. A bar of fancy pink soap sat in the rack above the sink along with a matching pink hand towel.

He wished the scene between him and Jacob hadn't happened. John told himself the other man had been out of line, putting his nose where it didn't belong. But the fact of the matter was, Jacob was right. The truth of that stung. Hit him in a place that was already rubbed raw.

Once upon a time, John had been a good cop. It was the one thing in this life he'd done well. The shooting had changed everything. It had left John with a fear he couldn't get a handle on and a terrible guilt that ate at him twenty-four hours a day.

So what in the hell was he doing here, taking responsibility for another life? Julia's life? Jacob was right. John was in no frame of mind to be taking on this kind of responsibility. He wasn't capable of protecting her, couldn't even pick up his gun. His attraction to her was skewing his objectivity. He was making the entire situation worse by drowning himself in booze every night. A losing proposition for everyone involved. Especially Julia. If the bastard stalking her decided to pay her a visit in the middle of the night, how did John plan to protect her?

Scrubbing his hand over his face, he walked to the duffel and opened it, found himself staring down at the fifth of gin he'd picked up at the liquor store on Bourbon Street. He could feel the need crawling inside him, taunting him with the promise of oblivion.

Next to the gin was the revolver. Even though the weapon was zipped in its case, John still felt a cold chill at the sight of it. The reaction shamed him. At one time he'd been a decent marksman. He'd made it a point to get to the range two or three times a month. He'd *enjoyed* shooting. Then came that terrible night in the warehouse. He still dreamed about the way the gun had kicked in his hand. He still saw Franklin Watts's pale-as-death face. He could still hear his final words. Feel the warm stickiness of the other man's blood on his hands.

Two weeks after *The Incident*, being a firm believer in facing the hair of the dog that had bitten him, John had gone to the range. But the instant he'd tried picking up his weapon, a cold sweat had broken out all over his body. His heart had pounded. He'd begun to tremble, and suffered with nausea so powerful he'd tossed his lunch. He's found himself in the throes of a fucking anxiety attack and left without the slightest clue how to overcome it.

He knew he should see a shrink. His captain had ordered mandatory counseling. Only John had quit the department after that first visit. He'd thought he could handle it on his own. What a fool . . .

Pulling the duffel closed, John turned away from it and

tried not to feel like hell. He wanted a drink. He wanted to be able to pick up his gun without fucking losing it. God-damn it, he wanted Franklin Watts to still be alive . . .

Restless and unsettled, he sat down on the cot and put his face in his hands. He closed his eyes, wishing he were somewhere else. That he hadn't screwed up his life and a dozen others. That Julia's safety wasn't his responsibility.

When he opened his eyes, he found himself looking down at the corner of her book, *A Gentleman's Touch*, which was sticking out from beneath the cot. He'd shoved it there the night before and promptly forgotten about it. He didn't feel like reading. But facing a long night and a host of demons, he figured it was better than spending the next eight hours bouncing off the walls.

He'd been curious about the book, anyway. He wanted to know what Julia had written that had angered someone to the point of wanting to hurt her.

Snagging the book off the floor, he folded the pillow and lay back on the cot. Misery settled onto his chest as he opened the book. Refusing to acknowledge its presence, he turned the page and began to read.

Julia knew better than to start a project as monumental as her taxes so late in the evening. But when she'd sat down at her laptop to work on her current project, *The Bride's Secret Dream*, the words refused to come. Usually she could find solace in her writing. Tonight, however, she hadn't been able to concentrate. She felt out of sorts. Out of touch with her characters. It didn't happen often, but when it did she knew there was no forcing the issue.

Now if only she could get a handle on these taxes.

Sighing, she pulled a fat hanging file from the drawer and set it on the desk. From within, she slid a manila folder marked "Deductions" and began sorting them according to type of expense.

The wall clock glared down at her, reminding her that if she didn't go to bed soon and get some sleep, tomorrow was going to be a tough day. Usually, she was a good sleeper and fell into slumber the minute her exhausted head hit the pillow. Tonight she felt keyed up. Restless. As if her own skin didn't quite fit.

She wanted to blame it on the latte she'd had after dinner. But caffeine had never bothered her before. As much as she didn't want to acknowledge it, she'd been thinking about John on and off all evening. She'd tried occupying her mind with other things. Her book. Taxes. Even the stalker. But time and time again she found her thoughts going back to John. She wanted to believe her preoccupation with him was nothing more than concern for a friend in trouble.

But the thoughts squeezing into her mind were a hell of a lot more complicated. She couldn't get him out of her mind. She liked the sound of his voice. The way he smiled. She wanted to know everything about him. Worse, she was attracted to him in a way she'd never been attracted to another man. Every time she was in the same room with him, she could feel the attraction tugging at her.

Of course she was too smart to succumb to something as mindless as hormones. There were a hundred reasons why she shouldn't let herself get tangled up in a relationship with him. He drank too much. He was moody and could be hostile. He had a dominating personality. It would never work. Still, she couldn't deny the chemical reaction that exploded inside her every time he so much as looked at her.

"Enough already," she muttered. "This is ridiculous." Sighing, she looked down at the file, and realized she needed her "Receipts" file, which was downstairs in her desk.

Julia glanced down at the lavender drawstring pants and matching T-shirt she wore and briefly worried about running into John. But he'd retired almost two hours ago. She could creep down the stairs, snag the file from her desk and be back without ever being seen. Holding that thought, she padded to the door and went down the stairs.

Pleasure fluttered inside her as she walked between the

aisles toward her desk. She loved slipping into the shop after hours when the place was dark and the smell of coffee and candles and old books lingered. She smiled at the memory of the customers she'd interacted with that day. The shop comforted her in a way most people found comfort in their bedrooms or kitchens or Labrador retrievers.

Her bare feet silent on the wood planks, she went directly to the desk and opened the file drawer. She flipped through several files, deciding to take the utility bills and credit card file as well as the receipts and other shop-related expenditures.

Satisfied she had everything she needed to at least put a dent in her tax work before she took it to the CPA, she closed the drawer and turned. She nearly dropped the files at the sight of John standing a few feet away, watching her.

"You startled me," she snapped when her heart slid back into her chest.

"Didn't mean to."

His voice was low and rough. He was wearing faded jeans. No shoes. The navy chambray shirt was untucked, unbuttoned and opened to reveal a chest she knew better than to notice. Disappointment whispered through her when she noticed the bottle of gin he held at his side, his fingers wrapped around the long neck.

"Are you all right?" she asked.

"I'm fine."

Julia let her eyes drop to the bottle. "I thought you were going to stop drinking."

"Just taking the edge off."

"Edge off what?"

He was looking at her oddly. As if she had somehow amused him. "You don't want to know."

"I wouldn't have asked if I didn't want to know." When he only gave her that odd smile, she stepped closer. "John, look, I'm your friend. If you need help—"

"Help isn't what I want from you, Julia."

At some point her heart had begun to pound. She could feel the rush of blood through her veins. Suddenly she was aware of everything around her, her senses heightened to a fever pitch. She heard the sound of heat coming through the furnace vents. The tick of the clock above her desk. The cold floor beneath her bare feet. The heat of his gaze against her skin.

"What are you doing up at this hour?" she asked.

"Just trying to wind down." His gaze flicked to the files in her arms. "I could ask you the same question."

"I'm just . . . getting started on taxes."

"Taxes, huh?"

"Yeah, you know. The IRS. April 15."

"Odd time for you to be working on taxes."

"I couldn't sleep."

"Must be something in the air."

She didn't know what to say to that. The way he was looking at her was making her uncomfortable. As if he could see right through the cotton pants and T-shirt.

"I finished your book," he said.

She didn't know what to say to that either. A ripple of surprise. A tug of discomfort. "Oh . . . well."

"You're talented."

"Thank you." Pride swelled in her chest. Too much of it. Too powerful. She shouldn't care so much what he thought of the book, but she did. "Did it give you any insights into why this goon is stalking me?"

"A lot of sexual content." He shrugged. "This guy is probably fantasizing. He might have created his own little world. Put you right in the center of it."

"Scary how someone could do that."

"Yeah, well, fantasies are generally harmless. It's when he starts acting on them that things get dangerous."

The thought made gooseflesh rise on her arms. "You think that's what he's doing?"

"Maybe. Probably."

She half-expected him to reassure her, but he didn't.

He stood his ground at the mouth of the aisle, looking at her as if seeing her for the first time. "Your book," he began. "It wasn't what I expected."

"Did it shock you?"

A smile curved his mouth. "It made me hot."

Julia laughed, felt the heat of a blush and found herself inordinately relieved for the dim lighting. She gripped the files tightly, used them to cover her chest because she was suddenly painfully aware that she wasn't wearing a bra. That she was chilled and her nipples were hard.

"Well," she said, hefting the files. "I've got to get these files upstairs. Good night."

Her heart was beating too fast when she started toward the aisle. She could feel John's eyes on her. She wanted to say something flippant and light and brilliant. But Julia was astute enough to know there was something happening between them that was none of those things, and she instinctively knew the smartest thing for her to do was get back upstairs and lock the door behind her as quickly as possible.

"Wait."

She stopped, but she didn't turn and look at him.

The silence was like an explosion. Julia could hear her heart thudding against her ribs. A little voice inside her head telling her to get the hell out of there before he did something inappropriate. Before she let him.

"Put down the files," he said softly.

She turned to face him, but didn't put down the files. "I don't think that's a good idea."

He started toward her at a slow, predatory tread. The urge to run was powerful, but Julia held her ground. She wasn't afraid of John, knew he would never hurt her. But her heart was beating so hard her chest hurt. She didn't know what would happen when he reached her. Didn't know what he would do or how she would react. The one thing she did know for certain was that they were probably about to do something stupid.

He stopped with scant inches between their bodies. Julia stepped back when he invaded her personal space, but he moved with her.

"Why are you backing away from me?" he asked.

"Because evidently I have more common sense than you."

Her bottom connected with the edge of the desk, halting her backward momentum. He stopped inches away, not touching her, but so close she could feel the heat of his body through her clothes.

"W-what are you doing?" she asked.

His eyes drilled into hers. "Screwing things up probably."

"Maybe we ought to just let this go."

"I've never been good at letting things go, especially when it's something I want." She jolted when he reached out and tucked a strand of hair behind her ear. "How long are we going to ignore what's happening between us?"

She blinked rapidly. "There's nothing happening between us."

"I guess that's why you're gripping those files like your life depends on it."

"John, you're drunk."

"Honey, I'm not even close."

"I have to go." But Julia didn't move. She couldn't take her eyes off his. She knew he was going to kiss her. She knew she shouldn't let him. But it was as if her feet were suddenly mired in glue.

"Don't go," he whispered.

"This is a mistake."

"Mistakes are my specialty."

He leaned close. The brush of his mouth against hers didn't feel like a mistake. The intensity of the pleasure shocked her system. All five senses jumped and began to hum, like electricity through a high-voltage power line. Every nerve ending in her body quivered with anticipation. Julia knew this was the moment when she should say something about consequences and pull away. But John's kiss was like a highly addictive drug. All her mind could think was that she wanted more.

His mouth was hard against hers. He tasted of gin and male frustration. She was vaguely aware of the masculine scent of his aftershave, the scrape of his whiskers against her face. He kissed her like she'd never been kissed in her life. Her toes curled. She could feel her body responding to his. Her breasts felt heavy and full. Blood pooled like hot mercury low in her body.

The files in her arms fell to the floor with a thump. Julia barely noticed the papers scattered about. The next thing she knew John moved against her. She could feel the ridge of his erection through her pajamas, hard seeking soft. Raking his hands through her hair, he tilted her head and deepened the kiss. Her gasp of surprise came out as a sigh when he entered her with his tongue. Julia opened to him. For an instant he seemed to hesitate, then cupping her face with both hands he went in deep.

Desire like she'd never known before pounded like a hammer inside her. Her body wept for his, and she felt herself go wet. The need was edgy and uncomfortable, a knot low in her belly that begged for release. Desperate for relief, she moved against him. His erection slid easily over her cleft. So close. Almost . . . Oh God, she couldn't stand it.

The next thing she knew his hands were on her hips, gripping her a little too hard. In the back of her mind she knew there would be bruises in the morning, but she didn't care. He lifted her onto the desk, stepped between her knees and spread her wide. Before she could react, he lifted her T-shirt over her breasts. An instant of cool air against hot skin. And then he scraped rough fingertips over her sensitized nipples. A gasp of pleasure escaped her. As if of its own accord, her spine arched, giving him full access to her breasts. Her hips jerked forward and then he was flush against her.

A groan escaped him as he began to move. Julia could feel her entire body trembling. The need rushing through her like a white-water rapid down the side of a mountain. She was no stranger to the power of human sexuality. But she had never imagined herself losing control like this.

He cupped her breasts, trapping the nipples between his thumbs and forefingers. Julia cried out as the sharp edge of desire slammed through her. All the while he kissed her, until she was mindless with pleasure. Until it was just her body and his body and the only thing that existed in the world was this moment between them.

The rhythm of his body against hers was driving her to the edge. She could feel the orgasm building, a violent storm shocking her with its awesome power.

She knew she should stop him when she felt him fumbling with the drawstring at her waist. But for the first time in her life, Julia had lost her grip on control.

The drawstring came away easily. Whispering her name, he slid his hand into the waistband of her panties. Julia couldn't think. Her heart was like a piston. Her pulse pounding like a locomotive in her ears. She could feel herself shaking, her breaths rushing between clenched teeth.

She went rigid when his fingertips touched the curls at her vee. She cried out when he slipped two fingers inside. Her arms went around his shoulders. He stroked her. Deep, steady strokes. Her hips bucked. Once. Twice.

"Easy," he whispered.

But there was nothing easy about the way he was touching her or about the way her body was responding. Her body went liquid around his fingers. She could feel the contractions building, high-wire tension winding toward an inevitable snap.

"I . . . can't . . . ," she panted.

"Let me," he said.

The rest of the world faded away as the sensations overtook her body and mind. For the span of several long seconds all she could do was feel. John's mouth against hers. His fingers inside her body, stroking her to madness. Her spine curled. The first wave swamped her, a tidal wave washing over her, tumbling her, a stone being tossed about by a violent sea. Her vision blurred as the blood left her head. She heard herself cry out his name. She heard her own name on his lips as his mouth moved over hers.

The sensations plummeted her into a wild free fall. She tried to pull back. To get ahold of herself and stop this before things went too far. But Julia knew things had already gone too far.

Vaguely, she was aware of the phone ringing. A shrill sound that drilled into her consciousness. She tried to pull away, but he held her tightly against him, his face buried in her hair. "Let it ring," he whispered.

But she knew if she didn't pull away now, she wouldn't stop. That John wouldn't stop. Turning her head, she broke the kiss. "I have to get it."

"It's midnight," he said. "Let it go."

"It's my home number," she panted. "It could be Claudia."

He stepped back. Intensity burned in his eyes. He looked as if he'd just been wakened from a dream. His mouth was taut and wet. His hair was mussed and she re- membered running her fingers through it just a moment be- fore. She wanted to do it again. She didn't want to stop.

The phone rang again.

Knowing if he kissed her again she would be lost to rea- son, Julia slid from the desk and retied the drawstring. Her legs shook when she crossed to the credenza. Unable to meet his gaze, she picked up the phone. "Hello?"

"You let him put his hands on you," came a hoarse, an- gry voice.

"What?" The fog cleared from her mind. "Who is this?"

"I am your savior."

Her expression must have relayed her shock, because an instant later John made eye contact with her and mouthed the words "Keep him talking."

Not knowing what to say to the caller, Julia stammered, "I-I don't know what you mean."

"You've got the devil inside you. If I don't intervene, he's going to win, Julia. Is that what you want? To spend all of eternity in hell?"

"I want you to stop calling me."

"I'm your last hope. You don't know it, but you need me. You need someone to save you from what you have become."

In her peripheral vision, she saw John slide behind her PC and hit a few keys. The monitor blinked and the tracing software filled the screen. "You're sick," she said. "You need help."

"Succubus," he whispered.

"You're wrong about me," she said.

But the line went dead.

She glanced at John. "He disconnected."

John glanced up from the monitor. "That's okay because I got the son of a bitch's number."

Eighteen

John dialed his brother's home number without setting down the phone. Mitch answered on the fourth ring, with a hostile "What?"

"I got the stalker's number."

A groan emanated through the line. "It's after midnight."

"Yeah, well, our stalker pal's a night owl."

Rustling sounded on the other end of the line and John imagined Mitch sitting up, tossing the covers aside. "Can you run the number for me?" John asked.

"Whaddya got?"

John tapped a key and recited the number.

"Probably a cell."

"Probably, but sometimes these guys are pretty stupid."

"Let me make some calls."

"I'll wait up."

John disconnected and turned to Julia. He knew he should be focused on the stalker, but the only thought his mind processed when he looked at her was how good she'd felt in his arms. How responsive she'd been. That he was still aroused . . .

"What did he say to you?" he asked.

Her eyes were wide and frightened and very dark against her pale complexion. "A lot of strange things."

"Give me specifics, Julia."

"He—he said he was going to save me. That I had the devil inside me. That he was my last hope. He called me a succubus." Her eyes widened. "When I first picked up the phone he said something like 'You let him put his hands on you.'"

Fury spread through him as realization dawned. "The son of a bitch is watching."

"How? The blinds are closed."

"I don't know."

Cursing, John crossed to the front of the store. He paused to run his hands along the blinds, but they were closed tightly. He flung open the door and stepped onto the sidewalk and looked both ways. The street was nearly deserted. How the hell did the bastard know what had happened between him and Julia?

Furious at being spied on, John walked back inside and closed the door behind him. Julia had walked to the blinds. "These blinds are tight, John. I was adamant about that when I had them installed last year. There's no way he can see inside."

The hairs at John's nape prickled. A feeling of near paranoia swept through him. He looked around the shop. If the blinds at the front window were indeed secure, how did the son of a bitch know what they'd been doing?

Without speaking, he walked the perimeter of the shop. He looked at the knickknacks scattered about. A bright red vase filled with greenery and orange and white silk flowers. The antique books squeezed between gargoyle bookends on the occasional table. A set of three colorful plates hung on the wall.

"What are you looking for?" Julia asked.

"I'm not sure."

But he found what he was looking for a few minutes later. The tiny wireless camera had been wedged between two books directly across from her desk. Something male and protective slithered through him at the thought of some scumbag spying on her, watching her when she was totally unaware.

"He's been in the shop." John stated the obvious.

Julia came up beside him. "My God." She reached for the camera. "Unbelievable."

John grasped her wrist before she could touch it. "Might have latent prints." All too aware that her wrist was small and warm in his hand, he let her go abruptly.

"This seems sophisticated," she said.

He hated it that the bastard had been spying on them. John felt as if he should have somehow known. He was getting rusty. Drinking too much. He'd lost his focus. The edge that had once made him a good cop.

"Wireless cams are becoming more and more commonplace." Using a pencil from the desk, he moved the camera so the eye could not watch them. "Any Joe can pick one up for under two hundred bucks."

"I wonder how long it's been there."

He studied her face, remembering what it had felt like to kiss her, pulled himself back. "When's the last time you moved these books?"

Her brows snapped together. "Claudia dusted this area last Tuesday."

"You sure? She dusted these bookends?"

She nodded. "She always dusts on Tuesdays."

"That means that at some point between last Tuesday and today, he's been in your store."

"That's creepy." She shivered.

The urge to reach out and touch her was strong, but he resisted. "Do you remember anyone hanging out in this area of the shop? Any of your customers behaving strangely?"

Julia shook her head. "I can check with Jacob and Claudia."

"I'll talk to them tomorrow." John looked at the camera again, felt another rise of male outrage go through him at the thought of some bastard getting his rocks off watching her. Watching *them*. And he wondered if seeing them together had added fuel to the flame.

"How did this guy sound when he called?" he asked. "The same as before?"

Julia thought about it for a moment. "He sounded . . . intense. A little breathless." Her gaze met his. "He was watching us like some sick voyeur."

John nodded. "Sounds like maybe he didn't like what he saw. Like maybe he didn't want things to go any further."

"That is so sick."

"Yeah."

He watched her cross to the desk. The baggy drawstring pants and T-shirt didn't do much for her figure, but he knew just how shapely she was beneath. She'd been incredibly responsive when he kissed her. He could still taste the sweetness of her mouth. Feel the softness of her skin. Hear the hiss of her breaths as he'd brought her to peak . . .

Still semi-erect, he found himself wishing they hadn't been interrupted. It was one thing to be attracted to a woman he couldn't have. It was sheer torture to come so close to . . . something.

But deep inside he was glad they had stopped. The last thing either of them needed was to send this guy over some edge—or complicate the situation by falling into bed.

"Are you all right?" he asked after a moment.

"I'm okay." She turned to him. "I just feel . . . violated."

"Julia, I can't tell you how important it is for you to be careful."

An unhappy sigh slid from her lips. "Come on, John. For God's sake, I'm not stupid."

"No, but you are a little too independent for your own good."

"John . . ."

"All I'm saying is stick to the plan we talked about, okay? Keep someone with you at all times. Be alert. Be aware of what's going on around you. Of who's in the shop. Above everything else listen to your instincts. Trust them. Most people don't."

She nodded. Her eyes went to the bottle of gin he'd left on her desk. John knew what he had to do. He knew it was going to be painful. But twice he'd nearly blown it with Julia. The last thing he wanted was for her to get hurt because of him. His conscience couldn't handle another death.

He crossed to the desk, picked up the bottle and carried it to the storage room. Trying not to think about what he was doing, he uncapped it and poured the gin down the sink. When he finished, she was standing at the door.

"Thank you for doing that," she said. "I know it wasn't easy."

"I'm not an alcoholic." He said the words, but figured they both knew the jury was still out on that one.

"I know what happened in Chicago has been hard," she said. "If there's anything I can do—"

"I don't want to talk about it." He could feel himself shutting down. His emotions crawling back into the deep, dark hole where he didn't have to deal with them.

"All right. You don't have to. Just know that I'm there for you if you need me."

Because he didn't want to need anyone, John turned away from her and walked into the storage room, closing the door behind him.

The whore.

Succubus.

If he hadn't called when he had, she and that second-rate ex-cop would have consummated the act. They would have had intercourse right there on her desk. Gone at it like a couple of dogs in heat.

It had been sheer torture for him to watch the other man kiss her, touch her, put his fingers inside her body. But even through the pain, watching them had aroused him in a way he'd never been aroused before.

The weakness shamed him. Made him realize he'd been

wrong about her. There was no goodness left in her heart. Nothing to be saved in her soul. The evil inside her had taken over, grown into something monstrous.

The realization hurt more than he'd ever imagined possible. He'd always seen the goodness in her. Evidently, he'd been blinded by his own weakness. She could not be saved.

His only recourse was to destroy her.

Nineteen

John didn't sleep, but for the first time in two months the insomnia was not because of the nightmare. At some point in the last couple of days, he had become preoccupied with Julia. He'd found himself watching her. Listening to her voice, the sound of her laughter. He enjoyed being with her, missed her when he wasn't. He knew it was a stupid waste of time and energy, but he wanted to know everything about her. What she liked to do in her spare time. Her favorite foods and movies. He wanted to know what her hopes and dreams were.

He couldn't remember the last time a woman had affected him so profoundly. He'd spent the entire night thinking about her, reliving the kiss, the way she felt in his arms, the way she'd sighed when he'd brought her to peak.

It was still dark when he gave up on sleep, kicked off the blanket and rose to start his day. Making his way into the shop, he dumped coffee beans into the grinder.

It was damn silly getting himself worked up over a

woman he had no intention of getting involved with. Someone should tell his libido that.

He guzzled half a pot of coffee, then began the task of replacing the old alley door with a new steel one he'd picked up at the hardware store. Julia had told him she wanted it painted glossy black, so he'd picked up a gallon of paint as well. He was about to apply the second coat when Julia came down the stairs.

"Good morning," she said brightly.

John looked up from the can of paint. She was wearing a red jacket and skirt with matching shoes. Beneath the jacket, he saw pink lace that should have clashed with the red, but didn't. It matched the color she'd painted her lips.

"Nice knees," he said.

She looked down at her knees and laughed. "Thanks."

"I made coffee if you want some."

"I knew there was a reason why I hired you."

"You might want to withhold the compliments until you've tasted it."

Smiling, she walked to the coffee station. John knew it was a mistake to watch her, but he did. Damn, she had the sexiest legs he'd ever seen on a woman, and she didn't even seem to realize it.

"You're up bright and early this morning," she said.

He glanced away from his painting. She was watching him with a little too much interest, sipping from a steaming cup.

"You look . . . rested," she said.

Or maybe it was the first time she'd seen him when he wasn't suffering with a hangover. "Overnight courier came a little while ago," he said. "You got a package from New York."

"Probably fan mail from my editor." Turning away, she started toward the counter at the front of the shop.

Setting the paintbrush on the bucket, John followed. He reached her as she tore off the top of the envelope.

"Let me." He eased the envelope from her hand and

pulled out a manila folder. He opened the folder on the counter. A short stack of letters stared up at them.

"What are we looking for?" Julia asked.

"Anything that strikes you as odd." He shrugged. "A disgruntled fan. A letter that crosses a line."

"A fan who thinks I'm a succubus?"

"That would be way too easy."

"Thought so."

They paged through several letters without speaking. Most were from female readers who were writing to let Julia know they'd enjoyed her story. Some were lighthearted and poked fun at the level of sensuality of the book. Some were deeply emotional. A few were scolding, but appeared harmless.

Halfway through the stack John came upon a letter from a man by the name of Nicholas Vester. The envelope was stapled to the letter. The return address was the Orleans County jail.

"What about that one?" Julia asked.

"Let's take a look." John skimmed the letter.

A Gentleman's Touch *is the best book I've ever read. You have a gift for storytelling. You certainly have a way with describing sex scenes! The story gave me hours of pleasure in a place where pleasure is hard to come by. You see, I'm currently incarcerated in the county jail on a bogus charge of stalking. Ridiculous!*

I would love it if you would send me an autographed picture of yourself. Are you as hot looking as your heroine in the book? As I read the book I imagined you as Chloe. It's killing me, I've got to know what you look like.

I'm being released next month and would love to meet you in person. Now, I know what you're thinking. But I'm not a criminal! The charges against me were false. Please write me back and let

me know if you are interested. I truly think I've
fallen in love with you.

"Does that fit the profile?" Julia asked.

John glanced at her. She looked uncomfortable. "Do you get many letters like this one?"

"A few."

Shaking his head, he read the letter again. "He claims he was convicted of stalking. That sends up a red flag."

"Look at the date of the letter."

"He wrote this a month ago." He grimaced. "If he wasn't lying about his release date, he's out of jail by now."

"You think this might be the guy?"

"I think he's worth checking out."

Their eyes met, held. "How do we do that?"

"I'll call Mitch and have him run the name through a couple of databases, see if anything pops."

"And if something pops?"

John shrugged. "I pay him a visit."

Mitch called with the results of the check at noon. "Hey, bro, I got the goods on Vester."

"He out?"

"Yup. Did six months. Got released two weeks ago."

"So what did our boy do?"

"He stalked a morning radio show host."

"Female?"

"Yup. He claimed he was a fan. But he thought she crossed a line when she said something on the air. He told the judge he wanted to talk to her about it in person."

John had dug up what he could on the Internet, but in a city as large and violent as New Orleans, there wasn't much out there on this one case. "How did she cross the line?"

"She faked an orgasm on the air one morning. That started the whole thing."

John couldn't help it. He laughed. "People will do anything for ratings."

"Ain't that the truth." Mitch chuckled. "Anyway, this guy Vester starts calling her at the station. He somehow got her unlisted number at home and called her several times. He found out where she lived and was spotted parked outside her house. He crossed the line the day he walked into her garage when she was home."

"He break in?"

"She left the garage door open about a foot for her cat. He saw that as an invitation. Get this, he says she was teasing him, inviting him in by leaving her door open. So he squeezes through the door. By the time he walked into the kitchen he had his pants down and a big hard-on."

"Guy sounds like a real winner."

"You like this guy as Julia's stalker or what?"

"She got a letter from him. Profile seems to fit."

"Looks like maybe six months in jail didn't rehabilitate him." Mitch was silent for a moment. "If this is the guy, then he could possibly be involved in the murder in the cemetery the other night."

"Can you get a warrant?"

"Yeah, but it's going to take a little time."

"Give me his address. I'll pay him a visit. Lean on him a little."

"I might do that if I felt like getting my chops busted."

"Come on, Mitch. You owe me. I gave him to you."

"If this guy is the killer and I let you go in there, some scumbag defense attorney is going to get him off on a tech."

Frustration made John sigh. Back when he'd been a cop, more than once he'd seen shoddy police work or an overzealous detective screw up a case. "How long will a warrant take?"

"I'll meet you there in an hour." Mitch rattled off Vester's address. "You know I shouldn't be letting you in on this, so don't screw it up, bro."

"Wouldn't dream of it."

Julia was watching him when he hung up the phone. "What did he say?"

John told her about the circumstances surrounding Vester's conviction.

"I guess that would qualify as a pop, huh?" she asked.

"And then some."

"The police are going to arrest him?"

"They're going to search his house. Probably his vehicle. And take him in for questioning. I'm meeting Mitch in an hour." He glanced at his watch. "Call Claudia and ask her to drive over and stay with you until I get back."

"I want to go with you."

John shook his head. "No way."

"Why not?"

"It's a police matter now."

"You're not a cop anymore."

The barb cut, but John let it roll off him. "I'm an ex-cop and his freakin' brother. I made the connection. He owes me, so he cut me some slack."

She went still, her eyes widening. "Does Mitch think this guy murdered that woman in the cemetery?"

"He won't know anything until he questions him, executes a search of his house and vehicle. But Vester has a history of stalking. I think he's a strong suspect."

"Maybe I could go with you to see if I can identify him." She looked excited.

Too excited, John thought, and frowned. "You didn't see the guy's face."

"That's true, but maybe I'll be able to identify him in some other way. Recognize his voice, or his mannerisms."

"Mitch may ask you to come in and take a look at a lineup. For now I think it would be best if you stayed away."

What he didn't want to reveal to her was that he was feeling protective. Maybe a little *too* protective. He didn't want her anywhere near Vester. "Let us handle this, Julia."

"Too dangerous for the little woman, huh?"

"That's not the way it is."

"Really? Then why don't you tell me how it is?"

Seeing temper in her eyes, knowing where the conversation was heading, John unsnapped his cell phone. "I'll call Claudia myself."

Turning away from her, he punched the number from memory. Claudia picked up on the second ring. John didn't bother with a greeting. "There's a possible break in the case. I have to leave, and I need you here."

A moment of shocked silence. "I can be there in fifteen minutes."

"See you then."

When he hung up, Julia was waiting. "You have no right to shut me out of this. This is my life, my business."

"What are you going to do? Close the shop?"

"Claudia can handle it until we get back."

"No." He turned and headed toward the storage room.

She followed. He could hear the sharp click of her heels against the wood plank floor behind him. "This is not your call."

He stopped and turned to her so fast she nearly ran into him. "Yes, it is."

She blinked. Because she was standing too close, because he was more pissed off than he wanted to be, John spun away and entered the storage room. Crossing to the shelf next to the cot, he snagged his keys. When he swung around, Julia was standing in the doorway.

John sighed. "Look," he began, "I'm asking you to trust my judgment on this."

"I'm asking you not to try to run my life or make my decisions for me. I won't tolerate it."

"I'm trying to protect you."

"I don't need that kind of protecting. It makes me feel smothered."

"Damn it, Julia, I don't have an ulterior motive. All I'm saying is that we don't know how Vester is going to react to the warrant. If he comes out shooting, it could be a bad scene. I don't want you there."

That seemed to deflate some of her anger. A breath shuddered out of. "I'm sorry. I don't mean to be unreasonable. I just hate feeling so damn helpless."

"I know. So do I." The urge to go to her was strong, but he resisted. He did not want a repeat of what had happened between them the night before. "You might try looking at the bright side."

A wry smile curved her mouth. "There's a bright side?"

"Yeah. If Vester is our man, this is about to be over in a very big way."

Vester lived in a halfway house on a quiet side street just east of the Quarter. John drove slowly past the run-down duplex, looking for signs that Vester was home. There were no cars parked in front, but he could see through the window that the television was on. He pulled up to the curb halfway down the block and shut down the engine.

Mitch and Detective McBride showed up ten minutes later. John got out of the car as his brother pulled the unmarked cruiser to the curb. They met on the sidewalk.

"I was starting to wonder if you were going to show," John said.

McBride scowled at him. "For the record, I don't think you should be here."

John scowled back. "I found him for you."

"That makes you a tipster, not a cop."

John wished everyone would stop pointing that out. Annoyed, he frowned at his brother. "You got the warrant?"

"Yup." His brother eyed his leather bomber jacket. "You're not packing, are you?"

John wondered what these men would think if they knew the truth about him. That he didn't have the guts to pick up his weapon. The shame that followed cut him to the quick. "No."

"Good, because you're here only as an observer," Mitch said. "You got that?"

"I got it."

"I mean it, bro. You're a civilian. McBride and I could find ourselves in deep shit if the lieutenant finds out we let you in on this."

"So don't let him find out."

Muttering an obscenity beneath his breath, McBride went around to the back. Mitch and John stepped onto the front porch. Mitch rapped hard on the screen door. "New Orleans Police Department. Open up."

John stood beside his brother and listened for movement on the other side of the door. He could hear the blare of the television. Behind him, the wind rattled a loose shutter. Somewhere in the distance a sax wailed a haunting tune.

"Looks like maybe he flew the coop," Mitch said.

"Since I'm a civilian, I could always find a way in and take a look around."

"Not on my watch."

Just then the door swung open. John's nerves went taut as a middle-aged man just short of six feet in height peered at them through the screen. Mitch's hand slid to the revolver at his hip.

"You Nicholas Vester?" John asked.

The man scratched his hairy belly and belched. "Who the fuck'r you?"

"Your worst nightmare." Mitch flashed his badge. "Open the door and step aside."

One side of the man's lip lifted as he glared at them through the screen. "I saw my parole officer yesterday."

"Open the door or I'll cart your ass off to jail so fast you'll get whiplash."

Vester glanced over his shoulder as he unlocked the screen door and opened it. "Don't you guys have anything better to do than fuckin' hassle me?"

"I live for hassling guys like you." Mitch pushed his way inside. "Keep your hands where I can see them."

John followed close behind, his every sense trained on Vester.

"Hey, you can't just barge in here without a reason,"

Vester said, but his attention seemed divided. As if there was something in the house he didn't want them to see. Drugs? He looked like a kid who'd been caught doing something he wasn't allowed to do. "I know my rights. You ain't got a warrant, you can get the fuck out."

Mitch slid the warrant from his pocket and slapped the man's cheek with it. "In case you can't read, it says we can come in and do whatever the hell we want."

Vester looked like a gas pain had hit him.

John looked around. The front door opened to the living room, where a television depicted a couple in the throes of what looked like an illegal sex act. A dead ficus tree sulked near a grimy window. A pile of what smelled like day-old cat shit clung to a stack of *Playboy* and *Hustler* magazines on the floor.

"There anyone else here?" Mitch asked.

Vester snarled, "No, man."

John didn't even realize it, but he'd already gone into cop mode. He crossed to the kitchen, unlocked the door and let McBride into the house. Then the two men worked as a team to clear each room. "Clear," McBride said.

"You armed, Vester?" Mitch asked.

"I don't like guns." Vester smiled nastily. "They scare me."

"In that case you don't mind if I check for myself, do you?" Quickly, Mitch ran his hands over the other man, then guided him to a ratty-looking recliner and shoved him into it. "Now we're going to have us a nice chat."

"I ain't got nothing to say to no cops." Vester looked stubborn and indignant.

While Mitch questioned Vester, John walked into the first bedroom and looked around. He wasn't exactly sure what he was looking for—a cell phone, a jester Mardi Gras mask, perhaps stationery that matched the letters Julia had received. But he knew this wasn't going to be that easy. It never was.

An antiquated PC sat atop a dresser. Someone had pulled up a plastic chair. The PC was running but the monitor had been turned off. *Interesting.* John hit the power button for the monitor. Disgust rose inside him when the nude photo of a young girl who couldn't possibly have yet seen her sixteenth birthday materialized.

"Aw, man," he muttered.

Shaking his head in disgust, John walked into the living room. Vester and Mitch looked up when he entered.

"Find anything?" Mitch asked.

John looked at Vester. "You want to fess up or shall I clue them in?"

"I didn't fuckin' do nothing."

Vester started to rise, but Mitch shoved him back into the chair. "Sit the fuck down."

John crossed to him and got in his face. "You like looking at pictures of naked little girls, don't you?"

"Those pictures ain't mine."

"Bullshit." Vaguely, John was aware of Detective McBride walking into the room. Mitch walked to the bedroom. "Where were you night before last?" John asked Vester.

"I was fuckin' here. I'm on parole, man. I got a curfew."

John thought about the bruises on Julia. The dead woman in the cemetery. The photos of the young girl in the bedroom. And he saw red. He felt his teeth clench. Before he could stop himself, he reached out and fisted the other man's collar. "You think this is some kind of joke? You think we're kidding around, you sick fuck?"

Vester's eyes widened. "I was here, man. I'm only allowed to drive to work and back. House arrest, you know? Where the fuck do you think I was?"

"I think you were skulking around the Quarter like the cockroach you are," John snarled.

Mitch walked into the room, his face dark. "You get a go-back-to-jail card free, Vester."

Vester started to rise, but John shoved him back down. "You know what they do to perverts like you in prison?"

"You can't put me in jail. I didn't do nothing!"

"How about child pornography for starters," Mitch said.

"How am I supposed to know she ain't over eighteen? She looks grown-up to me!" The belligerence had transformed into panic.

"I thought you said the pictures weren't yours."

"They're not!" Sweat was pouring off the man's scalp. "I swear!"

But Mitch was already on the radio, asking for a crime scene unit and a patrol car.

John pulled out a copy of the letter that had been sent to Julia. "Did you write this?"

Vester's eyes landed on the letter. "I wrote a lot of letters."

"This one is to an author by the name of Elisabeth de Haviland."

"What if I did? That ain't against the law, is it?"

"It is if you're stalking her."

"I ain't stalking no one, man."

"Have you had any contact with her?"

"No."

"Did you call her? Follow her?" Rough her up in the alley? a furious little voice added.

"No!"

Teeth grinding, John slapped him with an open hand. "You had better stop lying to me."

Temper glinted in the other man's eyes. John half expected him to make a move, half wished he would so he could work off some of this rage, but the other man only glared.

"Why did you write this letter?" John asked.

"I wrote it, okay? Jesus! She wrote a hot book. Not many chicks know the moves, but she does." Vester rolled his shoulder. "I wanted to meet her. She never wrote me back. That's it."

"You have an affinity for porn, don't you, Vester?"

"I been locked in a cage for six months," Vester said. "What do you think?"

"I think you're in deep shit."

"I didn't stalk no one!" Spittle flew from his lips. "That deejay bitch was lying through her teeth about the whole thing. She *invited* me inside."

John slapped him again, not hard, but enough to make the other man angry. "I don't believe you."

"Merrick." McBride's warning tone came to him as if from a great distance. "Cut it out."

John ignored him. Back when he'd been a cop, he'd had to abide by the rules of the department. Now that he was a civilian, he did not. The urge to cross a line with Vester was strong. This man was the worst kind of human being. A predator. A liar. A man who preyed on the innocent. But was he the man who'd been stalking Julia? Was he the man who'd murdered a woman in the cemetery?

"Easy, bro." Mitch's hand on his shoulder pulled him back.

John straightened and was surprised to see his hand shake when he shoved a finger in Vester's face. "Stay away from Elisabeth de Haviland. Next time they won't be here to pull me off you."

Vester's gaze swung from John to Mitch. "I'm telling the truth! I ain't done nothin'! I swear!"

Mitch's fingers dug into John's shoulders. "Can't take you anywhere, can I?" he growled as he hustled him to the door.

John let his brother shove him through the front door and onto the porch before he pulled away. He knew it was unprofessional of him to lose his cool, but he wasn't feeling particularly professional.

"Now, that was some smooth police work," Mitch said dryly. "Good job."

Shaking off his brother's hand, John turned back toward the house. "Can you take him in on the child porn charge?"

"Oh yeah." Mitch looked back at the house. "I don't know if it will stick. But I've got a crime scene unit on the way. They'll go over this dump with a fine-toothed comb, see if they can find some trace, match this loser with the vic."

"You think he's the guy?"

Mitch shook his head. "I don't know." His gaze went to

John's. "I'll probably need Julia to come in, do a lineup, see if she can give me some kind of I.D." Mitch glanced back at the house. "Why don't you go tell her the good news?"

It was Mitch's way of saying he'd outlasted his welcome. John knew better than to take it personally, but the words drove home the fact that he was an outsider here. That he was neither wanted nor needed. That the twelve years he'd spent as a cop didn't count for shit when it came to department policy and procedure.

"I'll do that."

John knew he should thank his brother, but he didn't even look back as he started toward the Mustang parked curbside.

He should have been relieved Julia's stalker had been caught. That he could put this assignment behind him and get on with the business of pulling his life back together and trying to figure out what came next.

But relief wasn't what he was feeling. John didn't want to analyze what he was feeling too closely. Emotions were generally pretty useless as far as he was concerned.

He thought about driving back to the shop and telling Julia the good news. He could already feel the anticipation of seeing her pulling him in that direction. But that kind of eagerness wasn't something he wanted to feel at this point in his life. For the last two days he'd done nothing but think of her. Fantasize about her. It had to stop.

Instead of driving to the shop, he opted for a drink at a relatively quiet bar on Bourbon Street. He'd give her a call from there. Tomorrow, he'd go back to the shop for his things. Maybe when she wasn't there, so he wouldn't have to see her or talk to her. So he wouldn't be tempted to do something stupid. He'd never been very good at good-byes, anyway.

Hell, a few days at the cabin and he'd forget all about Julia Wainwright and her gypsy eyes.

Yeah.

Right.

TWENTY

John called a few minutes before Julia closed the shop for the evening. Claudia was at the register, counting the day's receipts. Jacob was helping a customer find just the right antique cookbook for his wife's fiftieth birthday. Julia was at her desk trying to focus on work, but as had been the case for the last few days, her mind was bouncing between a dangerous stalker and a man who seemed every bit as dangerous, but in a very different way.

She caught the phone on the second ring, hating it that she was terrified it would be the stalker. "The Book Merchant. This is Julia."

"Hey. It's me."

John.

She sat up straighter, the file she'd been alphabetizing forgotten. She knew it was stupid, but a blush heated her cheeks at the sound of his voice. "Hi," she said.

"I think we got the guy," he said.

"That's great news! Was it Vester?"

"We think so. Mitch and McBride made the arrest a few hours ago. Took him into custody for questioning."

"Is he the one who murdered that poor woman in the cemetery?"

"Cops are looking into it."

"This is fabulous news, John. It's finally over. I can't tell you how relieved I am."

"You and a lot of other people."

"I should call Dad and let him know."

"That's probably a good idea."

Silence filled the line for the span of several heartbeats. Julia sensed a tension that hadn't been there before. She thought of what had happened between them the night before, and suddenly it dawned on her that once he picked up his things he probably wouldn't be coming back.

It shouldn't have mattered, but it did. A lot more than she'd anticipated. Julia had just received word that the man who'd been stalking her had been caught; she should have been ecstatic. She could go back to her old routine. No more looking over her shoulder. No more dealing with John's moodiness. His morning hangovers. But all she could think about was that he'd kissed her like she'd never been kissed before in her life . . .

Not wanting to think of that now, Julia reined in her thoughts and said the first impulsive thing that came to mind. "I think this calls for a celebration."

"You think everything calls for a celebration." He said the words teasingly, but he sounded distracted. More reserved than usual. She could hear music in the background. Blues, if she wasn't mistaken. People talking, laughing. The clang of glass against glass. And she realized he was in a bar. Probably with Mitch.

"Just some wine and cheese," she said. "Champagne with strawberries. Oh, and chocolate. Lots of it." She closed her eyes. "Can you stop by?"

"Uh, you mean tonight?"

"Everyone's already here. We're closing the shop for the day. I've got a wedge of Brie and a bottle of champagne in the fridge. I'll send Jacob across the street for some of Mr. Rossi's chocolate Piroulines." She knew she was blabbering, but she couldn't help it. She wanted him to be there, and the tone of his voice was telling her he wasn't going to make it. "I'm going to ask Dad to come. I'm sure he'll want to thank you in person."

He hesitated. The realization that he didn't want to be there disappointed her more than it should have.

"If you can't make it, it's okay," she said quickly. "It's not a big deal."

"I'll try to swing by a little later," he said. "I need to pick up my stuff, anyway."

"Oh." She closed her eyes briefly. "All right."

But he had already disconnected.

Julia loved entertaining. She'd always had a flair for it, however impromptu or short notice. After hanging up with John she brought her hands together and announced to Claudia and Jacob that the stalker had been apprehended.

"Does that mean we don't have to tolerate your cop buddy anymore?" Jacob asked.

Claudia elbowed him. "How did they catch him?" she asked.

Julia explained how John had traced the fan letter to Nicholas Vester. "It turned out Vester had just been released from prison for stalking a radio talk show host."

"I think I remember hearing about that on the radio," Claudia mused.

"I must admit, I didn't have much faith in Merrick," Jacob said. "But I'm glad he came through for you."

"I'll kind of miss having him around," Claudia said.

"Especially the puking in the alley," Jacob added dryly.

Rolling her eyes, Julia started for the phone. "I'll call Dad and give him the good news. Are you two up for a little celebration?"

"Do the French drink wine?" Jacob answered.

"Great idea," Claudia said. "I'll call Rory."

Benjamin Wainwright wasn't in, so Julia left a message

with his assistant, Parker, who promised to have her father call her as soon as he arrived back in the office.

Rory Beauchamp arrived twenty minutes later with a bottle of Chianti. Julia set out food while Claudia, Rory and Jacob wiped down wineglasses and draped the table with linen. She tried to work up some excitement, but for the first time in recent memory, her heart simply wasn't in it. She went through the motions. Linen tablecloth on the coffee buffet. Chocolate Piroulines set in a fan-shaped pattern. Chicory coffee with cream. Chianti in a flat carafe with matching tall tumblers. A crisp cabernet sauvignon with tall-stemmed glasses. Imported Brie and water crackers. Dark Swiss chocolates. French champagne on ice. She'd just chosen a haunting Celtic CD when Claudia came up behind her.

"The shop looks fabulous."

Julia turned to survey the place and found herself smiling despite her thoughtful mood. How she loved creating atmosphere and sharing it with friends. It would have been perfect if only John had agreed to come. "It does, doesn't it?"

"Only one thing missing."

"Hmmm? What's that?"

"John."

Julia's hand froze as she lit the last of a dozen eucalyptus candles she'd set in antique gold-leaf pillars. "Oh, I think he's had enough of this place. He probably has better things to do."

"You can pretend not to be disappointed, but I know you wanted him to be here."

"Why wouldn't I?" Julia hit her sister with a bright smile. "Thanks to him this nightmare is over. All of us are safe. We can get back to the way things were before."

"I don't think those are the only reasons you wanted him to be here."

"Don't be silly." But even to her the laugh that escaped her sounded forced. "Thanks to him I have a new alarm system. New locks on the windows and doors. It's only right that I thank him for helping me out."

"I'm sure it has nothing to do with his being attractive. You're far too astute not to have noticed the way he looks at you."

"You've been reading too many romance novels."

"Any fool can see there's something between the two of you."

"It's called friction."

"Or maybe you're so deep into denial you can't see the woods for the trees." Claudia topped a cracker with cheese and popped it into her mouth. "Rough around the edges suits him."

Because she was blushing, Julia focused on the carafe and wiped it down for the third time. "Rough around the edges or not, he's dealing with a lot of demons right now. I think he needs his space."

"Or maybe he needs someone like you to pull him out of whatever bottomless pit he's fallen into."

"He's the only one who can pull himself out of this particular pit."

The bell on the front door jingled. Julia looked up to see her father and his assistant, Parker Bradley, walk in.

"Saved by the bell," Julia said under her breath.

Claudia snagged a glass of Chianti off the banquet table and grasped her sister's hand. "Let's go tell Dad the good news."

The letters were waiting for John when he arrived at his apartment. He'd been riding a high since the scene at Nicholas Vester's place. Cops called it the rush of the bust. For the first time in months, he'd felt useful. As if he'd done something worthwhile. Something good. Something that had made a difference in someone's life.

The high was short-lived.

He knew what was inside the envelope even before tearing it open. The first letter was from the law firm of Perrin, Fair and Gay out of Chicago and had been sent via registered mail. John's stomach went queasy as he stared at the legalese. Dread and grief and a terrible, crushing guilt descended as the words registered in a brain that didn't want to believe:

> *Eva Watts [plaintiff] is hereby suing John T. Merrick [defendant] and the Chicago Police Department [defendant] in a civil suit for the amount of two million dollars for the wrongful death of DEA agent Franklin Watts.*

Two million dollars.

Jesus Christ.

A second letter was a formal notification from the Chicago PD informing him of the suit. He was to call the legal department as soon as possible. It was strongly advised that he obtain legal representation. Get his cards in order. His life was about to be ruined a second time.

John tossed the letters onto the coffee table and brooded. He wanted to believe he didn't give a shit. His life was already ruined; why sweat something small like two million dollars? He didn't have it. Not even close. What were they going to do? Take it out in blood?

But the reality of what his life had become struck a hard blow. The lawyers for the department had warned him that this day would come. It wasn't enough that his life was ruined. It didn't fucking matter that he couldn't sleep. That most days he was lucky just to get out of bed. Now they were going to financially ruin him, too.

Par for the course when you shoot a cop, a little voice reminded.

John didn't have much left. He hadn't drawn a paycheck in two months. Over the years he'd put aside a nest egg, a small 401K, a checking account that was dwindling at a rapid rate, the Mustang. He would probably lose it all. If he ever worked again, everything he owed would go toward paying for lawyers, the bereaved widow and her two father-less children.

He thought about the kids and realized there was noth-ing on this earth that would give them back what he'd taken away. Franklin Watts would never see his children graduate from college. He would not be there to give away his daughter on her wedding day. He would never hold his first grandchild.

At that moment, like a thousand other moments before it, John would have given his own life to rectify what he'd done. But he couldn't bring back Franklin Watts. He couldn't change any of what had happened that night. He was going to have to deal with this. Find a way to get through it. Get on with his life.

Yeah. Right.

Scrubbing a hand over his jaw, he looked around the derelict apartment. Like the rest of his life, the place was a piece of shit. A pigsty. Already, he could feel the walls closing in. The memory of that night descending. The guilt squeezing like a giant snake wrapped around his throat.

For the first time in a long time he wanted to call some-one. But for the life of him he couldn't figure out who. He didn't want to call Mitch. Didn't want to talk to his former partner from Chicago. The only person who came to mind was Julia Wainwright. Pretty, sweet, gypsy-eyed Julia. As of late she seemed to be the only person left in the world he looked forward to seeing. She was the only ray of light in a life that had become black with despair. The only per-son capable of lifting him out of the deep, dark hole he'd fallen into.

He wanted to believe his feelings for her were only the result of his sex drive kicking back in after a two-month hiatus. He knew it would only make things worse if he came to rely on her for anything. That he was only fooling himself by thinking her feelings for him were anything but friendly sympathy.

He'd always been good at keeping things in perspective,

particularly when it came to women. As far as John was concerned, a relationship with a woman meant sex on a regular basis. He'd never had a female friend. He'd sure as hell never gone off the deep end and gotten the two confused. Then along came Julia Wainwright with her pretty smile and kind heart and he'd started getting all kinds of crazy ideas. Like maybe this was the real deal.

He'd done the right thing earlier when he'd turned down her invitation. The last thing he wanted to do was hang out at the bookstore with a bunch of old codgers and eat hors d'oeuvres he couldn't pronounce. He'd done the right thing by practically hanging up on her earlier. He didn't want her gratitude. He sure as hell didn't want her sympathy.

Goddamn it, he didn't want to want her.

But he did.

He wanted to sleep with her. He wanted to act on the impulses running hot in his blood, even though he knew in the long run it would cost him something to walk away.

If he were a stronger man, he might have had the moral character to stick to his guns. Do them both a favor and stay the hell out of her life. Keep her out of the muck he couldn't seem to climb out of himself.

But when it came to Julia, John was a long way from strong. Snagging his bomber jacket off the chair back, he left the apartment and set off for the French Quarter, hoping he found a bar before his discipline crumbled and he ended up at the Book Merchant.

Julia wasn't going to let herself think about him.

If John didn't want to be here, so be it. She wasn't going to get caught up in something she had no control over. Damn it, she was going to have a good time if it killed her.

Except for her own misguided expectations, the impromptu get-together was a success. Everyone she'd invited had shown: her father; his assistant, Parker Bradley; Claudia's beau, Rory Beauchamp. Even Jacob had stayed late to socialize and celebrate the end of what had been a tough week for everyone.

Absently, Julia listened to the conversation around her as she replenished the tray of chocolates.

"I told you John Merrick would come through," Benjamin Wainwright was saying. "His daddy was a good man, and John certainly has the potential to follow the same path."

Parker Bradley nodded vigorously. "His references were glowing. Well, except for the Chicago incident."

Rory Beauchamp spread Brie on a cracker. "So what happened up in Chicago? He get fired, or what?"

Julia sipped her Chianti and tried not to look at the clock. It was nearly ten o'clock. John wasn't going to show. Damn it, she wasn't going to do this to herself . . .

"He was involved in a friendly fire incident a couple of months ago," she said.

"Claudia told me he accidentally *shot* someone?" Rory shook his head.

Parker grimaced. "Terrible thing, the guy was a cop. Died at the scene."

"Whoa. That's heavy."

Jacob shook his head. "I hate to put a damper on the praise for this guy, but in my opinion John Merrick has a drinking problem."

"I know he has a drink now and again." Benjamin Wainwright's eyes sharpened on Jacob. "What makes you think it's a problem?"

"Half the time he was here at the shop he was drunk," Jacob said. "The other half he was accusing me of being the stalker."

Julia had been hoping Jacob wouldn't go down that road, but he'd never been one to keep his opinions to himself. The worst part about it was that John wasn't here to defend himself.

"I think John is struggling with what happened in Chicago," she said.

Parker leaned closer and lowered his voice. "While I

was checking him out, I heard rumors of an impending lawsuit. The widow of the dead cop was considering filing a civil suit against him for negligence and endangerment. She had children, you know."

"I had no idea," Claudia said. "How terrible for everyone involved."

Benjamin Wainwright grimaced. "Very difficult situation to say the least."

"Hopefully, he wasn't drinking when it happened," Jacob put in.

Julia shot him a hard look. "I believe the drinking is a result of the tragedy, not the cause of it."

He looked contrite for a moment, but he wasn't deterred. "Look, Julia, I'm not saying he shot anyone on purpose. But some of the things I witnessed when he was here make me wonder about his competence." He looked at Benjamin. "Frankly, I was surprised you hired him."

Julia counted to ten. "I think that's enough idle gossip for one evening," she said. "And just in case any of you have forgotten, John is the one who apprehended the stalker."

Benjamin Wainwright nodded at his daughter. "Well said, Julia."

Parker nodded solemnly. "Maybe you should counsel him, Benjamin."

The elder Wainwright nodded. "That's a good idea. I'll give him a call when we get back from Baton Rouge. He's a good man. I'd hate to see him go down the wrong road."

Julia didn't think John would willingly let her father "counsel" him. But she agreed that it would be good for him to talk to someone about the shooting. If not her father, then someone else.

"So, Julia, have the police ascertained the reason why this guy targeted you?" Parker asked.

Her father grimaced. "We were wondering if it had anything to do with the ministry."

Julia had been raised never to lie, so she wasn't very good at it. At the moment she wasn't sure if that was good or bad. "From what I understand this guy is a serial stalker. He had already served prison time for stalking a radio talk show host. I don't believe it had anything to do with the ministry."

"There are a lot of troubled souls in this town," Benjamin said.

Parker nodded in agreement. "We've got our work cut out for us."

"Indeed."

"I'm just glad it's over," Julia said.

Claudia raised a stemmed glass. "I think this calls for a toast."

Six glasses rose. Glass tinkled. "Here's to the good guys," Benjamin Wainwright said.

Julia was thinking about John when a pounding sounded on the front door. She knew it was unnecessary now that the stalker had been caught, but a chill passed through her nonetheless.

"Did you put the CLOSED sign in the window?" Jacob asked.

"I did," Julia said.

"There's always someone who chooses not to read it," Claudia put in.

"Or doesn't care," Jacob added.

Setting her glass on the counter, Julia started toward the door, but Jacob stopped her. "You hang with your dad," he said. "I'll get rid of them."

She smiled. "Be nice."

He smiled back. "I'm always nice."

She returned to where her father and Parker were in the midst of a conversation about the upcoming convention. "My keynote," Benjamin was saying, "promises to be controversial, but if I've learned anything in the last sixty years it's that change isn't easy, even when it's past due."

Parker nodded. "I'm halfway through the speech and it's really powerful."

"I wrote a rough draft. But when I step up to that podium, I'm probably going to wing most of it." He rapped his hand against his heart. "What I have to say comes directly from here."

Out of the corner of her eye Julia watched Jacob cross to the front door. She was aware of him mumbling something beneath his breath. The rustle of the blinds as the door opened.

Claudia was speaking to her. Something about a new restaurant in the Quarter. But Julia's attention was on the visitor at the door, because at some level she knew who it was.

"What are you doing here?" came Jacob's voice.

She turned to see John push his way inside. "Where is she?"

His gaze clashed with hers. An unwanted thrill barreled through her when his eyes skimmed down the front of her. She could feel her heart thrumming against her ribs. Something primal inside her calling out to something even more primal inside him. But she was keenly aware of the other people in the room. The eyes on her. On him. The speculation this unexpected visit would bring.

"Oh. John. Hi." Brilliant greeting.

He didn't even acknowledge anyone else in the room. "I need to talk to you. It's important."

He ran the last two words together, and with a keen sense of disappointment Julia realized he'd been drinking. "Is everything all right?" she asked.

"Everyth'ns fine." Blinking, he looked around the room as if realizing he'd walked in on something. "Mr. Wainwright."

"John." There was no censure in her father's voice, but his eyes were watchful.

Shaking his head, Jacob stepped back, his questioning gaze going to Julia. "I can ask him to leave."

Julia wasn't sure why she felt compelled to keep John from making an ass of himself. Maybe because she cared. Because she knew he was a good man and that in spite of that fact he was going to make a bad impression on people whose opinion mattered to her.

Parker crossed to where John and Jacob stood just inside the door. "Maybe someone ought to drive him home," he said.

"I don't need anyone to drive me home." John didn't even spare the other man a glance. His eyes were on Julia. "I need to talk to Julia. Now. In private."

She stared back, wondering if he could see the hard beat of her heart, because it was going wild inside her chest. He didn't look very coplike standing there in his faded blue jeans, biker boots and black leather bomber jacket. He looked dangerous. For the life of her she couldn't fathom why he'd come to see her.

"We can talk in the storage room," she said.

"Maybe you ought to talk out here." Parker tried to sound casual, but Julia didn't miss the concern in his voice. "After all, you've got all this food."

John said nothing. Didn't even acknowledge the other man.

"Excuse us just a moment." Wiping palms that had suddenly become clammy on her skirt, Julia turned and started toward the storage room.

Her knees were shaking when she walked in. She turned to see John enter. She started when he closed the door behind him. Her heart began to pound out of control when he locked it.

"What are you doing?" she asked.

"Making sure we don't get interrupted."

"Interrupt what?" She was sorry she asked the question the instant the words were out. She saw his intent in his eyes as he started toward her. An unnerving intensity radiated from him as he moved. Julia sensed danger; the instinct to flee barreled through her.

She didn't even realize she was moving backward until her back came in contact with the shelf behind her. All she could think was that there was no place to run. That she wasn't equipped to handle this man, this situation.

He reached her a moment later. In one smooth motion he locked her in with his arms by grasping the shelf behind her. Julia got an impression of mile-wide shoulders. Lean hips encased in faded denim. She jerked her gaze to his face, caught a glimpse of heavy brows riding low over eyes glittering with dark intentions. Two days of stubble on a lean jaw. A sculpted mouth pulled taut.

"This," he said and lowered his mouth to hers.

TWENTY-ONE

Julia was no stranger to the power of lust. In her books, she explored the many facets of passion, delving into the darker, forbidden side of desire. But none of her writings had prepared her for this encounter with John Merrick.

The hot shock of pleasure stunned her. Every nerve ending in her body jumped to life the instant his mouth touched hers. Her blood heated and began to boil in her veins. A pang low in her abdomen transformed into an ache that was urgent and unbearable, a knot drawn inexorably tighter.

Never in her wildest dreams could she have imagined a simple kiss throwing her into such a maelstrom of physical and emotional upheaval. But she knew there was nothing simple about this kiss. About this moment. Or the man holding her in his arms.

Using both hands, she pushed against his shoulders. But the attempt was token, because deep inside her something called out to him. She wanted this and no false pretenses were going to change that. His shoulders were rock hard beneath her palms. His skin was hot to the touch. Sweat dampened his shirt beneath his bomber jacket. She ran her hands over his shoulders, down the muscled biceps of the arms that pinned her. All the while his mouth coaxed and teased and made promises she knew better than to believe.

She believed anyway.

It was wrong for her to want him. Wrong for her to respond here and now and with no holds barred. But for the first time in her adult life, Julia didn't think about doing the right thing. And even though in the back of her mind she knew this would cost her later, she didn't let herself think about repercussions.

A swirl of dizziness engulfed her when his body came flush against hers. She got the impression of hard planes and angles. She wanted to put her hands on him and explore all of them. A gasp escaped her when he moved against her, but he deepened the kiss and swallowed the sound.

For an instant she resisted, but the feel of his mouth against hers tore down her defenses. She wanted his tongue in her mouth. She opened to him. He went in deep. At some point he'd loosened his grip on the shelf behind her. His hands trembled slightly as he set his palms on either side of her face and angled her toward him. His palms were damp and rough against her skin. A tremor moved through her when they slid to her shoulders and skimmed down her arms to rest on her hips.

Gripping her there, he moved against her. Once. Twice. She was keenly aware of his arousal sliding against her pelvis. A groan rumbling up from his chest. Her own blood pounding like a drum in her womb. She shivered when he removed her shirt. A protest escaped her when he cupped her breasts.

But John didn't stop. He didn't give her time to catch her breath. His hand went to the front of her bra and for several seconds he struggled with the clasp. When he couldn't get it open fast enough, he used both hands and snapped the thin scrap of material.

Her breasts sprang free. Pleasure surged when he

brushed his fingertips over her swollen nipples. Julia arched her back, giving him unencumbered access. He cupped her breasts. She muffled a cry when he took her sensitized nipples between his thumbs and forefingers and gently squeezed. All she could think was that if he stopped she would surely die.

He broke the kiss. Her head lolled back. Then his mouth was on her breast, warm and wet and sucking. The intensity of the pleasure made her cry out. Her womb contracted and she wondered if a woman could orgasm from breast stimulation alone.

She wanted to touch him, explore every hard plane, take his breath the same way he was taking hers. Reaching out, she skimmed her hands over his chest. The buttons of his shirt seemed like a monumental task when she could barely think, so she used both hands and ripped his shirt open. Vaguely, she was aware of buttons popping and hitting the floor. He quivered when she skimmed her hands over his pebbled male nipples. His quick intake of breath told her he was sensitive there so she did it again.

The floor shifted beneath her feet when he reached down and cupped her between her legs. She felt herself begin to melt. Julia knew she should stop. The moment was rapidly spiraling out of control. It was a moment she would be sorry for later. But the pleasure was like a powerful narcotic racing through her blood. A drug that fed a ravenous need she hadn't even known existed.

John whispered something in her ear. But Julia was beyond hearing, beyond understanding. She was aware of his hand sliding down her hip. Cool air rushed over her thighs as he raised the hem of her skirt. Then his palm was flush against her belly, sliding lower into the waistband of her panty hose.

She knew what would happen next. But lost in a sea of sensation, she wasn't strong enough to stop him. If only he would stop kissing her.

But he didn't stop.

His fingers brushed the curls at her vee. Her mind ordered her to shove away from him and stop this madness before it veered into dangerous territory. But her body betrayed her intellect. She reveled in the smooth slide of his palm over her skin. When he reached the apex of her thighs a second time, she opened to him. Her legs went weak when his hand slid over her mound, separated her. She cried out when two fingers dipped inside and went deep.

"Easy," he whispered.

Julia went rigid for an instant, then her bones seemed to melt. "John . . ."

"That's it," he said and began to stroke her.

The world around her faded to monochrome and ceased to exist. All she could think was that she was at his mercy. That in all the years she'd been writing, she'd never even come close to capturing the power of true desire. The reckless heat of unencumbered lust. The tangle of emotions that went along with both of those things.

The pleasure built with breathtaking speed, with stunning intensity. Need tore down her intellect, piece by devastated piece. Her fingers dug into his shoulders. Her hips moved in time with his hand, each stroke driving her to a higher level of madness. All the while he kissed her like a man possessed.

The climax crashed over her like a tidal wave. Control fled. Every sense heightened to a fever pitch. Her body broke a sweat. Vaguely, she was aware of his name on her lips. Her fingers digging into his shoulders and back while the sensations coursing through her seemed to go on and on.

For several seconds Julia could do nothing but cling to him. At some point her legs had buckled. She would have slid to the floor, but he was holding her propped against the wall. Her entire body trembled with aftershocks. Vaguely, she was aware of their labored breaths. It was a harsh sound in the confines of the storage room—as if both of them had just run a marathon.

Slowly, her senses returned. John continued to hold her, but he gently slid his hand from inside her pantyhose and smoothed her skirt.

Julia let him hold her, but only because she didn't yet have the strength to stand on her own. She couldn't believe what she'd just allowed to happen. She couldn't believe she'd done something so utterly reckless. Her. Ms. I'm-always-in-control Wainwright. She who never veered from the straight and narrow. She who, at the age of twenty-nine, never kissed on the first date. What in the name of God had she been thinking?

But Julia knew what she'd been thinking. She hadn't, and that was the problem. She'd handed the controls over to John. Everyone knew men couldn't be trusted to make decisions when it came to sex.

Sex.

Oh God.

Embarrassment was the first emotion she could identify. Not only because she'd given herself to John with such reckless abandon, but because her father and several close friends whom she cared for and respected—people whose opinion of her mattered greatly—were standing just one room away more than likely wondering what the hell they were doing in the storage room.

Regret came in a blinding rush.

She disengaged herself from John. Because she couldn't meet his gaze, she looked down at her disheveled clothes and brushed at them frantically. When she mustered the courage, she made eye contact with John.

"What the hell do you think you're doing?"

He met her gaze levelly. "Screwing things up probably."

"Damn right you are."

"I didn't mean for things to go that far."

Spinning away from him, Julia tucked her blouse into her skirt. "I can't believe you did that."

"I can't believe you let me."   •

That was the worst part about the whole episode, she thought. As much as she wanted to, she couldn't blame it on him. She had partaken in the moment every bit as enthusiastically as he had.

"That's the most . . . inappropriate thing I've ever done

in my life." Not knowing what else to do, she began wiping frantically at the wet spot on her skirt.

He handed her a Kleenex from a box on the shelf. "Let me help—"

"I can do it." She ripped the tissue from his hand and dabbed at the spot. "My father is standing out there wondering what the hell we're doing in here." When the spot had been blotted, she looked at John. "What do you suggest I tell them?"

He rolled a shoulder, and Julia couldn't help but remember how that shoulder had felt beneath her hands when he'd been kissing her. "Tell them I came to you with a problem."

"That's not far off the mark."

He laughed. It was a rich, masculine sound. That he could be flippant about this ticked her off.

"This is not the least bit funny," she said. "You waltz into my shop drunk and . . ." She closed her eyes.

"It takes two to tango, Julia."

"I'm not saying you're the only one to blame for this, but you instigated it. Neither one of us is in a position to . . ." But the words failed her.

"Have sex?"

"We didn't have sex."

"One of us didn't."

The image of him bringing her to climax flashed in her mind's eye. She stared at him, her face flaming. Humiliation burned, but she didn't let herself look away. "Neither of us is in a place in our lives where we should be taking on a relationship. What you did by coming in here and . . . kissing me like that was . . . inappropriate."

He gave her a lazy smile. "Inappropriate?"

"To say the least."

"You can deny it all you want," he began, "but I know I'm not the only one who's noticed the chemistry every time we get within shouting distance of each other. You've felt it. All I did was act on it."

The blush came harder, hotter. "There is no chemistry,

John. Just bad judgment on both our parts. You're troubled. You reached out. I was there for you because I'm your friend. End of story."

"Or maybe I'm just being more honest about it."

"It shouldn't have happened." She blew out a breath. "It can't happen again."

For a moment she thought he was going to grab her and kiss her. She prayed he wouldn't, because with arousal still humming through her veins, she wasn't sure she'd have the willpower to push him away.

"I think you should leave," she said.

Without giving him time to respond, Julia straightened her shoulders and started toward the door. It crossed her mind again that the people she'd left standing in her shop were going to be curious. A dozen lame explanations scrolled through her mind. The only one that sounded even remotely reasonable was that they'd been talking. Of course that didn't explain the flush on her face or that damn wet spot on her skirt . . .

She was brushing at it again with trembling hands when a hard rap sounded on the door. She froze and watched the knob twist back and forth.

"Julia? John?" It was Jacob's voice. "You guys okay in there?"

Pasting on a smile she hoped looked real, she unlocked the door and swung it open. "Of course we're okay," she said brightly. "What's up?"

Jacob's gaze skimmed down the front of her. Julia held onto her smile, hoping he didn't notice the wet spot. It could always be explained away . . .

"The door was locked," he said.

"Oh." She shrugged. "Hmmm . . . the bolt must have engaged when I closed the door."

Jacob's eyes narrowed. "And you closed the door because . . ."

She glanced back at John and lowered her voice to a conspiratorial tone. "We just needed to talk for a moment, but everything's okay now."

"Uh huh."

"Julia darlin'."

She glanced past Jacob and felt a moment of panic when she saw her father heading toward them with Parker at his side.

Jacob shook his head. "If you want him to buy the same story you just told me, you might try buttoning your blouse."

Julia looked down, and was mortified to see there was only one button keeping her blouse closed. Gasping, she turned away and quickly buttoned up.

"Darlin', it was a lovely evenin', but Parker and I are going to call it a night."

Buttons engaged, Julia pasted a smile on her face and turned to her father. "Are you sure you've got to leave? There's plenty of food."

He'd stopped in the doorway of the storage room, his gaze flicking to John. "Parker and I are flying to Baton Rouge tomorrow to discuss the district's position on some of the issues I'll be addressing at the conference. We've got to catch an early flight. Five A.M. rolls around early."

John came up beside her and extended his hand. "It's good to see you again, Benjamin."

All Julia could think was that same hand had been touching her intimately just a few minutes earlier.

"Everything okay?" the elder Wainwright asked.

"Now that the stalker has been caught, everything's just fine."

Remembering she'd ripped the buttons from his shirt, Julia risked a glance at John. Relief flooded her when she realized he'd zipped his bomber jacket.

"Good work on the stalker. I appreciate you keeping my daughter safe."

"I was glad to help."

Grimacing, the elder Wainwright gave his hand a final shake and lowered his voice. "If you ever want to talk about anything at all, I hope you'll call me." He lifted a business card from the breast pocket of his suit and handed it to John. "Anytime, son. Day or night."

John glanced at the card, then dropped it into his pocket. "Thanks."

Wainwright turned to Julia and kissed the top of her head. "Darlin', I'll see you in a few days," he said and started toward the door.

TWENTY-TWO

"Details."

Julia looked up from the stack of books she was logging into the inventory database and frowned at her younger sister. "I have no earthly idea what you're talking about."

"You are *so* not good at playing dumb." When Julia said nothing, Claudia rolled her eyes. "I'm talking about you and John in that storage room last night."

"Oh. That. Well, I hate to disappoint you, but there's nothing to tell."

"That's interesting." Café au lait in hand, Claudia crossed to Julia's desk and plopped into the visitor chair. "Because nothing sure has you blushing."

Julia tried to hide the blush by looking at her computer screen, but her younger sister was far too astute. "He kissed you, didn't he? That's how all your lipstick got rubbed off."

"He didn't kiss me."

"Oh, my God."

Julia looked up. "What?" she asked irritably.

"You did more than kiss, didn't you? I see it in your eyes. Julia!"

"Oh, for Pete's sake!"

"Anyone with more than two brain cells can see you and John are hot for each other."

"Does that include Dad?"

"You might be able to fool Dad. I mean, come on, most father's wear blinders when it comes to their daughters' sex lives."

"Stop right there."

Claudia continued as if she hadn't heard. "He probably still thinks you're a virgin." She laughed. "Good grief, he probably thinks *I'm* still a virgin."

Julia looked at her younger sister, mildly alarmed. She knew it was probably naïve, but she'd also thought Claudia was still a virgin. "I do not want to hear this."

But evidently Claudia was enjoying herself far too much to let the subject drop. "When you opened that door last night . . . I swear, I've never seen you look so flustered." She sighed. "And John looked just plain adorable."

"John is a lot of things," Julia said. "Adorable is not one of them."

"I guess sexy would be a better term."

John was the one subject Julia did not want to discuss this morning. The memory of their encounter in the storage room had kept her up half the night. The erotic dreams that followed had kept her up the other half. This morning she felt bleary-eyed, exhausted and embarrassed.

"Talking about me again?"

Julia looked away from her computer to see Jacob enter the store through the rear door, looking snazzy in a vintage jacket and burgundy turtleneck. He shrugged. "I heard 'sexy' and just assumed."

Claudia rolled her eyes. "I'm talking about John Merrick."

Jacob smirked and shot Julia a knowing look. "Are we confessing our sins this morning?"

"I have nothing to confess," Julia snapped.

Claudia nodded. "She's sticking to the we-were-just-talking story."

"Well I guess that explains that wet spot on her skirt."

Julia shot him a warning look. "That's enough."

Claudia's eyes widened. "Oh, my God. Julia! You did more than kiss!"

"Both of you are just a word or two away from getting fired." It was an idle threat. One Julia made every so often when her employees pushed just a little too hard.

"Julia, I like him," Claudia said in a softer voice. "I think he's a nice guy."

"I think he's an alcoholic," Jacob put in.

Julia rose abruptly. "Nobody asked either of you for an opinion," she said and started toward the storage room.

She wasn't sure why she was so cranky this morning. She wanted to believe it was the lack of sleep. The troubling turn of events the night before. But as she turned on the storage room light and looked around, it struck her why her mood was dark. The room seemed empty without John. She didn't know where he was or when she would see him again. Both of those things bothered her more than she wanted them to, no matter how hard she tried to pretend otherwise. She knew it was crazy. He was the last man on earth she should be interested in.

But she was. More than interested, if she wanted to be honest about it.

Damn it.

Shoving thoughts of him aside, she went to the shelf for the box of manila folders, opened it and counted out a dozen for the files she needed to make. She happened to glance down as she counted and found herself looking at a half a dozen white buttons.

"Julia."

She started at the sound of her sister's voice, then turned to face her. "Don't start."

Julia moved away from the buttons, but her younger sister had already spotted them. Her expression sobered. "I didn't mean to upset you."

"I'm not upset."

"If you don't want to tell me what happened last night, you don't have to."

"Well, I appreciate your letting me off the hook." Tucking the folders beneath her arm, Julia started toward the door.

Claudia blocked her path. "I just want you to know that if you need to talk, I'm here."

"What I need to do is get these files made so I can open the shop."

And try to make it through the rest of the day without thinking about John Merrick.

John woke to the incessant blare of the phone and a headache that was in the process of grinding his brain into mush. He rolled onto his side and knocked the phone off the night table before realizing the sound wasn't the phone at all, but his doorbell.

He squinted at the alarm clock, wondering if it was five A.M., or five P.M., and tried not to wonder what that said about his state of mind. The doorbell blasted again and he decided it didn't matter. He was going to kill the son of a bitch ringing it.

Groaning, he threw his legs over the side of the bed. Nausea seesawed in his gut, and for an instant he wondered if he was going to throw up. After a few seconds the nausea passed. He got unsteadily to his feet and stepped into his jeans. Weaving drunkenly, he made his way to the living room, stumbled into the foyer and reached the door. He opened it without checking the peephole.

Mitch stood in the darkened hall looking pissed off and aching for a fight. "You missed your firearm proficiency test this morning."

John tried to close the door, but Mitch shoved it open and stepped inside.

"What the fuck is your problem?" he demanded.

"Can it, bro. I'm not in the mood." John started to turn away, but Mitch caught his arm and spun him around.

"I vouched for you," he said. "I told them you were a good cop. That you were reliable and they should hire you. You made a goddamn liar out of me."

"You made a liar out of yourself."

Mitch's lips pulled into a snarl. "You didn't even bother to call." He sniffed. "You smell like booze, John. You were fucking drunk, weren't you?"

"I told you I didn't want the job."

"What the hell are you going to do with the rest of your life? Crawl into a bottle and feel sorry for yourself until you die?"

Because the statement was so pathetically close to the truth, John turned away and started for the bathroom. "Something like that."

Mitch grasped his arm and spun him around again, then gave him a shove. "Don't fucking walk away from me. I put it on the line for you and you blew it."

John's temper sparked. Moving more quickly than he'd thought himself capable of, he slapped the other man's hands off him. But Mitch was ready. Using both hands, he shoved John against the wall hard enough to send a picture to the floor.

"I'm not going to stand around and watch you self-destruct."

"No one's asking you to."

"For God's sake, John, I'm trying to help you."

"I didn't ask for your help."

"There's a place for you with the New Orleans PD. I don't understand why you won't at least try to help yourself."

Something inside John broke open. Temper. Two months of regret and rage and grief. Moving quickly, he grabbed his brother by the lapels, spun him around and slammed him against the wall. "How the hell can I be a cop when I can't even pick up my fucking gun!" he screamed. "I don't have the guts to touch it. I can barely fucking look at it! How the hell am I supposed to deal with that?"

Mitch blinked, allowing himself to be pinned for several interminable seconds. Then he shook off John's hands and shoved away from the wall. When he looked at John, there was pity in his eyes. He might as well pulled out his revolver and shot him in the heart. Pity was the one thing John could not handle.

"Don't look at me that way," he snarled. "Don't fucking feel sorry for me."

Mitch shook his head. "I don't need to. You feel sorry for yourself enough for both of us."

Giving himself a hard shake, John flung open the door and turned away. "Get out," he said.

He heard Mitch moving behind him, but John didn't turn around. He didn't want his brother's sympathy. He sure as hell didn't want his pity.

"Maybe you ought to get yourself some help, bro."

"Words aren't going to fix the problem," John said.

"You can't let this beat you."

"It already has."

"What are you going to do? Run away? Crawl under some rock and hide for the rest of your life?"

"I'm going to the cabin for a few days."

"Oh, that'll fix everything. Go to the cabin. Drink a couple of bottles of booze."

When John said nothing, Mitch sighed. "I never had you pegged as a coward, man."

Slowly, John turned to face him. "Me neither," he said. "Looks like both of us will have to settle for less, doesn't it?"

Shaking his head, Mitch walked out and slammed the door in his face.

"You sure you don't want us to walk you home?"

"Are you kidding?" Julia stood with Rory and Claudia on the sidewalk outside Dannigan's House of Creole and breathed in the cool, damp air of the French Quarter. "After a week of having to look over my shoulder, walking home by myself is going to be a treat."

Dinner with her sister and Rory was the most fun she'd had in days. The three of them had spent nearly two hours in a dimly lit booth savoring Chef Dannigan's mirliton ratatouille, a bottle of merlot and a pot of chicory-laced coffee.

Now the food sat comfortably in her stomach. The wine buzzed pleasantly in her head. She could still taste the bitterness of the chicory on her tongue. Around her, the French Quarter buzzed with a rowdy pre–Mardi Gras crowd. She couldn't think of any place she'd rather be.

"Claudia and I are going to Ray's," Rory said. "Will you come with us?"

The offer was tempting. Ray's was a jazz club on the east side of the Quarter. The music—mostly local bands—was legendary. The atmosphere was all dark wood, palms and smoke. But Julia had always been in tune with her younger sister; she sensed Claudia and Rory wanted to be alone.

"Thanks, but I'll take a rain check."

Claudia's gaze met hers. "You sure? We'd love to have you."

Julia leaned close. "Your good manners are showing."

Her younger sister rolled her eyes. "I mean it. Come with us."

"I've got some work to catch up on anyway," Julia said.

Rory took Claudia's hand, and she smiled at him. The moment didn't elude Julia. She wasn't sure exactly when it had happened, but she was pretty sure her younger sister had fallen in love. The thought gave her a twinge that was both happy and melancholy. Rory might look Goth with his long black hair, pierced ears and funky trench coat, but the more Julia got to know him, the more she came to realize he was a good kid just trying to find his place in a world that could be confusing.

"You're sure you ought to be walking home after dark?" Claudia asked.

Julia didn't miss the concern in her sister's eyes and stepped close to hug her. "Don't worry, Claude. Nicholas Vester is in jail where he belongs. I'm perfectly safe." She motioned toward the Quarter with its wet cobblestones and ancient bricks. "It's a beautiful night, and I'm going to enjoy it."

Shoving her sister to arm's length, Julia turned to Rory and gave him a hug. She could tell by his expression the gesture surprised him. But if he and Claudia were getting serious, he was going to have to get used to it. The Wainwrights were a clan of huggers.

"Don't keep her out too late," Julia said.

He grinned. "I'll have her home by midnight."

"Be forewarned: Dad will hold you to it."

Julia left them at the corner and started down St. Peter toward home at a brisk walk, her denim skirt swishing against her leather boots. The night was mild, with a moist breeze that brought with it the earthy smell of the river. Around her, groups of tourists huddled on the sidewalk. Couples paused at storefront windows to admire merchandise or browse the menus posted by the restaurants. A lone saxophonist played at the mouth of an alley, the lilting notes floating like poetry on the night air.

Julia smiled as she took it all in. A sense of freedom engulfed her at the thought of walking home without having to worry about some crazy stalker jumping out of the shadows. The French Quarter was one of her favorite places on earth. Everything about it fascinated her. The people. The buildings. The river. The history. The food. No matter how many years she lived here, she would never become immune to its unique charm.

At Chartres she stopped at her favorite coffeehouse and ordered a café au lait and a praline to go. She'd decided to stay up late and finish the chapter she'd started earlier in the week. She chatted with the clerk for a few minutes while the praline was wrapped and the coffee poured into a paper cup, then took both and left. A right on Royal and then it was just a few blocks to the shop.

She should have felt celebratory as she strode briskly down the cobblestone street, passing by the quaint antiques shops and eclectic mix of restaurants. But not for the first time that evening she felt the weight of an emotion she couldn't quite identify pressing down on her. An emptiness she hadn't been able to put her finger on. When the welcoming lights of the shop came into view, she caught herself looking for John's Mustang, and with some surprise she finally realized the source of her emotion.

She missed John.

She knew it was silly. After all, they barely knew each other. He'd only stayed at the shop a few days. Not because he'd wanted to be with her, but because her father had hired him to find the man who'd been stalking her. It was stupid to make anything more of it.

But somewhere deep inside, Julia acknowledged the fact that she missed seeing him. She missed talking to him. Missed knowing he was there. It wasn't like her. Independent to a fault, she was not the kind of woman to go off the deep end over a man. She'd always prided herself on being levelheaded and focused. She could count on a couple of fingers the number of men she'd been attracted to.

But she couldn't deny there had been something powerful at work between her and the brooding ex-cop. Something edgy and uncomfortable and, as much as she didn't want to admit it, damned exciting.

The image of him kissing her—bringing her to climax—in the storage room the night before came to her unbidden. Even alone and walking a dark street, she felt the heat of embarrassment creep into her cheeks. She'd never done anything so wildly inappropriate in her life. She'd never let a man touch her that way. Never been so swept away that she forgot where she was.

She almost couldn't believe it had happened. But there was no way she could deny the memory of the intensity of the pleasure he'd given her. Nor could she deny that just the thought of doing it again brought a hot flush to her entire body.

"Oh, for God's sake get a grip," she muttered as she dug the keys from her purse and opened the door.

John might be an attractive man. He might appeal to her on so many levels she couldn't begin to count them. Both of those things were tempered by the knowledge that he was not in a place in his life where he could partake in a healthy relationship. Not that Julia was looking for a relationship. She wasn't. The shop and her writing kept her hopping seven days a week. She was happily unencumbered. She loved her independence. Loved the freedom of being able to come and go as she pleased. Of not having to answer to anyone but herself. She liked her life the way it was. Liked it too much to change it—or share it with anyone else. At least for the moment.

But when she stepped into the shop, the silence seemed as loud as a blaring horn. She breathed in the lingering scents of sandalwood and coffee like she always did, but the usual pleasure of coming home eluded her. Her celebratory mood dimmed. She didn't want to admit it, but the place seemed empty. And for the first time in her adult life, Julia felt . . . lonely.

It was a ridiculous notion. She led a busy life filled with good friends and a family she adored. She *wasn't* lonely. She didn't need a man to be happy or fulfilled or satisfied. She was all of those things alone. But she couldn't deny that for the few short days John had been here, he'd added something special and unexpected to her life.

"Do not go there," she said aloud, locking the door behind her.

She hit the light switch next to the door, but the overhead lights didn't come on. "Crap." Shaking her head, she crossed to the register and set her coffee and purse on the counter. "Damn stupid fuses."

She walked to her desk and switched on the lamp.

Nothing.

Muttering beneath her breath, she opened the bottom drawer and fumbled around for a fuse, then started toward the storage room at the rear of the shop. She was midway down the aisle when she stumbled over something on the floor. "What the—"

She looked down to see a copy of *A Gentleman's Touch* at her feet. "How did you get there?" she said aloud as she stooped to pick it up.

In the dim light slanting in from the front window she could see just enough to discern that the book was not intact. The cover had been ripped. Some of the pages were stuck together with something sticky. She stared down at the book, her mind scrambling for a logical explanation.

But there was nothing logical about finding the damaged book on the floor. The only explanation that came to mind was like the scrape of a cold finger down her back.

Someone had been in the shop.

Alarm zinged through her with the force of an electrical shock. Straightening, she squinted into the semidarkness, her heart bucking hard against her ribs. On the floor ahead she noticed the dark silhouettes of other books that had been torn from the shelves. To her right the coffeemaker lay on the floor, wet grounds scattered about like dirt. The carafe had shattered and the glass glittered like ice. Beyond, she could see that files and papers had been strewn about the floor.

Someone had ransacked the place. But who would do such a thing? What had they been looking for? Had they been after cash?

Slowly, she backed away from the mess. At the end of the aisle, she turned and crossed to her desk. Black dread rose inside her when she spotted the petty cash drawer open, the money inside untouched. Whoever had done this hadn't come in to steal. They'd broken into her shop to destroy.

Her temper flared at the thought of some mindless goon destroying her property. Her shop. Things that had taken her years of hard work to accumulate. Many of the books she carried were one of a kind. Priceless. Irreplaceable. What gave someone the right to destroy? To take something valuable from the world?

"You son of a bitch." Putting her hands on her hips, she shook her head and tried not to be frightened.

But the fear was like a fist clutching her gut. She looked down at the book in her hand. Something cold and unsettling went through her when she spotted the slip of paper sticking out from between the pages.

Her hand shook when she slid the paper from its nest.

Yet each man kills the thing he loves.

She read the words twice before their meaning penetrated the veil of denial. It was from "The Ballad of Reading Gaol" by Oscar Wilde. A poem about a man who killed the woman he loved . . .

Realization came like a punch. She tried reminding herself the police had caught the stalker. Nicholas Vester was sitting in a jail cell. But if that was the case, who had done this? Had Vester made bail and returned to exact revenge?

For the first time it struck her that the intruder could still be in the shop, watching her, and her blood ran cold. Julia spun and bolted for the front door. She was midway there when the scrape of leather soles against ancient wood planks sounded directly behind her. Alarm ratcheted into terror. She picked up speed. Four strides and she reached the door. Her fist slammed against the bolt lock, clicked it open. Her hand twisted the knob.

The next thing she knew two clawlike hands slammed down on her shoulders. Pain radiated down both arms when he squeezed. She screamed, but the sound was cut short when a smothering hand slapped over her mouth.

"Princess of Darkness," came a guttural male voice.

Julia tried to get the door open, but he was incredibly strong and yanked her backward so violently she lost her footing. His hand was so tight against her nose and mouth that she couldn't breathe. She tried to pry his hand from her face, but couldn't.

"Father, forgive her," he said in that terrible, whispered voice, "for she knows not what she does."

Julia clawed at the hand, gouging his flesh with her nails. Gasping, he jerked his hand away.

"Help me!" she screamed.

The blow came out of nowhere, so hard the impact

buckled her knees. Pain exploded the left side of her face. The room spun sickeningly. The next thing she knew she was lying on the floor, the wood planks hard against her cheek. Lifting her head, she blinked, shook her head to clear it. Vaguely, she was aware of the taste of blood in her mouth. Throbbing pain in her left cheekbone.

A lightning burst of adrenaline sent her upright. She caught a glimpse of her attacker above her. Black jacket. Black pants. The Mardi Gras mask gleamed like some macabre demon. She lashed out with her feet, made contact. Heard a grunt. The second blow snapped her head back. The floor rushed up and crashed into her back. Around her the room spun in a slow circle. The light slanting through the window from the street went dark.

The next thing she knew he was on top of her. She tried to twist, writhe out from beneath him. But he was heavy. At some point he had captured her wrists, and he was using something to bind them together. She tried to scream, but when she opened her mouth he stuffed something into it. She tried to bite his fingers, but he withdrew them too quickly.

She raised her head, tried to spit out the gag, but he stopped her with a hard, openhanded slap on the face. "Don't fight me," he whispered. "Let me save you."

Julia fought dizziness that was partly from the blows, partly from the surge of adrenaline. A terrible sense of vulnerability engulfed her when he shoved her hands above her head.

"Blessed are the pure in heart; for they shall see God," he whispered.

Julia tried to scream, but the gag muffled her voice and she ended up choking.

"Unto the pure all things are pure."

The words snapped her back. She was lying on her back. He was sitting on top of her, looking down at her through the eye holes of the hideous mask. All she could think was that she was at the mercy of a madman.

Never taking his eyes from hers, he reached down and

jerked her skirt up her thighs. She screamed into the gag. Twisted and kicked, but she could not dislodge him.

"And He said that holy water will reveal Satan's followers by blistering the skin."

She lifted her head to see the glint of something in his hand. He lifted the object above her, turned his hand as if to pour. Liquid splashed her throat. Her legs. At first she thought he'd doused her with water. Then she felt the sensation of heat on her skin. A heat that quickly exploded into a burning pain.

Renewed terror engulfed her. Julia twisted and lashed out with her feet. She caught his back with her knee hard enough to knock him off balance. He fell sideways, let go of her hands. She twisted out from beneath him, lashed out with both feet. Her left boot caught him squarely on the shoulder, sent him reeling back.

She scrambled to her knees. Fighting to free her hands, she spat the gag. Screamed as loud as she could. "Help me!"

Before she could get to her feet, his fist slammed into the side of her head. White light exploded behind her lids. The force of the impact knocked her to the floor. Darkness crowded her vision, and for an instant she was terrified she would lose consciousness. She lay still, unable to move, trying to gather her senses. Vaguely, she was aware of the pain in her head. The searing pain of whatever he'd splashed on her.

Rough hands fumbled with her shirt. She heard the sound of fabric ripping. Fighting dizziness, she opened her eyes, tried to focus. The man in the mask was on his knees beside her. He'd ripped open her shirt. He snapped the elastic of her bra. "No!" She raised her bound hands to fight him.

He snarled something unintelligible and slapped her hard in the face. Dazed, Julia fell back, her head snapping against the floor.

Dear God, he's going to rape me, she thought with a horrifying sense of clarity.

But instead of touching her, he thrust a small vial at

her, splashing more of the burning liquid onto her bare abdomen.

"God be merciful to me, a sinner," he said in a fervent voice.

The burn came instantly and with a ferocity that took her breath. Julia screamed, terrified that he was dousing her with some kind of acid.

"Shut up!" Roughly, he yanked up her skirt.

She caught a glimpse of something in his hand. The glitter of a crucifix covered in gold leaf. Then his fingers were tugging at her panties, tearing the fabric.

Panic clawed at her, a wild animal trapped and fighting for its life. Screaming, she twisted, kicked out with her legs. "Get away from me!"

"Whore!" He caught her around the waist, pulled her back, slammed her against the floor. "Succubus!"

Screaming, Julia went wild, hammering him with her bound hands. She raised her knees, caught him beneath the chin, sent him reeling back. But before she could scramble away, he lunged at her.

A fresh wave of terror descended when she felt the crucifix being rammed against her inner thigh, her groin, her pubis. Oh, dear God, he was trying to put the crucifix inside her.

Outrage and adrenaline sent her bolt upright. She twisted, tried to scramble away. He came after her. Only this time she saw the blow coming and rolled.

Bone crunched when his fist smashed into the floor. His scream came out as a roar. "You *bitch*!"

Before he could recover, she clasped her bound hands together, formed a double fist and swung as hard as she could. Her fist connected with his left ear. He yelped, raised his hands to protect himself. But his eyes were murderous within the mask.

Knowing he was going to react with extreme violence, Julia leaned back on her elbows and pummeled him with both feet. No time to aim. Just kick. Wherever she could get him. Chest. Shoulder. Throat. Kick. Kick. *Kick!*

"Bastard!" she choked out, all the while working frantically to free her hands.

An animal sound tore from his mouth when the heel of her boot caught him squarely in the solar plexus. He faltered. She heard the breath whoosh from his lungs. But she didn't stop kicking. The toe of her boot caught his neck. Making a strangled sound, he clutched his throat. A final kick to the chest sent him reeling back.

She scrambled to her feet and looked around wildly for an escape route. He stood between her and the front door. Between her and escape. Spinning, she used both hands to grab a row of books from the shelf to her right and fling them at him. By the time they hit the floor, she was sprinting down the aisle toward the rear door. Her boots barely touched the floor as she ran down the aisle, past the last shelf. She used the edge of the bookcase to fly around the corner.

"Help me!" she screamed. "*Please!*"

The twine binding her hands was loose. Working frantically to free them, she glanced over her shoulder. He'd already risen and started down the aisle. The Mardi Gras mask looked macabre in the semidarkness. A monster from hell bent on killing her. Her terror escalated, took her breath, threatened to paralyze her.

She reached the back door. Tried the knob. Locked. Breaths rushing between her clenched teeth, she brought her fist down on the bolt lock. "Help me!"

A heavy hand bit into her shoulder, squeezed.

Spinning, Julia lashed out with both fists. She used her nails, her body weight, her fury to drive him back. He swung at her, his fist coming within an inch of her face, but she lunged backward just in time to avoid being knocked unconscious.

She turned back to the door, twisted the knob. The door flew open. Hope made her giddy as she burst into the alley. No time to think. Just run.

She went left where the narrow courtyard teed. She ran as she had never run before. Every breath was a scream.

Every beat of her heart a surge of adrenaline. She heard him behind her. Hard shoes against asphalt. Insane rantings. The whimpering of a predator that had lost its prey and would go hungry one more night.

"Succubus bitch."

She ran blindly, stumbling over clay pots and past Dumpsters ripe with garbage. She'd taken this route a hundred times in the last two years, but the fear had jumbled her thoughts so badly she couldn't remember where the alleyway led. She needed a phone. A public place. Somewhere the monster in the mask would not follow.

When the lights of Bourbon Street came into view, she risked a look behind her. The alley was empty, but Julia didn't stop running.

TWENTY-THREE

John had just packed the last lure into his tackle box and snapped the lid closed when his phone rang.

A number he didn't recognize. "Yeah."

"Is this John Merrick?"

"Who wants to know?"

"This is Doug Lay, the bouncer over at Tequila Joe's on Bourbon in the Quarter. I got a lady here who's been roughed up pretty bad. Says her name is Julia. She needs someone to pick her up. Wants to talk to you."

Julia.

The muscles at the back of his neck went taut at the thought of someone hurting her. "Put her on."

"John."

He barely recognized her voice and knew immediately something was terribly wrong. She wasn't crying or hysterical, but there was a sharp edge to her voice he'd heard before from other crime victims. "What happened?"

"I need you to come get me."

"Julia, are you hurt?"

"I'm . . . okay."

He could tell from the sound of her voice that she wasn't. Worry swept through him. "I'm on my way." All thoughts of the cabin and a week of fishing forgotten, he dug into his jeans pocket for his keys.

There was rustling on the other end of the line, then the bouncer came back on. "She wants you to come pick her up here at Tequila Joe's. You know the place?"

But John had already disconnected and run out the door.

It took John four minutes to drive across the Quarter to Tequila Joe's. He parked illegally in front of the place and hit the ground running. The bar and dance club was packed with pre–Mardi Gras revelers. He strode purposefully to the bar, where a scantily clad woman the size of a tank toweled shot glasses.

"Where's Doug?" he asked.

Raising a puffy arm, she pointed toward the back. "You can't go back there, though."

John frowned at her and spun toward the rear of the club, where he could see light slanting in from what was probably the kitchen. The bass of the band kept time with his heart as he strode toward the double saloon doors. He hit the doors with both hands, sent them banging against the wall. The room was dimly lit and cluttered with boxes of canned goods and booze. To his right were a dozen shelves jam-packed with glasses of all shapes and sizes. To his left was a small kitchen dirty enough to keep the health department busy writing citations for a week. Straight ahead he spotted Julia and his stomach dropped to his feet.

She was sitting in a folding metal chair with her arms wrapped tightly around her midsection. She looked small and fragile and very alone. Her hair was in disarray and hanging in her face. She was wearing boots, a denim skirt and a pink blouse. But even from twenty feet away John could see that the blouse had been ripped.

He didn't remember crossing to her. Midway there her head came up. Her eyes met his and all he could think was that some son of a bitch had hurt her. Not just roughed her up. Someone had punched her. Really *hurt* her. How could some guy do that to such a lovely and fragile creature?

The fury came with unexpected force. An earthquake that moved through his body hard enough to make him shake. He knew that wasn't what she needed at the moment, but it was the kind of rage that couldn't be reined. He wanted to find the bastard and pound his face until it caved in.

The bouncer was standing over her with a baseball bat in his hand. He was a tall man with a crew cut and biceps the size of Volkswagens. "You Merrick?"

John looked from the bouncer to Julia and back to the bouncer. "What the fuck happened?"

The bouncer propped the bat against the counter. "I was out taking a smoke break and she comes flying out of the alley like the demons from hell were chasing her."

Judging from the way Julia was shaking, John figured the description wasn't too far from the truth. Jesus. He couldn't believe someone had done this to her. In the back of his mind something began to niggle at him.

Realizing he'd been putting off looking closely at her, he reeled in his temper and knelt in front of her. "Julia, how badly are you hurt?"

She didn't meet his eyes. "I'm not. I'm just . . . shaken."

He could plainly see that she was a hell of a lot more than just shaken. Reaching out, he touched her, ran both hands down her arms. Her skin was cool to the touch and she was trembling violently. "I need for you to tell me what happened," he said.

When she didn't look at him, he gently took her chin in his palm and forced her gaze to his. "Come on, honey. Help me out here. Who did this to you?"

She lifted large, fragile eyes to his, and John felt it like a physical touch. Within the depths of her gaze he saw the remnants of terror. The jagged edge of shock. A jumble of emotions he couldn't begin to decipher.

"It was him." She said the words in a voice so low he had to lean forward to hear.

"Who?"

"The stalker. He was . . . in the shop. He . . ." Her voice cracked. "He was waiting for me when I arrived home after dinner."

John looked her over as she spoke. Both knees were cut. Most of the buttons were missing from her blouse and she was clutching it together with a white-knuckled hand. Her slender throat looked as if someone had gouged the skin with his nails. But worst of all was her face. Her left cheek-bone was swollen and tinged purple. How could someone garner enough hatred and rage to hurt something so utterly beautiful? What kind of man could hurt such a generous, giving woman? A woman whose smile could light the night.

"Julia, you know Vester is in jail," he said gently.

Her gaze didn't waiver. "It was him, damn it. The same man who came at me in the alley."

John didn't believe in coincidences. But what were the odds that two men would go after the same woman in the span of a single week? "How do you know he was the same guy?"

"He was wearing the same mask as before. The Mardi Gras mask."

An unsettling chill went through John. He knew there was a possibility some scumbag defense lawyer had gotten a judge to grant Vester bail. But he didn't think so. With Vester sitting in a jail cell, that could mean only one thing. Vester wasn't the stalker. And John had left Julia alone and unprotected . . .

"Did you get a look at him?" he asked. "Can you give me a physical description?"

She shook her head. "It happened so fast. The shop was dark. The lights weren't working, but I figured it was just the fuse again." Her throat bobbed when she swallowed. "God, John, I was so scared."

He swallowed outrage, took her hand and squeezed. "It's okay."

"I tried to yank off the mask a couple of times, but he kept . . . hitting me."

Cold rage poured over him at the image of some sick fuck striking her. Julia wasn't helpless, but she was small-framed and probably didn't weigh much more than a hundred and ten pounds soaking wet. The very thought made him grind his teeth in fury.

"John, it was him, damn it. I'm sure of it."

Something cold skittered down John's spine. "Okay. I believe you."

Shaking her head, she put her face in her hands. "I tried to fight him off, but he was in a rage. I hit him, but he just kept coming."

John had never been much of a toucher. He didn't give hugs. He didn't much like receiving them, either. But for the first time in his adult life, the need to touch, to comfort, overwhelmed him.

He set both hands on her shoulders and gently squeezed, wishing he was man enough to do more. Like take her in his arms and hold her until she stopped shaking. "I'm going to call Mitch."

Her head shot up. Her eyes were alarmed when they met his. "I want to go home."

Taking in the extent of her injuries, he decided she would be going to the hospital first. But because he didn't think she was ready to hear it, he said nothing.

"Hey, man, you want me to call the cops?"

John looked at the bouncer. The man was holding his cell phone in one hand, a smoldering cigarette in the other. "I'll take care of it," John said. "Thanks."

"Sure thing."

John turned his attention back to Julia. She was shaking violently. Her arms. Shoulders. Legs. She wouldn't look at him. He couldn't stand to see her like this. "Honey, I'm going to drive you to the hospital and get you checked out."

She looked at him. "I don't want to go to the hospital."

An alarm went off in his head. Julia was too level-headed to think ignoring her injuries was going to make them go away. His experience as a cop reminded him that many times the victims of sexual assault were the ones who wanted to avoid a trip to the hospital. The thought made him sick.

He took her hand. "Did he . . ." Not wanting to finish, he let the words trail.

She closed her eyes tightly and shook her head. "I thought he was going to . . ." She drew a shaky breath, used it to pull herself together. "He had a crucifix in his hand." Lowering her head, she rubbed at the spot between her eyes. "He tried to . . . He tried to . . ."

The thought made him nauseous. "With the crucifix?"

She nodded. "If I hadn't gotten away, he would have raped me with it. I'm sure of it."

He squeezed her shoulder, then looked at the bouncer. "Did you see anyone in the alley?"

The bouncer shook his head. "If I had, it would be the last time he touched a woman. I don't tolerate that shit."

John handed the man one of his old cards from back when he'd been with the Chicago PD, with the old numbers crossed out and his cell phone number written in. "If you remember anything or see anything, give me a call, will you?"

"You bet."

John turned back to Julia. She was deathly pale. Probably close to going into shock. "Let's get you checked out."

"John—"

"I'll call Mitch on the way." Bending slightly, he reached out to lift her hair to get a better look at the angry red marks on her throat. "What happened here?"

"I'm not sure," she began. "It was . . . strange. I think he had some type of vial in his hand. He splashed me with something. At first I thought it was water. Then it started to burn and I realized it must be some kind of chemical." Her gaze darkened. "He kept calling me a succubus. Quoting things out of context from the Bible."

"Sounds similar to what happened before."

"That's what I thought, too."

"What kinds of things did he quote?"

"I was too scared to make sense of most of it." Her brows snapped together. "He called me a succubus. And he said something about holy water blistering the skin of Satan's followers."

He thought about the burns and shook his head in disgust. "Anything else you can think of?"

"No, but I think once he finished with me, he was going to kill me."

John had never liked hospitals. Ever since he was six years old and had had his tonsils removed, he'd known they were places he would try to avoid at all costs the rest of his life.

Even at one A.M., the emergency room was alive with activity. He guided Julia to the registration desk and hit the bell with his palm. A plump African-American woman looked from Julia to John and handed him a clipboard with a form to fill out. "Don't forget to sign at the bottom. A nurse will be out in a few minutes."

John found a relatively quiet corner in the waiting area and ushered Julia into a chair beside him. Beneath the lights, her complexion was alarmingly pale. He tried not to be obvious about it, but he was more than a little worried.

"Stop looking at me that way."

Realizing he'd been staring, he frowned but held her gaze. "What way?"

"Like you can't make eye contact because all you see when you look at me are the bruises." She stared at him with those wide blue eyes. "I'm not a victim."

"I didn't mean to make you feel that way."

Letting out a sigh, she leaned forward and put her face in her hands. "I didn't mean to snap."

"You're entitled."

She raised her head and looked at him over the tops of her fingers. "I hate that this happened."

"Me, too."

"I feel sick inside. I feel vulnerable and weak and I hate it."

"Julia, you had no control over what happened."

"I know. But that's just it. I had no control. I was totally at his mercy." Another sigh shuddered out of her. "It's the most terrible feeling in the world."

The need to reach out to her was strong, but something stopped him. "Mitch should be here in a few minutes." He paused. "Do you feel up to answering some questions?"

"No, but I'll do whatever it takes for them to catch this creep."

"That's the spirit." He paused. "I should probably call someone from your family and let them know what happened."

"Call Claudia."

Before he could answer, a nurse wearing green scrubs and pushing a wheelchair approached them. "We got an exam room open, so I can take you back now."

Julia winced when she rose, so John took her arm to steady her. "The police are on the way," he said to the nurse.

The woman looked from John to Julia. "Ma'am, were you raped?"

Julia shook her head. "No."

"Okay, honey, that's good." She usurped John's position and offered the chair. "Go ahead and get in the wheelchair and I'll cart you back to an exam room, okay?"

Julia nodded, her expression pained as she eased herself into the chair.

John wanted to stay with her, but wasn't sure if that was what she wanted, so he opted to remain in the waiting area and use the time to make some very difficult calls.

TWENTY-FOUR

Julia lay on the gurney in a wrinkled cotton gown and tried not to think about everything that had happened. Not an easy task considering she hurt all the way to the ends of her hair. She'd spent the last hour submitting to a battery of X-rays, needles and invasive prodding, and all she could think about now was going home.

"Yoo hoo."

She raised her head to see Claudia peek her head around the curtain. She wasn't sure why the sight of her sister brought tears to her eyes, but it did. "Hey," she said.

"Oh, honey." Shaking her head, Claudia approached the bed and took Julia's hand. "I'm so glad you're okay."

"Okay being a relative term," Julia said. "Do I look as bad as I feel?"

"Let's just say you're going to need some extra concealer for a while."

"Just what I wanted to hear." Tears averted, Julia lay back and sighed. "Did John tell you what happened?"

Claudia grimaced, jerked her head. "I'm so sorry you had to go through that."

"Thanks."

"How are you feeling?"

"I feel like I was run over by a truck on the way to the hospital. Twice." Julia sighed.

"Twice, huh?"

"Don't make me smile. It hurts."

"Sorry."

But she did smile, and she was vastly glad she had her younger sister to keep things in perspective.

"Did they give you something for pain?"

"Yeah, but I'm still waiting for it to kick in. No more jokes."

Claudia smiled, but it was brief. "Are they going to admit you?"

Julia raised her hand, inordinately pleased that it wasn't shaking. "Not if I have any say in the matter."

"What did the doc say?"

"If my test results come back okay, I can go home." Taking a deep breath, she asked the question she'd been avoiding. "Has anyone called Dad?"

"John called him after he called me. Dad and Parker are on the way."

Julia closed her eyes. She wasn't sure why, but for some reason she thought it was going to be hard to face her father. Maybe because for so many years she'd pushed so hard for her independence and now he could say "I told you so."

"He was always dead set against my moving into the Quarter," she said.

"He's overprotective," Claudia said.

"Maybe he was right."

Claudia gripped her hand more tightly. "Don't say that. You love the Quarter. You love your shop. Honey, this could have happened no matter where you were living."

"I wish I hadn't written that blasted book."

"Julia, just because some nutcase has taken it upon himself to make your life a living hell doesn't mean you should deprive yourself of something you feel passionately about."

"I don't feel safe in my own home anymore, Claudia. I don't feel safe in the shop. I don't even know how he got in. My God, if I hadn't gotten away, he would have—"

"Honey, you *did* get away. You're safe now, and you're going to be all right."

But for the second time in five minutes Julia had to blink back tears. Feeling restless and annoyed, she shook her head. "Where's John?"

"He and Mitch are in the hall waiting to talk to you." Claudia gave her a small smile. "He's been hovering like a worried mama."

A ray of warmth cut through the cold that had taken up residence inside her, and Julia smiled back.

"Do you feel up to answering some questions?"

Reliving the most terrifying moments of her life was the last thing she wanted to do, but Julia knew she didn't have a choice. She wanted them to find the man responsible, and then she wanted him to pay. "I'm ready."

"That's my big sis." Giving her hand a final squeeze, Claudia leaned close and pressed a kiss to her forehead. "If you need anything, I'll be right outside."

Julia knew it was silly, but she didn't want her sister to leave. "Thanks."

John and Mitch walked into the curtained treatment room the instant Claudia left. Julia worked up a smile, but she could tell by the men's collective expressions that they weren't buying it.

Mitch looked downright grim as he stepped up to the gurney. "How you doing, kid?"

"Doc thinks I'm going to live."

John held his ground at the foot of the bed. "Are they going to admit you?"

"They'll know as soon as the X-rays are back from Radiology."

"Do you feel up to answering a few questions?" Mitch asked.

"If it will help you catch him," she said, letting some of the anger into her voice.

Mitch pulled a pad from his jacket pocket. "Take your time. Start at the beginning. Tell us everything you remember, even if you think it might not be important. Okay?"

She barely recognized her own voice when she started to speak. She began with her leaving the restaurant, walking the Quarter and arriving at the shop. She could feel her heart pounding as she took them through every horrifying moment of the assault. It was extremely difficult, but she spoke candidly, telling them about the stalker tearing her shirt, splashing her with some kind of burning liquid, about him trying to rape her with the crucifix. She relayed the Bible quotes as best she could remember, but she'd been so terrified she wasn't sure she got all the words right.

When she finished, she was shaking so badly she could see the sheets quivering. Sweat slicked her forehead. She tried hard to look unaffected, but there was no way she was pulling it off.

"Did you notice anything about him that might help us identify him?" Mitch asked.

"I couldn't see his face because of the mask."

"Did anything about him look familiar in any way?" John put in. "The way he moved? Tattoos? Birthmarks? Teeth?"

Julia shook her head.

"What about height and weight?" Mitch asked.

"He was shorter than you," Julia said. "Not large, but very strong. I'd guess his weight to be around one hundred seventy pounds."

"Eyes? Hair color?"

A flash of memory jolted her. Murderous eyes staring at her though the slits in the mask. The memory made her shiver. "His eyes are blue. Light blue. I saw them through the mask."

"That's good. You're doing great." Mitch scribbled. "Voice?"

"Guttural. Deep. But I think he was disguising it."

Mitch and John exchanged a look she didn't understand, then Mitch continued. "Did he say anything else?"

Julia shook her head. Her mouth had gone dry. She was starting to feel sleepy.

"I think the painkiller the doc gave her is kicking in," said John.

She risked a look at him to find him standing at the foot of the gurney. His arms were crossed at his chest. His expression was inscrutable, revealing nothing of what he felt. Julia wasn't sure she wanted to know. She hadn't been able to look at him while she'd recounted the details of the attack. She hated feeling so vulnerable. She couldn't bear the thought of him seeing her as a victim.

"Yeah. Okay." Mitch shoved the notepad into his jacket pocket and handed Julia his card. "I'm going to file the report. In the interim, if you remember anything, even if it doesn't seem important, give me a call, okay?"

She nodded. "Sure."

John looked at his brother. "What about the shop? There might be something there."

"CSI is already processing it," Mitch said. "We got the book and letter."

"Let's hope we get some latents." John looked at Julia. "The CSI you talked to said you had tissue beneath your nails. DNA will take a couple of days, but if he's in the system we will identify him."

Julia nodded. The CSI who'd "processed" her was a woman not much older than Claudia. She'd made small talk and done her best to put Julia at ease as she'd swabbed beneath her nails and taken photos of the bruises and burns.

"Let's hope he's in the system," Julia said.

"I'll keep you posted. Take care." Nodding at Julia, Mitch turned and left.

Even through the haze of the painkiller, Julia felt the rise of tension between her and John. She couldn't pinpoint its source. Before either of them could speak, the curtain swished and a young man donning blue scrubs entered the exam area.

"I'm Dr. Rahimi. How are you feeling?"

"Better now that the painkiller has kicked in."

"Excellent." He turned and jammed three films onto the X-ray light on the wall. "You're a very lucky young woman."

Lying there with her body aching, all Julia could think was that she didn't feel very lucky.

He glanced at the chart in his hand. "You have no broken bones. No internal injuries. Lacerations and burns are minor. You do, however, have a mild concussion."

John stepped forward, his expression concerned. "A concussion?"

"Mild," the doctor repeated. "It doesn't warrant my admitting you."

Relief swirled through her. She'd been praying her X-rays would come back all right, because she did not want to spend the night in the hospital.

"Any idea what caused the burns on her throat and abdomen?" John asked.

The doctor nodded solemnly, his eyes going to Julia. "Tissue samples are being analyzed at the lab, but my best guess is that they were caused by acid."

The word struck her like a fist. "Acid?" she repeated dumbly. "My God."

John scrubbed a hand over his face and muttered an obscenity. "Are you sure?"

"We can't be certain without having some residue to test. But I've seen burns caused by skin exposure to hydrochloric acid." The doctor shook his head. "Your burns are very similar."

Julia closed her eyes, wishing her head would stop spinning so she could digest this latest information. Why in the name of God would someone douse her with acid?

"Do you have someone to stay with you tonight?" Dr. Rahimi asked.

"My sister," she said quickly.

"Me," John said simultaneously.

Dr. Rahimi's mouth twitched, then he addressed Julia. "In that case I'll sign your release papers." He looked at

John. "Just make sure she goes straight to bed. I want her to drink plenty of fluids. I'll write a prescription for some painkillers. You will need to wake her at least twice during the night."

"No problem," John said.

The doctor scribbled on the clipboard. "She's been sedated, so you'll need to use the wheelchair. I'll leave her prescription at the window."

"Thank you," Julia said and worked up a smile.

Smiling back, the doctor touched her arm briefly, then ducked past the curtain.

John walked to the bed and looked down at her, his expression taut. "I'm glad you're all right."

"Me, too." A sigh shuddered out of her.

"I'm sorry this happened."

"It's not your fault."

"I was wrong about Vester."

"All of us were wrong about Vester."

"I shouldn't have let you out of my sight."

The curtain surrounding the gurney swished. Julia glanced up to see her father barrel into the examination area. Parker trailed behind him, looking frazzled, his expression telling them he'd have had better luck stopping a train.

"Julia." Benjamin Wainwright's face went sheet white at the sight of his daughter. "Oh, darlin'."

"It looks worse than what it really is," she said quickly.

He rushed to her side, stopped and bent to kiss her gently on the forehead. "Oh, darlin'. You're hurt."

"Dad, I'm okay."

His hand shook when he reached for her. "You're obviously not okay, honey. You're covered with bruises. What on earth happened? John didn't tell me much over the phone. Just that you were attacked in your shop."

Leaving out most of the horrid details, Julia explained how she'd been ambushed.

"Thank God you're all right." Wainwright shook his

head. "Honey, how many times have I told you the Quarter is no place for you to have set up shop? The crime rate there is off the scale. It's no place for a lone woman to run a business."

"Dad, this doesn't have anything to do with the French Quarter or the shop."

The elderly Wainwright plowed on as if he hadn't heard a word she'd said. "Why don't you consider moving the shop to Metairie? Better yet, why don't you consider closing the shop and taking a position with the ministry? You've so much to offer."

Julia stomped on impatience. She loved her father dearly and knew his heart was in the right place. But they'd had this conversation before, always with the same results, and she did not feel up to having it again tonight.

"Dad, we think the man who was stalking me did this," she said.

"*What?*" Wainwright looked like he'd been punched in the nose. "That's impossible. The man who'd been stalking you is in jail."

"Vester isn't the man," John said.

"Isn't the man?" Wainwright repeated.

Before Julia could intervene, her father swung around to face John. His eyes went cold. "You told me you caught the man who'd been stalking her."

John met the older man's eyes steadily. "I was wrong."

"How could you let this happen?"

"I'm sorry."

"Julia could have been killed tonight and you're *sorry*?"

Julia sat up in the bed. "Dad, that's enough. John handled the situation the best way he knew how. Even Mitch and the police thought Vester was the guy."

But none of those things seemed to matter to her father; once he made up his mind about something it was impossible to change. He swung anger-bright eyes on John. "I asked you to keep her safe and what do you do? You nab the first suspect you find and wash your hands of it because you're too busy drowning your sorrows in alcohol. How would you have felt if this maniac had succeeded and killed her?"

John had been raked over the coals too many times to count in his lifetime. He'd developed a thick skin. But it wasn't thick enough to keep cruel images from creeping into his head, and he was brutally reminded that Julia wasn't the only person who'd been hurt because of him. She was the lucky one; she'd survived. Franklin Watts had not.

John couldn't defend what he'd done—or what he hadn't done in this case—so he remained silent while the older man dressed him down.

"I knew you were going through a rough time, but I didn't think it was so rough that it would affect your ability to keep her safe."

"Dad, Nicholas Vester fit the profile," Julia said.

"Stop defending him," Wainwright snapped to his daughter. "You're not thinking straight."

Anger whipped through Julia. "I'm thinking quite clearly."

But her father had already turned his attention back to John and lowered his voice. "I'm sorry, John, but I'm not willing to risk my daughter's life on the chance you'll come around. I think all of us would be better off if I found someone else to look after Julia."

The words shouldn't have shocked him, but they did. The humiliation that followed burned. But John couldn't dispute the man's logic. He should have stayed with Julia even after Vester was taken into custody.

"Dad!" Julia cried.

John raised a hand. "It's okay." But he didn't take his eyes off of Wainwright. "He's right."

He could feel Julia's eyes on him. He could feel the anger and disappointment coming off Benjamin Wainwright in hot, undulating waves. He could feel the shame pressing down on him with the weight of a thousand tons of earth.

He wanted to say something, but there were no words

left inside him. There was no defense for what he'd done, for what he hadn't done. As much as he hated to admit it, he'd failed Julia. He'd failed all of them.

He'd failed himself.

"I'm sorry," he said, then turned and walked away without looking back.

TWENTY-FIVE

There had been plenty of times in the past twenty-nine years when Julia had been angry with her father. But she had never been so angry as she was tonight.

The look on John's face when her father fired him had been like a bayonet run through her heart. For the first time since she'd known him he hadn't had a smart-assed reply ready on the tip of his tongue. He'd stood there, stoic and silent, his expression inscrutable. But she'd seen the pain and humiliation in his eyes. Emotions so powerful he hadn't been able to hide them. It had killed her when he'd simply apologized then turned and walked away.

"You had no right to do that," she said.

Benjamin Wainwright turned to her. "I had every right. I hired him. I can fire him."

"He didn't deserve that."

"You didn't deserve to be assaulted tonight!" he shouted.

Until this moment Julia hadn't realized just how upset her father was. The intellectual side of her knew he was reacting to the fear of her being hurt, because he loved her.

But the more emotional side of her couldn't sit by and let her father berate John when he'd done exactly what any cop would have done.

"Dad, John isn't the only one who thought the stalker had been caught. So did you. So did Mitch."

"I don't care. It was John's responsibility to keep you safe. He accepted that responsibility. He didn't deliver." The elder Wainwright shook his head. "For God's sake, he's probably on his way to some bar to drown his sorrows."

"Dad, he's dealing with a heavy load. He accidentally killed a man two months ago. Where's your compassion?"

"My compassion lies first with my family." His eyes narrowed. "You know, Julia, this isn't the first time I've gotten the impression there's more going on between you and John than you're saying."

"I'm twenty-nine years old, Dad. My private life is none of your concern." Despite the words, a hot blush heated her cheeks.

Her father pretended not to notice. "You are my daughter. Every facet of your life is my concern." He huffed. "You can stay in the guest room at the mansion tonight."

"That's not going to happen." Flinging the sheet aside, Julia sat up, wishing immediately she'd passed on the painkiller.

"Where do you think you're going?"

She turned away and looked at him over her shoulder. He'd stopped midway to the gurney, his expression part concern, part indignation. "I'm going to find John," she said.

"Honey, no. You need to rest. Come home where you'll be safe."

"You should have thought of all those things before you fired him." She pulled the sheet around her hips. "Now, if you'll please leave, I'd like to get dressed."

"Julia, honey, I wish you'd rethink this."

"Send Claudia in on your way out."

"Julia . . ."

When she ignored him, he finally turned and left the room.

* * *

"We're going to John's house."

"What?" Claudia looked away from her driving, her expression alarmed. "Just how many of those painkillers did the doctor give you?"

"Not enough to make me believe Dad did the right thing by firing him."

"Julia, it's one o'clock in the morning. You're exhausted and medicated. I need to get you to the house, where you can get some rest."

"I'm not staying with Dad."

"What? Honey, Dad's expecting you." Claudia jabbed a finger at the headlights behind them. "In case you've forgotten, so is Mitch."

Julia pressed her lips together. Benjamin Wainwright had asked Mitch to escort her and Claudia back to his Garden District mansion. "Dad is a control freak and I've had all I can take."

Claudia cut her a sideways look. "Please tell me you didn't have a fight."

"He shouldn't have fired John."

"I agree he could have been a little more diplomatic, but can't you deal with it tomorrow?"

"You didn't see John's face. He blames himself for what happened to me. The same way he blames himself for what happened to that cop in Chicago. He's got this guilt thing going on and it's eating him alive."

Spotting her sister's cell phone in the black bag next to the seat, she picked it up and punched in the number from Mitch's card.

"What are you doing?" Claudia asked.

Mitch picked up on the first ring with a curt utterance of his name. "Take us to John's house," Julia said.

A beat of thoughtful silence, then, "Julia, your father asked me to escort you to his house."

"My father had no right to fire him."

"John's a big boy. He can handle it."

"Cut out the macho bull," she snapped. "He's in trouble and you know it."

Another long beat of silence. "You sure you want to do that?"

"If I wasn't sure, I wouldn't be calling."

A sigh hissed over the line. "Okay. Have Claudia pull over and I'll take the lead. John lives on the other side of the Quarter." He paused. "You might want to call him and give him a heads-up that you're coming."

Julia knew Mitch was concerned that John had already picked up a bottle. That he was home alone and drowning his sorrows. Just like her father had insinuated.

"You know if I call him he'll only try to talk me out of this," she said.

"And that would be the first thing he's done right in days."

"He didn't deserve what happened. I want to make it right."

"Let's just hope he appreciates the effort," Mitch said and disconnected.

John didn't waste any time breaking the seal. He knew at some point he was going to have to end his jaunt down the superhighway of self-destruction. That wasn't going to happen tonight.

He felt like a fool. Worse, he felt like a failure. Not only as a cop, but as a man. Benjamin Wainwright had hired him to keep Julia safe. As in so many other areas of his life in the past few weeks, John had fallen short.

He poured four fingers of gin into a tumbler and took a long, dangerous pull. The alcohol burned all the way to his stomach, so he took another drink. Fighting fire with fire. John knew it wouldn't work, but the knowledge didn't keep him from finishing the glass and pouring again.

He tried not to think about Julia witnessing the entire humiliating scene. He couldn't imagine what she thought of him. He shouldn't care. Didn't want to care.

But he did.

That was when he realized his being fired was only part of the reason for his despondency. The real reason was a hell of a lot more disturbing. He missed her. He wanted to be with her. To be perfectly honest he wanted a hell of a lot more than that. The admission shouldn't have shocked him, but it did. Of all the times in his life to get tangled up with a woman, why did it have to be now, when he was so totally unraveled?

The laugh that followed was as bitter as the irony. He looked down at the glass in his hand, swirled the clear liquid, then drained it. He had enough problems to deal with without having to contend with a hard-on for a woman he could not have.

A knock on the door jerked him from his reverie. Mitch. Or maybe Wainwright stopping by to give him the name of some counselor.

"Fuck that," he growled and started for the door.

He swung open the door without checking the peephole. Shock rippled through him at the sight of Julia. She was standing in the hall in baggy sweatshirt and faded jeans. Her hair brushed the tops of her slender shoulders like a curtain of silk. She looked beautiful and vulnerable and sexy at once.

The sight of the bruises took him aback. He hated it that someone had done that to her. That he hadn't been there to protect her. Better to end this now . . .

"If you're here to apologize for your father," he began, "don't bother."

"I'm here to see you." Her gaze met his. "Can I come in?"

John's heart began to pound, but he didn't move. "I don't think that's a very good idea."

Her gaze flicked down to the glass in his hand. "You didn't waste any time."

"I'm an expeditious kind of guy. What can I say?" But there was a very big part of him that wanted to take her into his arms and kiss her until they were both mindless. It was the one thing he couldn't allow. Another encounter like the one in the storage room and no doubt the situation would get out of hand. He respected her too much to let things go any farther.

"Who was stupid enough to drive you here?" he asked.

Her mouth tightened. "I asked Claudia to drive me here."

"I guess that means Mitch was stupid enough to give you my address."

Julia said nothing.

"What the hell are you doing driving around when you should be home and in bed?" He gestured toward her. "Look at you. You're bruised and exhausted. Not to mention there's some sick son of a bitch out there who wants to finish what he started. Julia, what the hell are you thinking?"

"I wanted to see you." She bit her lip, looked away. "Set things straight."

"One of us has things straight, and it's not you."

She reacted as if he'd jabbed her with something sharp. "I came over here to rehire you."

John couldn't help it. He laughed. "That's rich." But he could see by the look on her face that she was serious.

"I mean it," she said. "After tonight I am very much concerned about my safety. My father was wrong to fire you. I'd like to hire you back."

Looking at her, it would have been easy to say yes. Invite her inside. Close the door. He'd have bet he could get her into bed. He knew it would be good. Better than good. Things had been heating up between them for quite some time. John knew an encounter would blow his mind.

But he couldn't do that to her. Hell, he couldn't do it to himself. He knew that once he got a taste he would only want more. It would be better, simpler, to fuck this up now instead of waiting until one or both of them invested any more emotions into whatever the hell it was happening between them.

"I'm not interested," he said after a moment.

"Or maybe you're afraid you might have to start living your life again."

"That's bullshit."

"Is it?"

"You're wasting your time here, Julia."

Her eyes flicked to the glass in his hand. "One of us is wasting time and it's not me."

"In case you haven't noticed, I'm in no shape to be taking on any kind of job." He motioned dumbly at the bruises on her face. God, he hated seeing them. "It's not like I did a stellar job of it."

"You thought it was Vester. So did everyone else."

"This isn't about Vester, damn it. It's about me. My state of mind. My lack of focus. It's about . . ."

What I did.

John stopped short of saying the words. But he could tell from the look in her eyes that she'd heard them. That she understood. That she wasn't going to let this go no matter how badly he wanted her to.

"For God's sake, Julia, I can't even take care of myself," he said after a moment. "I can't do this."

"Can't? Or won't?"

"Take your pick."

"Maybe that's because you're too busy blaming yourself for something you had no control over."

He laughed, but it was a bitter, incredulous sound. "I killed a man, goddamn it. I forgot my training and I fucking panicked. I overreacted. I pulled the trigger when I shouldn't have and killed a cop. A thirty-eight-year-old guy with a wife and kids. I turned a young woman into a widow. I left two kids without a father. If all of that isn't my fault, then who the hell's fault is it?"

The door to the apartment across the hall opened. A short man with a belly the size of a Volkswagen stepped out and glared at Julia. "You want to keep it down, toots? We're trying to sleep in here."

Eyeing the man with open hostility, John reached for Julia, tugged her inside and slammed the door behind her. "I'm going to call Mitch and have him take you home," he snapped.

"I'm not leaving." She spun toward him, put her hands

on her hips. "John, you put anyone in the same situation as what you were in that night and they might have reacted the same way."

"You don't know that. You weren't there."

"The department cleared you of wrongdoing."

"Yeah, well, they're covering their own ass because they don't want a civil suit eating up the budget."

"Can't you take anything at face value?" she shot back.

"I know how the world works, Julia."

"And I know what kind of man you are. I know how much you care."

"I don't want to hear this."

"Too bad because I'm not finished." Stepping close, she jabbed her finger in his chest hard enough to drive him back a step. "You're running away. From life. From me. All because you feel you don't deserve to be happy."

Suddenly furious, he stepped toward her and rapped his fist against his chest. "This isn't about my happiness, goddamn it."

"You're letting the guilt over a terrible accident ruin your life."

"I'm accepting responsibility for what I did."

"That's way too noble for what you're doing." She motioned toward the bottle of booze on the table. "You're letting it destroy you."

"I can't even pick up my own goddamn gun!" he shouted. "I haven't been able to touch the fucking thing since that night. How's that for fucking capability!"

The words shocked both of them to silence. He hadn't meant to say it. But now that his deep, dark secret was out, he was going to have to deal with it. He sure as hell couldn't take it back.

He told himself he didn't care what she thought of him. Things would be better for everyone involved if she knew the truth. That she was dealing with a head case.

"I'm calling Mitch to take you home." Turning away from her, he strode toward the kitchen, where an old rotary phone hung on the wall.

"John, don't . . ."

He didn't look at her as he started to dial.

Temper flared when she crossed to him and depressed the plunger with her forefinger. "We're not finished."

John wasn't exactly sure what happened next. One moment he was furious and determined to get her the hell out of there. The next she was standing so close he could smell the sweet scent of her hair.

The hot rise of lust stunned him. Shook him. He knew touching her now would make the situation infinitely worse. But in some small corner of his mind he knew being with her just one time would be worth the price he would pay later when he walked away.

Holding that thought, he wrapped his fingers around both her biceps and lowered his mouth to hers.

TWENTY-SIX

A kiss was the last thing Julia expected, especially from John in his current frame of mind. She knew he was kissing for her all the wrong reasons. Because he was angry and frustrated and didn't want to deal with her—on an intellectual level, anyway. Not a good reason to let a man kiss you. But the instant his mouth made contact with hers, she forgot all about inappropriate motivations and sank into the kiss.

He tasted of gin and male heat, laced with a thin layer of a desperation she didn't understand. There were no pretences with John. It was just him and her and the moment, with nothing between them except white hot fire.

The kiss was primal and raw, without the finesse a more pretentious man might have shown. But for the first time in her life, Julia didn't want finesse. She wanted John's mouth on hers. She wanted his hands on her breasts. She wanted his body inside hers.

Never taking his mouth from hers, he backed her toward the wall. Vaguely, Julia was aware that she was losing ground, that he was overwhelming her, both physically and psychologically. She tried to hold her ground, but he was too strong, too intense.

She gasped when her back made contact with the wall, but he didn't give her a respite. Grasping her hands in his, he slowly slid them above her head. All the while he kissed her. Hot, wet kisses that turned her blood to fire. She could feel the arousal coursing through her body. Her breasts swelled within the confines of her bra. Wet heat pulsed between her legs.

Julia had always prided herself on being levelheaded. She liked being in control. But when John pulled back and looked at her with heavy-lidded eyes, she knew the situation was about to explode into chaos.

"This is not going to help." His gaze was level and intense on hers. His chiseled mouth was wet, his jaw taut. "Damn it, Julia, this is wrong."

"This isn't about right or wrong," she whispered. "It's about us."

He blinked as if the words had shocked him. A dozen emotions she didn't understand scrolled in his eyes. She felt his restraint break as if it were a physical barrier between them. She cried out when he came against her. She could feel the steel rod of his erection against her belly. At some point he had begun to tremble. She could feel those same tremors ripping through her own body.

Vaguely, she was aware of his hands sliding down her body. Grasping the hem of her sweatshirt, he worked it up and over her head. Her hair brushed her bare shoulders. Chill air swept over her heated flesh. Wearing only her bra and jeans now, she could feel his eyes on her skin. She could see the male admiration in his expression.

All thoughts left her head when he raised his hand to the clasp between her breasts. One flick of his fingers and the tiny scrap of lace fell open. With a tenderness he hadn't shown seconds before, he gently tugged the straps from her shoulders. Julia shivered when the cups fell away. Anticipation was like fire in her blood. She could hear herself breathing hard. The blood roaring in her ears like a thousand jet engines.

Bending slightly, John kissed her neck then trailed his tongue over the tops of her breasts. Every nerve ending in her body zinged when he took her nipple into his mouth. Gasping, she arched her back, giving him full access. She cried out when he raked his teeth over her. Arousal turned sharp-edged and urgent. She felt herself go wet between her legs, the heat pounding with every wild beat of her heart.

He suckled her until she was insane with the need to feel him inside her. It was as if her body had been doused with gasoline and ignited. She writhed against the wall as he licked and sucked and drove her to near madness.

Julia had taken only two lovers in her life. Men she had cared deeply for. But neither of those men had even come close to making her feel the things that John was making her feel now. They'd never made her lose control.

Desperate for his touch, she unfastened the button of her jeans. Her hands were shaking so badly she could barely lower the zipper, but eventually she managed.

"Touch me," she whispered.

Raising his head from her breast, he made eye contact. Within the depths of his gaze she saw the deep well of emotion and a vulnerability he did his best to hide.

"You were hurt tonight," he said in a gruff voice. "We shouldn't be doing this."

"I'm bruised, not dead."

A smile curved his mouth. "You keep surprising me."

She tried to smile, but there was too much tension running through her body. Her heart was beating too fast, her breaths rushing in and out between clenched teeth. "I keep surprising myself."

He kissed the tip of her nose. "I like surprises."

"So do I."

He kissed her mouth then, driving his tongue deeply into her. Julia returned the kiss in kind, wondering how she was going to survive this encounter when she couldn't seem to catch her breath. Her attention went south when she felt him tugging her jeans and panties down and over her hips. Quickly, she stepped out of them and kicked them away.

A shudder moved through her when John knelt in front of her. She felt his mouth on her stomach, just below her navel, and her knees went weak. All the blood rushed from her head when he kissed the crisp curls at her vee. Then he opened her and her legs nearly buckled.

Wave after wave of sensation swamped her. She heard herself cry out when he slicked his tongue over her. Setting her hand against the back of his head, she moved against him. She knew it was wanton; she'd never done anything like this in her life. But her trust was complete.

He flicked his tongue over the most sensitive and private part of her body. Julia cried out his name. Once. Twice. Pleasure warred with the need to protect herself, but the pleasure won. It built inside her, as violent and powerful as any storm.

"Come for me," he whispered against her.

Her mind could barely process the words. There was too much sensation coming too quickly for her mind to absorb. He stroked her, harder and faster. The storm inside her broke with a violence that shocked her system. Pleasure wrenched a scream from her. The orgasm crashed over her like a storm surge. Her vision blurred. Stars exploded behind her lids. She could feel her body moving against his mouth. Heat and intensity burning her from the inside out. It was too much, but not enough.

When she opened her eyes, John was looking at her with an intensity that took her breath away. She was still breathing hard. Her body trembled violently. Heat pulsed between her legs with every hard thrust of her heart.

"I didn't know it could be that way," she said.

He brushed the hair back from her face. "I think they call it chemistry."

"Or a nuclear blast."

Julia smiled when he swept her into his arms. She laid her head against his shoulder as he carried her through the living room, down the hall and into the bedroom. She caught a glimpse of an old-fashioned iron bed, unmade. Dark, heavy furniture. Windows with the blinds pulled.

He laid her on the sheets, then stepped back. Never taking his eyes from hers, he pulled the shirt over his head and threw it aside. His chest was as wide and hard as an oak tree. He was broad in the shoulders and lean of hip. His limbs curved with muscle, but they were not overdeveloped.

Julia's heart pounded hard when his fingers went to his belt. He unbuckled it, unzipped his fly and tugged the jeans down. She caught a glimpse of white boxer shorts over lean hips. An abdomen covered with a thin layer of black hair. Her breath jammed her throat when he hooked his thumbs into the waistband of the boxers and eased them down.

Her cheeks heated at the sight of his jutting sex. His size intimidated her, made her feel like perhaps she was in over her head. John Merrick was not the least bit shy, and the sight of his body thrilled her in a way she'd never been thrilled.

"Come here," he whispered.

All the breath rushed from her lungs when he put his knees on the bed and started toward her. She walked on her knees to him. Then they were belly to belly. She could feel the sensitive tips of her breasts brushing against the hairs on his chest. The tip of his penis against her belly. Taking her hand in his, he set her palm against his shaft.

His jaw went taut when she wrapped her fingers around him. The breath rushed between his teeth when she began to caress. His eyes glazed when she leaned forward and ran her tongue over his flat male nipples. A surge of feminine power washed over her when he groaned. It excited her knowing she could do this to him.

Bending, she kissed him lower, leaving a wet trail from his chest to his hip. She could feel his penis against her breasts. She moved toward him, ran her tongue over the tip. He was slick with his own moisture.

His body jerked when she took him into her mouth.

"Aw, God," he ground out.

His shaft was like steel, the head like velvet. He set his hands on her shoulders as if to restrain her, but Julia didn't stop. She'd never taken a man into her mouth, never had the desire to do so. But with John everything was different. She wanted to give him pleasure. She wanted to ease his pain, remind him that life was worth living. She wanted to show him how much she cared.

He growled when she took him into her throat. His hips moved and he began to gently slide in and out of her mouth. Once. Twice.

"Stop."

Before she could, he pulled away. In a single, smooth motion he grasped her arms and eased her onto her back. "I've got to get inside you before I explode," he whispered.

His arms shook as he poised himself over her. Her heart raged as she opened to him. She could feel her entire body trembling. Then, surprising her, he lowered himself to her, took her face between his hands and looked into her eyes.

"No matter what happens, I want you to know I'll never forget this moment."

No matter what happens?

Julia had barely gotten her mind around the words when he pushed into her. Though her body was ready, an instant of pain made her wince. But John didn't stop. Never breaking eye contact, he went in deep, until she was filled all the way to her womb. The mix of pleasure and pain took her breath.

Before she could catch her breath, he braced his hands on either side of her and began to move. Her thoughts scattered as he pumped in and out of her with long, slow strokes. Suddenly Julia wanted him to know just how much this moment meant to her, but her body was so overcome with sensation her mind couldn't form a single coherent thought.

The tempo of his strokes increased. She looked into John's eyes. His gaze was unshuttered. She saw strength tempered with vulnerability. Emotional pain mingling with physical pleasure. The wounds of his past tearing down his hope for the future. A future she very much wanted to be part of.

She wanted to heal him, wanted to love him. She raised her hand. He winced when she touched the side of his face. "I love you," she whispered.

For an instant he looked taken aback. Then he closed his eyes, shutting her out. That he would do that at a time like this tore a hole right through her heart. She knew she should stop. But the physical sensation overrode her intellect. The tempo of his strokes increased. The pleasure came in blinding, crashing waves. She raised her hips to meet him, taking him all the way to her core.

Her control broke with an audible snap inside her head. The climax wrenched a scream from her and seemed to go on forever. But John didn't give her a respite. He drove into her until the floodwaters rose a second time. Still weak from her previous orgasm, Julia could do nothing but hold on. The crest came quickly and with bone-shattering force. Vaguely, she was aware of John calling out her name. Of his body going rigid against hers. His body pulsing and hot inside hers.

Julia closed her eyes and rode out the storm.

John lay in the semidarkness and tried hard not to think about what he'd done. He should have felt like a million bucks lying next to a beautiful woman after having the most mind-blowing sex he'd ever had in his life.

Instead he felt like hell.

He felt like hell because there was still a part of him that was decent enough to know this was going to hurt the one person he cared for most. Julia.

She was decent and kind, with a heart as big as Lake Pontchartrain. John wasn't even sure he *had* a heart anymore. He had nothing left to give. He knew if he forged a relationship with her it would end badly. She would end up hating him, and that was the one thing he simply couldn't handle.

But he'd slept with her anyway. He'd taken advantage of her big heart and hauled her to his bed for a few minutes of physical satisfaction. What the hell kind of a man did that make him?

A son of a bitch, a cruel little voice answered.

He ached as he lay on his back and stared at the ceiling. Next to him Julia slept. He could have taken comfort in the warmth of her body against his, but he didn't. He was in too deep for any of this to be comfortable. Evidently, she was in too deep, too.

I love you.

Her words echoed inside his head like the retort of a killing shot. He told himself she'd just been caught up in the moment. But he knew Julia wasn't the kind of woman who slept with someone just because it felt good.

How could he have let things go this far?

But John knew why, and the answer terrified him. He'd let things go this far because he hadn't been able to keep his own emotions out of it. If the irony hadn't been so bitter, he might have laughed. He'd never been in love before, so he didn't have a point of reference from which to measure. But the emotional turmoil inside him was off the scale.

Somehow, he'd fallen in love with her. She was the one bright light in a life that was as black as the darkest of nights. He didn't have the slightest idea how to handle it. He couldn't pursue it. All he could do was let her go and hope she didn't hate him for it.

"If facial expressions could speak, I'd be getting an earful right now."

John actually jolted at the sound of her voice.

Holding the sheet to her breast, she rose onto one elbow and set her hand against his cheek. "My God, John, you're trembling."

"I'm fine," he snapped.

"You're not."

Annoyed and embarrassed by her concern, he shoved her hand away and sat up. "I said I'm fine."

She went silent beside him and he felt like a jerk. Jesus, this was exactly what he didn't want to happen. He didn't want to lash out at her, but that's what he did best. That's what he did to the people he cared about.

Sighing, he scraped a hand over his face and turned to her. "Julia . . ."

"It's okay." She started to rise, but he stopped her by grasping her arm.

"Don't go."

She looked back at him then. The hurt he saw in her eyes devastated him. For no good reason he'd hurt this lovely woman who'd just given him so much. She'd made him feel human again. Made him feel like a man. He couldn't imagine why, but she cared for him. She wanted to be with him. And all he could do was push her away . . .

Relief slipped through him when she relaxed back into the sheets. "Why do you do that?" she asked.

"You mean act like a jerk?"

"I mean push people away."

"Because it's easier than getting too close, and a hell of a lot less risky."

"John, I think it's a little more complicated than that."

He didn't want to have his psyche sliced and diced by a woman who meant more to him than he'd ever imagined possible. He didn't want her to look inside him or get inside his head. Maybe he was afraid of what she might find if she looked too hard.

"If you're looking for something in return, you're looking in the wrong place. I don't have anything to give back." He turned to her, looked into her eyes. "I don't have anything left."

"I don't believe that." She raised her hand.

He winced when she brushed his cheek with her fingertips. "I don't want to hurt you," he said.

"Then don't."

Panic swirled uneasily in his gut. She wasn't making

this easy. She was saying all the things he didn't want to hear. She was too close. Too kind and beautiful and giving. They'd just made love, but already he was aroused again and aching for her. He wanted to believe this was all about sex, but he knew it wasn't. The truth of that was scaring the hell out of him.

"I'm not the kind of man you want to care about," he ground out.

"Too late," she whispered.

He stared at her, too shaken to react. The need twisted inside him. But the need to protect himself—to protect *her*—outweighed the physical. John reacted the only way he could.

Throwing off the sheet, he swung his legs over the side of the bed. Without looking at her, he reached for his jeans and jammed his legs into them.

Julia sat up, her eyes large and wary. "What are you doing?"

"I've got to make some calls."

"It's almost four A.M."

He didn't even spare her a glance as he started for the door. "Go to sleep."

"John—"

He reached the door and turned to her. "Don't."

"Why are you doing this?"

"Because I'm a son of a bitch. Better you learn that now than later."

Pulling the sheet around her, she rose. He stiffened when she crossed to him. "You're running."

"In case you haven't noticed, I'm good at that, too."

"That is such a cop-out."

"Call it whatever you want."

"John, you're one of the most courageous people I've ever known," she said. "For twelve years you put your life on the line."

"So do tens of thousands of other cops every single day," he snapped. "I'm no different. I'm sure as hell no hero."

She continued as if she hadn't heard him. "You can walk into a dark warehouse and face drug runners and murderers and God only knows what else. But when it comes to facing the one woman who loves you, you turn tail and run."

The fury that swept through him was so powerful that for a moment he was dizzy with it. He would never physically hurt a woman. Never Julia. But he was not above hurting her emotionally.

Grasping her arm, he spun her toward him. He caught a glimpse of wide eyes, her mouth parted in surprise. Before he could stop himself he ripped the sheet from her grasp and flung it to the floor. She gasped when he yanked her against him and crushed his mouth to hers.

Her body went rigid against his. He tasted shock and the bitter taste of his own shame. Need tangled with the knowledge that he was screwing this up. But he could not let this go any further.

A sound escaped her as she set her hands against his chest and shoved. For an instant he held her against him. He slid his tongue along her teeth, but she refused him entry. He told himself that was what he wanted. Go ahead, the little voice taunted. Scare her away. Disgust her. That's what you want, isn't it?

He released her with a tad too much force. She stumbled back. He told himself it didn't hurt to see the hurt, the accusation in her eyes. But John was getting good at lying to himself, and he didn't let himself analyze it any more deeply than that.

"I know what you're trying to do." Bending, she snagged the sheet from the floor and clutched it to her breast.

"Yeah?" He looked her up and down. "What's that?"

"Push me away so you don't have to deal with your feelings."

"The only feeling I have for you right now is lust," he said.

"Coward."

"Drop that sheet and I'll show you just how much of a coward I am, Julia."

In a subconscious gesture, her knuckles tightened on the sheet. "I'm not going to let you do this."

She spun away from him and began gathering her clothes from the floor. John stood his ground, his heart pounding, and swore he wasn't going to stop her.

This is what you wanted, hotshot. She's leaving. She won't be back. Now you can wallow in the muck your pathetic life has become and not worry about anyone but yourself.

"I'll drive you to your father's," he said.

"Go to hell." Glaring at him over her shoulder, she walked into the bathroom.

"You're not leaving alone, Julia." John was midway there when she slammed the door in his face.

Julia's hands shook as she quickly washed up and stepped into her clothes. She avoided the mirror as she ran a brush through her hair with a shaking hand. But it wasn't the bruises on her body that were hurting now. She remembered the words she'd uttered while in the throes of lovemaking. She knew those words were plastered all over her face.

I love you.

She closed her eyes against the pain. She'd never been in love before. Why now? Why John? How could her timing be so bad? She knew he would hurt her before all was said and done. But the fact of the matter was he'd already hurt her. All she could do now was salvage as much of her self-respect as she could and get out before she fell apart.

For a full minute she stood facing the door, trying to gather enough courage to step out. The man outside that door was not the same man who'd made love to her so passionately just scant minutes before. She didn't fully understand the motivations for his transformation. All she knew was that he'd purposefully been cruel to her, and she needed to get away from him. She'd figure out the rest later, when her head was clear. When her body wasn't humming with the aftermath of his touch.

Taking a deep breath, she opened the door. John looked up from where he stood at the bar, a tumbler in his hand. He'd put on his shirt, boots and bomber jacket.

"I'm going home." Snagging her purse from the kitchen table, she started for the door.

"You're not going anywhere alone," he said.

She didn't even pause. Just as she reached for the knob, he touched her arm. Furious that he would touch her after all that had been said, Julia spun. Her hand shot out to slap his face. But he was faster and grabbed her wrist.

For an instant, she stared into his eyes, trying to decipher what she saw. For the life of her, she couldn't.

"I'll drive you home," he said.

The urge to argue was strong. But Julia was exhausted and overwrought. She longed for the privacy of her little apartment over the shop, but knew she couldn't return there. Her father kept a room for her at his Garden District mansion. She had the overnight bag Claudia had packed. It was enough to get her through the night.

"If you don't want me to drive you, I'll call Mitch." His jaw flexed. "But you can't leave alone."

"I'd rather not drag Mitch into this," she said as coolly as she could manage.

Grimacing, he released her wrist, crossed to the door and opened it. "Let's go."

Julia walked out without looking back.

Twenty-seven

*Two days had passed since the ugly scene in John's apart-*ment, but it seemed like an eternity since he'd last seen her. He hated knowing he'd hurt her. Hated even more missing her so much some nights he wasn't sure he was going to make it through. He'd picked up the phone a dozen times in the last forty-eight hours.

He never made the call.

His heart jumped every time his cell phone rang. He couldn't stop thinking about her. Couldn't keep his mind from replaying the hurtful scene that had transpired between them. On an intellectual level, he knew she was better off without him. But on a more primal, selfish level, he didn't give a damn about right and wrong. He wanted her. He wanted to hear her voice. The music of her laughter. He wanted to feel her body next to his every night from here to eternity.

Goddamn it, why did things have to be so complicated?

John hadn't slept. He ate, but didn't taste the food. He drank, but only enough to take the sharp edge off the crushing pain in his chest. Not even alcohol could make him that numb.

The one thing he had been able to do was work the case, which he'd done like a man possessed. He'd kept in close contact with Mitch. He'd called Benjamin Wainwright several times, but the old man didn't return his calls. John didn't blame him.

Sitting at the kitchen table in his tiny apartment, he stared down at the copies of the letters spread out before him and read the chilling words for the hundredth time. *Yet each man kills the thing he loves.* To his right lay a legal pad upon which he'd written a list of suspects. He knew that many times the stalking victim knew the stalker, and so he'd started with the people Julia knew. Rory Beauchamp, Claudia's strange boyfriend. Jacob Brooks, her part-time clerk. Parker Bradley, Benjamin Wainwright's assistant. Skip Stockton, her scorned date. Even her sister, Claudia.

He'd run background checks on every name he could come up with, friends and family and acquaintances. All had come back squeaky clean. Although that didn't necessarily mean they were.

Out of desperation—and unbeknownst to anyone—he'd also run a background check on the Wainwright patriarch. Maybe the old man knew about Julia's book. Maybe he wanted her to stop writing without having to confront her. Maybe he'd hired someone to frighten her.

But John didn't buy it. He'd known Wainwright since he was a teenager, and even though the old man could be controlling, this wasn't his style. He could see the old man sending a few harmless letters for what he perceived to be the greater good, but he couldn't see him resorting to violence.

But if not someone she knew, then who? A stranger? A fan? A customer from the shop? A neighbor?

John closed his eyes and rubbed them. A glance at the clock above the stove told him it was after ten P.M. He'd been looking at the same scant evidence for almost two hours and he wasn't any farther along than when he'd started.

He thought about Julia and wondered what she was doing. He wondered if she missed him. Wondered if she would speak to him if he called . . .

"She's way too smart for that, buddy," he muttered.

His voice sounded strange in the silence of his apartment. The best he could hope for was that someday she would realize he'd done what he had to protect her. Because she deserved better. His life was a fucked-up mess. Not only was his career over, but he now had the civil suit to contend with. Best case scenario, it would financially devastate him. The last thing he wanted to do was drag her down with him.

It was the thousandth time he'd found himself thinking about her. The thousandth time he'd arrived at the same conclusion. He had to let her go. But dear God it hurt to think of never seeing her again.

Rising, he crossed to the counter and picked up the bottle of gin. He expertly twisted it open and proceeded to pour. Just a little to kill the pain, he told himself. Yeah. Right.

He'd just taken that first, dangerous sip when his doorbell rang. Odd for him to have a visitor anytime. Even odder at ten o'clock at night. Setting down the glass, he crossed to the door, checked the peephole. Surprise rippled through him at the sight of Parker Bradley standing on the porch looking like he'd rather be anywhere but there. Benjamin Wainwright was conspicuously absent.

John opened the door. "You lost or what?"

"No." The other man looked uncomfortable. "May I come in?"

John stepped aside. "Get you a drink?"

Bradley entered and shook his head. "I don't drink."

"What a surprise." John didn't miss the other man's quick perusal of his living quarters. If he hadn't been so damn depressed he might have smiled at the look of distaste on Bradley's face.

"Mr. Wainwright wanted me to deliver this in person," Bradley said.

"Why didn't he deliver it himself?"

"He would have, of course, but he had a meeting in Baton Rouge tonight." He glanced at his watch. "I'll be joining him there as soon as I finish up here."

"Well then by all means finish up."

Bradley actually flushed as he handed him the envelope. "For what it's worth, I tried to talk him out of it," he said. "For Julia's sake. For some reason unbeknownst to anyone, she cares about you."

John already knew what was inside the envelope. He opened it and looked at the check inside. Eight hundred and ninety-two dollars.

"That's final payment for your services."

Final payment. John did laugh then, but it was a bitter sound. "You can tell him to keep his check." He shoved both the envelope and check at Parker.

"Take it." Bradley raised his hands. "I'm sorry, man."

Shaking his head, John tossed the envelope onto the counter. Bradley started for the door, but John stopped him. "Has Mr. Wainwright hired someone to keep an eye on her?"

Bradley stopped and turned. "He hired a private detective."

John nodded. Now that Julia's safety was out of his hands, he should have been relieved. But he wasn't.

"How's she doing?"

He hadn't meant to ask. But he had to know. He met the other man's gaze. He saw knowledge and a damning amount of sympathy in them.

"She's doing well," the other man said. "Still bruised, but she's definitely on the mend."

"She open the shop?"

"Not yet."

"She still staying with her father?"

"Yes."

"Good," he said. But deep inside all he could think was there was nothing good about any of this.

He wanted to know more. He wanted to know how she was doing emotionally. He wanted to know about her frame of mind. What she was thinking. He wanted to know if she missed him as viciously as he missed her . . .

"I've got to go." Bradley started for the door.

John watched him leave, then walked to the bar, picked up the bottle of gin and took a long pull straight from it.

Julia stared at the blank screen of her laptop, but the words refused to come. She'd been trying to finish this same scene for going on two hours, to no avail. She wanted to think it was the turmoil in her life keeping her muse at bay. The stalker. Closing the shop. Temporarily moving in with her father. But she knew the reason for her writer's block had nothing to do with any of those things—and everything to do with a troubled ex-cop from Chicago.

Every time the phone rang her heart pounded. Even though she desperately wanted to talk to him, she never answered. But John hadn't called.

She missed him with a desperation she'd never before experienced. She longed to hear his voice. See his smile. She wanted to raise her hand and touch his cheek. For the first time in her life she understood what it was like to have an addiction. A compulsion. In the last few days John Merrick had become both.

Sighing, she looked down at the blinking cursor on her screen. She tried to concentrate, tried to put herself in the scene. But her muse refused to cooperate.

"Damn. Damn. Damn."

Closing her laptop lid, she rose and left her bedroom for the kitchen downstairs. She wanted to talk to Claudia, but her sister was out with Rory. It would have been nice to pass the time with her father, but he and Parker Bradley were in Baton Rouge at an overnight meeting. As a last resort, she decided to make coffee and take a tall mug to the private detective parked outside the house. She'd only met

Ellis twice. He was an ex-cop from Houston. Nice enough, but his personality was about as engaging as a head cold.

"Tonight you're going to have to do," she muttered as she entered the kitchen and flipped on the light.

A glass of wine would have been nice. Her father didn't condone the use of alcohol, but he tolerated it. If she wasn't mistaken, one of his non-church friends had given him a case of Portuguese wine for Christmas last year. If she was lucky, he'd forgotten about it and it was still in the garage gathering dust.

She ground beans and started a pot of coffee. While the coffeemaker hissed and bumped, she went to the garage and flipped on the lights. Her father's Lincoln was gone. Her Volkswagen looked small and lonely sitting in the big garage all by itself.

"Looks like it's just you and me, kid," she said as she crossed to the shelving unit on the far wall. Spotting the case of wine on the top shelf, she looked around for something to stand on. The stepladder was nowhere in sight, so she opted for the wooden crate next to the garbage can. Removing the balled-up newspaper inside, she was about to turn it upside down when she noticed the mask.

Her blood froze in her veins when she realized it was a Mardi Gras mask similar to the one the stalker had worn. She told herself it couldn't possibly be the same mask. But her heart quickened as she reached for it. Then she spotted the purple feathers at the crown and her heart began to pound. It wasn't merely *similar* to the mask her stalker had used, it was the *very same* mask. But how in the name of God had it ended up here?

"I knew you'd figure it out sooner or later."

Julia yelped as she spun. The mask fell to the floor when she saw Parker Bradley standing in the doorway that led back into the kitchen. A sense of impending danger overwhelmed her when she spotted the nasty-looking pistol in his hand.

"Parker."

"I see you found the mask." He shook his head. "Silly of me to leave it where you could so easily discover it, but your father almost caught me with it when I was about to dispose of it."

Her entire body began to quake as the situation crystallized. "I-I don't know what you're talking about."

"Oh, I think you know exactly what I'm talking about." He raised the pistol, pointed it at her chest. A chilling smile curved his mouth. "I see it in your eyes. You're frightened of me, aren't you?"

The roar of blood in her ears was so loud she could barely hear him. A terrible realization had taken root. Icy fear spread through her body.

"Why?" was all she could manage.

"I thought that would be obvious."

"It's not."

"I love you, Julia. I've loved you since the moment I saw you almost three years ago. Do you remember that night?"

She didn't. Thin and ordinary, Parker was not the kind of man a woman remembered. He'd been her father's executive assistant for three years.

"Parker, you don't even know me. You can't possibly love me."

"I know all I need to know." Gooseflesh prickled her arms as his gaze swept slowly down her body. "Your religious convictions are strong, like mine. Your beliefs parallel mine. You're kind and beautiful. The kind of beauty that elicits lust in a man, you know?" The smile turned self-deprecating. "Even a wimpy guy like me."

"You're not—"

He cut her off. "But we all know beauty is only skin deep. I fell in love with you the instant I met you. I knew that one day we would be married. That we would have children. All this time I've been saving myself for you."

Julia couldn't believe what she was hearing. Never in a million years would she have suspected Parker Bradley of being her stalker.

The kind of beauty that elicits lust in a man . . .

The words made her shiver. She glanced around the garage, seeking an escape route. There was one window on the north side of the garage, but there was no way she could open it and get through before he reached her. He was standing in the doorway that led to the kitchen and the button for the garage door opener. There was no escape.

"I'm thirty-two-years old and I've never had intercourse with a woman." He looked intense and embarrassed at once. "But I'm only a man. A sinner. I've lusted. After you mostly."

"Parker, don't do this."

"God knows I tried to fight it," he said. "I tried to exorcise these feelings from my psyche. From my body. Then you came to me in a dream and I saw you for what you really are. It was a message from God, Julia. A message telling me it was my responsibility to save you from yourself."

Julia could hear herself breathing hard. Her heart hammered like a freight train in her chest. She measured the distance between her and the door. The nearest phone was in the kitchen, on the wall next to the bar. Her cell phone was charging in her bedroom. There was no way she could reach either . . .

"You were so innocent. Virginal. So . . . perfect." His lips peeled back, revealing small, straight teeth. "Then I found out about the book and everything changed."

"Parker, how did you know?"

"You think I'm stupid?"

"No, it's just that—"

He cut her off. "I heard you and Claudia! At the shop. Whispering about the book. You were *laughing*. I didn't understand at first. I didn't want to believe you could write filth. To prove myself correct, I went to the post office where Elisabeth de Haviland's address is listed in the bio of her book. And I waited." His voice cracked. "My heart broke when I saw you. When you used your key and opened the box for your dirty fan mail." Fervor of the righteous gleamed in his eyes. "Immoral filth. Writing of fornication and lewd acts between unmarried men and women. Masturbation. Oral sex. Anal sex." A dark red blush colored his cheeks. "You *glorified* it." He wiped his mouth as if the words had dirtied his lips. "My God, how could you do that to your father? How could you do that to God? To *me*?"

"It's just . . . a novel, Parker. A fantasy—"

"A fantasy that is perpetuating the downfall of a society."

"No—"

"I saw you with Merrick!" he shouted abruptly. "You let him put his hands on you. You took him into your bed. Into your body. It is his seed inside you, not mine!"

A profound sense of violation shook her. Julia stared at him, her only thought that he had somehow seen them together. That he was insane and there would be no reasoning with him. At least not in rational terms. "Parker, it isn't too late to stop this. Let's go outside and get Ellis and we'll talk about it."

"Don't talk to me as if I'm crazy," he said calmly. "I'm not insane. Far from it, Julia. God has bestowed upon me the responsibility of saving you from your own immorality, and that's exactly what I intend to do."

She thought about getting into the Volkswagen and locking the doors. But then what? The keys were in her purse inside. He would probably just break a window. Then she remembered her father had given her a garage door opener. She'd clipped it to her visor. If she could get into the car and hit the button she could run out the door and find Ellis.

"Parker, let's go inside and talk about this." Reaching out as if to take his hand, she stepped closer to him, closer to the driver's side door. "Please."

He looked confused for a moment and lowered the gun. "You're not going to talk me out of what I have to—"

Julia dashed to the Volkswagen and yanked the door open. Bending, she slammed her fist against the garage door opener clipped to the visor. Behind her she heard Parker's shoes against the concrete floor. The garage door groaned and began to rise. One foot. Two feet. Not taking time to look back, she threw herself at the small gap between the garage door and the floor and rolled.

"Stop!"

She didn't stop. In the driveway, she lurched to her feet and looked around wildly. Ellis's Ford was parked in the circular driveway twenty yards away. "Help me!" she screamed and sprinted toward the car.

She could hear Parker behind her, but she didn't stop. She didn't slow down. She reached the car seconds later, darted around the hood, slapped both hands against the driver's side window. "Help me!"

When the door didn't open, she reached for the handle, yanked the door open. "Ellis!"

The private detective lay against the seat back, his face slack. The blood on his jacket looked black in the dim light from the street lamp. Horror and disbelief slammed into her like a giant fist. Julia tried to scream, but no sound came.

She sensed Parker behind her. She was about to turn and run when pain exploded at the back of her head. Black and white lights flashed before her eyes. She managed to grab the side-view mirror before her knees buckled. The world dipped and spun as she tried to crawl away.

"Help me!" she cried.

The second blow sent her into total darkness.

TWENTY-EIGHT

John had never been good at letting things go. It was his scourge and, some would say, his saving grace. After Parker left, he threw the copies of the threatening letters in the trash. He poured half a glass of gin and carried it to the living room, where he turned on the television and stared blindly at the screen.

Old man Wainwright should have given him the opportunity to brief his replacement. It was PD protocol when a detective handed a case to another. Was the private detective capable of keeping Julia safe? Was he taking the assignment seriously? If no one would listen to John, perhaps he could ask Mitch to give the private detective a call and fill him in. Or at least get of sense of whether or not the man was competent.

But John knew that while all of those things were valid concerns, what he really wanted to know was how Julia was faring through all this. Picking up his cell phone, he scrolled through the numbers until he found Julia's. He didn't hit Send, but he was thinking about it. He could feel the desperation tugging at him. He hadn't eaten dinner and the alcohol was going straight to his head. Not a good thing considering he was an inch away from making a call he had no business making. He was probably going to say things he had no business saying.

"What the hell," he muttered.

Taking another long drink, he hit Send and waited. Her voice mail answered on the third ring. His chest actually went tight at the sound of her voice. He left a message asking her to call him and hung up.

For a crazy instant he considered driving by the Wainwright estate, just to make sure she was all right. But on some level he knew it would only tempt him to do more. Like walk up to the house and knock on the door. The Wainwrights had made their position on his being there perfectly clear.

But that didn't mean he couldn't continue to work the case. It wasn't like he had anything else to do these days. Setting down the glass, he went to the kitchen, dug the letters out of the trash and spread them on the table.

> *Her tainted pen spills sin onto the page*
> *like the fevered blood from a sickle slash.*
> *Soon thine blood will be hers*
> *and vengeance will be mine.—Author unknown*

> *Death is here and death is there,*
> *Death is busy everywhere,*
> *All around, within, beneath,*
> *Above is death—and we are death.—Shelley,*
> *"Death" [1820]*

> *The wages of sin is death.—The New Testament*

> *Yet each man kills the thing he loves.—Oscar Wilde,*
> *"Ballad of Reading Gaol"*

The sins ye do by two and two ye must pay for one
by one.
—Rudyard Kipling, "Tomlinson"

He stared hard at the characters, thinking about the writer, trying to get inside his head. A tiny blotch of toner on each paper revealed that the letters had been printed from the same printer. It was barely larger than a comma and appeared at regularly spaced intervals on each paper. He stared at the blotch. Something pinged in his brain. Suddenly he was pretty sure he'd seen the blotch before. But where?

He slid the check Parker had given him from the envelope and laid it beside the letters. His heart began to pound, the way it did back when he'd been a cop and knew he was about to break a major case. The same blotch appeared on the check Wainwright had sent to him as final payment.

Disbelief and a cold new fear coursed through him. John stood abruptly, nearly knocking his chair over. He couldn't take his eyes off the check. Was Benjamin Wainwright the stalker? Parker Bradley? John hadn't eliminated them from his list of suspects. But neither were strong contenders.

John's heart went into overdrive when he realized Julia was in imminent and grave danger. She was staying at the Wainwright estate, a place John had always believed safe.

"Shit," he hissed as he sprinted to the living room and snatched up his cell. He hit Julia's number as he grabbed his keys off the counter. Three rings and her voice mail answered. "Julia, this is John. You're in danger. Lock your bedroom door and don't let anyone in. Not your father. Especially not Parker Bradley. I'm on my way."

Cursing, he hit the End button and quickly called Mitch. His brother answered on the first ring.

"I think Parker Bradley is the stalker," John said without preamble.

"Bradley? How do you know?"

Quickly, John explained about the blotch of toner. "I'm on my way over to the estate now."

"Stay put, John. I'll handle it."

"Not going to happen."

"They don't want you there. Damn it, you're not a cop anymore."

But John was already out the door and sprinting to his car. "She's there alone, Mitch. There's no way I can sit this one out."

"Goddamn it, John, let me handle this. If Bradley is the stalker, that means he's now a strong suspect in the murder case. I can be there in ten minutes with a couple of patrol cars and a warrant."

"I can be there in two," John said and disconnected.

John hauled the Mustang into Wainwright's driveway, skidded to a halt in front of a massive ornate steel security gate and hit the intercom button with his fist.

"This is John Merrick," he said. "Open the gate."

A minute ticked by, but it felt like an eternity. He glanced through the massive gate. The mansion was large and surrounded by stately live oaks. There was no sign of Julia's Volkswagen. A Ford sedan was parked in the circular driveway. It was too dark for John to see if there was anyone inside. In the back of his mind he wondered if the car belonged to the private dick. If it did, where the hell was he?

He hit the intercom again. "This is Merrick. Open the goddamn gate or I'm coming through it."

He laid on the horn and watched for lights, but nothing happened. Getting out of the Mustang, he strode to the gate and tested it with a vigorous shake. But the mechanism held strong and secure.

Not letting himself consider the consequences of what he was about to do, John climbed back into the Mustang, secured his safety belt and put the car into reverse. Halfway down the driveway, he slammed it into drive and floored the gas. The big V-8 roared. The car shot forward. Zero to thirty in three seconds flat. The bumper hit the gate. Steel screamed against steel. The impact jolted him, but he didn't let off the gas. The gates exploded open. The one to his left was ripped from its hinge and clattered to the cobblestone. The one on the right slammed against the fence hard enough to bend steel.

John brought the Mustang to a screeching halt outside the three-car garage. He was out of the car and running for the front door when headlights played over the stucco exterior. A glance over his shoulder told him Mitch had arrived. "Shit," he muttered, not sure if that was good or bad. The only thing he knew for certain was that his cop's instincts were telling him something was terribly wrong. He wasn't going to let police protocol keep him from finding out what.

He tried the front door, but found it locked. Cupping his hands, he looked through the beveled glass sidelight, but the interior was as dark as a cave.

"What the fuck do you think you're doing?"

John turned to see Mitch jogging up the sidewalk, his face incredulous and angry.

"She's in trouble."

"How do you know?" Mitch looked around.

"I can't get her on the phone."

"Maybe she's not taking your calls. For God's sake, John, can you blame her?"

"The bedroom light is on, but she's not answering the intercom."

"So you obliterated their security gate?" Mitch gestured angrily toward the gate. "How are you going to explain that to the old man?"

John started toward the garage, but Mitch stepped in front of him, blocking his way. "Not so fast, hotshot."

"Get out of my way." Shoving his brother aside, John started toward the back door that opened to the garage.

Mitch stayed on his heels. "What are you going to do now? Break in?"

"If that's what it takes." John reached the door and tried the knob.

"For fuck sake, John, don't make me arrest you."

At the door John halted and spun to face his brother. "Look, if I'm wrong about this I'll cover the damage."

Mitch didn't look appeased. "If you're wrong about this I'm going to make damn sure you get some help."

"Fine. Deal." John looked toward the garage door. "I'm not wrong. Something isn't right here. Where the hell is the private dick the old man hired?"

Mitch glanced toward the street. "I didn't see a car."

"Check the car in the driveway."

Turning on his heel, Mitch started for the Ford sedan. When his brother was out of earshot, John removed his shoe and broke a windowpane on the door. He reached in, disengaged the bolt lock and stepped inside.

In the dim light slanting through the window, he could see the silhouette of Julia's Volkswagen. He found the light switch, flipped it on. At first everything seemed to be in order. Car parked neatly in its bay. Tools hung on a rack against the wall. Dual garbage cans next to the door. But as he drew closer to the car, two small dark droplets on the concrete outside the driver's side door caught his eye. Kneeling, he looked more closely at them. The hair at his nape prickled when he realized it was blood.

He'd started toward the door to get Mitch when his brother burst into the garage. "The PI is dead," he said.

The words struck John like a punch. *"What?"*

"His throat was cut. I called it in." Mitch was breathing hard. "Goddamn it."

Vaguely he was aware of Mitch speaking on his radio. John stood there dumbly, his heart pounding, his mind scrambling wildly for explanations. But there was no explanation that would keep his worst nightmare from coming true.

The stalker had Julia. The blood on the floor told him she'd already been hurt, maybe even murdered. And nobody had the slightest idea where he might have taken her.

*   *   *

Consciousness returned one sense at a time. The first thing Julia was aware of was the cold. She was shivering with it. Her clothing was wet. She was lying on her side. Whatever was beneath her was hard and cold and damp. The second thing she became aware of was the pain in her head. The back of her head throbbed with every beat of her heart.

In the next instant everything that had happened at her father's mansion rushed back. Finding the mask in the crate. Parker accosting her in the garage. The dead private detective. The ensuing struggle . . .

Terror and adrenaline sent her bolt upright. Panic went through her like electricity when she found her hands bound in front of her. She looked around wildly and realized she was on the floor of some dilapidated church. To her right, rows of old-fashioned wood pews stretched toward a boarded-up doorway. To her left stood a high altar surrounded by several rickety wood pallets and an old tire. Beyond, the cross of Christ sat against a broken stained glass mural.

"Welcome to Our Lady of St. Agnes."

Julia gasped at the sound of Parker Bradley's voice. Hindered by her bound hands, she scrambled awkwardly to her feet and faced him. A shock went through her at the sight of him. He'd changed into a white robe that was belted at the waist with a gold sash. Except for the pistol in his hand, he looked peaceful and eerily priestlike as he approached her.

"What do you think of my church?" he asked.

"Parker, you don't want to do this." Her throat was so tight she barely recognized her voice.

"You have no idea what I want."

"Let me go."

He raised the pistol, his eyes going hard. "I asked you a question, Julia. Show some respect and answer it."

Blinking back tears, she looked around. "I don't know where I am."

"This is St. Agnes. You know the place. Just off of Rampart. You've probably driven by here a hundred times and never so much as spared it a glance."

"The abandoned church and cemetery," she said.

"Ah, see?" Turning in a circle, he raised his arms to the altar. "I've always thought this place was special. A little work and it would make a fine house of worship, don't you think? I've thought about turning the rectory into a shelter. Your father had his eye on this place before he became so involved with the directorship position. Once I saw it I knew I had to have it."

"Parker, I don't understand why you're doing this," she tried. "Untie me. Please. Let's talk about this."

Intensity glittered in his eyes when he approached her. He stopped a few feet away. Close enough for her to see the light of insanity in his eyes, the sweat beading on his forehead. "Don't treat me like some stupid peasant, you wicked little whore."

Julia couldn't believe what she was hearing. "Parker, what is it you think I've done? Why are you doing this?"

He studied her with an intensity that unnerved, then he made a sweeping motion toward the pews. "Do you know the story behind St. Agnes, Julia? Like so many stories that have taken place in New Orleans, it's tragic."

She stepped back when he moved closer. She glanced toward the front door, wondering if she could reach it before he caught her. But she could see the gleam of a padlock from where she stood.

"A hundred and fifty years ago Our Lady of St. Agnes Church was used as a mortuary during yellow fever outbreaks. There's a cemetery out back. The crypts are dilapidated for the most part. But they house hundreds of souls lost to the disease."

"I d-didn't know."

"A lot of people of the era believed only the sinners were afflicted with yellow fever. Can you believe that? But then New Orleans has always been full of sinners. Some believed death was the only way God could save their souls."

She jolted when her backside made contact with the chancel rail.

"That's one of the reasons this place is so special. So perfect," he said. "The House of Lost Souls."

"Parker, you need to let me go."

Every muscle in her body went rigid when he reached out and brushed the side of her face with his hand. "You used to be so full of goodness and innocence, Julia. You could walk into a dark room and light it up with nothing more than your smile. It was the innate goodness of your heart, the innocence of your soul that drew me to you. Those things set you apart from other women and I've always loved you for it."

Her heart was beating so hard she could barely hear him speak. "I c-care for you, too, Parker. You know that."

"A year ago I entertained the idea of pursuing a relationship with you. My God, you were so *perfect*. I could barely get through the day without at least one glimpse of you. But now . . ." Shrugging, he let the words trail. "Now it's too late."

"I don't know what you mean."

"The book, Julia. That ungodly novel you published. It crushed me. I will never understand how you could write something so depraved. No wonder you wrote it under a pseudonym."

"It's only a book."

"No, Julia. It's a lot more than a book. You see, I read it. It's filled with sin and depravity. It made me weak. Made me question my morals . . ." His voice broke and he looked away. "It reminded me that I am a mere mortal. A sinner. It made me lust. For you."

"Parker, the book is a work of fiction. It's harmless. A fantasy—"

"It's not harmless!" he screamed abruptly. "It's more than that! It changed everything. It changed the way I felt about you. You see, Julia, I've seen your real face. I know what you are. After you came to me that night . . . God told me what I had to do."

Julia slid along the rail, but he followed. "Don't do this."

"I tried to make you stop. I sent you the notes, hoping they would frighten you. Make you realize that your words were perpetuating immorality. Because of you, how many men committed rape? How many women committed adultery?"

She looked around for a route of escape. There were two doors behind her and to her left. The doors were closed. She didn't know if they were locked. The stained glass windows in the nave were too high for her to get through.

"And so," he said, "I have agreed to do God's work and save both our souls."

"Parker, I won't write any more books. I promise. In fact, I'll talk to my father. I'll have him counsel me. Help me work through this."

"Don't patronize me, Julia."

Her gaze flicked down the flowing robe. He had a cell phone clipped to the sash. She looked quickly away, terrified he would know what she was thinking. But when she made eye contact with him, he was still staring at her, only it was as if he no longer saw her as a person. She was an object. An object he wanted to remove from this earth.

"God knows I didn't want to hurt you," he said. "I never wanted it to come to this. I love you. And I'll spend the rest of my life praying for both our souls."

"God forgives all of his children." It was a weak attempt to play along with his sick dialogue, but Julia couldn't think of any other way to buy time. First chance she got she was going to grab that phone . . .

"I've prepared everything you will need for your journey." Crossing to a table he'd set up near the altar, he yanked off a sheet.

A shudder of horror swept through her at the sight of the table and instruments. From ten feet away, Julia could see rope restraints attached to the table legs, as if he planned to tie her down.

"I will purify you before I send you to God." He gestured toward several glass vials. "I will bathe your body in holy water."

Gooseflesh raced along her skin as she identified several items in the table. The sight of them sickened her. Drove home the fact that there would be no reasoning with this man.

"Get down on your knees." He held out his hand as if expecting her to comply. "Let us pray before we begin."

Heart pounding, Julia moved slowly toward him. In the back of her mind, she wondered if anyone had discovered Ellis's body back at her father's mansion. She thought about John and wondered if he'd tried to contact her. If anyone had even realized she was missing . . .

A few feet away from Parker, she lowered her head as if to pray, but her eyes were on the cell phone clipped to his sash.

Three feet separated them. "Which prayer?" She knelt. Her hands shook as she folded them.

He looked at her as if her sudden cooperation had surprised him. Blinking, he knelt beside her and bowed his head. "Our Father, Who art in heaven . . ."

Without raising her head, she sidled closer. "Hallow'd be Thy name."

Her heart thundered in her chest as she recited the words from memory. But her every sense was homed on the man kneeling beside her. On the phone clipped to his sash. She visualized herself lunging, snatching the phone, bolting for the door. She would only have a few seconds to make the call. Her best bet was to call John; he lived only two blocks to the north. She knew he would respond faster than any 911 call.

"And lead us not into temptation, but deliver us from evil—"

She lunged at him. Using both hands she snatched the phone from his belt. Parker lurched to his feet and swung at her. But she'd gone in low and the blow glanced off her shoulder. Before he could hit her again, she spun and threw herself into a dead run toward the double doors behind the altar.

She punched John's number as she sprinted. The phone rang once. Twice. Her heart surged when she heard his voice. "*John!*" she screamed. "It's Parker Bradley! He's taken me to Saint—"

The violence of the blow sent her reeling sideways. She reached out to break her fall, felt the cell phone slip from her grasp. Around her the lights dimmed. The next thing she knew she was on her knees. The cell phone lay on the floor three feet away. Vaguely, she was aware of John's voice coming through the phone. He was shouting her name. Then Parker's boot came down and crushed it.

"That was a stupid thing to do," he snarled.

Julia didn't see the next blow coming. One moment she was on her knees, trying to get her bearings. The next she was reeling backward. Her cheekbone felt as if it had been ripped from her face. The floor rushed up and slammed into the back of her head. Red light flashed before her eyes.

For an instant she struggled for consciousness.

But the darkness won and she tumbled headlong into the abyss.

TWENTY-NINE

"*Julia!* Julia!"

John heard panic in his voice. He felt it running the length of his body like a thousand volts of electricity.

"Julia!" he shouted.

But the line was dead.

"Fuck! *Fuck!*"

"What is it?"

He spun at the sound of Mitch's voice. He was still clutching the phone. He felt wild and out of control inside. His brother was staring at him as if he were exactly that.

"Parker Bradley has Julia." He looked down at his cell phone. "Jesus Christ, that was her on the phone. He fucking has her."

"Easy, bro."

"Goddamn it, Mitch. She was . . . screaming my name. Got cut off."

"Easy." Never taking his eyes from his brother's, Mitch approached John and reached for the phone. "Give me the phone. Let me see what CIS can do with it."

Before handing it over, John pressed Received Calls and checked the number, but it was Unknown. "Damn it."

Mitch pulled a plastic Baggie from his pocket and dropped the phone into it. "What did she say?" he asked.

John could feel his emotions beginning to spiral. He couldn't think. His mind kept replaying her scream over and over. "She screamed my name."

"Okay." Mitch scraped a hand over his jaw. "Anything else? Did she say where she was?"

His brain pinged. "She said the word 'Saint.'"

"Saint what?"

"Just Saint. We got cut off."

"Okay." Mitch hit a number on his cell phone. "I want patrol units dispatched immediately to all three of the St. Louis cemeteries. Bolo for Julia Wainwright. Twenty-nine-year-old white female. Brown hair. Blue eyes." He cut John a look. "What kind of car does Bradley drive?"

"A 2006 Lexus."

Mitch repeated the year and model to Dispatch. "Possible kidnapping." Clipping the phone to his belt, he turned to John. "We've got patrol cars en route to the three St. Louis cemeteries. If Parker is there with Julia, they'll bring them in."

John couldn't shake the feeling that he was missing something vital. Something locked inside his head that would make everything *click*. Some piece of information he'd run across in the course of the case but couldn't put his finger on.

"You going to be okay?"

Deep in thought, John caught the last word and nodded at his brother. "I'm fine."

He was a long way from fine. He was panic stricken and terrified. He couldn't stop thinking about Julia. What she might be going through at that very moment. He had to find her. If only he knew where to look.

"Do you think she could have said St. Louis Cathedral?" Mitch asked.

"Worth checking." John pulled his car keys from his pocket.

Mitch glanced down at the keys and frowned. "I'll get a unit out there. Why don't you find Wainright and tell him what's happened?"

John didn't appreciate being relegated to dealing with family members. Telling Wainright his daughter had been kidnapped by a killer wasn't going to be easy. He wanted to look for Julia. But John figured the police were better equipped to cover more ground more quickly. Once he took care of Wainright, he'd join forces with the cops. Or else launch his own search.

"I'll call him," he said.

Mitch patted the bagged cell phone. "I'm going to run this to the lab myself. See if they can give us a proximity on that last call."

John nodded, feeling frustrated and ineffective and unable to do anything about either.

Frowning, Mitch started toward his car, then stopped and turned. "If anything pops, you call me, bro. You got that?"

"I got it."

"And stay out of the crime scene. Let the cops do their jobs."

As he watched his brother walk away, John realized staying away from the scene was the one thing he could not do.

Julia fought to reach the light, but the dizziness kept pushing her back to the dark tunnel of unconsciousness. Vaguely, she was aware of Parker touching her hands, cutting the restraints on her wrists. She opened her eyes to see him kneeling over her, his face sweaty and red and less than a foot above her.

"Ah, you're awake."

She was lying on the floor with her left leg twisted to one side. The back of her head hurt. A gasp escaped her when he grasped her arm and roughly rolled her onto her stomach. She fought him, but the blow to her head had weakened her. She lay there, breathing hard, like a beaten animal waiting for slaughter, as he tied her hands behind her back.

"Don't do . . . this." A new fear crept through her when her words slurred.

"I tried to be kind to you." Jerking her arm, he flipped her onto her back. "I tried to get you to stop writing that filth! But you refused to see the signs I sent to you, Julia. You refused to listen to me! Now, because of you, both of us are going to have to pay a terrible price! Do you think I want to do this?"

Spittle flew from his lips as he spoke. He was grinding his teeth so hard she could hear the molars grating together. Julia stared up at him, wondering why she couldn't focus. Wondering why her head wouldn't stop spinning. She wanted to fight him, but her arms and legs felt leaden.

"What have you done to me?" she whispered.

He reached for something on the table. His mouth twisted when he held up the disposable syringe. "I gave you something to make you a little more manageable."

Drugs. Horror spiraled inside her. "What did you give me?"

"It's just a little Demerol, Julia. In a few minutes I'm sure you'll be thanking me."

She couldn't believe the quiet young man who'd worked so diligently for her father for the last three years had transformed into the raving maniac kneeling over her.

In the back of her mind, she thought about John. She wondered how much of her call he'd understood. At the very least, he knew she was in trouble. That the stalker had her.

Would it be enough to save her life?

"Who did you call?"

The question jerked her back from the hazy world inside her own head. "I dialed 911," she said. "The police are on their way."

"You're lying."

"No—"

"Do you think I'm *stupid*?" he shouted. "I know who you called! You called Merrick, didn't you?"

When Julia didn't answer, he leaned close. So close she could smell his breath, hear his teeth grinding together. Lips peeled back in a snarl, he slapped her face with an open palm.

The blow snapped her head back, brought tears to her eyes. "*Didn't you?*" he demanded.

Julia closed her eyes, determined not to let him see her cry. "He's coming, Parker. Give this up. Please. He won't let you get away with this."

"Yes, he'll come for you, won't he?" An odd light entered his eyes. "You see, Julia, I saw you with him in the shop that night. I saw both of you going at it like a couple of dogs in heat. You're nothing but a lustful little whore."

"Stop it," she said.

"That night was a turning point for me. That was when I knew I had to stop you or your soul would be lost forever."

"You're wrong about me," she said breathlessly. "You're wrong about John."

"Merrick is just a man. Weak and lustful." He spat the words as if he were spitting spoiled meat. "But you . . . You came to me in my sleep. You seduced me. By the time I saw you for the monster you are, it was too late. I saw your real face. The things you did to me—" His voice broke. "You evil, evil bitch. Instrument of Satan. Succubus whore."

The hatred in his voice stunned her. How could he believe what he was saying about her? "Parker, please, listen to me. You're wrong. You need help—"

"I'm not crazy!" he shouted. "You raped me that night. You did vile things to me. You tried to steal the breath from my lungs."

"Parker, it doesn't have to be this way."

"Yes, it does." Roughly, he yanked her to her feet.

Off balance, Julia stumbled and nearly went to her

knees. His fingers dug into her shoulder as he shoved her toward the table.

"Get on the table."

She blinked, focused on the table next to the altar. It was a wooden rectangular table covered with a white sheet. On a battered pulpit beside the table lay an array of items. A syringe. Vials of what she could only assume was holy water—or his version of it. An over-the-counter douche product. Enema bag. Oh, dear God, no . . .

"Parker, please don't do this."

He went on as if he hadn't heard her. "I will first purify your body with holy water."

"No," she croaked.

"Only my seed will cleanse the impurities from inside your body. Your soul will be purified only when your blood runs red over the altar. You will be pure inside and out when you stand in judgment before God. You see, Julia, I have prepared a crypt just for you . . ."

THIRTY

A second NOPD cruiser arrived as John walked to his car. The collision with the gate had torn up the grille and dented the hood, but he didn't think the radiator was breached. Not that he gave a damn about the car; he just hoped it started.

Behind the wheel, he used his cell phone and dialed Wainwright's number from memory. The old man picked up on the second ring.

"Mr. Wainwright, it's John Merrick."

A cool silence ensued. "What are you doing calling me at this hour?"

John closed his eyes, wishing the other man weren't out of town so he could tell him this face to face. "I'm afraid I've got some bad news, Mr. Wainwright."

A beat of tense silence followed. "What? What are you talking about?"

"Julia's missing."

"*What?* That's impossible. I talked to her earlier this evening and she was fine."

"I'm sorry, Benjamin, but she's missing."

"That can't be! I hired an armed private detective to look after her."

"The PI is dead," John said.

The old man made a strangled sound. "Holy mother of God. How did this happen? Who's taken her?"

"We think Parker Bradley is the stalker."

Wainwright made a sound as if he'd been punched in the stomach. "Parker? That simply isn't true. He's on his way here." Heavy breathing came through the line as he paused. "Dear Lord, he should have been here an hour ago."

"Look, Benjamin, I need to ask you some questions."

"Anything." A sob escaped the old man. "Oh, Julia. God . . ." The old man choked out the words. "I've got to get to New Orleans. If I leave now I can be there in an hour."

"Julia called me." John looked at his watch. "About twenty minutes ago. She was in trouble. We were cut off but not before she said the word 'Saint.' I think she was trying to tell me where she'd been taken. Can you think of a place Parker would take her?"

"The old church."

"What old church?"

"Our Lady of St. Agnes. I was considering renovating it at one point. Parker lobbied heavily for me to buy. But the place has extensive water damage. It's scheduled for demolition."

John's heart began to hammer. He hit the gas and the car shot out of the driveway. "Where?"

"Rampart near Bayou Road." The old man choked back an anguished sound. "Go get her, John. Bring my girl back to me."

But John had already disconnected.

Even with the fertile imagination of a writer, Julia could never have imagined herself in such a terrifying situation. She fought Parker with all of her strength as he forced her to the table. She twisted and lashed out with her feet, knocking several items from the pulpit. "Help me!" she screamed.

"Shut up!" Lips peeled back in a snarl, he spun her around and shoved her to the floor.

Julia hit the ground so hard the breath was knocked from her lungs. Straddling her, he grabbed duct tape from the pulpit shelf and tore off a piece with his teeth.

"No!"

Her scream was cut short when he slapped the tape over her mouth. Lowering his weight onto her stomach, he reached for the syringe.

The sight of the syringe sent an electric shock of panic through her. She bucked beneath him, tried to twist away, but he was too heavy. An evil smile split his face as he thumbed off the cap.

"This is what happens to sinning little bitches when they misbehave," he said and jabbed the needle into her hip, right through her jeans.

Her body bucked beneath him as the needle penetrated fabric and skin and muscle. The Demerol burned but Julia knew the pain of the injection was the least of her problems. She knew once he disabled her he was going to put her on that table and do unspeakable things to her.

Before he killed her.

The drug hit her brain like a locomotive moving in slow motion. One moment she was twisted and lashing out beneath him. The next it was as if her body had floated two feet off the floor. Her brain ordered her to keep fighting; she knew that was her only chance of surviving. But as the drug wound through her system, she felt her muscles go slack.

"Ah, that's better. Yes, that's it. Relax." Rising, Parker looked down at her. "You're strong for your size."

Julia stared at him, trying to focus, but the drug was making her lids heavy. She wanted to speak, but the tape held her mute. All she could do was look at him and pray someone stopped him before things went too far.

Her eyes drifted closed. Only for a moment, she told

herself. Just enough time to gather her strength and come up with a plan. But there wasn't any plan that would save her from what he planned to do. Her only hope was that someone would find them.

She thought of John and a sob rose into her throat. She could feel the tears welling in her eyes and spilling onto her face. She didn't want to cry, but the thought of never seeing him again was too much to bear. She'd fallen in love with him. She wanted desperately to prove it to him. Now, she'd never get the chance.

Please come for me, she prayed.

Vaguely, she was aware of Parker moving around, banging things around on the table. Every nerve in her body snapped taut when she felt his arms slide beneath her. She tried to twist away when he lifted her, but her muscles refused to obey.

"Don't fight me," he whispered as he laid her on the table.

Julia lifted her head, fought to open her eyes. She caught a glimpse of Parker standing over her. She tried to scoot away, but he set his hand against her stomach and pushed her back. "Don't move or I'll hurt you."

Her eyes wanted to roll back, but she fought to keep them open. She felt his hands at her left ankle and kicked at him, but missed. He removed her boot and, using a soft gold sash, secured her ankle to the table leg.

She tried to sit up when he grasped her right ankle, but he lunged and slapped her hard. "I said don't move!"

The impact of the blow sent her back down. Closing her eyes tightly, she screamed into the tape as he secured her right ankle.

Oh, dear God, please don't let this happen!

It was as if she were trapped inside her own head. Unable to speak or scream. Unable to move or protect herself. Somehow her eyes had drifted shut. Her mouth was bone dry. Her lids flew open when she felt his hands on her bound wrists. At first she thought he was cutting the ropes, then she realized he was pulling them above her head to secure them to the table.

A terrible sense of vulnerability crashed over her as he jerked the ropes taut. Screaming into the tape, she struggled against her bindings. Her struggles were not only futile, but also seemed to give him a twisted sense of pleasure. Bound, drugged and gagged, she was totally at his mercy.

But Parker Bradley did not have any mercy in his heart. She saw fanaticism and hatred in his eyes when he looked down at her. She wondered how someone who called himself a man of God could be so cruel. How someone she thought she'd known for three years could hide such utter and complete insanity.

"He's not going to come for you."

His whispered voice jerked her out of the hazy world she had sunk into. Even drugged and terrified she knew he was talking about John.

Never taking his eyes from hers, he undid the sash at his waist. At first Julia thought he was going to expose himself to her. She could handle that as long as he didn't touch or force himself on her. Then she realized he'd removed the robe to show her what he wore beneath it.

"It's a Kevlar vest and is designed to stop a bullet even at close range." He rapped the vest with his knuckles. "Just in case Merrick gets any ideas about trying to play hero."

Lower, she saw the wood grip of a pistol sticking out of the waistband of his jeans. She stared at the butt of the gun, wished desperately there was some way she could get to it. She fought the binds, but the ropes held. She wanted to scream and rage; she wanted to tell him she would do whatever he wanted so long as he didn't kill John. She knew he would come for her. And she knew with terrible certainty that when he did this man would kill him.

"I begin the ceremony by bathing you in holy water," he said.

He was standing over her. Sweat beaded on his forehead and upper lip. The robe he wore was wet with sweat at his chest and back and armpits. His hand shook uncontrollably when he picked up the vial of holy water.

She jerked against her binds when the water splashed onto her face and neck. Expecting the burn of acid, she closed her eyes and cried into the tape. But the burn didn't come.

"Now for the rest of you."

She opened her eyes to see him pick up a long-bladed knife. A scream exploded from her lungs, but the duct tape muffled it. Her body bucked against the table when he set the blade against her sweater.

"The holy water must have contact with your skin." A flick of his wrist and the first button popped. "I hope you know there is no enjoyment in this for me, Julia. I am doing the work of God. And He has told me you must atone for your sins."

No!

An odd expression of sympathy entered his eyes. He removed the knife and stroked her hair back with his hand. "I'll make this as comfortable as possible for you, Julia. But I must make certain you are pure when you leave this world."

Julia threw her head back and screamed into the duct tape.

The Mustang's tires screeched against asphalt as John hauled the car onto Bayou Road. He put the accelerator to the floor and the car flew over potholes the sizes of basketballs. To the south he could see lightning flickering through the trees. The air was leaden and still with the promise of a storm.

He had no idea what he would find when he got to the old church. He didn't even know if that was where Bradley had taken her. But it was his best guess, and at the moment it was all he had.

Uncertainty taunted him as he sped through the old neighborhood. The area had been on the decline for half a century. Dilapidated warehouses banked by a deep canal ran parallel with the street to his left. To his right, ancient Victorian homes that had once been stately stared at him with hollow, dark eyes. Our Lady of St. Agnes stood among hundred-year-old live oaks at the end of the street, like some fallen saint.

Cutting the headlights, John idled past. The weeds were knee-high in the gravel lot; he didn't see a vehicle. There were no lights on inside. The place looked deserted. But John knew that didn't mean it was.

He made another pass then parked curbside twenty yards away. As he silently jogged to the front of the building, it crossed his mind that he was going into a potentially dangerous situation unarmed. Stupid thing to do considering Bradley was probably packing a gun. But John was all too aware of his limitations when it came to his service revolver. He was just going to have to make do without it.

He was midway to the rear when a flicker of light from inside caught his eye. It was coming from a broken stained glass window six feet above the ground. If he stood on the sill ledge, he would be able to see inside.

Light rain began to fall as he walked to the window. Standing on a rusty five-gallon bucket, he heaved himself onto the narrow sill and put his eye to the hole. The light inside was dim. The hairs on the back of his neck stood on end when he realized the light was coming from dozens of candles. His heart began to pound when he spotted Bradley standing near the altar. He was too far away to discern what the man was doing. He was wearing some type of robe. But where the hell was Julia?

His gut twisted when he spotted her lying on the table spread eagle. Duct tape covered her mouth. Shock and outrage and a terrible new fear stormed through him when he realized Bradley was cutting away her clothes.

John closed his eyes and struggled to get a grip. Shaking himself, he stepped down off the sill, his heart hammering hard against his ribs. He knew he wasn't going to be able to stop that son of a bitch without a weapon.

Breathing hard, he stepped into the shadows of the trees, whipped out his cell phone and called Mitch. His brother answered on the first ring.

"Bradley has her at the old church on Bayou Road. Saint Agnes. I'm here now. He's going to . . ." But John's voice broke and he couldn't finish the sentence.

"Take it easy, bro."

"He's going to hurt her, Mitch. For God's sake, he's got her tied up. I'm going in."

"Stay put. I'm in my car. I can be there in five minutes."

"She doesn't have five minutes." John disconnected and jammed the phone onto his belt. Not giving himself time to debate, he sprinted back to his car. Sweat slicked his back and face as he pulled the nylon zip case from beneath the passenger seat. His hands shook uncontrollably as he stared down at the gleaming barrel of the H&K .45. The same gun that killed Franklin Watts. The only tool he had that would save the life of the woman he loved.

He envisioned himself picking up the gun and chambering a bullet, the way he'd done a thousand times in the years he'd been a cop. But his mind's eye flashed back to the night Franklin Watts died. He saw gray flesh and staring eyes and a pool of blood the size of an ocean. He saw two children and a woman too young to be a widow. Nausea seesawed in his gut. Cold horror raced through his blood like ice water being pumped into his veins.

Pick up the gun, you fucking coward, a little voice ordered.

But his hands refused. His knees hit the ground. He retched and lost the contents of his stomach. Cold sweat covered his body, but he was shivering with a chill that seemed to emanate from his bones.

"Pick it up, goddamn it," he choked out.

He closed his eyes, tried to will away the horror of that night. In the dark recesses of his mind, he saw Julia. He felt the goodness of her soul. The kindness of her heart. The undeniable connection to his. He thought of all the terrible things that would happen to her if he didn't do this.

Giving himself a hard mental shake, he got unsteadily to his feet and reached for the gun. The blue steel felt foreign and deadly in his hands. The fear rose like vomit in his throat. Sheer determination allowed him to maintain his grip. He pulled back the slide and chambered a bullet. His hands were wet on the grip as he shoved the gun into the waistband of his jeans.

His legs felt rubbery as he sprinted toward the church, but he didn't let himself think about the fear. He knew it would overwhelm him, render him useless. He wasn't going to let Julia die because of him.

Midway to the church, the skies opened up. The rain came in a sudden and blinding torrent, soaking him instantly and washing the fear sweat from his face. The gun felt huge and heavy against him. But John didn't let himself think about it. He didn't slow down. He didn't stop.

Come hell or high water he was going to keep a madman from killing the woman he loved.

Thirty-one

John found Bradley's Lexus parked behind the church.
He sloshed through ankle-high water to a door on the north
side of the building. He tried the knob, but found it locked.
Through the pouring rain he spotted another door, possibly
leading to what had once been the rectory. He jogged to it,
tried the knob, found it locked.

Frustration hammered at him as he looked around. He
thought about shooting off the lock, but nixed the idea. He
had to find a way in without alerting Bradley or he risked
the other man killing Julia before he could reach her. The
thought filled him with a horror so black that for a moment
he was frozen.

Hang on, he silently told her. I'm coming for you.

Struggling to stay calm, he looked around and spotted a
row of jalousie windows. Crossing to them, he cupped his
hands and tried to peer inside, but saw only darkness. If
this was the rectory, there was probably a door or two sep-
arating it from the main part of the church. The perfect
place to make entry without being discovered.

Blinking back rain, John reached for the glass slat closest the crank inside. He tried to work it free, but the glass remained snug. Cursing, he abandoned the first louver and went to the next. Hope surged when he found it loose. Quickly, he forced it from the sash bar and tossed it to the ground. Thrusting his hand inside, he found the crank and opened the window. It seemed to take forever to remove the remaining slats, but in less than a minute he was through the window.

The interior was as dark as a crypt, but John's eyes adjusted quickly. From the dim light slanting in from the street lamp he could see that he'd entered the chancel. The air was stagnant with the smell of rotting wood and mildew. Water dripped from his clothes as he crossed to the door that would take him to the nave. The door was open several inches. He peered through the crack. He saw the yellow glow of the candles. A fluted pillar stood between him and the high altar. But he could see Parker Bradley silhouetted against the light. Lying on the table before him was Julia. Rage coursed through John when he saw that Bradley had cut the clothes from her body. He fought a surge of desperation, reminding himself he wouldn't do either of them any good if he charged in without some kind of plan.

He opened the door another inch and tried to get a better look, but the wide pillar partially blocked his view. He could hear Bradley chanting. Julia, he realized, had been gagged. John could hear her whimpering, screaming into the tape.

Hang on . . .

His hands shook as he reached for the H&K in his waistband. He didn't acknowledge the old fear, but it was there, taunting the fringes of his consciousness. He could feel his heart pumping hard in his chest, the slick of sweat on his skin even though he was soaked to the bone and shivering with cold.

Slowly, he shoved open the door and stepped into the transept. He could see Julia struggling against the binds now. She was wearing nothing but her underpants. Her flesh looked as white as snow in the dim light coming off the candles. The sound of her cries shook him badly. But he reminded himself that she was still alive. As long as she was still alive, it wasn't too late.

Hang on.

He silently chanted the words like a mantra. He gripped the pistol with the desperation of a man hanging onto a lifeline. But no matter how hard he tried, he couldn't keep his hand from shaking.

Never taking his eyes from Bradley, he slinked along the wall, the H&K ready in his hand. The hard ping of rain against the old roof was deafening, but the roar of blood through his veins was louder. John thought about taking the shot now. He so badly wanted to kill the other man he could taste it. But the pillar blocked his shot.

Every nerve in his body went taut when Bradley trailed the tip of the knife down Julia's throat and between her breasts. She wrenched at the ropes binding her. Her cries grew more frantic. The knife glinted in the candlelight. And John knew that if he were discovered now, he wouldn't be able to get to her in time to keep the other man from stabbing her in the heart.

Or cutting her throat . . .

He was in plain sight now. Thirty feet separated them. One wrong move and Julia would die. He was debating whether to take the shot or try to get closer when the sound of sirens carried over the pounding rain.

Bradley swung around, his eyes seeking, seeking . . .

Twelve years of training kicked in; John brought up the gun, took aim. "Stop or I swear to Christ I'll put a hole between your eyes."

Bradley didn't look particularly worried. More like he'd been interrupted by some unruly child. But the tip of the knife was against Julia's throat, less than an inch from her carotid artery . . .

"Put down the knife, you sick little prick."

An eerily calm smile split Bradley's face. "It you care about her, you will let me purify her before she stands in judgment before God."

John decided on a body shot. Even with his hands shaking, he figured it gave him a fifty-fifty chance of hitting his mark. Two months ago, he would have already taken the shot and ended this. But his hand wouldn't stop shaking. He could feel the sweat dripping down his temple and between his shoulder blades. He could hear his breaths echoing off the walls of the cavernous church. The old fear gripping him with sharp talons. Goddamn it, not now, he thought. *Not now!*

"Your hands are shaking, Detective Merrick."

"Drop the knife. Now."

"Or what? You'll shoot me? Look at you. Do you actually think you can hit anything when you can barely hold that gun?"

John flicked his gaze to Julia. Her glazed eyes told him she'd been drugged. Evidently the drug wasn't strong enough to dull the terror. He saw it in her eyes, as sharp-edged as any razor. He hated seeing her like that, but he steeled himself against it. "You're going to be all right," he said to her. "Mitch is on his way along with SWAT."

But even to him the words rang hollow . . .

"This would probably be a good time for me to mention I'm wearing body armor, as you cops like to refer to it." Using his free hand Bradley untied the sash at his waist to reveal the Kevlar vest.

"In that case I'll go for a head shot."

Bradley looked amused. "From a man suffering with hoplophobia, that's not a viable threat."

John knew better than to engage him; he didn't let himself react. But the fact that Parker knew his most private fear surprised him.

"Ah, yes," Parker continued, "I know all about the cop you shot in Chicago. Fascinating reading. Benjamin was quite concerned and wanted to counsel you. After all, taking the life of an innocent man with a wife and children . . ." He tsked. "It can mess up a man's head, can't it?"

John said nothing, instead focused on moving ever so slightly to his left for a better angle.

"Ben thought your taking on the job to protect Julia would help you get back on your feet." His gaze flicked to John's shaking hands. "Had he known you were afraid of your own gun, I'm afraid he never would have hired you to protect his daughter." The smile sharpened. "Lucky for me you failed to mention your little problem, wouldn't you say?"

John should have already taken the shot, but the gun wobbled uselessly in his grip. He willed his hand to stop. Fear sweat dripped into his eyes.

Stop it, goddamn it!

But he didn't trust his aim. Didn't trust this son of a bitch not to do something crazy. If he missed . . .

"I'm sure the alcohol isn't helping. I hear you've become quite the alcoholic. I hear the DTs can be quite . . . shall we say, uncomfortable."

He focused on slowing his breathing, calming himself so he could take the shot. But when Julia cried out into the duct tape, his eyes flicked to where she lay bound. Within the depth of her gaze he saw terror and the will to live in its most primal form.

Hang on . . .

"She's quite lovely, isn't she?"

John looked at him. "Let her go and I'll let you live."

The other man only smiled. "She's a whore, you know. A succubus. Once she seduces you . . . well, I'm sure you know the story."

"You heard the sirens, Parker. It's over. The cops have this place surrounded." John sidled closer. "You have two seconds to drop that weapon or I'll kill you where you stand."

Bradley ran the knife from her navel to the top of her underpants. "I could have this knife through her heart before the bullet reaches me. I could cut her breasts. Perforate her uterus and, if she doesn't bleed to death first, render her barren."

A drop of sweat trickled into John's eye, and he wiped it away with the sleeve of his left arm. In his right hand, the H&K wobbled uselessly.

Bradley saw it and his smile turned knowing. "Do you remember how it felt when you blew a hole through Franklin Watts's belly? While you were sitting with him, trying to keep his intestines from spilling out all over the floor? Are you sure you want to risk *this* shot, Detective? Judging from the way your hands are shaking, you'll miss. This knife is razor sharp. One slice and I'll eviscerate her right before your eyes."

"I won't miss."

"Ah, such utter certainty. But you lie." Abruptly, Bradley reached out and ripped the tape from Julia's mouth. "Would you like to hear her scream?"

"John!" Julia choked out his name. "Oh, God! He's got a gun! He's insane!"

The terror in her voice shook him badly. John knew that was what Bradley wanted. Why he'd removed the tape. He tried to steel himself against her screams, but he couldn't stop the shaking.

She was still screaming when Bradley slid a chrome semiauto from beneath his robe. A triumphant light entered his eyes as he aimed it at John. "Now we even the scale," he said.

Take the shot.

The pistol wobbled in John's hand. Bradley ran the tip of the knife along the hollow of Julia's throat. She screamed and yanked against the ropes. A thin trail of crimson followed the point this time. The sick fuck was cutting her, hurting her. And John knew that no matter what he did now this was not going to end well. The best he could do was pull off a shot and hope his aim was true enough to stop Parker.

"Such a pretty throat, don't you think?" the other man

cooed. "You've run you tongue along it, haven't you? You've been inside her body, felt the heat of her lust wrapped around you."

John fired. The weapon exploded like a stick of dynamite going off in his hand. He'd gone for a head shot. The other man's body jerked like a puppet on a string. At first John thought he'd hit his mark. Then the other man's hand went up. John caught a glimpse of chrome and a second explosion rocked his brain. The bullet slammed into his bicep like a baseball bat slamming in a home run. He felt the bone snap. An electrical shock of pain zinged down his arm to his fingers.

The pain sent him to his knees. He looked down, saw bright red blood dripping from his fingertips to the floor.

"John! *John!*"

Julia's voice pulled him back from shock. He looked up, saw her struggling against the binds, her eyes wild with terror, her face as pale as death.

"I'm okay," he ground out.

But he wasn't. The amount of blood on the floor told him he was seriously injured. He looked at Bradley, noticed the blood on the right side of the other man's head. John had hit his mark after all. Only Bradley was still standing.

"You shot off my fucking ear!" Bradley screamed, his voice high-pitched with panic. "You shot it off!"

Blood leaked between the Bradley's fingers and dripped onto his shoulder. He'd dropped the knife; it lay on the floor at his feet. He held the pistol at his side, but his finger was no longer on the trigger.

Take the shot.

John glanced down, spotted the H&K on the floor two feet away. In one fluid motion, he bent and scooped up the gun with his left hand, brought it up. His vision tunneled on the spot between Bradley's eyes. The other man lunged at his gun, but he wasn't fast enough.

John fired four times in quick succession. He didn't hear the blasts. Vaguely he was aware of the dark spray of blood on the altar. Parker Bradley collapsed. His body heaved twice and then he lay still.

Julia.

The room dipped as John crossed to her. He could hear her crying openly. Saying his name. His vision was beginning to gray. He prayed he could hang onto consciousness long enough to untie her . . .

"John." She raised her head as he approached the table. "You came. I knew you would. Oh, dear God, you're bleeding."

"I'm okay."

"No . . . your arm."

"Doesn't matter." He tore off his jacket as he crossed to her. Even though it was wet, he covered her with it. "How badly are you hurt?"

"He cut me. I don't think it's bad. He drugged me."

Using his left hand, John tugged down the jacket and looked at the thin trail of blood that ran from her throat to her collarbone. Relief swept through him when he realized the injury was minor.

"You're going to be all right." Using his left hand he untied the ropes binding her wrists. He couldn't stand seeing her like that. More than anything he wanted to feel her arms around him. He wanted to feel her warm and alive against him.

Once her hands were free, she sat up and threw her arms around him. He could feel her trembling. Her tears were warm and wet against the side of his face. Her breaths came in fast, shallow bursts in his ear. "I'm so glad you're okay," he whispered.

"Me, too."

"I'm sorry I missed the shot," he said.

"You stopped him. John, you saved my life." Pulling away, she gazed into his eyes. "I knew you would."

"You were smart for making that call."

"I couldn't bear the thought of dying without ever telling you how much I love you."

He wanted to respond, but he didn't have the slightest

idea what to say. There were too many emotions jamming up the pipeline. Blood loss was making him dizzy.

In the distance, he heard the cops making entry. Shouting. The sound of boots against concrete. He wanted to turn around, tell them everything that had happened, but he couldn't seem to let go of Julia.

"Never . . . going to . . . let you go." But he could feel his grip on her waning, his strength leaving him with every drop of blood that hit the floor at his feet. Surprise rippled through him when his knees buckled. He blinked at Julia, trying desperately to keep her face in focus. The face he loved more than his own life.

"Easy does it, bro."

Somehow he'd ended up on the floor. He looked around. Mitch was kneeling beside him. "Let's see if we can get that bleeding stopped," Mitch said.

"Fucker shot me," John murmured.

"No shit."

"Bradley?"

Mitch shook his head.

"Good." John looked for Julia; he didn't like having her out of his sight. "Julia . . ."

"She's okay, bro. You saved her life. You just lay still. You're bleeding like a damn stuck pig."

"Nice . . ."

Fighting dizziness, John raised his head and looked around. Julia was being tended to by a female patrol officer who'd brought her a warming blanket. A few feet away, Parker Bradley stared into eternity.

"You're going to be okay," Mitch said. "Ambulance is on the way. Just hang tight, buddy."

Vaguely, John was aware of his brother taking his hand. He wasn't sure why he thought of Franklin Watts at that moment, but he found himself wondering if he'd been as much of a comfort to the man as his brother was at that moment.

God, he hoped so.

And then he slipped into darkness.

EPILOGUE

Julia stood behind the counter at the Book Merchant counting petty cash and humming along with Frank Sinatra's "Fly Me to the Moon." Six days had passed since the terrible night Parker Bradley had tried to kill her. It was her first day back at the shop, and she was trying hard not to think about it. Hard to do when a single, violent event had changed her life so dramatically.

But it was incredibly healing to be back and doing what she loved. Some people might think that was a small thing, but not Julia. This tiny, dusty shop with its creaky floors and drafty windows was the center of her life. It was her home and her family rolled into one. She would never again take any of it for granted.

The nightmares were bad, but the therapist her father had recommended told her they wouldn't last. It was her mind's way of dealing with an emotional and physical trauma and putting it into perspective. Eventually, her therapist had said, Julia would be able to put it behind her and move on with her life. She hoped so.

She wasn't the only person who'd been hurt that night.

She certainly wasn't the only one suffering. So was her father. The instant John called and told him about Parker Bradley, Benjamin Wainwright had chartered a private chopper from Baton Rouge and flown directly to the hospital where Julia had been taken. He'd rushed to her bedside like a protective mama bear fearing for an injured cub. He blamed himself for what had happened. After all, he had been the one to bring Parker Bradley into her life. Julia had tried to reassure him that was not the case. He'd had no way of knowing that beneath the benign facade lay the twisted heart of a killer. It was the first time in her life she'd ever seen Benjamin Wainwright cry.

The police had linked Bradley to the cemetery murder. Evidence found in his apartment also linked him to several other unsolved crimes in Baton Rouge and Shreveport. Crimes including stalking, sexual assault and murder. Julia had learned just that morning from Mitch that Parker Bradley had journaled much of his twisted obsessions and fanaticism. The journal told a chilling tale of an abused boy, a troubled teenager and a man's decline into insanity.

She hadn't seen John since that night when the EMTs had carried him away, bleeding and unconscious. He'd been transported to Charity Hospital; she'd been taken to Tulane. Only later did she learn that John had spent the first twenty-four hours in critical condition.

He was the one bright spot in the darkest period of her life. Even before she'd been released from the hospital, she'd wanted desperately to see him. To touch him and thank him for saving her life. When she'd been released the next day, Claudia had driven her directly to Charity. John had been transferred to a regular room. But like a sentry, Mitch had come out and told her John didn't want visitors. The rejection had hurt, but Julia had respected his wishes.

She waited another day before trying to call him. But once again Mitch was there to screen his calls, telling her John would return her call.

But he never did.

Once he was released, she'd called his apartment number and left messages, but he hadn't returned her calls. She'd tried his cell phone, only to discover it had been disconnected. She might be a little hardheaded, but she could take a hint.

As long as she had the shop and her friends and family, she would get through this. As long as she stayed busy, she could endure the nightmares. Someday she might even be able to put the terrible night behind her. But there was no way she'd ever get over John.

Her heart broke every time she thought of spending the rest of her life without him. Such a decent man. So courageous. So willing to accept responsibility, even when he didn't have to. She missed him with a ferocity that took her breath away. The ache deep in her chest wasn't lessening with each passing day as her therapist had suggested. Instead it seemed to grow a little more every day, like a cancer that would eventually leach the life from her and leave nothing but a shell.

Finishing with the petty cash, Julia looked up at her sister, who was sitting at her desk, punching computer keys and grumbling about the new inventory system. Jacob was using a feather duster on the antique set of encyclopedias she'd purchased from Mr. Thornbrow just that morning. Life went on. Everything was going to be fine. She could take comfort in that. Like her therapist said, healing was just going to take some time . . .

The bell jingled, announcing a customer. Julia looked up from the cash register, a smile she didn't feel pasted to her face. Every nerve in her body went taut when John came through the door. He was wearing a battered brown bomber jacket, black boots and faded blue jeans. The right sleeve of the jacket hung unused at his side. Beneath she could see the blue and white fabric of a sling. He looked thinner, his face a little more lean. But he still filled the entire room with his presence.

He scanned the shop. Julia's heart began to pound when his gaze met hers. She knew it was a silly response considering he was probably here to officially break things off.

That would be just like John. Do it face to face even if it was going to hurt more.

"Hey," he said, crossing to her.

Feeling her cheeks heat, Julia looked blindly down at the cash in the drawer and promptly forgot the figure she had yet to jot on the daily sales form. She wanted to say something witty. Something that would let him know his showing up now to end things before they'd ever really had a chance to begin wasn't affecting her one way or another. But her voice had suddenly taken leave.

"Julia?" She started at the sound of her sister's voice. Only then did she realize Claudia must have noticed her discomfort and come up behind her. "You okay?"

"I'm fine." But Julia wasn't fine. Her heart was pounding. Her face was hot. Her chest was aching so bad that if she hadn't known better she might have thought she was having a heart attack.

"You're shaking." Jacob set a reassuring hand on her shoulder and squeezed.

"It's cold," Julia said dumbly.

"That's it." Jacob raised his hands. "I'm asking him to leave."

If Julia hadn't suddenly been so nervous, she might have laughed at the absurdity of the situation. At that moment she honestly didn't know what she'd do without Claudia and Jacob. But this was one thing they could not handle for her. She needed to do it on her own. "Guys, thank you. But I can handle this."

Shaking his head, Jacob shot John a withering glare as he went back to his dusting. "I'll be right here if you need me."

Giving her a final, knowing look, Claudia squeezed her hand. "Same goes," she said and slowly walked back to the desk.

Julia's heart was still pounding when she turned to face John. He was standing at the counter, looking at her as if she were some complex math equation he'd never learned about in college. From two feet away, she could smell the masculine tang of his aftershave. The familiarity of it wrapped around her heart and squeezed until she felt she couldn't breathe.

"How are you?" he asked.

She tried to smile, but felt her lips tremble and she pursed them instead. "I'm good. Great, in fact. This is my first day back and things couldn't be better." Even to her the proclamation sounded phony.

His eyes narrowed as if she'd just told a big fat lie and he didn't believe a word of it. "You look good," he said. "I mean, aside from the bruises."

"Thanks." It was difficult, but she forced herself to meet his gaze. "How's the arm?"

"Hurts like a son of a bitch." His smile nearly disarmed her, but she steeled herself against it. "They put in a titanium pin and a few bolts."

"Going to be fun at the airport."

"Yeah."

He spotted the copy of *A Gentleman's Touch* on the counter and smiled. "How did Benjamin take to the idea of his daughter being an author?"

"He's still getting used to the idea."

"Might take some time."

"A couple of centuries."

John smiled.

Julia cleared her throat. "Any news on the civil suit?"

He sobered, looked away. "My lawyer believes the widow will settle out of court."

"That's good, isn't it?"

"Yeah. It's good. She's . . . a good person. She called me. At the hospital."

"So you're no longer only the man who killed her husband, but a real person who's suffered more than his share."

"Something like that." He looked sheepish for a moment. "The department is going to help pay."

"And you?"

"I'll pay some, but it won't financially devastate me. I can live with that."

"I'm glad it worked out."

He looked around the shop. "I like what you've done with the place."

She'd spent the morning rearranging everything from bookshelves, to knickknacks, to the coffee service. It was either that or go insane . . .

"The place needed some sprucing up," she said quickly. "I've got new shelving units on order—"

"Julia," he said abruptly.

She cut the sentence off mid-word and looked at him. "What?"

"Cut it out."

"I don't know what you mean."

"We're not strangers, damn it. Let's stop acting like it."

She blinked at him, wondering why the hell he didn't just say what he'd come here to say and get it over with. She could handle it. She'd spent the last days preparing. But she didn't think there was any way a woman could prepare for having her heart ripped out.

"Why don't you just say what you've come here to say?" she snapped. "I'm tired of waiting."

He arched a brow. "Well, I haven't gotten around to it yet."

"I'd appreciate it if you'd just stop beating around the bush. I've got things to do."

The brow went higher. For the first time realization entered his eyes. A smile that was a little amused, a little uncertain touched the corner of his mouth. "What is it you think I came here to say?"

"John, please. It's obvious, okay? I haven't seen you for a week. You refused to see me when you were in the hospital. You didn't bother to return my calls. You didn't even call to let me know you were out of the hospital. Damn it, you didn't even call to see how I was doing."

"I kept tabs on you through Mitch."

But now that the door was open, Julia couldn't seem to stop talking. So many words and emotions had built up inside her during the last week she couldn't stanch the flow.

"I know you have some issues to deal with. I can accept that. What I can't accept is your shutting me out, avoiding this."

"Whoa." He raised his good hand. "I'm not avoiding anything."

"It's been six days."

"I was in the hospital for five."

"You could have picked up a phone." A breath shuddered out of her. "At the very least you owed me the respect of letting me know where I stand."

A tense silence fell over the shop. Julia was only vaguely aware of Sinatra's voice in the background. The tick of the grandfather clock against the far wall.

John was looking at her oddly. Like a man who'd just realized he'd flubbed something he'd thought he had sewn up. "I'm sorry I didn't come to see you."

"Don't be. I got the message loud and clear."

"I didn't want you at the hospital because I didn't want you to see me like that. I get prickly when I'm in pain." When she didn't smile, he sighed. "I needed some time to think."

Julia closed the cash drawer with a snap. "Is there a point to dragging this out?"

Before she even realized he was going to move, he rounded the counter and was moving toward her. "There's a point," he said.

Stepping back to keep a safe distance between them, Julia blinked. She'd thought she had this all figured out. But the way he was looking at her, now she wasn't so sure.

She jolted when he raised his left hand and set it against her face. "Wh-what are you doing?"

"Making my point." Bending slightly, he brushed his mouth across hers.

Every pleasure center in her brain lit up like a Christmas tree. She marveled in the firmness of his lips. The warmth of his breath against her cheek. The scratch of his whiskers against her chin.

When he pulled away, his eyes were dark and serious.

"My point," he said, "is that I love you. I didn't want to tell you that while I was lying in a hospital bed feeling like death warmed over. I didn't want to tell you over the phone. I wanted to tell you in person. So, here I am."

The floor shifted beneath her feet. She stared at John, her heart jigging in her chest. And in that moment, everything else in the shop faded to babble. Her every sense tunneled on the man standing before her, looking at her as if she were the only woman in the world.

"I've waited six hellish days to tell you that," he said. "The least you can do is say something back."

But Julia couldn't find her voice. She could feel the emotions expanding and tangling in her chest. "I thought . . ." Her voice broke.

"You thought what?"

Taking a fortifying breath, she looked at him. "I've been expecting you to waltz in here and tell me it's over because your life is too screwed up to let me get involved with you."

"I won't tell you I didn't consider it." His hand trembled when he caressed the side of her face. "But I'm not that selfless." One side of his mouth curved. "I'm greedy when it comes to you, Julia. My life may be screwed up, but I want you in it." His jaw flexed. "You're the best thing that's ever happened to me."

She closed her eyes against the tears building behind her lids. The surge of happiness in her chest took her breath away. "In that case, maybe we ought to try to work on this communication thing."

"Not my strong suit, but I'll give it my all." Using his left arm, he pulled her to him and looked into her eyes. "I know I'm not an easy man."

"You're a quick study, though."

He grinned. "Trainable."

"Yeah." Blinking back tears, Julia smiled at him. "I love you."

"I know that now." Taking her face between his hands, he looked into her eyes. "I love you, too," he said and lowered his mouth to hers.

Turn the page for a look at

HARD EVIDENCE

BY

PAMELA CLARE

Available now from Berkley Sensation.

Tessa walked through the main entrance to the hospital, feeling uneasy, her conversation with Chief Irving still playing through her mind.

"If I were you, Ms. Novak, I'd take a long vacation," he'd said. "Failing that, I'd buy a gun and learn how to use it."

"I already own one—a twenty-two."

"Good. Pack it. I've already ordered extra patrols for your street."

Tessa told herself Chief Irving was just being cautious. There was no evidence to suggest her life was in danger. Kara had been getting death threats for a while before they came after her. Tessa hadn't gotten so much as an impolite e-mail. She had nothing to worry about.

Then why are you carrying a handgun, girl?

Like Chief Irving, she was just being cautious.

Tom had all but gone apoplectic when Chief Irving

promised to give her an exclusive when the killers were caught, provided she dropped the story now. He'd launched into the thousandth rendition of his "Watchdogs of Freedom" speech, bringing a look of bored resignation to Chief Irving's face. Obviously, Irving had heard this speech before, too.

"This is outrageous! No journalist at this paper has ever caved to pressure from the city, and I can assure you Novak won't be the first!"

Chief Irving hadn't been pleased. "We'll be as helpful as we can be, Ms. Novak, but we're playing this one close to the vest. And don't go on a charm offensive against my men with that sweet Southern accent of yours, because I've warned them all not to discuss this case with you. If you want information, you come to me."

Tessa had agreed to that much.

She stopped at the hospital's front desk and asked one of the volunteers for Bruce Simms's room number. She'd spent the morning working on a routine story about the recent ketamine robberies and had planned to start researching Denver's gang history, as most drive-bys in Denver were gang-related. But when she'd learned the gas station attendant had been moved out of Intensive Care, she'd known she had to speak with him.

"Room three-thirty-two, miss."

"Thanks."

Tessa found Mr. Simms sitting up in bed in a blue-and-white hospital gown watching a soap opera. He was pale but alert, an oxygen tube beneath his nose, deep reddish bruises on the backs of his hands from multiple IVs. He glanced over and saw her, and his eyes widened.

Clearly he recognized her.

"Mr. Simms? I'm Tessa Novak. I hope you don't mind my stopping by."

"You like *Days of Our Lives*?"

"I don't watch much television." She took that as an invitation and sat in the chair next to his bed. "I work during the day."

"It's all crap anyway." He clicked off the television. "You're that reporter. You came in for coffee. I read your piece. You come here to interview me? I got nothing to say."

"I'm here for personal reasons, Mr. Simms. You and I watched someone die. I thought—"

"I didn't see nothing." His mouth was clamped shut, but his eyes—hazel eyes more gray than green—told a different story.

"Oh, well, I imagine you were fighting your own battle for survival, weren't you?" She gave his arm a sympathetic squeeze. "I'm terribly sorry that you became ill as a result of the shooting. I must say the whole thing nearly frightened me to death."

Charm offensive? How dare Chief Irving reduce years spent studying deportment and communication to mere manipulation!

Even though Mr. Simms had read the article, Tessa went through the story again, told him what she'd seen. The car. The rims. The blood. The man in the leather jacket.

"She was so young, Mr. Simms. We were the last two people to see her alive. That matters to me."

For a moment there was no sound but hospital noises from out in the hallway.

"She used to come by most every Sunday afternoon with the others." Mr. Simms looked up at the dark television screen. "There were four of them, girls about the same age. They'd come in, buy gum, candy, maybe shampoo or lip gloss, then they'd go again. Never smiled. Never said a word till that night."

It was the first real information Tessa had gotten about the girl. "Did you know her name? Do you think she lived nearby?"

"I told you they never said a word, didn't I?" He glanced sharply at Tessa. "No, I didn't know her name. But, yeah, I think she must have lived nearby. They always walked to the store together. Never saw her by herself. It was always the four of them, and they were always dressed kind of shabby."

Curious, Tessa couldn't resist asking, "Did you ever see her with anyone else—a man, someone who looked like a gang member? A man in a black leather jacket perhaps?"

His eyes narrowed. "You're fishing for an article. I don't want to be in no newspaper."

She met his gaze, held it. "No, sir. I'm trying to find some peace of mind. Besides, I would never quote you without making it clear you were being interviewed."

He seemed to measure her.

"There was an older woman who sometimes came with them, but she never entered the store. I always figured her for one of their mothers. But . . ." He paused for a moment. "I always thought it was strange the way she watched them—like a hawk. I figured maybe she wanted to make sure they didn't steal nothing."

"Did they ever try to steal anything?"

"Nope."

"How about the black car? Did you see it or its driver before?"

"Can't recall. The place is a damned gas station—cars

coming and going all goddamned day and night." He picked up the remote, clicked the television back on.

Tessa stood, took a business card out of her purse, and scribbled her home phone number on the back, knowing her time with Mr. Simms had ended. "I hope you're feeling better soon, Mr. Simms. If you think of anything else, or even if you just want to talk, you can reach me at this number."

He took the card, glanced at it, then looked up at her face. "I'm leaving town as soon as I get out of here. Going to stay with my brother in Omaha, maybe move there."

And Tessa knew he was being cautious, too. "Good luck. And thank you."

She walked out of his room and down the hallway, running what he'd told her through her mind. Four girls about the same age, always together, most of the time under the watchful eye of an older woman. Never spoke. Never smiled. Walked to the store dressed in shabby clothes to buy candy.

Perhaps they were sisters or best friends, and the older woman was someone's mother. It wasn't surprising that they didn't talk to anyone else, given that they probably spoke little or no English, but it was a little odd that they didn't chatter with each other. Teenage girls were not exactly known for being quiet. It was strange, too, that they never smiled. Whoever heard of teenagers on a somber candy binge?

The shabby clothes pointed to a life of poverty. Perhaps the girls were wearing hand-me-downs or Salvation Army cast-offs, cobbling together a wardrobe out of bits and pieces no one else wanted, seeing scorn and pity in other people's eyes, feeling ashamed just to be seen. Maybe that's why they kept to themselves.

Tessa knew only too well what that felt like.

¡Por favor. Señor, ayúdeme!

The girl hadn't been wearing shoes—a dangerous thing on city streets. That tended to support Mr. Simms's belief that she lived nearby. So perhaps that's where Tessa should start.

She glanced at her watch, saw that it was nearly three. That gave her a good hour and half before dark to walk the streets, knock on doors, look around for signs of gang activity. The victim was a teenager and poor, both of which fit a gang theory.

Tessa lifted her gaze and saw *him* come around the corner. He was wearing a dark blue cable-knit sweater instead of a black leather jacket, but she would have recognized him anywhere. And she could tell from his scowl that he recognized her, too.

The breath left her lungs in a rush. She took one step backward on unsteady legs, then another, her heart slamming in her chest, her lungs too empty to scream. Then beside her, she saw the fire alarm.

She lunged for it, found herself hauled up against a rock-hard chest, a steel hand clamped over her mouth, her feet lifted off the ground.

Julian saw she was about to pull the fire alarm and did the only thing he could—clamped a hand over her mouth and pulled her out of the hallway and into the nearest room, a large closet full of linens. He kicked the door shut behind him and worked to subdue 120 pounds of desperate, terrified female that kicked, twisted, and struggled in his arms.

He turned her to face him, held her fast. "I'm not going to hurt you, Tessa."

At the sound of her name, she froze, and Julian found himself looking into the biggest, bluest eyes he'd ever seen. Framed by long, sooty lashes, they stared up at him in unblinking horror. Her face was pale, her skin creamy and translucent apart from a few tiny freckles on her nose. She felt small in his arms, fragile and soft. Holding her this close, he could feel her heart pound, smell her fear, taste her panic.

"If I wanted to kill you, you'd already be dead." He'd said it to calm her, realized when her pupils dilated that his words had somehow had the opposite effect. "I'm going to release you, and you're going to stand here and listen to me, got it?"

She nodded.

He lowered her to her feet, let her go—and found himself staring at the working end of a sweet little .22 revolver. Where the hell had that come from?

Smooth, Darcangelo. What's your day job again? Special agent, you say?

"S-stay away from me!" She was trembling—not a good thing when her finger rested on the trigger of a gun pointed at his chest. It hurt to get shot, even wearing Kevlar. "I-I saw you that night! I know you were there!"

"Put it down, Ms. Novak. I told you—I'm not going to hurt you."

"Why should I believe that? I know you're carrying a gun. I felt it beneath your sweater!" Her voice quavered, hovering somewhere between rage and terror. She gripped the handle of the gun with two hands, steadied it.

He weighed his options. He could tell her he was a federal agent—except that she was a reporter. How could he be sure she wouldn't splash his name all over the damned paper? He could disarm her, but there was a chance he'd hurt her or she'd pull the trigger either accidentally or on purpose. Neither option was ideal.

He took one slow step toward her. "Put down the gun."

"Not a chance! You came here to kill him, didn't you? You came here to kill Mr. Simms so he couldn't talk to the police!"

He'd come to question the old guy, but he didn't want to tell her that. "If that's what you think, shoot me. Here, I'll even make it easy for you." He took another step forward, stretched his arms out to his sides. "Aim just to left of my breastbone. A little twenty-two round will ricochet inside my ribcage, shred my lungs and heart, and I'll be dead before I hit the floor."

She gaped at him in surprise, and her gaze dropped to his chest.

It was the break Julian needed.

He pivoted out of the line of fire, grabbed her wrist, and wrenched the .22 from her grasp. It took less force than he'd imagined, and he heard her gasp—whether in surprise or pain, he couldn't tell. He turned to face her, found her rubbing her wrist and watching him fearfully through those blue eyes.

"I told you to put it down. You should have listened." He popped out the cylinder, tapped the bullets into his hand, and pocketed the rounds. Then he snapped the cylinder into place and handed the gun back to her.

The damned thing had been fully loaded and ready to fire.

She dropped the little pistol into her purse, her wary

gaze never leaving him. "H-how do you know my name?"

"I know almost everything about you." He recited what he'd learned after doing a digging on her this morning. "Born in Rosebud, Texas, on March 9, 1979, to Linda Lou Bates, age fourteen. Father unknown. Grew up on welfare and food stamps with your mother and maternal grandfather. Graduated Rosebud-Lott High School in 1997 with a GPA of three-nine-eight and left Rosebud behind the next day."

No longer pale, her cheeks had flushed red with what Julian supposed was anger or embarrassment. He continued.

"You earned an associate's degree in English from Austin Community College in 1999—the year you changed your last name to Novak. Moved to Athens to study journalism at the University of Georgia and graduated Phi Beta Kappa. Then you took your first reporting job at the *Savannah Morning News*. You moved to Denver three years ago to take a seat on—"

"I-I don't know who you are, but I'm getting security!" Quick on her dressy little feet, she darted past him toward the door.

He caught her easily, turned her about, and hauled her against him—just as the door opened and two middle-aged women wearing blue cleaning uniforms walked in. Unsure what she might say and wanting to avoid a scene and get rid of the women, Julian ducked down and silenced her with his mouth.

Tessa heard the door open behind her, felt the hot shock of his lips on hers, and in dazed disbelief, realized what he was doing. He was trying to shush her, trying to control her. It was nothing less than assault, and it both stunned and enraged her. She pushed against his chest to no avail, tried to scream, but when she opened her mouth, his tongue invaded, turning her scream to a stifled squeak.

A bolt of heat, unexpected and unwanted, shot through her, and her insides seemed to melt as he attacked her senses, his tongue teasing hers with stolen strokes, his lips pressing hot and unyielding against hers. She couldn't stop herself from noticing how hard his body felt, couldn't stop the minty taste of his toothpaste from flooding her mouth, couldn't help taking in the scent of him—spice with just a hint of leather.

He's a stranger, Tess—maybe even a murderer.

Tessa's mind knew it, but her body didn't seem to care. The adrenaline in her blood warmed to pheromone, icy rage to steam. And before she realized it, she had quit fighting him, quit fearing him, quit breathing. Worse, she'd begun to kiss him back, her tongue curling with his, her bones going liquid as his hand slid slowly up her spine.

Behind her, the women gasped, giggled.

Tessa had forgotten all about them.

"*¡Perdónenos!*" *Pardon us!*

The door closed, and Tessa realized dimly that the women had gone.

But he didn't quit kissing her, not all at once. He nipped her tongue, drew her lower lip into his mouth, sucked it. Then, abruptly, he grasped her shoulders and held her out before him.

"I hope you listen closely, Ms. Novak, because I'd hate to see you on an autopsy slab." His eyes were darkest blue. His dark brows were bent together in a frown, his square jaw clean-shaven, his lips unusually full for a man's. "I know you get paid to sensationalize other people's suffering, but this is one crime you'd better leave to the cops. You've already stirred up enough trouble with today's article. It would be best for both of us if you don't write another."

"Sensationalize—? You—! Oh!" She was so furious she could barely speak. "I watched that girl die! She begged me to help her, and I couldn't! But I'm going to do my best to help her now. I'm going to find out who killed—"

He gave her a little shake. "What you're going to do is get yourself killed! Let the cops do their job. Go chase an ambulance or something."

"Let go of me!" She jerked away from him, wiped a hand across her mouth, tried to erase the lingering evidence of his kiss. "You drag me in here, assault me, insult me, and then try to tell me how to do my job? Who *are* you?"

"Are we on or off the record?"

"On."

"You don't need to know who I am."

"Off the record, then."

He seemed to hesitate. "I'm Julian Darcangelo, and I'm one of the good guys."

"That's a scary thought." Tessa thought he looked like one of the bad guys—a shadowy criminal type. She didn't realize she'd spoken those last words aloud until the corner of his mouth turned up in a sardonic grin.

"You know better than to judge people by appearances, Ms. Bates. Oh, I'm sorry—it's Novak, isn't it? And next time you hold a gun on someone, don't let him get so close. Never take your eyes off his."

Then he brushed past her, opened the door, and strode out into the hallway.

By the time her legs were steady enough for her to follow him, he was gone.

From *New York Times* Bestselling Author

LINDA CASTILLO

DEAD RECKONING

Kate Megason was attacked eleven years ago, and she is still haunted by the experience.

Now an assistant DA, Kate starts receiving mysterious threatening messages that sound as if they could be from the same person who attacked her years ago.

Her boss assigns investigator Frank Matrone to keep an eye on her. Kate and Frank dislike each other from the moment they meet—they're opposites in many ways. But as the threats on Kate start to escalate, it's clear someone wants her dead, and Frank and Kate begin to realize they're more alike than they had imagined.

Don't miss this gripping romantic suspense
from *New York Times* bestselling author

LINDA CASTILLO

OVERKILL

Marty Hogan comes from a family of cops and
never wanted to do anything else. But when she lost
her temper and beat a murder suspect on camera,
her career was put on the line. She was fired from
the Chicago force, and the only job she could find
was with a police force in a small town in Texas.

Police Chief Clay Settlemeyer doesn't know why
he's willing to give Marty a second chance to prove
herself—but even he has grappled with guilt and
past mistakes. Now the violence of Marty's past
has come back to haunt her, and everyone who's
caught in the cross fire may not escape harm.

M587T1009